# DEATH
# IN THE
## OFF-SEASON

# DEATH
# IN THE
## OFF-SEASON

## FRANCINE
## MATHEWS

SOHO
CRIME

Copyright © 1994, 2016 by Francine Mathews

Published in 2016 by
Soho Press, Inc.
853 Broadway
New York, NY 10003

Library of Congress Cataloging-in-Publication Data

Mathews, Francine.
Death in the off-season / Francine Mathews.

ISBN 978-1-61695-726-1
eISBN 978-1-61695-727-8

1. Folger, Merry (Fictitious character)—Fiction. 2. Women
detectives—Massachusetts—Nantucket Island—Fiction. I. Title
PS3563.A8357 D43 2016  813.54—dc23   2015042662

Printed in the United States of America

10 9 8 7 6 5 4 3 2 1

*This book is dedicated with love to my mother,*
*Elizabeth MacEntee Barron,*
*who always believed*

# Introduction

*Death in the Off-Season* is the first mystery novel I wrote, many years ago in 1992. I was working as an intelligence analyst at the CIA at the time, had no children, and was not yet thirty. The book began as an experiment of sorts—my husband challenged me to write a novel—and I chose to set it on Nantucket, a place I had long loved. It seemed to me that the island's rich history and relative insularity—in the off-season, at least—were similar to those of small English villages immortalized in classic British detective fiction. Or, as Jane Austen once advised, "three or four families in a country village is the very thing to work on."

I did not really expect the book to be published. It began as an exercise in form, and that is where I thought it would end.

*Death in the Off-Season* found an audience, however, and precipitated a change in my career. I left the CIA, and three more books featuring Detective Meredith Folger and her circle of friends followed in swift succession. Other work claimed my attention over the ensuing decades—the raising of two sons and the writing of other books. It was only recently, when Soho Press asked me to write a new novel in the series and planned to reissue the previous Nantucket mysteries, that I looked with new eyes at the stories I had told.

I decided that a twenty-year gap in the lives of Meredith Folger, Peter Mason, and their families was too great for most readers to support, and that the fifth book ought to pick up where the fourth left off. That meant, however, that I would have to revise the existing novels in the series to make them compatible with a new story in the present time frame. Much has changed on Nantucket Island since the mid-nineties, and much has changed about American life in general. My personal style of writing has also evolved. This new edition of *Death in the Off-Season* is therefore something of a departure from the original.

I hope that those readers who first met Meredith at publication in 1994 will find her only more interesting in this version, and enjoy the streamlined series—several of the books under new titles—as each is reintroduced.

Francine Mathews
Denver, CO
October 2015

## Prologue

A PERFECT NIGHT for feijoada. The thought came to him unbidden as he stared through the windshield at the fog, a fluid blackness wrapping the car like a mourning sheet. *Feijoada*. Pungent rice and black beans with bits of pork and sausage, it was food intended to comfort—like most of his life in Brazil's decaying paradise.

His life. The car creaked into a pothole, lurching on its ravaged shock absorbers, and the motion sent blood pounding into his temples. He was exhausted, and his thoughts darted like fish in a disturbed pool; the nine-hour flight and the night ferry were catching up with him. He shivered in the creeping dampness. *His life*. He had to hold on to it, despite the insidious enemy, the threat coursing through his veins. He had to do more than escape. He had to win.

He'd always hated this island. Hated the fog, the way it masked his sight, made him stumble, and turned the familiar into something threatening. He felt vulnerable on Nantucket, something no Mason could ever endure. Masons destroyed the vulnerable, for God's sake.

The car came to a stop, engine idling, its headlights picking up the glint of the livestock gate's gray metal bars. He stared at it an instant, taking in the words MASON

FARMS, painted in a red semicircle on a square white sign-board; and then he bared his teeth at the family domain.

"Open the gate for me," his driver said.

"Why?"

"Because that's how you were raised."

He hesitated an instant, then shoved the door wide. The car was filled with the smell of salt and pine. He stepped tentatively into the opaque night, breathing his discomfort in quick bursts, the fog smoothing his brow with a wet hand. Only a few steps to the gatepost and the wire loop holding the bars closed against the sheep.

He crossed in front of the headlights, feeling exposed and backlit, and glanced over his shoulder. The glare blinded him momentarily, as he had known it would, and he blinked, thinking for an instant that the car's sudden movement was a trick of the light, something to do with the fog, and not the hurling of wheels and metal toward his body. The first stab of fear and understanding came just as the hood of the car crashed into his spine, throwing him up and backward, snapping his skull against the windshield.

He skittered off the roof into a darkness that was filled with searing pain, unbounded by the edges of his body. *The fog*, he thought, fighting for sense even as it left him; and knew with anguish that he was lost.

*Chapter 1*

WILL AWOKE, AS he did every day, a few seconds before his mother turned from the muffins she was mixing in the kitchen two floors below and walked to the stairs. He lay still, his eyes closed in the semi-dark, listening for her voice.

"Will! Will, it's past six!"

Labor Day. He hugged the stillness of the early morning to himself for a few seconds longer; tomorrow he'd be torn from sleep and thrust into the long tedium of the school year. With it would come winter—shorter days, fewer ferries to the mainland, and the disappearance of the summer people, whose energy and strident voices broke the island's isolation for a few months.

"Tomorrow, and tomorrow, and tomorrow," he murmured sleepily, and then stopped, self-conscious. His voice had changed a year ago and its new depth still had the power to startle him. He thrust his head deeper into his pillow and groped for the strands of a dream that had drifted across his brain an instant before his mother's voice turned night to day. No good; it was gone. His eyes flicked open.

The attic room high above the restaurant faced east, into the morning sun, but today a livid white light filtered through the shade, and the groan of horns, human and suffering, rose off the water. That meant fog, his favorite weather. He felt a rush of satisfaction as he threw back the bedclothes and swung adolescent legs, lanky and beautiful, onto the rag rug. It was boom day at the bog, and Peter would need him early to work the flooded cranberry beds.

He pulled on a pair of jeans and a sweatshirt and ran down the two flights, three steps at a time, passing his mother's second-floor living area and the freshly painted dining rooms at the stairs' foot. The kitchen sat at the back of the house, down a length of narrow, aged corridor that smelled of dry rot; the off-islanders considered it quaint. He pushed open the swinging door and a rush of air blew his dark bangs back from his forehead.

His mother turned from the sink and gave him a brief smile as he slid a stool over to her butcher block. She'd already set out his blueberries and cream. He threw himself down before them and yawned hugely. The kitchen windows were shut against the damp, and the heavy smell of sausage fat hanging in the warm drafts from the stove reminded him of winter. His face creased uncontrollably in another yawn. He could feel his mother's eyes on the back of his head, and dug into the berries.

Tess Starbuck studied her boy an instant, and then pulled up another stool.

"Get enough sleep?"

"Yep."

"You were up until all hours. It was twelve-thirty when I fell off."

"I was reading," he said. "That book on the Egyptian campaign is really good."

"Peter lend it to you?" she asked, reaching for a towel. Her fine hands were reddened like a waterman's, or a chef's. She had been both, among many things. Will loved his mother's hands. He dropped his eyes to his breakfast.

"Yeah. He's got awesome books out at the farm. I could spend a week there."

"You could spend one in bed, too, by the look of those circles under your eyes. Read all winter, Will, when there's nothing else to do on this godforsaken island."

Will gave her a doleful look from his dark blue eyes, and then grinned. Despite herself she grinned back. He knew that however she cursed Nantucket, Tess loved the island as he did and his father had, a native love deep into the bone.

At the glancing thought of his father, Will felt the familiar burst of pain shoot through his gut, and breathed deeply to push it away. When would it stop?

He wiped his mouth on his napkin and shoved back his chair. "It's boom day, Tess," he said. "Gotta get out there."

She kissed him swiftly on the cheek and brushed a hand across his forehead, needing to feel the silkiness of the hair spilling into his eyes. Fifteen. Growing up and away from her, and she'd never have another. "Take a change of clothes. You don't want to ride back in wet jeans."

He was already out the door.

HER BROW FURROWED, Tess followed him through the kitchen window as he swung a leg over his bike and sped off down Quince Street. One of these nights, maybe he'd be able to sleep without dreaming, she thought. Until then, she'd have to live with the dark circles, the pallor underneath his late-summer tan, and have faith that the passage of time would ease his nightmares.

She watched as the fog rolled up from the harbor, silent and unstoppable, blotting out the gray shingle of the neighboring house, and crossed herself, once, for luck. Then she shook her head angrily and turned back to her pans.

She rarely indulged the pain of Daniel's death, one way she and Will were very much alike. She had mourned the man she loved from the night his body was found on the beach at Siasconset until she buried him three days later; then she had turned her energies to survival. She could brood, cultivating the terrors of the unstable future, and go slowly mad in the emptiness of her queen-sized bed; or she could cook until she was mindless and weary. Tess had undertaken to feed the island.

Daniel's partner had bought out her share of the scalloper. God knows it was worth less these days than when Dan had mortgaged his soul three years ago to buy it. But his partner had pitied her, something she hated and bore because she had no choice; he had given her enough to clear the debt and get out from under the bank. She had thrown Dan's insurance money—how little she'd thought of actually having to use it, the day he'd signed the policy—into a professional kitchen, moved her life upstairs, and opened for business three months after the storm that killed her husband. The Greengage was a home away from home for the men who fished Nantucket's waters, and it was a tourist find as a result. Tess had been so busy from the day she opened that the nights she had feared—the stillness in her room, the dread reckoning of all she had lost—had been consumed by exhausted, dreamless sleep. Now she steeled herself against the arrival of winter, when the crowds fled, the island battened down against endless wind and damp, and she would have only Will, fighting his own demons, between herself and the memories.

The oven's timer shook her out of sadness. She opened the door and inhaled the scent of bursting cranberries, then glanced at her watch. Four hours until the lunch crowd.

WILL COVERED THE mile and a quarter from his house to the rotary at the end of Orange Street in about five minutes. The bike was a three-year-old Trek, one of his prized possessions and a gift from Peter, who had bought a new Yeti early in the spring. Tess had almost made him give it back, too proud to take charity from one of the Masons, but Peter had told her it was a fair exchange for Will's help at lambing. Peter had hired him outright after that, paying fifteen dollars an hour. Will was saving his money for college.

The tall captains' houses that lined Orange Street were silent this morning, their backyards blotted out, the colors of the late dahlias bleached and flattened by fog. Already most of the summer people who owned or rented them had left the island, beating the rush for spots on the car ferries at the end of the season. A few hardy souls waited until late September, but the ones with kids his age, bound for school tomorrow, were long gone. At the rotary at the end of Orange Street, he took the Milestone Road bike path toward Siasconset, not trusting the road in the fog.

He had close to four miles to pedal before the turnoff to Altar Rock, through the gently rolling moors whose wind-gnarled scrub, on clearer days, had begun to show the first of fall's intense color. Here in the middle of the island, beyond the town's closely huddled houses, the heath stretched almost unimpeded to the sea. The occasional gray-shingled saltbox, rising amid the moor like a ship cresting a wave, was invisible now in the fog.

The bike path was empty. Up ahead, a single gull huddled in the middle of the road, its feathers fluffed into a ball against the damp, examining an indeterminate roadkill flattened on the macadam. Will felt moisture on the back of his neck, already warm with exertion, and shivered. Even in the height of July the island had weather like this, but today the air bore the scent of dying grass and beach plum past its prime, a sure sign summer was at its end.

He slowed the bike, anxious lest he miss the turnoff in the fog, but his sense of timing hadn't failed him. Ten yards ahead a swirl of sand showed where the road to Altar Rock cut through the heath into the center of the island. Will stopped the bike and glanced to either side, wary of cars looming suddenly out of the mist, then shot across. It took him ten minutes to travel the mile and a quarter before Altar Rock appeared on his right. He stopped the bike an instant to look at it, but today the granite slab was lost in fog. The radar station, his earliest memory of alien technology, hovered nearby. Most days, at ninety feet above sea level, this was one of the best spots for viewing the whole island. Today, the rise and fall of foghorns, a lament steady as his own breathing, carried across the moors from the invisible harbor a mile to the east.

He pushed the sleeves of his sweatshirt above his elbows and labored on, past Altar Rock to the intersection of three sandy trails. He took the right-hand fork—less than a mile now to the farm. He felt a sudden burst of happiness at the thought of the day ahead. Wet harvesting was much more fun than dry. This year, Peter would give him a beater and let him wade through the flooded bog, the whirling machine sending a carpet of blood-red berries bobbing to the surface in his wake. Will was just young enough to relish having water up to his knees. To be paid for it was too much to be believed. Lunch would be something hot, given the coolness of the day and the drenching nature of the work: quahog chowder, maybe, with corn bread and fried scallops, followed by blueberry pie. Rebecca, the housekeeper who was old enough to be Peter's mother, would serve him second helpings. Then they'd haul in the booms, skimming acre after acre of red berries from the water.

Will felt a shifting current of air graze his cheek, and the fog cleared slightly: he'd passed the entrance to the farm. He thrust out a leg to stop the bike, his heel kicking up a whorl of damp sand, and studied the tangle of scrub pine to his right. No wonder he'd almost missed it. The aluminum gate that stood closed most of the day—to keep the sheep from roaming too far—was wide open this morning. Rafe must have been out early. Will's forehead wrinkled slightly in puzzlement. Then he put his head down and pedaled up the unpaved drive toward the old saltbox.

A mouse darted from the undergrowth to his right and shot in front of his wheel. He clutched at the hand brakes so suddenly that the bike skidded to a stop, throwing him off balance. In a desperate bid for stability, he dropped his left leg; but the bike went down. He slid on his side in the sand perhaps five feet before his momentum ceased, and then he lay, slightly dazed by the early hour and the sudden panic, staring at the gray sky. He hoped devoutly that the mouse wasn't ground to a pulp beneath his left hip. When he thrust the bike upright and eased himself to a standing position, slapping his jeans, his hands came away bright with smears of blood from one torn knee. Great. Now he'd have to tell Tess, and she'd never believe he hadn't been reckless.

A bobwhite called its name from the undergrowth opposite, and Will glanced up. Water lapped at the edge of the cranberry beds running along either side of the drive. The vines were completely submerged. A fragment of bright fabric, caught on a large piece of driftwood half sunk in the shallow pool, drew his eye. He walked closer and strained to make out its shape.

And then he cried out, hands over his mouth to stifle his terror. He turned in panic and dashed back to his bike, scraped leg forgotten, screaming for somebody.

RAFE DA SILVA surveyed the flock of merino sheep bunched up around the hay bale and counted them mentally. Fifty-three, ewes and lambs, with the ram fifty-four. Not a major concern, but not a shabby bunch, either. With this year's shearing—and a good price from Nantucket Looms, their major customer—they might begin to pay for their keep. Not that Peter cared; Rafe knew the sheep would stay whether they made money or not. Peter raised the merinos for the same reason he did everything on the farm: for the love of it. The sight of sheep dotting the moors around the bog satisfied Peter's sense of history, the way his life in the two-hundred-year-old saltbox seemed a direct link to Masons dead and gone. Rafe didn't question it, and he didn't waste much time thinking about it. He understood very little of Peter's class of people, but everything about Peter's way of life.

The dog Ney sauntered toward him, his tongue hanging out lazily now that his work was done and the sheep were busy eating. Part cattle dog, part bearded collie, Ney looked like pure mutt. Peter had picked him up in the parking lot of the South Street ferry in Hyannis, where the bewildered pup had been circling a crowd of embarking Nantucketers waiting patiently in the rain. Peter had watched as Ney herded the passengers into a tight knot next to the gangplank, and then he'd grinned. He had been on his way to the Boston Marathon. He hadn't needed a dog. He'd thought about an animal shelter, and then he'd thought better of it. He could usually find a use for strays.

"You and me both, fella," Rafe said to the dog. He dropped his hand to Ney's snout and scratched either side of it, knowing the dog loved it. Ney thrust his nose deeper into the man's hand and snorted deeply.

"Come on, pup." Ney pivoted as though joined to Rafe's body, then loped off ahead, disappearing into the fog.

Rafe strolled without hurry toward the barn where the bog equipment was stored. He and Peter had opened the shunts of the reservoir across ten of the farm's fifty acres at sundown last night and flooded them with several feet of water. He glanced up at the gray weather. Not pretty, but not bad. There were worse things than a cool day of farming.

He stopped suddenly and cocked his head, listening. Since well before dawn he had been half conscious of the moan of foghorns, a sound he had known from birth; but now a long, thin note spiraled through the air. Ney was howling, a high-pitched keening Rafe had never heard in the three years of the dog's life. It came from the driveway. He broke into a run.

"I THINK IT'S Peter, Rafe," Will said. He was bent over, staring at the bog, one hand on his knee and the other on Ney's collar. Rafe glanced at the boy's ashen face and then back at the body floating facedown in the water, seized by the same fear. The hair was Peter's dark brown, the body long and muscled. The man was dressed in khaki shorts and a rugby shirt, black-and-orange, that looked vaguely familiar. The calves were discolored with what at first glance appeared to be splotches of grease, but as Rafe moved to the edge of the bog and put one foot up to his knee in water, reaching for the man's hair, he realized the legs were badly bruised. He lifted the head. Wide and staring, the dead eyes looked toward the bank.

"It's not Peter, Will," he said gently, and let the corpse fall back into the water. "Let's get back to the house."

"You're not going to leave him here, are you?"

"It's better not to move anything until the police arrive. I shouldn't even have touched him." Rafe shook his wet hand and felt suddenly sick, not wanting to dry it on his own clothes. He shot a look at Will. The boy was watching him, his eyes filled with worry. And something else, Rafe thought—the memory of pain.

"I'd tell you if it were Pete, Will. Believe me. Come on, let's get to the phone."

It was not unusual for Peter Mason to be out of the house early. He spent a good part of his nonworking hours on his bicycle or running through miles of Nantucket's moors. A light sleeper, he'd been awakened at five today by the horns off the water. He'd stared at the beams running across the low ceiling of the upstairs bedroom, unable to doze. At six, abandoning all hope of sleep, he'd thrown on some clothes and headed out the back door for an easy run. An hour later he was making the turn for home at Altar Rock when he heard the sirens.

The ambulance and police car came up behind him suddenly in the fog, driving him into the underbrush as they went by. He narrowed his eyes and slowed to a near-walk, assessing what the sirens meant as they diminished in the distance. Then he began to sprint.

## Chapter 2

DETECTIVE MEREDITH FOLGER surveyed the trampled drive, the flooded bog, the bent backs of the two police sergeants, and Rafe da Silva standing silently in the distance; then she ran her fingers nervously through her blonde hair. Barely seven in the morning, and no evidence to speak of. Her first murder might have been kinder to her.

For a few moments after arriving with the crime scene unit, she had held out hope that the sodden body meant nothing more than a drunken slip and a drowning, or even an inglorious suicide. She had dismissed those options fairly quickly. The bruises on the dead man's legs and the broken underbrush raised too many questions.

She fished in the depths of her shoulder bag and came up with the slim packet she was looking for: her half-glasses. Useful for detail work—and maybe they'd even lend an air of professionalism to her face. She perched them on the tip of her nose and walked in a half-crouch down the gravel drive to the livestock gate, stopping to study the spot where Will's bike had met the mouse. Then she surveyed the unpaved road beyond that ran perpendicular to the Mason Farms entrance. Multiple car tracks—a heavy four-wheel-drive and several passenger cars of varying sizes—had crisscrossed its sandy surface. She walked back along the road several feet, following the intertwined treads closely, and veered left. Near the right-hand side of the gate a car had gone off the road, stopped abruptly—spraying gravel on the grass—and then executed a three-point turn in order to drive away.

Merry crouched motionlessly above the scattered gravel an instant, thinking, and then stood up. She removed her reading glasses and stuffed them into her coat pocket, staring abstractedly at the roadbed. Then, impatiently, she pulled out the glasses again and retraced her steps.

Bent double, she walked slowly along the bog's edge from the turnoff to where the body still lay in the water twenty feet down the drive. It was obvious something heavy had recently been dragged through the gravel—the corpse? Or harvesting equipment? She paced back along the driveway more carefully, and was rewarded: a small wooden object, tossed haphazardly in the high grass by the bog's edge, caught her eye. She dropped to the ground.

"Clarence!"

Clarence Strangerfield, head of the crime scene unit, was up to his knees in the bog, camera poised, taking multiple shots of the corpse from various angles. He glanced across the drive at Meredith. "Ayeh," he said.

"C'mere. I found something."

Clarence hitched up his trousers with one hand, balancing his camera in the other. "What is it?"

"Looks like—" Merry hesitated. "Looks like a small wooden rat. I need a shot of the way it's lying. Make sure you get the pattern of the breakage in the underbrush all around here, too."

Clarence was pushing sixty, and he enjoyed his wife Emmeline's dinners; with a grunt of effort he pulled one bog-laden boot out of the water and heaved himself onto the bank. He took one last shot of the dead man from above, and then ambled down the drive toward the detective.

Her hands were on her hips, and her dark brows, always so startling in contrast to her tow-colored hair, were furrowed. "Looks like an oversized charm from a bracelet. Any ideas?"

Clarence eased his bulk down onto his work-worn knees and hovered over the scrap of wood. There was a pregnant pause. Then he cocked an eyebrow gravely at Merry. "Ayeh," he said, "thaht's a raht."

"Never mind, Clare," Merry said. "Just shoot the thing." When he had finished, she reached into her purse for tweezers and a plastic bag, and lifted the rat from the grass.

"Okay," she said. "We have a button. With a thread of yarn still stuck in the buttonhole—looks like it's from a sweater. The wood's smooth enough to dust for prints." She slipped the button in the bag and handed it to Clarence for labeling. "You'll probably want to vacuum the corpse for matching fibers, too."

Merry turned toward the spot at the side of the driveway that she could no longer avoid: the corpse, floating gently on the water's surface. She took a deep breath and forced herself to walk over to the broken underbrush and the lifeless body, wondering for an instant at the way the outflung arms seemed to embrace death. She had expected murder to look less thankful.

"You've triangulated the position of the body?" she asked Clarence.

"Used the gate and thaht tree ovah there," he said, "and I've had young Coffin sketch the scene." If he was aware of any irony in the surname of his chief assistant, Nathaniel Coffin, the crime scene chief did not betray it. "We're 'bout ready for Doctah John, I should think. He's already seen the cahpse in situ. Told me to bring it to the van when you wahr done. Guess he doesn't want to get his trousahs wet."

Dr. John Fairborn was the island's medical examiner. Merry glanced over to the rescue squad's white van, useless now to the man floating in the flooded cranberries, and caught the doctor in the act of discarding a cigarette as he lounged against the truck's open back door. She made a mental note to pick up the butt—to prevent Clarence's boys from cataloguing it as evidence—and wondered again how doctors could smoke after studying cancer in medical school. A God complex, probably. She turned back to Clarence. "We'll need Coffin's help," she said.

Clarence motioned to his assistant, who came at a run, and the three of them stepped up to their knees in bog water and vines. "Let's lift him out and over the bank, Clare, and carry him directly to Dr. John," Merry said.

"Yah know he'll look rathah bahd," Clarence said carefully. "The blood'll have pooled in his lowah tissues."

Merry nodded impatiently. "Lividity. Let's get it over with."

She took hold of the man's sodden rugby shirt just under his left armpit, while Clarence took his right; Coffin placed himself near the corpse's pelvis and legs.

"On the count of three," Merry said. "One, two . . ."

Protesting like a sleeper torn from his dreams, the body

lifted free of its watery bed. They staggered, foot over stumbling foot, to where Dr. John lounged.

The medical examiner slapped his hands together in mock glee. "The iceman cometh," he said. "I'll let you know how long he's been dead, give or take a few hours."

Merry wiped her wet hands on her khakis and opened her mouth to say something, then thought better of it and turned away. She had always liked Dr. John, and in the past she had taken his black humor as one of the survival techniques of police work. Today she felt differently. The dead man must have been loved by someone; perhaps even now a wife or a friend was dialing the station frantically, wondering why he hadn't come home last night. He might be someone she'd bumped into exiting a shop, apologizing as he held open the door for her before moving on in his separate life. That life was over.

She forced herself to look at the purple face. "Any idea who he is, Clare?"

Clarence's ample stomach rumbled. He had missed his breakfast, but Merry was crawling toward the end of the night shift at eight-fifteen. On a normal morning they'd have met over coffee and doughnuts at the Downyflake. "A-no, I don't. You?"

She shook her head. "What a lousy way to die. He's not much older than me, for Chrissake." She paused, looking at the crime scene chief, her arms folded protectively across her chest, and then looked away. "Think about it, Clare. We're supposed to help people. And while I was sitting in the station last night, killing time, this guy was out here dying in the dark. *Violently*."

"Makes yah feel like yah lahst a contest yah didn't know had stahted," he agreed.

Merry stood still for a moment in her red slicker, the cheery color belying her weariness. Clarence, who had a streak of the mother hen in him, would want to throw an arm around her and send her home. To forestall him, she rolled her neck a bit to ease her muscles, and then moved past him toward the white van where the murdered man was lying. Clarence fell into step beside her. She could feel his worry nipping at their heels like a small dog. He was uneasy about this body. First of all, it was on Mason land—and though Clarence might consider them "summah people," the Masons had been powerful islanders for more years than Merry could remember. Secondly, the corpse hadn't died by itself, and that meant Merry had some difficult days ahead of her. Despite years on the Nantucket force, she had never investigated a violent death.

*So what*, she thought. *I'm a Folger. That's always stood for competence on this island.*

"Maybe he's a tahrist," Clarence said matter-of-factly.

Merry shook her head. "What tourist would be this far out of town, alone at night? Doesn't make sense—"

"—and it's *too easy*, in yahr opinion," Clarence finished.

Merry smiled at him wanly. *It's too easy* was her father's favorite phrase, as Clarence well knew. "I'd like you to shoot the spot out on the road where the car went into the grass, Clare. There's a faint set of footprints you might be able to lift. Also the drag marks in the gravel. Then, as soon as you can, get somebody on the Mason car, or cars—particularly the bumpers."

Clarence's face grew sober. "The bruises on the legs."

Merry nodded. Her eyes drifted back to the dead man,

and Clarence saw her blink rapidly. "When you're done there we'll deal with—"

"Baggin' him," Clarence said.

HE HAD EXPECTED them to pull up in front of the house, and so he ran right into the official knot gathered behind the yellow police barrier.

"Peter!" It was Will's voice, young and filled with relief. Peter looked for the boy and saw instead a blonde woman in a bright red raincoat, her booted feet firmly planted in his bog. Then he found Rafe, standing next to Will by the police car, and started toward him.

"What's going on, Rafe?"

"That's what we'd like to know, Mr. Mason."

Peter turned. The woman ducked under the police barrier and walked toward him, fumbling in her pocket for a badge. She flashed it half-apologetically at him. "Detective Meredith Folger, Nantucket police."

Peter held out his hand. "Peter Mason."

She seemed to shake it for a fraction of a second longer than was necessary, as if she found his hand comforting and didn't want to let go. He registered wide-set eyes the color of moss, heavy dark brows, and a high forehead. A face an artist would love, all bones and angles beneath a translucent skin. She was made for the forties, he thought, made for Cecil Beaton to photograph. She wore no makeup. Probably smart—if she did, the station house would explode.

"I'm afraid we've got some bad news, Mr. Mason," she said. "Someone's been killed in your cranberry field. Under the circumstances, I'll have to ask you some questions."

"Killed? Who?"

"He's carrying no identification, and I'm afraid he's a stranger to me and everyone present. Did you have any guests on your property last night?"

Peter started to brush past her, headed for the ambulance parked near the farm's entrance. She laid a hand on his arm. "Answer the question, please."

He stared at her a moment, considering whether she was worth obeying. The green eyes were hard and steady. "No," he said. "I didn't expect anyone, and nobody dropped by the house." He turned to Rafe. "Any midnight callers?"

The foreman shook his head. "And I've never seen this guy before, Pete." His voice held a note of uneasiness.

Peter's eyes narrowed. "But what, Rafe?"

"The guy looks familiar. Maybe you know him."

For an instant, Peter's instinct was to run in any direction. *Rafe was afraid for him.* He glanced at Meredith Folger, then walked toward the black body bag laid on a stretcher. A lanky paramedic was in the act of zipping it shut.

"Wait a minute." Peter pulled back the edge of the bag and looked hard at the dead face. The eyes had been closed. He was sharply aware of the smell of his own sweat, vividly alive, as he studied the blue lips.

"Finished, sir?" the paramedic asked.

Rafe was standing next to him suddenly, one hand on his back. "Who is it, Pete?"

"Rusty."

Meredith Folger looked up sharply. "Rusty?"

Peter nodded. "My brother."

*Chapter 3*

"CAN YOU TELL me what happened, Will?" Merry said. She was trudging with the boy and Rafe da Silva, a police summer intern in tow, up the quarter-mile of sand-and-gravel drive to Peter Mason's saltbox on the moor. They had left Mason behind with the paramedic.

Will looked imploringly at Rafe, who seemed to have retreated into himself. He was striding purposefully toward the house, head down, lost in thought.

Merry had known Rafe all her life. She suspected that this routine walk over familiar territory allowed him to think without interruption. The careful lack of expression on his Portuguese features camouflaged a very active anxiety. *He's worried not about the body, but about what it implies*, she thought.

This close to Rafe, she felt a rush of dread that had nothing to do with the dead man that had brought her onto his turf; she bit her lip and wished he would look at her. He studied the ground instead.

She gave up and turned back to Will. He was walking between the two of them, slightly bent as he held firmly to the collar of a large, indiscriminate dog. He looked peaked and too old for his fifteen years, and something tugged at the back of her brain. She did not know the

Starbuck family well—in fact, she knew Tess Starbuck only by sight—but there was something about the father's death that she ought to remember.

Will cleared his throat. "I wouldn't have seen it if it weren't for the mouse," he said.

Merry nodded encouragingly, not understanding him in the slightest. "Let's start before that. Why were you here at all, and so early?"

"I'm supposed to work. That's why the bog's flooded. We're wet-harvesting today." At the prospect of the promised job, Will's face brightened momentarily. "It was pretty foggy, you know, so I had to ride really slow. I almost missed the drive, because the gate was open, which it never is, and in the fog you couldn't tell there was a road there, even."

Merry made a mental note to ask Rafe about the gate. "And so?"

"There was this mouse on the driveway—it ran out in front of the bike, and I tried to stop and couldn't. The gravel makes it hard with the brakes. Anyway, I wiped out." He stopped.

"And that's when you saw the body?" Merry asked gently.

Will's head dropped to his chest, and he shrugged. "I didn't know that's what it was, right away," he said. "I thought somebody's T-shirt had got caught on a piece of driftwood, you know? In the fog, nothing looks like it should."

"Or maybe when you don't expect a body to be there, your eyes tell you it's something else," Merry said. "You didn't touch anything? Didn't pick anything up?"

"Nope." Will was studying his running shoes as he walked. "And then Rafe came."

At the sound of his name, Rafe looked over Will's head at Merry, a warning in his eyes. "Ney was howling," he said carefully. "That's something he never does. So I got there pretty quickly." Merry nodded slightly. Rafe was protecting the kid.

Rapid footsteps crunched along the gravel behind them, and Mason's tall frame loomed suddenly out of the fog at Merry's side. His tanned skin gleamed with moisture, part sweat and part condensation. He reached urgently for her elbow. "I need you to talk to the paramedic," he said. It was a command, not a request.

"What's wrong, Mr, Mason?"

"He won't let me go with Rusty's body. He wouldn't even let me search his pockets."

"I'm afraid that's police procedure," she said, not unkindly, and waited for him to drop her arm. She had expected something like this. Next-of-kin rarely took a death well; and they all handled it differently, men being the most unpredictable.

"Well then, change police procedure," he said.

Merry drew herself up to her full five feet ten. She still had to look up to him. "Mr. Mason," she said, "you're probably feeling grief and a bit of shock. Maybe even anger. I know I would in your place. I'm sure your brother meant a lot to you, and the idea that he's been killed is pretty difficult to accept—"

"I don't need you to tell me what to feel," Mason said, his anger in his voice. "*I need you to talk to the paramedic.*"

Merry stopped short. His strong chin, jutting brow bones, and sweep of jet-black hair were attractive, certainly, and his gray eyes held intelligence, even when he was in a rage. But he was decidedly arrogant—an attitude

she put down to off-island wealth, years of family authority, and the male desire to run things. It was hard to know
whether he felt any sorrow. Probably that would come
later. Now he was in a mood to take charge, as generations of Masons had done before him. She glanced over
at Rafe and Will, the one looking wary, the other, confused; and knew she'd have to fight this one alone.

"I'm afraid I can't change police procedure, Mr. Mason,
because the body is evidence," she said firmly. "There will
be an autopsy. A coroner's report. We'll probably have to
send fluid and tissue samples to the state police crime lab
in Boston. After a while, a couple of days at a minimum,
we can release your brother to you for burial. We'll do our
best to speed the process along, but you're going to have
to live with some delay and some red tape."

"I don't have to like it," Peter said. "Rusty may be evidence to you, but he happens to be my brother." He was
furious, his lips compressed. "I want the name of your chief."

Merry felt the faintest finger of amusement tug at the
corners of her mouth. "I guess that'd be John Folger," she
said. "He'll be in the station in another hour or so. But
I'll save you the trouble, Mr. Mason. He's a bigger fan of
the book than I am."

"Folger? Is he—"

"Any relation? Yeah. He's my dad. Police work is kind
of a family tradition on the island." She turned and began
to trudge up the drive, glancing at Mason from the corner of her eye to see how he was taking it. Momentarily
checked, but not beaten. He'd want to run this investigation himself.

They reached the saltbox's geranium-colored door. The
dog bolted out of Will's grasp and into the house, bound

for the kitchen with the boy in pursuit. Peter Mason stood back and waited for Merry to enter. She stepped inside the low-ceilinged entrance hall. A smell peculiar to the island—pine, salt water, roses, the fragrance of the moors, and something else she could only describe as the odor of time—drifted up from the floor. The house reeked of finished lives and the passage of years.

Mason led them to the study at the back of the house and sank into an armchair. Rafe took up a leaning position by the door to the kitchen. Merry refused a seat and stood squarely in the middle of the sea-blue rug, rummaging in her work bag for her laptop and half-glasses. The intern, a Northeastern criminal justice student named Howie Seitz, stood a reluctant three paces behind her. Seitz was six feet four and his limbs were straining out of his regulation-blue uniform. He had abandoned his hat, and his tanned face under an unruly mop of dark curls managed to look bored and exultant at once. He had spent his summer internship on a bicycle in Siasconset, giving directions to day-trippers and making sure some hedge-fund manager's drunk kid didn't crash his sports car on the way to the beach. Now, in his final week, Howie had something to talk about.

Merry abandoned her slicker, revealing khakis and a pale green crew-neck cotton sweater above the black rubber knee boots she still wore. She flipped her hair behind her ears and seemed not to notice when it slid just as quickly back down her cheekbone. An old boyfriend, in a burst of ill-advised fervor, had told her once that the soul of Medusa lived on in her hair. Her most striking feature—dark brows—had caused her endless grief in her younger years. She had tried to bleach them blonde in high school, and had suffered the horrors for a good six months. Those who did not know her well mistook her shyness for aloofness and thought her proud. It was one of the many miscalculations made about Meredith Folger.

She set her bag on the floor next to the sofa, withdrew a laptop from its depths, and after a second decided to sit down. She was starting to feel the hunger of an all-nighter, like a crab clawing its way out of her stomach. She shut her eyes and said a quick prayer that she wouldn't forget to ask anything important. Then she glanced around the study. Old maps in bird's-eye-maple frames flanked the fireplace. A partner's desk occupied one corner, while a comfortable sofa and a russet-colored leather chair were drawn up to a table with an inlaid chessboard. The chessmen were soldiers of some kind, and there was a game in progress. Books were everywhere. The room—comfortable, expensive, and entirely personal—was Peter Mason's defense against the world, and she had invaded it with her officiousness and her questions. She felt lightheaded, and swallowed.

As for Peter, even at rest in his chair, his body conveyed grace and power, qualities that Merry assumed were part of his genetic material. Masons had walked the world for centuries with just his brand of self-assurance and ownership; it was their birthright. His chin was resting on one palm, and he seemed to be gazing at nothing, his mind working furiously. Time to ask him some questions. She opened her laptop and turned it on.

"Since no one recognized him, I take it your brother doesn't live here, Mr. Mason?"

He laughed suddenly, shortly, and looked at Merry. "No, my brother did not live here, Miss Folger."

Merry hesitated, then decided to press a point for authority's sake. "I prefer Detective, Mr. Mason."

"Detective. I prefer Peter, but perhaps you have rules about calling victims by their first names."

"Victims, in my experience, are beyond being called anything," Merry said. "I prefer to maintain a professional relationship with those involved in an investigation, if that's what you mean."

Peter's expression of bitter amusement widened. "So now I'm under investigation? That's perfect. How like Rusty." He rose and crossed to the bookcases that lined one wall, filled helter-skelter with old leather-bound editions and dog-eared paperbacks, and reached for a bottle of Glenfiddich doing duty as a bookend.

"I'm sorry, Detective Folger. I'm not being very helpful, and now I'm drinking in the morning." The door next to Rafe opened, and Rebecca, the housekeeper, entered on a tide of warm air and comfort. She carried a tin tray with a coffeepot, five mugs, and a basket of cranberry bread. Will followed with the cream and sugar. Rebecca pointedly ignored Merry and Howie Seitz as she set the tray on the low table in front of the fireplace.

Peter downed the scotch, neat, and sighed as the liquor hit his empty stomach. "Thanks, Rebecca," he said.

Rebecca shook her closely cropped gray head disapprovingly at the drink, but, showing unusual self-restraint, said nothing and disappeared back into the kitchen.

Peter crossed to his chair and sat down again, eyes alert, face in control.

"When did you get up this morning, Mr. Mason?" Merry asked.

"About five-thirty."

"How do you know?"

"I didn't check the clock, if that's what you're asking. I awoke about five—which I know from long experience of what five o'clock feels like—and couldn't get back to sleep. I lay in bed awhile and then decided to go for a run."

"Do you often run at that hour?"

"I always run at that hour. The afternoons are for biking or swimming. I'm training for a triathlon."

Merry suppressed the impulse to ask him when he got any work done, and shot a glance at Rafe. The force behind the farm, obviously. "Did anyone see you leave?"

"Rebecca was in the kitchen. I said hello to her as I left."

"Did you call to her, or did she actually see you?"

"Why does it matter?" he said irritably.

Merry didn't answer.

"I left by the kitchen door. I assume Rebecca heard the door slam. She was standing with her back to me, at the kitchen sink."

"So you left the house in the direction of the moors," Merry said. "You didn't come around the house and take the drive? Perhaps leaving the gate open as you ran?"

"No. If I'd wanted to go in the direction of the drive, I'd have used the front door. I'm sorry I didn't make it easy for you and discover the body myself, but I'm a creature of habit. I run through the moors."

"Where did you go?"

"First north, toward the sea, and then down the Polpis Road toward town, and then back up the Milestone Road bike path to the Altar Rock turnoff. I was just beyond there when you roared past me in your SUV."

He'd done close to eleven miles in about seventy minutes. "Did you see anyone while you were running?"

"No. It wasn't a morning conducive to sightseeing. More to breakfast in bed, I imagine."

"Mr. da Silva," Merry said, dismissing Peter and turning to Rafe, "could you describe your movements this morning for me?"

Rafe's lips twitched at the use of *Mr. da Silva*. "I got up about the same time, five-thirty," he said, "and saw to the sheep."

"Meaning?"

"Meaning I got the dog and we herded them up off the moors and drove 'em in to feed. Came in for breakfast after. That'd be about six."

"And did anyone see you?"

Rafe gave the ghost of a smile. "Herding's nothing to get up for, unless you own the sheep," he said.

"And then?"

"I went back to the barn to check out the harvesting gear. That was when Ney started terrorizing the neighborhood. I ran up the driveway and—saw Will."

"When would that be?"

"Six forty-five, thereabouts."

"What did you do at that point?"

Rafe looked uncomfortably at Peter, and then at the floor. "We wanted to see if it was someone we knew, so I lifted the head a bit outta the water, just enough to check, and then we left everything and came back to the house."

Peter's gaze was riveted on Rafe. "Who found the body?" he said.

"I did, Peter." Will's voice was very small and seemed

to come from a farther distance than his cross-legged position in front of the coffee tray.

"Oh, Will," Peter said, turning to the boy. "Not you." He paused, looking at Will's white, stiff face.

Will flinched. "Like it matters who found him, Pete. I don't care." He stopped suddenly, and the set lines of his face crumpled and reddened. "I mean, I'm—I feel really awful about your brother, Pete, I do. I'm really sorry."

"I know, Will. It's all right." Peter held the boy's eyes, then glanced at Merry, who was watching, and waiting. She adjusted her half-glasses on the end of her nose.

"If you could give me your brother's contact information, Mr. Mason—"

"I'm afraid I can't help you, Detective. Rusty left the country ten years ago, and we fell out of touch. I think he was living in Brazil at one point, but I can't even be sure of that."

"Brazil?" She was momentarily startled, and showed it. "What was he doing in Brazil?"

"I've no idea," Peter said.

Rafe drew in his breath sharply, and Merry glanced at him. *He thinks Mason is deliberately stonewalling*, she thought. She turned back to Peter.

"Had he contacted you recently?"

"No."

"How about anyone else in the family? Who else is there, by the way?"

"My mother lives in Hobe Sound, Florida. I have a sister—Georgiana Whitney—who lives in Greenwich, Connecticut."

"And they said nothing about your brother coming home?"

"I think if either of them had heard from Rusty, I'd know about it. Particularly if he had it in his head to come here." Peter was staring at the floor again, his left leg crossed on his right knee, one hand drumming the tanned skin of his thigh. As if suddenly conscious of his fingers, he stopped the staccato and reached for a mug. "How do you take your coffee, Detective? Black or white?"

"White, thank you. No sugar. In other words, all of this is a surprise."

"Yes." He poured the coffee very carefully.

"Not just your brother's death, but the fact that he was here at all," she persisted.

"Right. In fact, I would go so far as to say that any news of Rusty, alive or dead, would come as an unpleasant shock." He handed her the mug.

An appalling thought entered Merry's mind as she took her first sip: *Peter Mason wasn't sorry his brother was dead.* In fact, the very sight of his brother seemed to have made him furious. It was incomprehensible. The body that had filled her with the abrupt finality of death had only enraged him.

"Mr. Mason," she began, "how well did you get along with your brother?"

"I can't see that that has anything to do with this, Detective Folger."

"Bad blood between brothers was good enough for Cain," she said mildly. Mason did not reply, which was an answer in itself. She glanced at Rafe, whose face was carefully wiped clean of all expression. *Either he knows more about this than he's telling, or he's turning it over in his mind,* she thought. She would have to talk to him later, alone.

"I have to ask you, Mr. Mason, whether you killed your brother."

Peter closed his eyes. "It's the obvious question, isn't it? No, Detective, I did not."

"Even without meaning to? By accident, or on the spur of the moment?"

"If I had, would I have left him there in the ditch for anybody to find? Give me some credit for intelligence, please!"

"I've tried to do that. I'd ask for the same in return," Merry said, exasperated. "It's pretty hard to believe that your brother's been gone for ten years, and you didn't know he was going to show up the night he got murdered. It looks, as we'd say down at the station, like an implausible explanation."

Peter said nothing, his face darkening.

Merry flipped through her laptop as though searching for Rusty's life somewhere among its files. She waited, guessing Peter Mason would offer nothing further.

"Did anyone here at the farm know your brother?"

He picked up his coffee cup. "I think we've established that Rafe and Will never knew him," he said. "Rebecca's in the kitchen. You're welcome to talk to her on your way out. But to my knowledge she's never seen Rusty. She's only worked here since I moved back to Nantucket permanently, ten years ago. Rusty was here every summer as a child, of course, as I was. But as an adult he lived in Manhattan and rarely visited the island." He took a deep draft of coffee, wincing slightly as it burned its way down his throat. "Tell me something, Detective, if you're allowed to. How did he die?"

Merry paused an instant, weighing her answer. Her training warned against allowing Peter Mason to ask the questions. But at the moment she was wracking her brain for an opening to all that he was withholding, and maybe some give and take would help. "I think your brother drowned, basically, but I can only speculate how that happened."

"Couldn't it have been an accident? A stumble in the dark, a blow to the head, a roll into the water, something like that?"

Meredith pulled her glasses away from her face and met Mason's eyes. "I doubt it. The crime scene unit is wrapping up its work right now, and we won't have the autopsy report for a couple of days. But from the bruises on the body when we pulled him out, I'd say he was struck with some violence behind the knees and thrown backward onto a hard surface. His skull is cracked."

Peter frowned. "Struck by what?"

"A car bumper, I'd guess."

"A hit-and-run?" Will's voice broke.

"I don't think so," Merry said. "At least, not in the sense of an accident, which is what you mean, Will. There are no tire tracks coming to a sudden stop anywhere near where you found the body. He wasn't hit on the drive."

"You said he drowned, Detective," Peter objected.

"I'd like to wait for the coroner's report, of course, but it looks to me as though he was struck squarely by the middle of the front fender—a few feet in front of the livestock gate—went into the air, and slammed his head on the hood of the car. He'd have rolled off to one side. It's clear he didn't go under the tires—there's no sign of crushed bones, as there would be if the car had actually driven over him. I'd bet he was knocked senseless by the impact."

Peter looked at her levelly. "So whoever hit my brother

deliberately opened the gate, hauled him up the drive and placed him facedown in the bog to die."

There was a small silence. "That's about it," Merry said. "He didn't walk into the bog. There's a fairly distinct drag mark, as though someone had pulled the body up the drive by the shoulders and rolled it into the water. Fragments of gravel from the drive are stuck on the fabric of your brother's shirt. It's possible there are microscopic paint chips from the vehicle that struck him lodged in the fabric as well. We just don't know yet. There's also a nice, deep set of footprints on the soggy edge of the bog that I'm having my colleagues cast right now, and a single print out on the main road. They were made by the same shoe. A set of what I think are Rusty's prints are near some tire-track patterns on the road, but there are none of his anywhere near the bog itself."

Peter stood up and crossed to the diamond-paned window that took up most of the study's far wall. Roses, coming into their end-of-summer bloom, trailed from the low eaves beyond it. The window looked out on the vivid moor, but today the view was obscured by fog.

"Are these bogs always flooded, Mr. Mason?" Merry asked.

"No," he said, "just at certain times of the year—in fall, for wet harvesting, which is harder on the berries than dry. Wet-harvested product goes to processing; dry, to the grocer. Then in winter, we flood the vines slightly and the water freezes over them. It's a form of protection. Why?"

"Could anyone have anticipated that the bogs would be flooded today?"

Peter turned to look at her, pausing to think. "We hire

a team of day laborers to wet-harvest," he said, "but it's Labor Day weekend, and half of them are on the Cape shopping for their kids' back-to-school clothes. Rafe and I decided to start on a few acres today without them. Only we knew the bog would be flooded—and Will, of course, and his mother presumably. And Rebecca," he added, as an afterthought.

"Once these things are under water, can they be drained off again?"

"I suppose so. Why?"

"I'd like you to do that. Some of your brother's effects may have sunk to the bottom. We should do a thorough search."

Peter's jaw tightened. "That'll delay my harvest, Detective."

"Not by much," Merry said brusquely. "I think you can spare a day. Use it to plan a funeral." She pulled on her glasses again and re-addressed her laptop. "How many people work here at Mason Farms?"

"You're looking at the staff, Detective, with the addition of Rebecca. She lives in the cottage out back. Rafe lives over the barn. Will, of course, just comes over when he can spare the time."

"I'll need to know where each of you was after eleven P.M. last night," she said.

"I can't even drive!" Will's face was white, the blotchy shadows under his eyes that much darker.

"I didn't think you could, Will. Were you in bed at home?" she asked.

Will nodded.

"Rebecca and I were here," Peter said, "but of course, we could be covering for each other." Merry ignored the acid in the remark and turned to look at Rafe. He was leaning forward over his work boots, studying the patches of mud on the worn leather laces.

"I'd guess I was at the Greengage until eleven," he said carefully. "Dod Nelson ran me home in his truck."

"Did he drop you at the door?"

Rafe shook his head and smiled crookedly. "At the end of the drive. And he didn't run anybody over doing it. But I guess you'll want to see his bumper."

"Will said the gate was open when he arrived. Did you close it after you last evening?"

Rafe hesitated, then nodded. "And I didn't open it this morning."

"Notice anything unusual as you walked up the drive?"

"Not a thing."

"Did either of you hear anything out of the ordinary last night—a car jamming on the brakes, a cry, a fight of any kind?"

The two men glanced at one another, but said nothing. Will Starbuck hung his head and pulled at the threads of his torn jeans.

"It's a half mile to the road, Detective. When you're inside, it's hard to hear much," Peter said.

"Is the dog loose at night?"

"He stays in the loft with me," Rafe said.

"Did he bark last night?"

Rafe shook his head.

Merry glanced down at her keyboard, stalling for time, wondering if she'd missed anything. She looked up and thought she saw a small expression of amusement cross Rafe da Silva's face. Her stomach contracted. "What time would you say you turned in?"

"Around eleven-thirty, or near enough."

Peter nodded. "All tucked in, Detective. Not that that lets us out. We sleep alone, after all." There was a bitterness in his voice, Merry thought suddenly, that had nothing to do with his brother's murder. Peter turned back to the fog beyond the window. "I wish I could tell you why Rusty was here and why he died," he said. "But I haven't a clue."

Merry closed her laptop. "I'm not sure that's true, Mr. Mason. It's possible you know more than you realize. I'd appreciate it if you'd think about who'd want to kill your brother on this island where no one supposedly knows him. You say he spent some time here as a kid. Maybe it's something from the past." She picked up her red slicker from the leather chair. Howie Seitz retrieved his hat.

"I'd like to talk to Rebecca now, if I could."

Peter nodded distractedly, his back to the room.

*As though I were invisible*, Merry thought. *One of the domestic help.*

"Detective Folger," Peter said. "Please keep me informed."

It was not, Merry reflected, a request.

## Chapter 4

PETER MASON CONTINUED to stare blankly through the study window, his arms folded across his chest.

Rafe and Will did not intrude on his thoughts. Rafe chose a mug from the coffee tray, tousling Will's hair as he reached past him. The corners of Will's mouth flicked upward in a poor attempt at a smile. "Have some bread, kiddo," Rafe said. Will shook his head. His knees, showing through the torn jeans, were drawn up to his chin and his arms were wrapped tightly around them. Warding off the bogeyman, Rafe thought.

"Rafe," Peter said, "do me a favor and run Will home in the Rover. We're not going to harvest today."

"But school starts tomorrow, Peter!" Will protested. "I'll miss everything!"

Peter turned to look at him. He sat down in his armchair and leaned toward Will, his eyes intent. "You heard the good cop, Will. We're not harvesting anything for the next few days."

"Can I come over after school and help?"

"If your mom thinks you've got the time, sure," Peter said carefully. "Now run home and spend the last day of summer vacation the way you should." He looked up at Rafe, who was staring at him over Will's head.

"Go say goodbye to Rebecca and meet Rafe at the Rover," Peter said, clapping the boy on the shoulder. Will rose reluctantly and headed for the kitchen, casting a doubtful glance backward at the two men.

When Will had disappeared into the kitchen, Peter sat back in the armchair. "What is it, Rafe? Think I killed my brother?"

"Of course not, Pete," Rafe said. "But somebody did, and I don't feel that great about leaving you alone."

"What do you mean?"

"I know you. You'll head right out of this house to look for Rusty's killer. You know a lot you're not telling, and it's going to get you into trouble." He stopped short and took a swig of coffee. "That's one theory. The other's simpler, but it's much worse."

"Meaning?"

"Meaning someone's going to be surprised as hell when you show up in town today. And not very happy."

Peter ran a finger around the edge of his mug. The coffee was cold. He frowned in distaste and set it back down on the tray.

"You mean the person who thought he was killing me when he killed Rusty," he said. "I thought of that, too. But it doesn't make sense, Rafe. Who'd want to kill me?"

"Who else would they be trying to kill? Never mind why your brother showed up here last night. That's weird enough. It's too much of a coincidence to think he could get himself to your place and killed all in one day." Rafe threw himself down on the sofa and leaned forward, elbows on his knees. "Pete, the fog hadn't come in yet last night when I got home, but believe you me, you can't see the end of your nose at the end of that drive after sundown. It's black as all get-out. Anybody who caught Rusty in his headlights, wearing a Princeton rugby shirt like yours, hit the gas thinking it was you they were mowing down. *Betcha*." He stood up and fished for his keys in his jeans pocket. "Remember that when you go looking for the guy."

Peter glanced up at his foreman and smiled crookedly. "Thanks, Rafe," he said.

The vehemence faded from Rafe's heavy features. "Aw, hell," he said. "You're not going to listen to me. But you better watch your back." He pulled open the door to the hallway. Merry Folger was saying goodbye to a friendlier Rebecca at the front door. He ducked back inside the study. "Nantucket's finest is on her way out," he said. "Think I'll give her time to get on down the drive."

Peter smiled again, genuinely this time, and Rafe grinned back.

Rafe knew very little about Peter's life before his return to the island. The youngest Mason had purchased the land with its abandoned saltbox ten years earlier, when he was just twenty-four, and had spent the next four years waiting for his fifty acres of cranberry vines to bear. He hired Rafe as foreman after that first harvest, and Rafe had been happy to stay. Over the past five years the Portuguese waterman and the Ivy League farmer had forged a deep friendship, born of common labor and love for the island. Rafe respected Peter's intelligence and strength, and counted on them to steady his own life. He was grateful to him for giving his days some structure and purpose, and he would sacrifice much to preserve Peter's peace. That Peter needed peace Rafe understood very well. He felt, rather than knew, that Peter carried a

weight he never spoke of, something unhealed and fester-
ing from the past. On days when simple work and hours
spent outdoors drained him of energy, the ghosts were far
away. But during the winter months, when the islanders were housebound and farm work was less demanding,
Peter withdrew into his books and his memories. Rafe was
perhaps more necessary to him then, as friend and silent
presence. Peter often wondered how he had survived the
winters before Rafe came.

"Well, you're right," Peter said. "Whether I'm supposed to be dead or not, I need to find out why Rusty is.
And to do that, I have to find out why he was here."

"You could let the police do their job, Pete," Rafe said.

Peter laughed. "You mean the island's answer to Ingrid
Bergman?" he said. "I don't think so. The closest she'll
get to figuring this out is what she told us this morning:
how he died. She won't have a clue as to why."

"I'm not so sure." Rafe's voice was quiet. "She comes
from tough stock."

Peter looked up. "You know her?"

"I grew up with her. Heck, everybody knows the Folgers. Her grandpa was chief before her dad. Her brother
Billy was probably my best friend." Rafe thrust one large
hand through his mop of black hair awkwardly. "He saved
my life in Fajullah, and died doing it."

There was a short silence. Peter nodded. "I'll try not
to disparage the local force, of whatever gender. If they
display some talent for investigation, I'll even work with
them." He bent down and unlaced his running shoes.
"But if we assume I'm the one somebody wants to kill,
I'd be an idiot to sit here and wait for him to try again.
Action may be my only means of survival."

"Or a flare gun for the killer."

Peter appeared not to have heard him. "I'm going to shower. When you get back, we'll pull out the pump and start draining the fields," he said. "Wouldn't want to obstruct justice."

"Or have the cops do it for you, and ruin the fruit," Rafe said. He sighed heavily as he stood up. Merry Folger was probably long gone, and Will would be waiting patiently by the Range Rover. He'd better get the boy back to Tess. "Whistle if you need me," he said, opening the study door. Peter nodded in dismissal. The door closed quietly behind Rafe.

PETER STUDIED THE chessboard in front of him for a few seconds, and moved Napoleon—the king piece— one square to the left. Marshal Ney, his horse rearing, was about to be taken by a Russian hussar. He could not let that happen. It seemed blasphemous to fight the Russian campaign over and over again on this circumscribed board, particularly with casualties that hadn't occurred in history, but he loved the opposing chessmen. A gift from his father, two years before his death, one of the many tokens by which Max Mason had tried to show that he understood his son.

He straightened Ney's horse, and then made for his bedroom. After the shower he had some phone calls to make. He considered waiting until he had a funeral date before contacting his mother and his sister George, wanting to delay the inevitable, and then decided against it. Rusty had the right to be mourned by someone other than himself.

## Chapter 5

MERRY FOLGER GLANCED over at Will, sitting beside her in her Explorer. She had spotted him waiting patiently for Rafe and had seized the opportunity to take him home herself. Howie Seitz was hunched in the backseat, crammed next to Will's bike, his head shaking rhythmically to the rap music coming through his earbuds. Merry was relieved. She had expected him to cross-examine her interrogation technique during the ride back to town. She asked the questions that occurred to her as they entered her mind, and had never done it any other way. After six years as the only woman on the Nantucket force, having worked her way up to detective, she wasn't about to follow the suggested guidelines in one of Howie's college texts. She had learned that stuff, retained what was important, and forgotten the rest. Not that you could argue with Howie. Massachusetts spending cuts had whittled the Nantucket budget for Summer Special Officers from fifteen down to one—Seitz—and he thought he was God.

They were almost to the house on Quince Street when Will spoke. "They were trying to kill Peter, weren't they?" he said. "Nobody wants to say so, but I guess that's what's going on. No one knows his brother. It doesn't make sense they'd run him over."

"They?" Merry asked. She assessed Will's profile. He was still too pale, and his brooding fascination with the horizon wasn't encouraging. "Who's they?"

"You know. Whoever did it. The murderer." He turned and looked out the side window, apparently riveted by the shop windows on Centre Street.

"I don't think we can say anything yet about who killed Rusty or why," Merry said carefully. "But that's an interesting idea, Will. Why would someone want to kill Peter?"

"I dunno. It's not like he's got any enemies. Everybody thinks Peter's awesome. Maybe it was somebody who can't stand him for that. It's how things work—if they're going well, you can't trust it. You've got to watch for trouble all the time, or it'll find you when you're not looking."

Merry pulled into the gravel drive in front of the Greengage. "Will," she said, and waited for him to look around at her. He did. She was struck by the raw worry suffusing his face. "If you can think of anything that might help me find out who killed Peter's brother, come see me." She fished into her slicker pocket and found a scrap of paper. Her pen was in her purse on the car floor. She reached for it. "Here's my phone number. You know where the police station is out at the Rotary on South Water. Call first to see if I'm around, and we'll talk."

She opened the door and stepped out. "Howie," she yelled, trying to penetrate the rap. "Help Will get his bike out of there." Howie unfolded his bulk from the backseat and lifted the bike from the cargo area. He was good for something.

Tess Starbuck was standing at the kitchen door, holding the screen open with one hand and a towel with the other. She was a red-haired woman in her late thirties with tigerish eyes and a sprinkling of freckles on her nose. Merry waved in a friendly fashion. Tess nodded coolly back.

Will took the bike from Howie and held out his hand. "Thanks, Officer," he said, and turned the wheel.

What a pathetically sweet kid, Merry thought, and then reminded herself that he was entering his sophomore year of high school. He seemed both younger and wiser.

She followed him to where his mother stood and smiled at Tess. "Don't worry, Mrs. Starbuck, Will hasn't gotten into any trouble."

"Oh, Lord, you had a fall," she said, bending down to examine his torn knee. "And these are your new jeans for school." She was exasperated, and showed it.

A spot of color came out high on Will's cheekbones, and he pushed past her into the kitchen, clearly a teenager now. "It's nothing," he said. "Torn jeans are cool."

Tess Starbuck looked inquiringly at Merry. "He was on his way to Peter Mason's cranberry farm," she said. "He left not two hours ago. Where did you come across him?"

"Could I come inside for a moment, Mrs. Starbuck?" Merry asked. "I'd like to have a word with you."

"Of course."

Merry turned back to where Howie Seitz stood by the jeep. "Take the town shuttle back to the station, Howie," she said, "and start typing up your notes. I'll see you later."

Tess led her into the kitchen and motioned to a chair. She was clearly in the midst of prep work for the noon meal. Live lobsters, their claws bound with rubber bands, struggled to climb the sides of a galvanized tin bucket. Chopped melons and fresh mint stood near a bottle of balsamic vinegar on the butcher block counter, and the smell of a corn chowder filled the air. "I was just making some melon salsa for the swordfish," she said, motioning to the counter. Will was nowhere to be seen.

Merry sat down, the kitchen's odors reminding her sharply that she hadn't eaten in twelve hours. She shrugged herself out of her slicker. The morning had turned humid, and the coat was too heavy.

"Will did have a fall, Mrs. Starbuck, but that's not why I brought him home. I'm afraid he found a body."

She was unprepared for the impact her words had on Tess Starbuck. Her weathered face drained of color, and Merry was afraid she was going to faint. She pushed back her chair and reached for Tess, but the woman motioned her away and groped for the stove behind her for support.

"I'm all right," she said. "It's just that what you said, almost word for word, is how I heard of my husband's death."

"I'm sorry," Meredith said.

"Will found him, you see. Dan was washed overboard during that nor'easter last year. It took a week for him to turn up on shore." Her strange golden eyes sought Merry's. "Will was frantic. I couldn't keep him in the house. He never stopped looking for his dad." She paused, staring sightlessly at her own reddened hands. "He's never spoken of it to me. I don't really know what he saw, how Dan looked. But Will's never been the same since."

A body lost in the ocean for a week wasn't a pretty sight, and it smelled like nothing on this earth. Merry had heard that Will hadn't spoken for a month after his father's funeral. Tess had sent him to the mainland, to a cousin who was a psychiatrist, and Will hadn't finished out the school year. "I should have remembered that, Mrs. Starbuck," she said. "It helps explain Will's reaction."

"My God, I haven't even asked you," Tess said, coming suddenly back to the present. "Was it someone he knew?"

"No—at least, not really. I think he may have thought it was Peter Mason at first, but it turns out the man was his brother."

"Peter's brother? He has a brother? I didn't know."

"Apparently no one did. He hadn't been to the island for a while."

Tess Starbuck looked anxiously toward the hall and the stairs leading to Will's attic. "It must have been a horrible shock," she said, "if he thought it was Peter. He adores Peter. He's been like an older brother to Will."

Merry rose. "I won't take any more of your time, Mrs. Starbuck." The woman seemed not to hear her. "I'm sure he'll be okay," she said, with a cheerfulness she didn't feel. *Just in time for school to start again*, she thought, *and he had to be the one to find the body.*

Tess showed her to the door. As Merry walked down the gravel drive she turned and waved. The woman raised one hand, a gesture eloquent in its loneliness.

As she turned her car into Centre Street, a red Range Rover sped past her, headed for the Greengage. Merry looked over her shoulder. The Rover jerked to a halt, and Rafe da Silva got out. Tess met him at the door. Merry saw the woman crumple and begin to weep, her face buried in Rafe's shoulder. His arms came up around Tess's back.

And suddenly, her face crimson, Merry drove quickly on. She felt ashamed, unsettled, and, dare she admit it, hurt. She thought she had forgotten Rafe da Silva.

PETER TOWELED OFF his hair and picked up the phone. He had called his mother and discovered she was in Capri, temporarily out of reach. He left a message to call him as soon as possible, and dialed Georgiana's number in Greenwich, hoping she, at least, was around. She had sense and compassion, and he had always valued both.

Four rings. Voicemail kicked in. His youngest niece, charming and almost unintelligible at four, crowed in his ear. "Please—leave—a message!" Much giggling followed. Casey had clearly been coached. He sighed inwardly and waited for the beep. He had barely finished leaving a message when his phone rang—George calling him back.

"Peter! Sorry I didn't pick up. How's the island? Miss us?"

The entire Whitney clan had descended on the Mason ancestral home, high on the Cliff Road, for the month of July, and Peter had played surrogate father. Hale Whitney, a director of Salomon Brothers, flew in for only two of the four weekends, while George spent much of the time at work on her lifestyle blogging. So Peter built sand castles, led bike caravans to Surfside, and rented a boat for the boys' first bluefishing. He had loved every minute of it. Yes, he missed them.

"George, I've got bad news." He felt rather than heard her small silence on the other end of the line, and knew she was gathering strength for calamity.

"Is it Mother?" she said.

"No. Rusty."

"Rusty?" She sounded decidedly relieved. "What's he done now? Led a coup in Central America?"

"He's dead. His body was found here at the farm." Peter shut his eyes and waited for her response.

Unexpectedly, she laughed. "But that's impossible. What would Rusty be doing on Nantucket?"

Peter said nothing.

Georgiana hesitated. "You're not kidding, are you?"

"No. He was murdered, George."

"Jesus. By whom?"

"We don't know. You hadn't heard from him lately, had you?"

"Me? Rusty hated me. Why would he get in touch now? No, I hadn't heard a thing. My God, murdered? That's just like him."

"I know," Peter said, and reflected that only Georgiana could understand that essential fact about Rusty: he'd victimize them all if he got the chance. "But as you can imagine, it's made things rather awkward. Rafe seems to believe someone was trying to kill me, and got Rusty instead."

"Not likely," George said. "I imagine some of his unsavory friends followed him up here and knifed him in the back. He probably welched on a drug deal. Was it a knife, by the way?"

"No, the bog. He was run over by a car and left to drown, apparently."

"And Rafe thinks whoever drove the car intended to hit you," George said. "Be careful, Peter. Do you need me to come?"

Peter thought of the ringing noise level of the Whitney

household, weighed it against George's energy and intelligence, and said regretfully, "I'll let you know when the funeral date's set. Don't worry about anything until then."

"Peter."

He waited for the inevitable.

"Have you talked to Alison since—"

"No," Peter said. "Listen, I've got to go."

"Don't you think perhaps you should—"

"I'll be in touch." He punched off his cell before she could continue, and stared in front of him. It had to be faced, and sooner rather than later. But first he would talk to Sky.

*Chapter 6*

MERRY WAS TRAPPED in holiday traffic on Broad Street, where a line of cars was snaking toward the Hyannis ferry and the last of the season's tourists were setting out from the Jared Coffin House in sneakers and cotton sweaters. Probably headed to the Whaling Museum, she thought, to hear about Great-Great-Great-Great-Grandpa Ezra and the rest of the famous Folgers who'd made fortunes, built houses, and left their names on the island's streets, before kerosene put an end to fishing for oil. Museum business was invariably brisk when the island was fogbound; the horns and the shifting damp drove home the threat of the sea and invested the whaling past with a glamorous power. Glancing up at the gray sky, Merry decided that the island was mourning summer already; from now on even the brilliant days of September would have a note of sadness in them. She had lost her summer in relentless hours of work, compensating, she told herself, for the state budget cuts and the smaller staff. On sleepless nights, she admitted she was trying to prove something else: that she merited her promotion to detective, regardless of her father's influence or any unspoken gender quotas; and she would keep it.

On impulse, she abandoned her official Explorer in

a no-parking zone, aware that she was abusing police authority, and trudged toward Water Street and breakfast. Her reflection rippled in the storefront windows that lined Broad Street. The expensive goods catering to the off-island trade were plastered with sale stickers. Another month, and some of the shops on Main and Centre would limit their hours; after Christmas, others would close for the winter. Her steps slowed as she approached Mayling Stern, the New York designer's island store, which she had never entered but could not pass without surveying. No sale stickers here. The window display had changed from late summer to early fall, with a collection of hand-knit sweaters spilling out of a scarred iron-and-leather trunk. She peered into the shop, not yet lit for the day's business, and decided that if she ever became extremely rich she would buy everything inside. Her eyes strayed back to the sweater display. Perhaps if she solved the Mason murder she'd spend her fall clothing budget on one of them. Merry looked closer.

Someone had propped a discreet card, penned in calligraphy, against a glass vase full of cattails: *Island Wool from Mason Farms.* Of course. With his family's retailing connections, Peter Mason's fleeces would go to nothing less than a New York designer. She eyed a mulberry-colored cardigan. An abstract geometric pattern in gray trailed across one shoulder and ended on the right front edge, where a leather toggle caught a single button.

Merry's jaw went rigid, and she felt a wave of heat wash over her. The button was of wood, cunningly made to look like ivory, and carved in the shape of a pig's head. A quick check of the other three cardigans draped across the trunk's edge revealed similar buttons, all of them representing different animals—a rabbit, a cat, and something she could only call a dragon. In her mind's eye she saw a similar button, carved in the shape of a rat, half hidden in the grass by the side of an unpaved road. She dodged around the window to the door and tried the knob, unsuccessfully, only then noticing that the shop opened at the reasonable hour of ten. She moved on toward Water Street, lost in thought. She had glanced at it only briefly, but she would swear the button she'd picked up by the dead man in the bog had been one of Mayling Stern's.

"'The fact of the matter is, Noah Mayhew,' I said to him, 'you've not enough faith in technology. Sure it's true that a hurricane tore your garden to pieces. And it cannot be denied that I harvested my tomatoes two days before. But let us not forget that I surf the internet, while you'll not have it in the house, and so were caught with your proverbial drawers down. There's no cause to hold a grudge because you're too dim to see a hurricane coming, even when it leaves calling cards all up the coast.'" The monologue was followed by a rich burst of laughter.

Merry stopped and turned around. "You're talking to yourself again, Ralph Waldo," she said.

The white-haired man striding briskly along behind her looked up and smiled. "I thought I was talking to you, Meredith Abiah. Why did you leave your vehicle in a no-parking zone?"

Merry waited until he reached her and then stood on tiptoes to peck him on the cheek. She was tall, but her grandfather was over six feet, with a trim white beard and deeply tanned cheeks. "Habit, I guess," she said. "I'm starving, and too exhausted to fight this traffic. You can issue me a citation."

"Only if you'll stop at Fog Island first."

It was after nine o'clock, and the Fog Island Cafe had a line of breakfasters out the door.

"Let's get coffee and a cinnamon bun and eat by Old North, Ralph," Merry said. "I need to talk to you."

He shot her a sharp glance from under his thick eyebrows—*her* eyebrows, as she well knew—and said, "Half a moment." She watched as he edged past the tourists waiting for tables and made for the counter. He stood upright and distinguished despite his eighty years, khaki trousers clean and pressed, his shoulders broad in a teal-blue Patagonia fleece pullover that sharpened the whiteness of his hair and the darkness of his skin. In his twenties, before he'd returned to the island and joined the force, he'd trained as a Shakespearean actor. Traces of the stage were visible still in his bearing and the cadences of his speech.

Bertha Shambles, who ruled Fog Island, beamed at him. There wasn't a woman on the island who hadn't carried a torch at some point for Chief Ralph, as he was still called, even after his son had taken over and he'd begun to talk to himself, spending his hours growing tomatoes, or scalloping in Madaket Harbor. Merry wondered if he recognized his charm, if he was conscious of his minor eccentricities, and felt a fierce love for her grandfather

"You look schnockered," he said, appearing at her elbow.

"Night shift." She reached for one of the steaming coffee cups he held precariously in his right hand and led him to the marina that bounded Water Street and Old North Wharf. Most of the boats were safe in their slips, gleaming palely in the fog.

Ralph eased himself stiffly onto the dock, his legs

dangling over the side. Merry sat down next to him and breathed deeply of salty sea, boat tar, and rotting fish. She summoned her flagging energy. "I need you to dredge your brain for Mason family history, Ralph."

He cocked one eyebrow at her and took a massive bite of bun, chewing ruminatively before he answered. "I assume you're not asking idly. Masons, Masons. So many stories to tell, so little food. Hang on, I'll go get us some more and think about it on the way back." He rolled to his feet before she could protest, and left her to glance at her watch and appraise the quality of the fog. She never managed to sleep during the day before a night shift, and at this point she had been up for twenty hours. A Forster's tern glided to a landing on a piling five feet away from her and eyed her breakfast. She broke off a bit of bun and tossed it to the bird, knowing Ralph Waldo would disapprove.

She considered the button. If the designer and Peter Mason did business, it was possible it had been dropped long before the murder, during some sort of fashion consultation. Or Rusty Mason could have been killed by a wealthy socialite who favored Mayling Stern clothing. Or, she supposed, Mayling Stern could have taken a sudden, violent dislike to Mason Farms wool and decided to kill Peter, but had gotten Rusty by mistake. None of it seemed even remotely plausible. Perhaps she needed more coffee.

"I got you some more coffee, too," Ralph Waldo said, sliding down beside her, "which I recommend you get inside of you. Eat this bacon sandwich instead of feeding the gulls. How far back in Masonry do I have to go?"

"You can skip the founding of the island," Merry said, "but not the founding of the empire."

"That would be somewhere around 1840, I do believe, and canny John Paul Mason. Saw the handwriting on the wall when kerosene was discovered in 1839 and got his money out of whaling. By the time the rest of the island figured it out ten years later, the sandbar had started to block the harbor, and a lot of fortunes went out with the tide. By then, John Paul had moved to New York permanently and his department store was quite the rage. Pretty much ignored Nantucket for the rest of the century, except for visiting relatives. He was married to your Great-Great-Great-Aunt Hermione, by the way, which makes us some sort of relation."

"You're kidding. Masons related to Folgers?"

"Masons had been marrying Folgers for two centuries at that point. But once the two families' fortunes parted ways, what with the island economy in decline and John Paul moving Hermione to New York, the habit kind of died out."

"I suppose so," Merry said shortly, thinking of the quiet, but clearly moneyed, elegance of Mason Farms. "I can't imagine two more different worlds." She felt oddly cheated. She had disliked Peter Mason enough to readily suspect him of murder. Knowing he was a distant relation brought her up short. She wondered if her antagonism was solely in response to his arrogance and apparent lack of grief—or if she had been intimidated by his status and her own lack of experience. That thought made her uncomfortable.

"Next we come to Fletcher Mason, and his son August—Fletcher's first wife died childless and then he married a German girl around 1890, but he only lived a few years after August was born. The family fortune, by the way, diversified and multiplied and revivified and whatnot. I think they set up the newspaper chain around the turn of the century. Anyway, August went off to World War I and came back a flying ace, only to die in the influenza epidemic of 1919. Poor kid. His bride was pregnant at the time and was sent off to Saratoga to avoid the flu."

Ralph chewed his sandwich ruminatively and cocked a bushy white eyebrow at his granddaughter. "Sarah Mason was a pistol, I'll tell you that, Meredith. She was a spirited young thing with a steel-trap mind who grew into a grand old dame. She ran the Mason empire—no minor feat for a woman in those days—and sent her son, Joe, to learn the business on the retailing floor. You didn't fool with Sarah."

"You knew her?" Merry asked, startled.

"She kicked off the family habit of summering on Nantucket. Bought the ancestral home on the Cliff Road and had it restored—I'd say Sarah Mason single-handedly launched the island's tourist trade, what with all her New York society friends streaming in for those summer parties. Joe Mason kept up the tradition, and made sure his kids knew their roots were in New England. That's why Max and I learned to sail together."

"Ralph Waldo Folger, you do not sail," Merry said severely. She put down her coffee cup and turned to gaze at his profile. "And if you do, how come you never taught me?"

Her grandfather broke off a bit of bagel and, contrary to philosophy, threw it to the Forster's tern. "Owning a sailboat and knowing what to do with it are two different things, young woman," he said. "Somehow I never managed to scrape together the price of the whistle."

Ralph Waldo viewed Ben Franklin—and his aphorisms—with affection, in part because Franklin's mother was a Nantucket Folger, albeit of cousinage much removed. He had insisted Merry's parents give her Abiah Folger's name, and disliking it, they'd compromised and placed it second. He was the only one who called her by it, and in fact one of the few people alive who knew what her middle name was. Merry exhaled gustily, her breath lifting the stray strands of blonde hair plastered to her forehead, slightly clammy from the fog. "Tell me about Max," she said.

"Max." Ralph Waldo steepled his fingers and thrust his long, knifelike nose into their midst. "Max is—was—a chip off the old block. Meaning his grandmother Sarah. He was a proud and lonely youngster, always wandering off into the moors by himself with a book and a sack of lunch, like as not gone for hours. I think, when I look back on it, that I was his only real friend; and that, probably, because I accepted the friendship on his terms."

"I don't understand," Merry said.

Ralph Waldo turned and looked at her fondly, if somewhat speculatively. "No, I daresay you wouldn't, dear heart," he said. "No one is ever likely to make you conscious of your class." He laughed shortly and clasped his arms around his knees. "Max knew he was several levels above me on the social scale. He chose me to be his tagalong, as a lord might enthrall a vassal. I was happy enough to be sword-bearer and general dogsbody to the highest liver on the island. Lord, we had fun. We raced around the island in his boat and swam naked in the surf; we buried pirate treasure in the Hidden Forest, made maps, and dug it up again; we ate cranberry tarts purloined from Mrs. Hodge's window and gave the miller fits with loosening the windmill sails. For a couple of years I got through the island winters just by making plans for the summer when Max would be back. The play-acting lasted until we were suddenly too old for it."

"Meaning?"

"Meaning," Ralph said, "until women and real money entered the picture."

The tone in her grandfather's voice made Merry angry, and she was uncertain why. She mentally thrust Max Mason away and said, "You got the girl, right?"

Ralph Waldo smiled. "More or less," he said. "He went off to Princeton. I took to the road and hoofed it a bit, did some vaudeville, spouted Hamlet. It was a lark while it lasted. Then I came home, married your grandmother, Swedish beauty that she was, and took a dose of real living." He glanced around him for his coffee cup, which Merry saw was empty. He raised it to his lips anyway for something to do.

"What'd Max do after Princeton?" Merry asked, relentless.

"Well, he didn't marry for another twenty years, matter of fact. Guess he carried a torch for a while. Came into his fortune, which, carefully shepherded by his father, had made money hand over fist. He won a contract for military uniforms during Vietnam, took the company public after the war, and never looked back. And we never really spoke again. Oh, once in a while, if we passed on Main Street in one July or another, I'd raise a hat and he'd nod." He paused. "I never asked your grandmother if she had any regrets."

"You know she didn't," Merry said. "He sounds like a real prick."

Her grandfather threw back his head and laughed out loud, a clear and joyous sound that came from his depths and washed away her annoyance. "Oh my, yes," he said, "as his poor kids no doubt discovered."

"Why didn't you ever tell me any of this?" Merry asked him.

"I don't like to talk about my failures. And, somehow, Masons never had much to do with our lives."

"They do now," Merry said. "One of them got himself killed last night."

"Not young Peter?" Ralph Waldo turned to her with real concern.

"Don't tell me you're in love with him too," she said. "And he's not that young."

"He's all right, then?"

"If you consider being a suspect for murder all right. Will Starbuck—a local kid—found his brother drowned in the Mason Farms cranberry bog, and Peter isn't talking."

"Rusty dead. Well, well. And it couldn't have been an accident?"

Merry shook her head. "Not that Mason cares. I've never seen such indifference in a next of kin."

"His kind of people don't show emotion to strangers." Ralph Waldo's voice held a note of reproof.

"He made it very clear that he hadn't seen his brother in ten years, didn't know why he'd turned up, and couldn't care less that he's dead; and he doesn't even seem to realize that makes him look guilty as hell."

"This begins to be interesting," Ralph Waldo said.

"Peter and Rusty were inseparable as boys. Peter was younger, of course, and trailed around after his brother with that pathetic adoration most teenagers exploit unmercifully—you did it to Billy, remember, and he had you washing his car every week until your mother found out—"

"—and lectured me about feminism for the first time in my life," Merry interjected.

"I'd have thought Rusty's murder would be a terrible blow. Sure he wasn't in shock?"

"Shock my foot."

"But he was surprised?"

"Yes, to be fair, I'd say Rusty's body was the last thing he expected to run into this morning. My gut says he had no idea it was there." Merry met her grandfather's eyes. "But I can't ignore the impression I got that he hated his brother. Do you think this falling-out's for real?"

Ralph Waldo pursed his lips. "Meaning, he could be trying to put as much distance between himself and the corpse as a good story can buy him? I grant you, it's possible, but not likely. I've watched Peter for years, and he's never given cause for worry. Rusty, now . . ." He paused, stroking his jaw. "Rusty's the last person I'd expect to end up dead. But then, I've been wrong about Rusty his whole life."

"You know, Ralph," Merry said, "it's safest, as a general rule, to assume we'll all end up dead."

"Rusty would have argued that point, my dear. He understood power. Maybe he confused it with immortality, I don't know. He certainly pursued it relentlessly. If you'd asked, I'd have said Rusty Mason would rule the world one day, whatever world he chose. I had him pegged as Max's successor—Peter wasn't enough of a shark." He dusted his hands free of crumbs, his finger-tips gleaming with bacon grease. "I figured Rusty would eventually enter politics—not electoral campaigns, you understand, but the sort of back-room influence that means real power. A cabinet member, maybe, or a presidential adviser. I never thought he'd die young. He must have lost his hold on Fate." The lines in Ralph Waldo's skin settled more deeply into his face. He had watched over a number of untimely ends.

"What else were you wrong about, Ralph?"

"Well, he didn't succeed Max, for one thing," Ralph said. "I can't tell you why. And he's never been back to the island since the heart attack that killed his father. That'd be about nine, ten years ago now, which squares with Peter's story."

"The island's Living Memory, Ralph Waldo Folger," Merry intoned. "I didn't even recognize the guy this morning."

"You forget. I was police chief when those boys were kids."

"What was Rusty like? Beyond being power-hungry, I mean?"

Ralph hesitated. "I could say one thing or the other, and they'd both be partly right and partly wrong," he said finally. "He was a tricky customer. Very good at the poker face and the unemotional voice, and next to impossible to know. He was bright in the way that's clever more than brainy, if you know what I mean—good at seeing people's vulnerabilities and using them to get what he wanted."

"Your basic privileged snake," Merry said.

"That's too easy, Meredith," her grandfather said

sharply. "It ignores his most useful skill—his charm. People would do anything for Rusty. That's what made him dangerous."

"Stop indulging your dramatic side, Ralph," Merry said.

"I'm not, young woman. I'm telling you what I've seen. I ran into Rusty once or twice on what I thought was the wrong side of the law, and was never able to pin him down to it."

"Like?"

"Well, there was one bad month twenty years ago when the Mason household petty cash disappeared and Martha Shambles, Bertha's niece, was dismissed for it. I think Rusty took it."

"But the Masons are made of money," Merry broke in.

"Sometimes there are things you don't want to ask for," Ralph Waldo said. "Like fixing a girl's trouble when you've caused it."

"That happened? You knew that?"

"There's knowing, and there's proving," Ralph Waldo said. "Let's just say that when a sixteen-year-old summer kid started hemorrhaging one night, and had to be rushed to Mass Gen in a helicopter, some of us started to think about the Mason theft. Rusty had spent a lot of the summer with the girl, and the timing fit pretty well. But rumors never washed much with Max; he stood by his kids, I'll give him that." Ralph Waldo fell silent, as Merry turned over his words in her mind.

"And you say Peter never gave any trouble?"

"Classic case of a completely different personality admiring, in his older brother, all that he wasn't. I can't blame Rusty for his sneaky ways, all the same. I saw some of his problems—his love of money, and the way he had of manipulating people to get what he wanted—as Max's fault. Max believed kids their age had too much money and too much freedom, so he kept them all on a short rein. Peter and the daughter could take it. Rusty fought it any way he could. I thought that was youth, something he'd grow out of."

"Like you think Peter's innocent now," Merry said.

"Perhaps. At my age, I'm allowed to want tragedies to have happy endings."

A deep-throated horn blared across the harbor, dominating the voices of other craft obscured by the fog. Somewhere beyond the curtain of damp, the Hyannis car ferry was rounding Brant Point. Merry shifted restlessly. Her backside was numb from sitting on the dock. "The thing is, Ralph, I'm of two minds, and I've got to pull them together if I'm going to move on this investigation."

"Sounds like sense."

"I can assume Rusty was the intended victim and try to find out who'd want to kill him, what possible motive he could have, and how he knew Rusty would be back on the island last night."

"Or?"

"Or I can look for a killer who thought he got Peter Mason and killed Rusty instead. You can see there's a certain sense of urgency in that."

Ralph Waldo meditated an instant, then slapped his knees, hoisted himself to his feet, and extended his hand to Merry. "Can't think of anyone who'd have any reason to kill young Peter," he said. "There's not a fellow with more integrity and sense on the island. No, Meredith Abiah, there is a tide in the affairs of men, which, when taken at the flood, can send entire families spinning off into separate eddies. Something snaps the line that binds them together. Maybe there's a tug when it happens, maybe it's so gentle the line just slips apart. But mark my words, it's the severed ends of the rope you're looking for."

Merry stood up and mechanically dusted off the seat of her khakis with one hand. When had the tide taken Rafe da Silva? Somewhere in the deserts of Iraq, or later, in a holding pen in New Bedford? A sudden wave of dizziness washed over her, and she closed her eyes, stars bursting against her lids. When she opened them, Ralph Waldo was gazing at her sternly.

"I'm going down to the wharf to buy bluefish, young woman, and I expect you to turn right around and head for home. Forget your report for a few hours and get some sleep." He pulled her close in a rough embrace. She yawned hugely against his shoulder.

"Can't, Ralph. I've still got to deal with Dad."

"I was wondering when you'd mention that," he said carefully. "Let me know if you need reinforcements."

*Chapter 7*

MAYLING STERN SAT cross-legged in a red leather chair, looking out at the sea. She was susceptible to weather; today the gray of water and air had driven her up and down the studio in restless pacing or left her huddled wordlessly, mug in hand, before the enormous and woeful sky. The house sat high on the Siasconset bluff, its historic front facing into the island's past and its contemporary back staring across the Atlantic. Mayling had furnished each half as befit its age, seventeenth-century and twenty-first, two faces of her divided soul.

She had awakened with a groggy head, the foghorns reverberating in her skull, and stumbled for the shower. She would get nothing done today. Desultory sketches that trailed off the paper, unfulfilled; much sighing and snapping of charcoal; the knowledge that her season's creative burst was done. Time now for the shift to New York, smacking of life, of brilliant harlotry, of details too rapid to absorb.

She wore black, her best color, suited to the quality of light and the richness of the chair. In her lap were the discarded pages of a letter. She had profited from Sky's early-morning urge for surf casting: waiting until he disappeared into the mist; lighting a burner for the cold, full, kettle; and then, tea in hand and the envelope flap carefully steamed, opening the letter with her nail file. She had read it three times and knew the words by heart.

At the sound of the light footsteps springing up the staircase from the ground floor, she shot to her feet, scattering the pages. A black head rounded the doorway, and she gave a small gasp.

"Peter!" She reached for the back of the chair.

Peter's smile of greeting faded. "Mayling," he said, crossing to her side. "What's wrong?" The color had drained from her face. "Sorry I scared you. I knocked, but you probably can't hear me up here."

"Forget it," Mayling said. "I'm fine. I startle easily when it's foggy. Everything's both muffled and louder than usual, if you know what I mean."

"Let me help you with those," Peter said, as she bent quickly to pick up the discarded letter.

"I told you I'm *fine*." Her brown eyes were furious, and he flinched as though he'd been slapped. She scuffled the loose sheets into a pile, found the envelope beneath the chair, and left the room.

PETER SAT DOWN on an ottoman, stifling the impulse to follow her. Mayling was moody enough, but rarely without reason. He was convinced she had thought he was someone else. Who? Sky? And what could be so important about a letter?

He glanced around the studio, his eyes adjusting to the dim light, wondering why she hadn't bothered to turn on the bronze lamps that hovered, UFO-like, in the space of the vaulted ceiling. He stood up restlessly and wandered over to the drafting table, where a single black spotlight threw a pool of brightness onto the paper. He had lied when he told Meredith Folger no one on the island knew Rusty. But he was determined to talk to his oldest friends first before he subjected them to her questions. They deserved to hear of Rusty's death from him. The detective could grill them in a few days. Maybe by that time he'd know who had killed his brother.

He glanced down at the drafting table. Mayling hadn't done much. A heavy red cross was drawn through the only sketch on the page. He leaned closer to examine it, curious, and saw that it was the last thing he had expected: a wedding dress. He felt suddenly self-conscious, as though he'd gone through her drawers, and turned away from the table. She'd never done a bridal line before. There was no hint of one in the works when he surveyed the bolts of silk and wool from her winter collection, stacked in the studio's corners. He reached out to finger a length of mohair the color of oxblood and smiled involuntarily. He was starting to speak Mayling's vernacular. Her names for colors—Anthracite, Ming Blue, Pomegranate—had never come naturally to him.

She had recovered when she returned to the room, her eyes clear and her smile carefully sustained. He decided not to probe.

"I hope I haven't missed Sky," he said.

"No, but only just. This is a twenty-four-hour trip—he's flying back tonight."

"He may not be going anywhere if the fog holds."

"That'd be nice, Peter. I'll hope for it. It's good to see you," Mayling said. "Every summer I envision weeks of things we can do together, and then summer disappears." She threw herself down on the chair and swung her legs over one side. "It's gone for good now, and I'm ready to be back in New York. It happens that quickly. I may go home with Sky."

"When I was a kid I hated this weekend," Peter said. "Because it meant loss—the end of my time here and the start of ticking off the months until I could return. I never really felt home was anywhere else."

"Except Princeton," Mayling said.

"Except Princeton. At night, when the past and the ghosts were all around you."

"You're a romantic, Peter. A romantic with sense."

"That sounds like a fast trip to hell."

"No!" Mayling protested. "You have sense enough to know when you're at home, and stay there. Most of us hunt for it all our lives." She looked wistfully out at the sea. "Sky is fishing," she said. "You can't see him from here because of the fog."

"Up or down?" Peter said.

"I assume toward Sankaty Light. It's one of his haunts." She looked back at him and for the first time seemed really to see him: the exhaustion around the eyes, the smile on the lips not reaching above them. "This isn't a social call, is it, Peter? Is something wrong at the farm?"

His gaze met hers, slid away. "Yes," he said carefully. He looked behind him for the mate to her chair, and eased himself into it. "It seems Rusty came back to Nantucket last night. His body was found in the bog early this morning." He paused. "I figured Sky was the person to tell. No one else here knew him as Sky did."

"Or loved him like that," Mayling said. Her voice sounded as though she found it difficult to breathe. "I'll come with you."

Peter looked at her narrowly, and then laughed, a short, harsh sound. "Nine out of ten people would have asked two questions, Mayling," he said. "What was he doing here, and how did he die. But not you. You've already gone mentally ahead, to Sky, and you can feel what he'll feel. You're saving your worry for him. What is it like to lose yourself in someone that completely?"

"You should know, Peter," she said. "You lost your soul to Alison years ago."

He saw that she regretted the words as soon as they left her mouth.

"I'm sorry, I've been impossible all morning," Mayling said in a rush. "Just let me get a sweater."

"Don't, Mayling." He reached out his hand to pull her back. "I'd like to see him alone, if I could."

"I said I was sorry, Peter."

"I know. But I want to talk to him by myself. The death is only half of it, Mayling. You can deal with that later. It's the murder I've got to discuss with him now."

SCHUYLER TATE-JACKSON'S JEANS were rolled up to his knees. The Atlantic Ocean swirled around his calves and numbed his toes, raising gooseflesh he disregarded in his eagerness to land a bluefish. Never mind that they preferred deeper water. His line, cast twenty yards into a wave, was taut as a bowstring, and his rod was curved into a question mark pointing out to sea. Something, blindly, had taken the hook, and Sky was determined to know what it was. He played the fish, letting it tire, praying the line would hold. The wind had ruffled his hair into a feathered mess of gray and black. He wore the oilskin hunting jacket Mayling had given him for Christmas, and he looked, Peter thought, completely happy.

Peter stood just out of line of Sky's peripheral vision a few seconds longer, avoiding what he'd come to do and wishing that his friend's day could continue as he'd planned it. Unexpectedly, Sky glanced sideways and saw him.

"Peter! I think I've got a big one."

Peter kicked off his Sperrys and walked splashily into the surf. "This the new rod?"

"Yep." Sky kept up the battle with his line. The fish was almost done, its darting runs less vigorous and panicked, as though a gear inside were running down. Sky reeled it in, stopped, reeled some more. "It's coming," he said.

Peter watched in silence, and then bent for Sky's net. As the fish reached shallow water he scooped it up, gills heaving, eyes blind in the waterless air, its body jackknifing in the mesh. Sky threw down the rod and carefully lifted the blue out of the net in triumph. "All summer," he said, "*all summer*, and not a one. You free for dinner?"

"You'll have to catch more than that if you're going to feed three, buddy," Peter said. "I think I'll let you have it all to yourself."

Sky bent down and started working the hook free from the fish's mouth.

"I need to talk to you," Peter said.

Sky hefted the fish in his hands, estimating its weight. "Something wrong with the farm?"

"No."

Sky looked up and focused for the first time on Peter, his teal-blue eyes wide and steady. He waited.

"It's Rusty."

"Rusty. He got in touch with you." He said it as if it were expected, although he knew Peter had never given his brother his contact information.

"He didn't. But he may have been trying to," Peter said. "Sky—somebody killed him last night. We found his body in the bog this morning. The police think he was run down by a car and left to drown."

Sky stared at him wordlessly for several seconds, the fish dangling. "Rusty," he said again. He sat down suddenly in the surf, salt water cascading over his jeans. "The bog? My God, what was he doing there? You say he drowned?"

Peter nodded. "We'd flooded the cranberries yesterday for wet harvesting."

Sky looked down at his fish, its gills still fighting for air, and abruptly threw it back into the water. He turned his head aside and vomited.

Peter waited until Sky stopped shuddering, then extended a hand to help him up. Sky filled his hands with salt water and doused his face. He kept his hands over his eyes a moment, letting the cold shock of the water clear his head.

"Peter," he said, somewhat unsteadily, "tell me you didn't do it, for God's sake."

"I didn't do it," Peter said. "I've given you cause to think me capable of anything. But I didn't do it, Sky. Never."

Sky nodded, and looked around vaguely for his fishing tackle.

"I'll walk you back," Peter said, picking up the rod and net. "I've already told Mayling."

"I always thought if there were news of Rusty," Sky said, "that I'd be the one telling you. Why was he on the island? Why didn't he call me?"

"I was hoping you knew," Peter said. "That's why I'm here."

Sky looked ruefully at his jeans, which clung to his body like a wetsuit. "Let's get back to the house. We can talk after I change."

THE STATION ON Fairgrounds Road had the air of a retail store on Christmas Eve: the end of the high season was almost in sight, with peace and sanity hovering on the horizon. Labor Day meant the summer people were on their way home—all excess fifty thousand of them. Another week and the island population would settle into its winter numbers, with the drug dealing and the drunk driving, the boat thefts and the petty shoplifting, receding for another year. The traffic that choked Main Street would trickle away; the boatloads of day-trippers would dump fewer and fewer tourists in need of directions, public bathrooms, and first aid. Errant bikers going the wrong way on the town's one-way streets would have fewer head-on collisions with New York lawyers' BMWs. Off-island teenagers would cease drinking on the Jetties on Saturday nights. And after a week of relief, the force would be restless and bored.

Ten of the island's finest were lounging around their desks like runners at the end of a race, some with their feet up and their chairs tipped back, others preparing to head out onto the streets for the season's final patrols. They were deeply tanned, solidly built, fresh-faced, and fairly young; most were off-islanders to begin with, and few stayed on the island longer than five years. They were all male. Several pairs of eyes glanced casually at Merry as she walked into the main office, then looked down. Word of the murder was out.

The division of criminal investigation had eight officers assigned to it. She knew Randy Garrett was following up a case of arson; Wendell Case was on leave for the next two weeks; Phil and Tom Potts, brothers and islanders, were about to close a sting operation targeted against cocaine dealers working both Nantucket and Martha's Vineyard from a fleet of yachts. Everyone else was too junior. She could make a case.

Merry threw her red slicker over the back of her desk chair and dumped her large, shapeless plastic leather bag on the floor of her cubicle. She locked her fingers together and thrust them toward the ceiling, stretching to her full height and looking more than ever like a lean and fine-boned cat. It was important to seem relaxed, confident, instead of exhausted and nervy as she really felt. To ignore Matt Bailey—*the snake*—sitting twenty feet away and staring at her over his coffee cup, as he calculated her chances of holding on to the case. She picked up her laptop and then felt around vaguely for her reading glasses. She'd left them in the pocket of her slicker. She reached for them and smelled the fog—wet macadam, damp car interiors, the animal odor of soggy hair—rising from the coat.

"Thanks for the legwork, Merr," Bailey said. "Send me the file of your case notes, okay?"

Merry turned. Matt had finished his coffee. He was leaning back in his desk chair, his dark head cradled in his arms and his feet up on his desk. He was grinning. She felt her face begin to flush crimson.

"What the hell are you talking about?" she said slowly.

"That call you logged around seven A.M. The Mason murder. "

"I know when I logged the call, Matt. You were still in bed."

"Yeah, well, you can head home and get some rest. Your dad gave me the case. I'm glad you went out there, Merry—none of the guys types as well as you do."

"My *dad* is Chief Folger to you, Bailey," Merry said through her teeth. She slammed her chair into her desk and turned away from him in a rage. She made straight for the glass-walled office in the corner of the room where her father sat reading the paper over his second cup of coffee.

Matt watched as the glass door shook behind her. He chuckled softly.

"YOU CAN'T KEEP doing this to me." Merry was rigid with anger, her hands braced on the edge of her father's desk. He looked at her over his paper, and his light blue eyes were flat and icy.

"Control yourself, Meredith. I have nothing to say to you—"

"The hell you don't."

"—until you can speak in a normal tone of voice. Let's try this again. Good morning, Detective Folger."

Merry turned away from his desk and raked her fingers through her hair. She reached for the doorknob and then dropped her hand. She took a deep breath and turned back to face him. "Good morning, sir. It looks like a fine day, sir. A perfect day to resign, sir."

John Folger's expression didn't change. He motioned

to the wooden captain's chair shoved stiffly against one wall. Merry hesitated. She felt more powerful standing. Her father didn't blink. She took the chair.

"Now tell me about the Mason case," he said.

"You mean the one you took away from me?"

"I didn't know I'd assigned it to you."

"Yeah, well, anyone else who was first on the scene, and who had my seniority, would be put in charge of the investigation. Not to mention that I'm the only one free right now. Or did you take Bailey off the Atwater vandalism?

"Bailey expressed an interest in handling a murder. Vandalism isn't up to his talents."

"What about mine?"

A muscle in her father's cheek twitched. He was beginning to get angry. But otherwise, his face betrayed nothing. He was adept at suppressing emotion—particularly when dealing with his daughter.

"Your talents are considerable, Meredith. So are your vulnerabilities. I don't think you're ready for murder."

"No, that's not quite true. You just don't think *any* woman is ready for murder."

"I wonder if this island is ready for a murder investigation headed by a woman, but that's different. I don't have any control over the confidence of the public. I *can* control my officers' caseloads. I gave the case to Bailey because I think he's tougher than you are." As Merry started to protest, her father raised one hand. "The Masons draw a lot of attention, on-island and off. They're also the sort of people who demand results fast. I'm not sure you need that kind of pressure."

She had certainly been nervous this morning, Merry

thought, but she had overcome it and asked Peter Mason the right questions. She deserved her father's trust. "I've got two years' seniority on Bailey. I've logged more hours of training and crime scene unit experience." She glared through the glass wall at Matt, whose feet were still propped on his desk. He seemed less than eager to pursue her case. "Hell, I've got more balls than that guy, Dad!"

"Meredith."

She faced the hard blue eyes. "My problem is that I've got my father for a chief. I've got a boss who's so worried he'll be accused of favoritism that he treats me as if I'm the worst officer on the force. I had to fight you for promotion to detective. I'm not going to fight you to be allowed to do my job. Maybe I need to move off-island and work for somebody who'll treat me with trust and respect."

John Folger shot out of his chair, and the pencil he held in his right hand snapped in two. "I'm going to assume you need sleep, Meredith. I'm sending you home to get it. And I'm giving you two weeks of paid leave to get your head on straight."

"I don't need a vacation, I need your confidence." She met his eyes and held them. "You've got to stop protecting me, Dad. Let me do my job."

"You think murder is your job," he said.

"Solving crime is what I've been trained to do. When are you going to accept it?"

John Folger glared at her. Then he sat back down in his chair. There was a pause while he carefully fitted one shattered end of the pencil into the nub of the other. "I never wanted this for you, Merry." His eyes flicked up to hers. "Your mother didn't want this for you."

"Oh, God, how long is that going to matter?" Merry cried out in exasperation. "I'm *your* daughter, too. I'm not going to slit my wrists when things get rough!"

She stopped abruptly, appalled at what she had said.

Her father's face had turned to stone. "Get out of here, Meredith," he said quietly. "Just go, now."

*Chapter 8*

SKY'S STUDY WAS in the old half of the house. It was a small room, and dark, overlooking Baxter Road—a room better suited to lamplit reading on cold November nights, of a kind Sky never spent on the island. Mayling had used cherry silk for the drapes that hung against the mahogany wainscoting, and picked up the warmth with a paisley print on two large easy chairs drawn close to the fire. An orange-and-black Princeton banner hung on one wall.

Peter slouched against the massive desk, idly looking at pictures, while he waited for his friend. Mayling's face shone out of one frame; in another, she stood next to a fashion runway, a slightly bewildered expression on her face. Peter imagined that she was searching beyond the lights for Sky, even as he took the picture.

He picked up a black-and-white shot of a college rugby game, an exhausted Sky throwing his arm around an exultant Rusty. Peter remembered that year. He'd been a freshman standing on the sidelines to cheer on the senior god, his brother. Rugby hadn't been Peter's sport. He'd tried rowing instead.

When Rusty disappeared, Sky had attempted to make Peter his friend. He had not been completely successful.

Hurt and lost without a brother he'd once loved, Peter had resented Sky's efforts to take Rusty's place. As he had gotten older and come to know Sky better, he understood that the lawyer had needed him to fill a void, and that he had failed him. Mayling, who had never known Rusty, was necessary to both of them, a buffer against their memories.

"What do the police think?" Sky asked from his study doorway. "They've been out there, of course."

Peter set down the picture frame. "They practically woke me this morning."

"You found the body?"

"No, that's the real tragedy. The one person who should never have seen it—Will Starbuck—discovered him. Rafe called the police. I'd gone out for an early run, and only got back after the ambulance and cop cars arrived."

Sky threw himself into a chair and reached for the box of foot-long matches. "And?"

Peter pressed his fingers against his eyes. "They think he was hit by a car sometime after eleven P.M., then dragged unconscious to the bog. He was left facedown to drown."

"A car?" Startled, Sky stopped short in the act of lighting the fire, then assumed a professional mask. In the time it had taken to change his clothes, he'd managed to distance Rusty's death in order to assess it as Peter's lawyer. "Who's handling the case?"

"A Detective Folger. A woman."

Sky's eyebrows shot upward. "What's she like?"

Peter shrugged. "A little abrupt. She struck me as tentative and aggressive at the same time, but maybe that's my discomfort with being a murder suspect. She's around thirty. Police chief's daughter. Rafe says she's competent."

"And what do you think?"

There was a pause. "First thing that comes to mind? She's a hottie, Sky. Swedish bones and blonde hair—with the most striking black eyebrows. And yes, if she'd been a man I wouldn't have noticed. So shoot me."

"Peter—"

He threw up his hands. "I don't know! Christ, I've never done this before. I have no idea how to judge detectives."

"This is important." Sky was in deadly earnest. "She's going to want to know why Rusty was here."

"And I can't tell her," Peter said evenly. "I may never find out, now."

"If the extent of your—falling-out—were known, it could place you in an awkward position. You realize that, of course."

"Yes," Peter said impatiently. "But right now it's not the main thing on my mind. I know I didn't kill him, and I don't give a fuck if the Nantucket police don't believe me. That'll sort itself out. Right now, I've got to figure out why Rusty was killed. Because there's a strong chance someone thought he was me."

Sky gazed at the fire, which was catching slowly, the wood too green. His long, thin fingers were loosely clasped in his lap. "No one has the slightest reason to kill you, Peter."

"I like to think not," he agreed "But the whole thing is so insane. It feels too random. If Rusty wasn't killed by mistake—why was he here last night? Did his murderer follow him to my door? Was Rusty on the run? I can't answer those questions because I know nothing about my brother's life, after all this time. "

"Was there anything on him that might tell us something? A cell phone? Any—papers or letters?"

"The cops wouldn't let me check his pockets and the detective didn't tell me what she'd found. I'll have to wait until they decide to share their information. She mentioned an autopsy."

Sky shifted in his chair. "If you're worried about the abilities of the Nantucket police, we could call in a private investigator. The firm uses a number of them."

"Rusty wasn't a cheating spouse, Sky."

"So far as we know." The lawyer's tone was sharp. "But the truth is, Rusty could have been anything in the past ten years. We need more information. Contacts in Brazil—"

Peter stared broodingly into the fire. "Rusty came back here to die. He was in trouble, and for whatever reason, he needed to see me. He didn't get in touch with you. Nothing but desperation would have brought him to me or this island."

"Unless your premise is wrong," Sky said.

Peter looked up. "Meaning?"

"Maybe he'd made a fortune and wanted to brag. Or maybe he wanted to settle old scores. Hell, maybe he just wanted to see his brother again. And just happened to stray into the path of a killer . . . who thought he was you."

"So you haven't ruled that out," Peter said.

Sky gave him the ghost of a smile. "I'm a lawyer. I can make a case for every contingency. So who *might* want you dead?"

"I'm not that interesting."

"No rival cranberry farmer who'd kill for your market share?"

"Right." Peter pulled a face. "You know the only other bog is a collective on preservation land. You drew up our agreement for sharing the water rights to Gibbs Pond. Nobody connected to it has any reason to want me out of the way. Dollar for dollar, I spend more maintaining the sluice gates than they can afford to."

"Scorned any women with bad tempers and big cars?"

"I'd have to look at them first, and you know I haven't done that in years."

"Other than the detective," Sky said, then added swiftly, "If I remember correctly, Georgiana's children are the main beneficiaries under your will."

"I left some stock to Princeton and the cost of a college education to Will Starbuck."

Sky studied him a moment. "I'd put that at about three hundred thousand dollars by the time he's ready to go," he said. "Does his mother know you did that?"

"Come on, Sky, Tess isn't the type to hang around my gate at midnight hoping I'll just happen to walk in front of her pickup," Peter said.

"Did she know her son would benefit by your death?" Sky persisted.

"I may have mentioned I'd like to help him with school at one time or another," Peter said grudgingly, "but she dismissed it. She's got a lot of pride. She knows nothing about my will."

Sky sighed. "That would be incentive to keep you alive, then. We can rule out material gain as a motive. Barring a psychopath, we've come up with nothing."

"Which brings us back to Rusty. And all that you know that I don't."

Something in the line of Sky's shoulders stiffened, and

the set expression he adopted for particularly difficult clients came over his features. "If you mean the background to Rusty's business ventures, Peter, I probably know very little more than you do," he said.

"Rusty's dead, Sky. You don't have to protect him any longer. Tell me what you know."

"Nothing more than you do. You're still the little brother, aren't you? Wanting to share Rusty's secrets? They're probably not pretty. I'd rather live in ignorance."

"He must have told you something about his break with my father."

"He showed up in Cambridge, in a snowstorm, the night it happened," Sky said. "But he didn't give me details. All he wanted was help to get out of the country."

"My dad and Rusty never got along that well," Peter said. "Both of them knew Rusty was intended to take over the business; Max needed him, and Rusty had the kind of instincts my father valued. Acumen and guts. Ruthless judgment and a will to power. But they were always looking at each other out of the corners of their eyes, like two guys circling a boxing ring. I don't think Dad fundamentally trusted Rusty. He knew there was something missing."

"Integrity," Sky suggested.

"Integrity." Peter studied him. "Is that why Max cut him off? What could Rusty have done to warrant that? Something criminal?"

"I suggest you ask your mother."

"I did. She doesn't know. Neither does George."

"And you were the one person Rusty would never tell," Sky said. "How ironic it is. What's the time, Peter?"

Peter glanced at his watch. "Ten of three."

Sky cocked an ear toward the Atlantic, his entire body listening. The faint bellow of horns drifted into the stillness of the room, and a log in the grate hissed. "The fog persists," he said. "They'll have closed the airport anyway—I'm not going to get out tonight. Where do I start?"

"How about that night in the snowstorm?" Peter stretched out his long legs. His calves ached from that morning's run; amid the confusion and police, he'd forgotten to stretch.

Sky gave him a sidelong glance. "After Alison. Okay. Rusty had been working for three years at Salomon. He'd made an enormous amount of money for someone twenty-five years old." Sky stood up and poured himself two fingers of bourbon, his favorite drink when fog engulfed the island. The liquor's gleaming depths glowed in the firelight as he lifted the glass to his lips. "But I think he sensed the downturn was coming and decided to bail. He was applying to business schools for the following September."

"I remember. I was filling out law school applications around the same time."

"Fortunately, you didn't mail them," Sky said, and for an instant the expressionless mask shifted and he smiled at Peter. "The world would be much diminished without Mason Farms."

"Thank you. I would be, too."

"I think he intended to sit out the economy for a couple of years, earn a degree, and then join your father at Mason Enterprises." He paused, swirling the bourbon, then looked searchingly at Peter. "But maybe that began to seem too safe. I don't really know what he was feeling or thinking at the time, I only know what he did. Can you understand that?"

"Perfectly. I always felt that way about Rusty. He was impossible to read."

"He kept himself under tight rein. When he was in the grip of some passion, he was extremely volatile. I'd seen it for years, under different circumstances: before a really big game, or when he was about to pull off a major deal, he'd have an air of genius—and of danger, of instability. During those times I felt like he'd gone beyond me, and that I didn't really know him at all. But to be around him then was the most exciting living I've ever done. Rusty could enslave anyone in that mood."

Peter shifted uneasily in his chair. He'd been pretty enslaved himself, once.

"How much did you know about the family business?" Sky walked over to his desk, fishing in a cubbyhole for tobacco and a cherrywood pipe. His restless progress through the room struck Peter as a way of warding off anxiety.

"Not much," he said, "and I wasn't in particularly good shape that Christmas. I'd spent most of the fall holed up here in the Cliff Road house, licking my wounds."

"That's right, you did. Rusty lived dangerously most of that year, didn't he?" Sky turned back to the fire, looking, Peter thought, curiously relieved. He sat down. "But Alison was nothing next to power."

"What do you mean?"

Sky struck a match and cupped it closely over the bowl of the pipe. Peter waited.

"This is all guesswork," Sky said, "but I think he tried to profit from a merger Max was planning, and screwed up."

"Rusty didn't work for Max."

"Exactly," Sky said. "From what he said before the whole thing blew apart, he got wind of a deal Max was putting together and tried to buy a chunk of stock."

"Insider trading?"

"Basically."

Peter glanced at Sky impatiently. "I figured out that much on my own. It had to be insider trading, given the business Rusty was in and the fact that a lot of traders got in over their heads around that time. Even though the federal grand jury came down with a sealed indictment, it was pretty clear that securities fraud was the issue." He paused. "But that's not enough. Max would have fought something like that with the best lawyers he could buy. He'd have loved the challenge, even if it was Mason Enterprises stock Rusty'd played with. Instead he cut his son's legs out from under him and went home to die. Can you see what that means?"

Sky drew on his pipe and said nothing.

"It must have happened before Christmas," Peter said. "I remember. I'd gone back to Greenwich for the holidays and when Max showed up that night, Rusty wasn't with him—I flattered myself that he was avoiding me. But I'd never seen Max look like he did that entire holiday. He was in the grip of a cold, white-knuckled fury. On Christmas Eve he stood up and raised a toast to Masons dead and gone, and he added Rusty's name to the list. That was it. A flat announcement that he'd cut my brother off. My mother went nuts. But he never told her anything."

Sky's face was impassive.

"Max wouldn't even hire a lawyer for Rusty. By January, my father was dead," Peter said. "A massive heart attack. Rusty had skipped town. No one knew how to reach him with the news."

"It's a year we've all tried to put behind us."

Peter chose his next words carefully, studying Sky's face. "We got almost no information out of the grand jury that investigated Rusty. We weren't even allowed in the room. But you were deposed by the prosecuting attorneys, Sky. What did you tell them?"

He pulled his pipe out of his mouth, then slapped the tobacco into the grate. "Nothing but what I've told you, Peter. Rusty didn't share much. Probably didn't want to incriminate me."

"I've thought for years that it must have involved a personal betrayal so monstrous, that Max could never bear the sight of Rusty again. It seemed the only thing that could explain the rage—the profound bitterness—that marked his last months."

"They're both dead," Sky said. "But what happened ten years ago has nothing to do with last night."

"Wait. Let's think for a minute as Rusty would have, before he was prosecuted. Max has a deal going down—no surprise, he lived and breathed them, but this one is special. Something risky, something Max was betting the store on." He stopped, his brows knit in concentration. "Let's call it a hostile takeover. Rusty's at Salomon—Max's major underwriter. Somehow Rusty knows when Max is going to move, he knows the target, he knows the status of negotiations with the banks; he stands to make big money on commissions."

"I think we've already established that," Sky said.

"If you had that sort of information, and you were Rusty, what would you do?"

"Neither of us has ever been Rusty," Sky said flatly. "This doesn't get us anywhere. Go home, Peter. I'll be in touch when I've talked to the police."

Sky was warning him off. The late-summer day was ending prematurely, the sun lost in the fog, and the old house felt drafty. Peter got to his feet.

"You're right, of course. What happened ten years ago only matters to me, doesn't it?

"You know that's not true," Sky said. "Take the back way home, and expect reporters at your gate. You're the closest thing to the Kennedys Nantucket's got, and people love a murder."

PETER TOOK SKY'S advice and made for the Polpis Road, the frame of his bike bucking stiffly over the occasional stone and his progress swift in the windless air. He pedaled unconscious of the effort involved, past Sesachacha Pond, his mind wrestling with the dark tangle of his brother's past. He was certain Sky knew more than he would say. He dismissed the reasons for his silence—loyalty to Rusty, a lawyer's innate discretion, fear of some kind—they could wait. More important was the thread he had picked out of the past, the fragile link between all that had gone before and the blood on his doorstep.

Rusty had used what he knew about a pending hostile takeover before it happened. He'd made a lot of money in his few short years on the Street. Money was always nice; but power was better. Rusty wanted what his father had: influence over markets, entire economies, and lesser men. And he wasn't willing to wait for it.

Suddenly, as Peter neared the Polpis Harbor Road, it

seemed obvious. This particular deal must have given Rusty power over *Max*. He'd tried to take down his *own father*. Nothing else would have made Peter's dad so unforgiving or so bitter.

How did Rusty find out about the deal? Not from Max; the control of information was one form of protection, and Max never shared his plans. Peter considered Salomon briefly, and ruled it out. When ME went to its underwriter, it counted on Salomon's practice of encoding clients' names—to limit the spread of information among insiders and shield it from speculators.

"There must have been a source," Peter muttered to himself, the wind generated by his passage tearing the words from his lips and throwing them over his shoulder. Someone close to Max, someone vital, who had betrayed him for a reason and lived to regret it. Once Rusty had the knowledge he needed, the source's credit with Max would be worthless. Had he tried to salvage what he could by telling Max what he'd done? Had that been Rusty's undoing? And had the source then lost everything—his job, Max's trust, maybe even his freedom?

A motive for murder, once Rusty returned to American shores.

Peter slowed the bike to take the left-hand turn-off past Almanack Pond and down toward the farm. He knew now what he had to do. There was one man who might be able to help him—Malcolm Scott, Max's former chief financial officer, who was spinning out his remaining years patiently at home in Westchester County. He would pay Malcolm Scott a call.

He dove for his driveway neatly, slowing the bike as it hit the unpaved surface. The wheels steadied and he glanced up, then came slowly to a halt, his right leg dropping to the ground. The dim bulk of parked cars loomed through the fog. Sky was right. He had company.

## Chapter 9

THE SLAM OF the kitchen door woke Merry abruptly
from a dream that she was underwater. She had been
pushing her way through brackish weeds in a swimmer's
crawl, her eyes clouded by mud, searching for something.
*The bog*, she thought hazily, and opened her eyes.

Her Swedish grandmother used to say it was bad luck
to dream of water. From the shifting patterns of leaves
thrown on the wall by the beech tree beyond her window,
she judged it to be five o'clock. She lay back on the pillow, eyes closed, and listened to Ralph Waldo humming
among his vegetables in the yard below. Her father's face
rose in her mind, and with it, the residue of anger filling
her head like bad gin. She opened one eye, groped for her
watch on the bedside table, and discovered it was past six.
She was fuddled with daytime sleep.

By now, the bog would be drained and the crime scene
unit would be crawling among the sandy vines searching for anything man-made that might have belonged
to Rusty Mason. Bailey would be with them. A wave of
anger and remorse washed over her. Her father would
never forgive her for the scene she'd made today. She'd
have to resign. But where to go? Back to New Bedford? It
was too much to think about.

The Folger house sat on Tattle Court, one of the
warren of lanes that sprang from Fair Street. It was a
Federal-style cottage of six rooms, with a slate-blue door
placed asymmetrically in the clapboard facade—a "three-
quarter" house in Nantucket parlance. The shingles that
sheltered it from salt air and the island's winter winds had
mellowed to a soft charcoal over the years, and on the
shady north side, sea-green moss grew thick on some of
them. The white trim was peeling and the windowpanes
were clouded with age. The house sat close to the street
behind a picket fence whose gate opened onto the driveway running along one side. The gate was weighted with
an iron ball and chain, staked in a bed of dahlias. In the
backyard, hydrangeas and herbs were ranged in riotous
disorder around a mirrored lightning ball. Ralph was a
desultory weeder.

Inside, the house was a mass of clutter. Boxes of junk
mail, never opened, but hoarded over decades, sat on the
dining-room table. The living-room curtains—removed
for cleaning before her grandmother's death three years
earlier—lay folded over a wing chair whose silk upholstery
fell in tattered streamers around its legs. Wrought-iron
blacksmithing tools, owned by some nineteenth-century
Folger, stood in the corner of the stairway. An easel sport-
ing a half-finished canvas straddled the hallway next to a
large Boston fern.

Merry descended the stairs, stepping over Tabitha,
the calico cat, and her latest litter of kittens, and picked
her way through a collection of prewar ladies' hats on her
way to the kitchen. Ralph Waldo had raised her father
here, and when Merry's mother and brother died, she and
John had moved back into the house. The clutter drove

her father mad. The prospect of clearing it away, how-ever, was too daunting. Every winter began with a vow to sort through the accumulation of years, and every spring found the house in its usual state. Nothing had changed; it had merely increased.

"What's for dinner, Ralph?"

Her grandfather, splendid in a red butcher's apron, held a fillet knife in one hand. There was a smell of lem-ons and freshly ground pepper. Ralph turned and smiled when he saw her.

"Bluefish. With tomatoes and basil. Potato salad. Iced tea with mint. There may be some ice cream left, but then again, you may have eaten it when I wasn't looking."

"I'm starved. Got any cheese?"

"You can look."

Merry considered the icebox, which sported the profu-sion and decay of the rest of the house, and gave up. She pulled out a rush-seated chair and slumped over the table, feeling cranky.

Her grandfather raised an eyebrow and turned back to his fillet. "You're looking cranky, Meredith. We'd better start with the iced tea."

"Dad gave my case away."

Ralph stopped his work on the fish and shook his head. "That boy," he said. "Never fails to lay the wrong foot."

"So you think I could have done it?"

He looked at her: mouth wistful and uncertain under the cool green eyes, hair tousled like a child's from sleep. "Of course you could have done it. I intend to tell your father so when I see him."

"Don't humor me, Ralph. This is important. I was ner-vous as hell out there today; I almost couldn't look the corpse in the face. Do you think I'm tough enough to handle a murder?"

"Toughness has its downside, Meredith. It can keep you from feeling. Assurance is what you want; and that'll come with experience. If you believe in yourself, that is." He shot her what she called his wrath-of-God glance from under his white eyebrows.

"I have to get Dad to believe in me first."

"I *do* not agree," he said firmly. "Work on your self-confidence, and you'll give him a reason to back you. You've never quite trusted your abilities, Meredith Abiah, and for the life of me I cannot see why. You're smart, you're dedicated, you're thorough—and better than that, you've got the best instincts I've seen in a long time. I flatter myself they're hereditary." He pulled out a chair and sat down opposite her, one gnarled hand supporting his chin and the other stroking her blonde head. The unruly waves were springy beneath his fingers, like ferns or feathers. "What is it you're so afraid of?"

She laid one cheekbone on the table's scarred surface and let herself be a child. With Ralph, she was open as she never could be with her father. "Failing."

"—To solve your first murder? Or to fill your brother's shoes?"

"There's some of that."

"Why?"

"Dad was so proud of him, Ralph. Of his *son*. He still is. I'm always struggling to be what I'm not."

"Bullshit," he retorted. "You're more your father's child than Billy ever was. He was one of the loves of my life, Meredith, but he had your mother's romanticism and her impetuosity. That's why he enlisted and jumped on an improvised explosive device as it went off. You're too rational to be a hero. That will take you far in the police business."

Merry laughed hollowly. "Unless I'm fired. I lost my temper in Dad's office. I was probably on a caffeine-and-sugar high from Fog Island."

"So we'll call it my fault."

"He mentioned Mom, and I said something stupid." Merry ran her finger around the rim of her iced tea tumbler, her face flushing as she spoke. The tea was the color of mahogany and smelled like the inside of a cedar closet.

Ralph got up and busied himself at the counter. "How bad was it?"

"I told him I wouldn't slit my wrists the first time things got rough. Or words to that effect." Her voice was very small. "I thought he'd punch his fist through the door."

Ralph set down his fillet knife and wiped his hands on his apron. "You've had more intelligent moments, Meredith. Your mother was the sweetest woman who ever lived."

"You think I don't know that?" she burst out. "You think I don't feel like crap? And the truth is that he's partly right. He shouldn't trust me. I nearly flunked out of my forensic anthropology class. I can't stand to look at 'human remains.' I hate the smell, the bloating, the obscenity of a murdered body."

She pushed aside her glass of tea. "I follow every case in the state with a horrible fascination. Dad thinks I'm morbid. Other cops can depersonalize murder—they talk about the killing's statistical group, or the modus operandi of a case compared to one last year—but I can't. I think about the victim. What his life might have been like. What she must have thought as she was dying. Whether he died in fear and pain, alone. And I think about how I'd have felt if it happened to me."

"You ought to. A lost life should mean something."

"That's why I can't understand Peter Mason's reaction," Merry said. "He's so cold, Ralph. It's as if he's dismissed the fact of his brother's death and moved on to worrying about his harvest. It's not normal. In fact, it makes me angry. So maybe I shouldn't be in the police business."

"'Any man's death diminishes me, because I am involved in mankind,'" Ralph Waldo mused. "I don't think that's bad, Meredith. I think it's a form of grace too often lacking in police work."

The backyard screen door swung open abruptly, and Merry looked over her shoulder. John Folger stepped into the kitchen, nodded to her wordlessly, and handed a brown paper bag to Ralph. "Picked up some melons from the produce truck in town this morning. Whole office smells like them."

"Thanks, son," Ralph said. "Well, I'd better get these fish on the fire." He slathered the fillets with mayonnaise and then disappeared into the foggy yard, where a charcoal grill smoked gently.

"I'm sorry for what I said to you this morning," Merry attempted. "All of it. You're probably right to give the case to somebody with more experience. I was just so tired, so—"

"—fed up with banging your head against the wall," her father said. "I know. I used to have to fight Ralph for every case I worked on. I should be better at this than he was." He dropped his keys on the kitchen counter and stood looking at them blankly for an instant. "But we don't learn, Merry. I look at you and I see the little girl who used to make me bury dead seagulls in the backyard. I see the young woman who dragged around for months when her brother didn't come home from war. Death makes us careful with our children. I don't want anything, ever, to happen to you. You're all I've got left. You're the most important thing in my life. And so I protect you too much." He put his hand on her shoulder. "Don't resign, kid."

"Sometimes it seems like the only thing left to do."

"You could try working on the Mason murder instead. I told Bailey I needed him on the vandalism case."

"I bet he loved that," she said carefully.

"He didn't share his feelings with me."

"Probably a good thing. Thanks, Dad. You won't be sorry."

Her chief kissed the top of her head lightly, something he rarely did. "Eat your dinner and get back out there." He made his way through the cluttered kitchen to the stairs, cursing as his shin met the edge of a blacksmith iron.

Merry shot out of her seat and thrust her head around the screen door. "He gave me the case, Ralph! What in the *hell* do I do now?"

Upstairs, as he folded his discarded uniform and reached for a towel, John Folger smiled.

## Chapter 10

TWO HOURS LATER, bouncing over the sandy trail through the moors to Altar Rock, Merry made a decision. Peter Mason's safety was paramount, and therefore she would have to operate on the assumption that he was the killer's intended victim and his brother an unlucky double. If in the course of investigation she was proved wrong—if Rusty in fact was the target—she'd have erred only on the side of caution.

She had done the obvious where Rusty Mason was concerned—furnished a description of him to the ferry service, the taxi stands, and the airlines in the hope that someone would identify him and she could trace his movements. She had sent Howie to the rental car companies out at the airport to ask whether Rusty Mason had picked up his ride there. And she had told Clarence Strangerfield to arrange for divers to search the kettle hole ponds that dotted Nantucket over the next few days. It was possible the killer had just submerged his weapon in one of them. Short of a garage-to-garage hunt, she was unlikely to find the damaged car any other way.

Clarence had texted her the results of his bog search. Three hours of combing an area within a hundred-yard radius from the body, with a party of three sergeants on hands and knees, had produced fifty-six cents in pennies, nickels, and dimes; a multitude of scratches; a rusted piece of metal, presumably from Peter's harvesting equipment; crimson juice stains on four uniforms; an ancient beer bottle; and colds in several heads. Clarence had vacuumed the clothes and body for fibers before they were sent to the forensic center on the mainland. The pockets were empty, as though Rusty Mason had left Brazil with only the clothes on his back. His watch, however, had stopped at two forty-seven.

"That doesn't mean he went into the water then, Merry, only that the movement stopped at that point."

"Fine," she'd said impatiently, wondering why the man had traveled to the island like a day-tripper, without a wallet, passport, or cell phone, not to mention a ticket stub—and recognized it was impossible. Either he'd left all his belongings in a hotel room on the mainland, or the murderer had gotten rid of them. Something else to look for.

Clarence had found a single print on the wooden button; they did not match the dead man's, nor those taken from Rafe da Silva's and Peter Mason's fingers that morning. "So we've got a non-suspect ident," she'd mused. A print from an unknown person—who might be the murderer. Or not.

"Ah'll search the database," Clarence told her. "Maybe we'll get lucky."

Finally, there were the photographs taken at the scene. She lingered over the shot of Rusty Mason's dead face, revising her earlier opinion of his resemblance to his brother. His hair was brighter brown, shot with red where Peter's tended to black, and the lines on the face were deeply etched.

"Looks like he lived hard, Clare," she'd said.

Now, as she guided the car along the still-foggy trail through the moor toward Peter Mason's house, it was Rafe da Silva she was thinking of. The prospect of bumping into him gave her a thrill of terror and nausea coupled with wild hope. Despite the smallness of the island, the two of them had been out of touch for years—because Rafe wanted it that way. She had tried to pump her grandfather for information over dinner, to little purpose.

"Ralph, you know anything about how Rafe da Silva wound up out at Mason Farms?"

"Nope. But I imagine like most folks he answered a want ad."

"The da Silvas are watermen. Not farmers."

"In this economy, you're lucky if you're apt for more than one trade. Mason Farms pays a salary, and I'll bet the board is thrown in. Shoot," Ralph had said, as he pulled a bone from the bluefish. "You know old Jose hasn't spoken to Rafe since he got back from New Bedford, Meredith. He's not likely to have him on his boat. The best Rafe can hope for is that the old coot will kick off one of these days and leave him the scalloper. Not that I wish the man ill. Still, I get tired of fellows who've no time for their own sons. Death ends enough conversations."

"They just seem like an odd pair," Merry had said. "Mason and Rafe, I mean."

Ralph had grunted assent, his attention on the beefsteak tomato he'd picked from the plants next to the fence. He'd held it in the palm of his right hand, a paring knife in his left, and sliced the dark red flesh into wedges. Tomato juice had run over his fingers and dripped to his elbow. He'd mopped at it with his napkin. "You thinking Rafe went for Peter and got his brother?" Ralph had said.

"Ralph! That's crazy. Rafe's not the killing type, whatever people think."

"I know that. I'm just wondering why you're worried about what the man does for a living."

BECAUSE I WANT *to know why he's so distant toward me*, Merry said to herself. *It's all part of the changes in his life since Iraq, since nothing seemed right to either of us with Billy gone. I'm just worried about him. And I don't like him so close to another murder, either. He's got some pretty deep scars.*

Somewhere behind the fog, the sun was in decline. Merry switched on her low beams and saw the air solidify in front of her, dual arcs of opacity thrusting into the darkness past the radar station. Her police radio squawked static suddenly into the quietness of the car, and she jumped involuntarily in her seat. She reached over and turned it off, then thought better of it and turned it back on, at low volume. A car passed her heading back to town, its high beams flooding a wall of fog, the motorist hunched over the wheel in a desperate effort to see. *Tourist*, Merry thought. Nobody used to fog would throw on the high beams. Must be lost, too; there was no good reason to be driving back in the moors tonight. Other than Mason Farms, the road led only to Nantucket Conservation Foundation lands. As she approached the driveway to the farm, she frowned, puzzled. A crowd of vans and cars had pulled up, helter-skelter, near the turnoff.

"Great night for a barbecue, Mason," she said to herself. She made the turn into the driveway and came to an abrupt halt. A crush of people with cameras were huddled near the yellow police cordon, flashes exploding in the darkening fog. Merry threw the Explorer into neutral and pulled up the handbrake, searching for the Nantucket police sergeant Clarence had left on duty. He was nowhere to be seen.

As she got out of the car, a knot of excited gawkers broke from the spot-lit area in front of a television crew and moved toward her in a wave. Merry stopped dead. "Seitz," she muttered. "Of course."

Howie Seitz was in the midst of his fifth exclusive interview, his trademark smile in full force. He stooped slightly to hear the questions posed by a breathless blonde in red linen, who held her earphones in one manicured hand and a microphone in the other. Merry glanced at the camera crew's call sign. A Boston station. They must have helicoptered when the news hit the wire.

She marched over to the charmed circle, reached out a hand, and said, "Sorry, ma'am, we've got work to do here. Seitz!"

"Detective Folger! Hey, Madeleine, this is the woman who's handling the investigation!"

The blonde newswoman turned to Merry eagerly and shoved a microphone next to her chin. "Could you comment on the death of Rusty Mason, Detective? Were drugs involved? Do we know whether this was an accident, or murder?"

"We'd know a lot sooner if you'd let us do our job," Merry said, scowling. "Now turn that thing off and leave my intern alone."

"Cut that, Steve," the blonde said coolly, turning to her cameraman. "We'll have to go with the kid."

Merry took Howie by the elbow and marched him over to her car. She reached into the back and pulled out a bullhorn. "Start talking with this," she said. "I suggest the phrase 'Clear the area.' It generally works. If you're talking to anyone—anyone at all, do you understand me?—when I come back down this driveway, you're fired."

"I'm going back to school at the end of the week, for Chrissake," Howie said.

"And you can leave without a recommendation, too," Merry shot back. She turned on her heel and pushed her way through the crowd.

The quarter-mile of driveway was relatively clear. At the geranium-colored door, however, another knot had gathered, hoping for a glimpse of Peter Mason. Merry glanced at it and paused, thinking. Then she turned and headed around the house to the barn. A light glowed from the loft.

After the chaos at the gate, the barn's stillness seemed unnatural. Merry paused at the huge, half-open doors, allowing her eyes to adjust to the dimness of the interior. The sweet smell of hay blended with the mustiness of sheep's urine and old wood rising from the floor. She sneezed once, and then again. A chair scraped against the flooring over her head, and heavy footsteps crossed the platform. From the barn's far corner, Merry heard the unoiled hinges of a door whine open. She turned in the direction of the sound, and saw a staircase leading from the threshing floor to the hayloft.

"Turn right around and head back where you came from," a man's voice said. "This is private property."

"Rafe." Her voice was tremulous. "It's Merry."

He paused, a dark outline against the glow of the doorway. "Hell," he said, "thought you were the Press."

RAFE'S ROOM STILL looked like the hayloft it had once been. He showed her the bolted trapdoor in the flooring, partially covered by a trunk that served as his coffee table. A single bunk in one corner was neatly made up, and a desk across the room was strewn with papers—feed orders, wool counts. The lamp hanging from the low rafters sent swinging shadows against the walls, but threw steady light on the armchair Rafe had clearly just vacated. Next to it on the floor stood a beer bottle and an open book, facedown. The windows cut in three walls were bare of curtains. She imagined the sun pouring in on clear mornings, slanting across the sharp planes of Rafe's face, causing his dark brows to furrow over crinkled lids, and then corrected her mental picture. The sheep on the property meant he'd be up long before dawn, something farming had in common with fishing. Maybe his new life wasn't so different from the old after all. As if he felt her eyes on him, Rafe turned and looked at her, and she dropped her gaze. The sight of his face undid her.

Rafe waited for her to speak. When she didn't, he motioned to the chair. "Have a seat," he said, and pulled out the desk chair for himself. He straddled it backward, arms folded along the top rail, and waited again. Rafe was accustomed to silence, and it did not compel him to speech. He'd learned long ago that if you didn't rush to fill a gap, people were likely to fill it for you.

"How long have you been here, Rafe?" Merry asked, with effort.

"Bit over five years."

"It doesn't seem that long." *Since we both left New Bedford*, she meant, but didn't say.

"Time goes."

Merry nodded, and looked around the room again. It looked as though no one really lived there, much less for five years. She glanced back at Rafe, hugging his chair like a safety barrier. It had been months—maybe a year and a half—since she'd had a reason to say more to him than hello. With a sense of shock she saw that he looked older than she remembered. She did a quick calculation and realized Rafe was thirty-nine, Billy's age if he'd lived. His body was still fit and powerful, his perpetually copper face and deep brown eyes as controlled and calm as ever, but lines of weariness ran from the corners of his mouth to his nose, and the mink-brown hair was shot with gray. It seemed inconceivable to her that she had touched that hair once, that he had cried in her arms like a child. Since New Bedford he'd opened a steadily widening distance between them.

Merry realized he was aware of her appraisal, and suddenly self-conscious, she looked away from him. "It's really good to see you. I'm sorry it takes a murder to get me out here."

Rafe didn't answer. He reached for the beer bottle and took a long drink. "What can I do for you, Detective Folger?"

As if they were strangers. "You could talk to me like a friend, for starters," she said. "What's wrong?"

A muscle in his cheek twitched. "Let's just say it's been a long day, and the morning comes early. Whatever you need, let's get it over with."

Merry looked down at her hands, which were tightly

clenched, and forced herself to loosen her fingers. "Tell me what you think happened here."

"I think Peter's brother bought it last night. What do you think?"

"I think you're being hostile for no reason," she retorted, "and if your boss ends up dead, too, one of these days, I'm going to have to ask some tougher questions."

Rafe's face darkened. He set down the bottle with a quiet clink that somehow managed to sound ominous. "So ask 'em now," he said.

Her throat tightened. This meeting wasn't going at all the way she'd hoped. "What do you know about Mason's life? Any reason somebody'd want to kill him?"

"No."

"That's not good enough, Rafe."

"Maybe not, but it happens to be the truth. I've watched the guy for five years. He's got no personal life. No women. He's not growing controlled substances down on the farm. He's a nice guy trying to make a living out of Ocean Spray."

"Know anything about his brother?"

"Didn't even know he had one."

"Has Mason seemed like himself lately?"

"Yep. He works out, sees a few friends, runs the farm. Plays a lot of chess, listens to his music. He keeps to himself."

It was remarkable, Merry thought, that someone you had once loved could become a complete stranger you no longer knew how to talk to. She shoved her hair behind her ears and tried again.

"No weird phone calls? Emails? Nothing out of the ordinary? No sign or code from his brother telling him he was due in town?"

"They teach you espionage and witchcraft at the police academy, too?"

"Answer the question, Rafe."

"No. Not so's I noticed."

*He's protecting Peter Mason,* Merry thought, *and he's afraid of me.* What an extraordinary thing. She'd have to keep forcing him to talk to her. "Do you like the guy?"

For the first time, Rafe dropped his gaze, and his face became carefully expressionless. "Yeah, I like him. He's a good boss and a good friend. Why do you think I'm so worried?" He stood up and started to pace around the loft. "I'm pissed as hell that I didn't hear something last night. That could've been Pete out in the bog, you know that, Merry? And I heard nothing."

"Can't take care of everybody, Rafe," Merry said gently.

He stopped in his tracks and looked at her, his dark eyes shadowed. "Yeah, well, it'd make a change from everybody taking care of me," he said. "But I'll be ready tonight."

"Meaning what?"

"Meaning if the clown comes back, he'll regret it." He pointed to a Browning nine-millimeter that stood on a gun rack next to a twelve-gauge shotgun.

"I didn't know you had an arsenal."

"They're Pete's. He wants them stored in the barn, not the house."

"So you can't think of who'd want to kill him, or why, but you think Peter was the target just the same."

"Nothing else makes sense," he said.

Merry shifted in her chair. "Unless he killed his brother."

Rafe gave a short bark of laughter. "Not a chance."

Merry leaned forward. "Mason seems to be the only

guy in town—besides my grandfather—who remembered Rusty existed. And he isn't hiding the fact he couldn't stand him."

Rafe ran his left hand over his stubble. "There's something there, something with the brother. I could see it today. The man's got a grudge. He won't talk about it, Merry, and it bugs me."

"You're afraid Peter did it," she said.

"Maybe I am. Aw, shit, listen to me—he's the last guy to get violent."

"Really? Would either you or Rebecca know if he left the house in the middle of the night?"

Rafe studied his hands.

"Rafe."

"I'd hear a car, wouldn't I?"

"Not if he met Rusty somewhere on foot—a prearranged spot, fixed in a text you never saw or a voicemail you didn't hear."

"Rusty was killed on the road, walking toward the gate," Rafe said.

"Maybe Peter offered him a room at the house, and insisted on driving because of the fog and the strangeness of the moors. And when they got to the gate, Rusty got out to open it, as any passenger would. Something inside Peter snaps—whatever it is he's been holding on to for so long. Maybe Peter hits the gas."

Rafe sat silently for a minute, then shook his head. "If Peter wanted to kill him, why would he wait until he got home to do it, and then leave the body in his front yard? And where did he leave Rusty's car? Strangerfield has checked all of ours and they're clean. You're working overtime, Girlscout."

It was a name from childhood Merry had almost forgotten. The memory of her brother washed over her in a sweet, painful rush. "These friends," she said. "When he sees people, who does he see?"

"A few islanders, some off." Rafe was being careful again. "Guy named Sky Tate-Jackson and his girlfriend. She's part foreign, makes clothes. Has a shop in town."

"Mayling Stern," Merry said. Rafe nodded.

"Then there's Lucy Jacoby, the English teacher at the high school."

"How's he know her?"

Rafe shrugged. "And the Starbucks, of course. He was a friend of Tess and Dan's first and got to know Will when Dan passed away. He's been good for the kid."

"Like you've been good for the widow."

Rafe's head came up and his eyes narrowed. "You watching what I do, Meredith Folger? You got a squad car following me?"

"No. I just checked your alibi for Sunday night. Dod Nelson spent Labor Day weekend on the Cape. You said he drove you home. But you were coming from the Greengage. Weren't you?"

Rafe sighed.

"Next time, think before you lie," Merry suggested. "You spent most of Sunday night with Tess Starbuck, I'd guess. You just didn't want to say so in front of her kid and your boss." She waited, but he did not reply. "You couldn't have stopped Rusty Mason's murder, because you weren't even here."

"Man, I am so sick of being tailed by police," Rafe said. His voice was low and taut with contained anger. "I'm perpetually guilty until proven innocent. God knows my dad thinks so. And somehow you're always around when things go south, Merry. Like a bad luck charm."

"Right. This is my fault," she said tiredly and turned to go. "Don't hold out on me again when there's a murder involved."

"I'll do as I goddamn please," he said. "You're not my parole officer or my grandma. And you're wasting your time checking up on me, Meredith. I had no reason to kill the guy."

"If the body had a knife wound, maybe I'd check harder," Merry shot back, and then stopped, horrified. "Rafe, I'm sorry, I didn't mean it," she said.

His face was expressionless. He seemed not to have heard her. He moved almost indifferently to his desk and rifled through the feed orders and wool counts. "Yeah," he said, "but part of you will always think it, Meredith. And whenever I see you, I'm back in a holding pen in New Bed. So just get out of my house, will you?"

*Chapter 11*

MERRY STUMBLED IN the darkened yard as she made her way from the barn to the gravel drive, and the sharp stab of pain unleashed the obscenities she'd barely held back in Rafe's presence. "You're such a fucking idiot, Merry Folger," she muttered furiously as she massaged her turned ankle. She had reminded Rafe of something he'd never done and a shame he couldn't erase. He didn't miss her, didn't want her, and didn't need her. He just wanted to be left alone.

She looked up, searching for her bearings. The night was moonless, the fog still holding, and the yard had no spotlights.

A dog gave voice suddenly close at hand. A dark, moving shape hurtled around the corner of the house and shot directly toward her. She stopped short, reaching for the service pistol she carried but had never had to use, her heart beating fast with fear.

"Ney!" A man's voice called through the darkness, followed by a whistle. The dog slid to a halt just in front of Merry, jaws snapping and ears back, holding her until his master approached. She froze. A man's hand came down over the dog's collar. Ney whined, sat, and turned his nose up to Peter Mason.

"The freak show is closed and you're trespassing," he said, not recognizing her in the darkness. "I'd appreciate it if you'd leave the property."

"That's some dog, Mr. Mason," she said. "How come he didn't catch a killer last night?"

"He probably would have, Detective," Peter said, "if I didn't keep him inside. I was just taking him over to Rafe's. The crowds have been driving him nuts, so I locked him in the kitchen all afternoon. He's a little jumpy. Thank God that cop at the end of the drive finally cleared them out." He paused. "Wait here a minute and I'll be right back."

He walked off in the direction of the barn, Ney moving with him like a shadow against his leg. Merry breathed deeply and closed her eyes. The last thing she wanted now was an interview with Peter Mason, but his requests had a curious way of sounding like commands, and she didn't have the energy to fight him. She heard the barn door open, and, after a pause, squeak shut. She waited for the light footsteps through the long grass to reach her and then turned.

"Let's go inside," Mason said.

He led her around to the back kitchen door. A single light over the sink gave it a deserted feeling. Rebecca had left pots and a coffee cup to drain in the dish rack. As Merry passed it, the dishwasher cycle kicked into rinse with a roar. The sound was vaguely comforting.

She followed Mason into his study and came to a halt in front of the fireplace, where driftwood was burning brightly.

"It's early in the season, I know, but the fog cuts through you," he said. "The fire's half for mental comfort."

She held out her hands to the blaze.

"Can I get you a drink? Or tea?"

Merry glanced over her shoulder. "Tea would be great."

"The cognac's on the shelf," he said. "I'll be right back."

ACROSS THE ISLAND, in Siasconset, Mayling Stern stood by her studio's wide window. Foghorns were booming over the night sea from the international shipping lanes to the southeast. Off to her left, up the beach, Sankaty Light sliced through the dark, but its reach was truncated by fog, its passage illuminating nothing but a swirling cloud. With one hand she drew her sweater closer around her slender body and with the other closed the vertical blinds against the night. "I hate this island in bad weather," she said. "It feels as though all the lost souls in the world have converged in the air above us, and are waiting."

"For what?" Sky asked.

"For Rusty to join them, perhaps." She glanced at Sky. Sitting in the red leather chair, he was backlit by the glow of her drafting-table spotlight, and she could not read his features. It occurred to her that he wanted it that way. He had turned off the overhead lamps when he entered the room.

"The first and last sign of an off-islander," he said. "Arrive with the sun, leave with the fog."

She had willed him to reach for her, and instead, he offered her scorn. She waited.

"Mayling," he said, "Did Peter tell you how Rusty died?"

She shook her head. "He was angry when I didn't ask."

"He was run down by a car, then dragged to the bog unconscious and left to drown."

Mayling folded her arms protectively across her chest.

"Don't drive the Mercedes," Sky said evenly. "Keep it in the garage. We'll get it fixed later, after all this has blown over."

Mayling searched for his eyes in the gloom, gave up, and turned to the door. "Take me home to New York, Schuyler," she said. "I can't bear to be here alone."

"RAFE TELLS ME you two go back a long way," Peter said delicately as he handed Merry the tea.

"I'm surprised he remembers. Most of the time he treats me like Summer People."

"I see." Peter settled back in his chair and reached for the cognac. "What happened?"

"Every possible thing that can drive two people apart." She took a sip of tea. "We've been friends since I was a kid —Rafe's one of the last links to my brother, Billy, who was killed in Iraq. You knew Rafe was deployed there?"

Peter nodded. "Two tours."

"But we didn't get involved with each other until about six years ago. Probably right before he started to work for you. I'm not surprised you never heard of me— Rafe cut his losses pretty quick where I was concerned."

"And you didn't?"

She laughed harshly. "Let's just say I haven't dated anybody since." She swirled the tea bag in the mug, staring into its depths.

"I think oracles use loose tea," Peter said.

"The future's not really worth knowing, is it?"

"I can't think of anything worse."

"Your brother, for instance. If he'd known he was going to die last night on this island, would he have stayed away?"

"No," Peter said. "Rusty thought he could beat all the odds."

"So he was a gambler."

"A very accomplished one." He did not want to talk about his brother. He deliberately turned the subject. "I met Rafe around the time of my first harvest. He'd been crewing on and off for Dan Starbuck, but the boat couldn't really support another guy, and Rafe knew it. That first job turned into a series of things—I was rebuilding this house, putting the addition on the back. Then the sheep came three years later. At this point Rafe's indispensable. I live in terror of losing him."

"You won't," Merry said. "He's loyal to a fault. He only went to Iraq because he wanted to protect Billy."

"And couldn't. I'm sorry for your loss."

"My brother was ready to get off the island and see the world," she said carefully. "I can't fault him for the impulse. I certainly don't fault Rafe."

"But I'm guessing he does," Peter said thoughtfully.

"Enlisting wasn't entirely a mistake. Rafe's dad, Jose, thought he should fish like all the da Silvas before him, but you know as well as I do that there's no fleet left on Nantucket. So he tried the army instead."

"He's not the first."

"No." She grimaced. "It was a nightmare when we heard about Billy. And then Rafe reenlisted. He wasn't the same when he came back."

"Most guys aren't."

"But only a few end up being tried for murder."

Peter choked on his cognac and set down the glass. "What did you say?"

"Rafe. The year before you hired him from Dan. In

New Bedford. He was crewing on a trawler owned by some Portuguese cousins. It was a real mess. A real media circus."

"Go on," Peter said.

"Three guys had been drinking in a bar, one of those places by the pier the New Bed fishermen hang out in. Turns out one of them—it had to be the guy with a petty rap sheet a yard long, a reputed wife-beater, and the ringleader of the group—was about to lose his boat to the bank. So the more the guys drank, the louder and angrier they got, the more vows of group honor and solidarity they took, the more obscenities they threw at the rich banker types in their BMWs who've never fished a day in their lives."

"Rafe was one of the three men?" Peter asked.

She shook her head. "No, but as luck would have it, he was in the same bar. And he got into a fistfight. Later, as many people swore he was with the three guys as didn't."

"So what happened?"

"The fishermen got tired of the beer and left, looking for some trouble. They found it about three blocks away."

Merry took a swig of cold tea. The slightly metallic flavor tasted like the stale nausea she'd felt in the courtroom every day of Rafe's trial. She looked at Peter. His patrician face was expressionless. How could he know what it had been like?

"There was this couple pulled up to a money machine. The street was pretty deserted—it was three in the morning. The guy was working his card while the woman sat in the car looking at her makeup in the visor mirror. It happened to be a BMW. At a bank. The three guys went nuts. The wife-beater had his gutting knife in his jeans pocket, and he held it to the guy's throat while he withdrew the maximum allowable on his card. Then they forced him into the car, drove to an empty warehouse, and made him watch while they raped his girlfriend." Merry paused and looked at her hands. "Then they slit both their throats. And went home to their wives to sleep it off."

Peter sat back in his chair. He remembered the incident dimly, but he rarely followed crime stories in the news; they had so little to do with his life. "And Rafe was charged with this?"

"He stood trial."

"That's unbelievable. Why? "

Merry smiled faintly. "He'd dated the dead girl."

"Jesus."

"She was from a Portuguese family—it's a pretty tight community in New Bed, you know, and they can close ranks around their own. First they accused a local homeless guy, but then the girl's sister came forward and fingered Rafe. Said he'd killed her because she'd left him for a yuppie with money and a great car."

"The sister must have known it wasn't true," Peter said.

Merry looked at him. "You know, when you hear stories like this it's easy to say men are animals. They're sick. But women are worse, sometimes. That girl had a crush on Rafe and he'd never once looked at her. So she brought him down. That's my theory, anyway. Don't try to understand it."

Frowning, Peter reached for his cognac.

"Turns out Rafe didn't have a very good alibi. He lived alone, and all he could say was that he'd left the bar and gone home to bed. People had seen him hit a guy that night. The prosecutor even used the fact that he was an Iraq vet to make it look like we were all lucky he hadn't taken out a movie theater with an assault rifle. What saved him was forensics—his DNA didn't match any of the sperm or hair samples found on the woman's body. But for months, until the wife-beater was picked up for domestic assault and had his DNA routinely taken, half of New Bedford believed Rafe was guilty. He was thrown off his cousin's boat, and when he came back to Nantucket, his dad cut him loose. He was probably pretty desperate around the time you gave him a job."

"How do you know all of this, Detective?" Peter asked.

"New Bedford was my first posting after I got out of the police academy. I wasn't on Rafe's case—too junior—but . . ." She hesitated. "I watched the whole thing, day after day. I've never been so terrified of mob justice in my whole life. I decided then that the difference between the wrong man going to jail and the right one was good detective work, and that's what I wanted to do."

"But not in New Bedford."

"I followed Rafe back here." She laughed brusquely. "Pretty pathetic, isn't it? To fall in love with a guy because he's wrongly accused of murder?"

Peter took a sip of his drink. "There were probably other reasons."

"I thought I'd helped him stay strong during the darkest time in his life. But it turns out, I just remind him of it." She set down her tea. "And if he knew I'd told you all this, he'd never forgive me. I'll have you thinking he's dangerous, next."

Peter poked at the driftwood with his fire tongs. A shower of sparks exploded into the chimney. "What a nightmare," he muttered. "The powerlessness, the fear he must have felt. I've never really known him, have I?"

"You know the man he's become," Merry said, "not the man he was. And maybe that's a good thing. Rafe's trying to build something new here at Mason Farms."

"Then I'll let him do that. There's no reason to talk about New Bedford. It never fails to trouble and amaze me how much sadness we cultivate, and hide, and carry with us from the past. How do you sustain your belief in people, Detective, when you spend your days digging into our collective unhappiness?"

"I was asking myself that this morning," she said, "although not exactly in those words. Nantucket doesn't witness a lot of violent crime. Drugs, of course, and burglaries. But what happened to your brother has really hit me—this being my first murder investigation."

Peter's reserve dropped for one startled instant. "Mine, too. But I hope it will be my last. You don't have that luxury."

"We all make our choices in life. This is mine."

"I've thought a lot about Rusty's murder in the past few hours. I don't know what your working hypothesis is—"

"But you've formed one? Go on."

"My brother was a black sheep, Detective. He hasn't been in touch with my family for years. As crazy as it was to find him in my bog this morning, I don't think he was killed by mistake."

"You mean, murdered in your place?"

"Exactly. I think Rusty pissed off some dangerous people in Brazil, ran for his life, and didn't escape. I think you should consult the FBI or Interpol."

"I already have, Mr. Mason," she said.

"You have?"

"When you mentioned he'd been living down there,

it seemed the logical thing to do. If there's anything in the response I think you should know about, I'll fill you in. And by the way," she added, "did you know the Department of Justice has a sealed indictment outstanding against your brother? He should have been picked up wherever he entered the US. Which says one of two things to me: he used a fake passport, or he entered illegally. We found no passport, fake or otherwise. Not that that means much. We didn't even find a wallet."

"I wondered about that," Peter said. "The killer must have taken everything Rusty had. So what's next?"

"Suppose we talk about your role in this investigation. How do you see it?"

Peter sat very still. "I want to help in ways that only I can."

"What does that mean? As patron of the criminal arts?"

"I'm sorry?"

"Could you explain how you envision helping? Because if it means you're going to wander around asking random people where they were last night, or that you're planning to fly to Brazil and hunt up your brother's old buddies, or that you're going to drag the harbor in search of his luggage, I'm going to have to ask you to stay home and let us do our job."

Peter's face darkened. He set down his cognac.

"And now I should be going. Thanks for the tea." Merry rose from her seat and glanced around for her red slicker.

"I hung it in the closet," he said. "I'm not going to get it until you listen to me."

"I think I could find it myself."

"Got a search warrant?"

"Yes, as it happens. This is a crime scene." Merry glared at him. Then she sat down. "Okay. Shoot."

"I happen to believe I'm uniquely qualified to help. Since this is your first murder investigation—I'm not questioning your ability, I'm only stating a fact," he said, as she started to rise—"I suggest you take all the help that's offered. I promise not to butt into your methods. I won't screw up your investigation. I merely intend to supplement it with my knowledge of Rusty's personality, his contacts, and his history."

"The severed ends of the rope," Merry said.

"Excuse me?"

"—that used to hold your family together. Somewhere it snapped, right? But you don't trust me enough to tell me what happened. I understand that. We don't know each other."

"It's just that it's personal," Peter said.

"Nothing's personal where murder is concerned. I have to keep in mind, for instance, that as pleasant and plausible as you seem, Mr. Mason, you could have killed your brother yourself."

There was a tense silence.

"I'll get your coat," he said.

SKY STOOD UP and opened the studio drapes Mayling had closed, and stared for a moment out over the Siasconset bluff. The sea was obliterated from view, and no stars were discernible above. Unlike Mayling, he found this comforting. Some nights, the knowledge of the sea lying just beyond his sleep, ceaselessly eating away at the shoreline, sent him tossing through the hours until dawn. The bluff had been Mayling's choice. Left to himself, he'd have moved into town, or built something solid and comfortable on the moors outside of Madaket. A house on peaceful Madaket Harbor, perhaps, with a view of furled sails and faded wooden docks to ease the mind before bedtime. The sea off Siasconset was never calm in the dark. It stretched to the horizon, to Europe, over the bones of the *Andrea Doria* and other ships that had fallen to wrack in centuries of storms.

Nights like this, with the sea obscured by fog, Sky knew what had set him apart from Rusty. Violence of feeling, violence of action, the night sea or the turbulence of the upper air tossing a small plane—he avoided these whenever possible. Rusty had thrived on them. And violence had ended his life.

Sky leaned toward the broad window and rested his forehead against the glass. He closed his eyes. The image of the Mercedes's mangled front end hung in his brain. *The fog*, she had said. *I hit a deer in the fog.* "The police would have understood that, Mayling," he'd told her. "Why didn't you explain? Never, never leave the scene of an accident again."

That was a conversation from this morning, before the news of Rusty lying in the bog, his legs bruised from the front end of a car. This morning, before Sky had a reason to doubt her. And why should he, after all? Mayling had never known Rusty. She had no motive for deliberately killing him. Sky jerked the drapes closed again and turned in the darkened room. Maybe it had been an accident. Mayling striking something in the fog, panicking, and leaving Rusty without even knowing what she'd hit . . .

But no, an inner voice reminded him, Rusty died face-down in the water. His murder was no accident.

Why would Mayling drive the unpaved roads near Mason Farms at night, anyway?

Was it possible she'd meant to kill Peter?

Madness.

Sky moved toward their bedroom. He had to get Mayling away from here. God help him, he couldn't face what it all might mean.

"Forgive me, Rusty," he whispered.

WHEN MERRY FOLGER'S SUV had disappeared down the driveway, Peter turned off his desk lamp and put his head in his hands. It seemed a year since he had pulled open the body bag and seen Rusty's face.

He pressed his fingers to his eyes. In the darkness behind the closed lids the image of Alison's face rose unbidden. One long winter before Rafe came to the farm, when his loneliness was stronger than his pain, he had written to her sister for news. Molly had told him everything and nothing: Alison lived here and there, doing this or that, neither happy nor unhappy; but she was alone, it seemed, and she never spoke of him. He had tried since then to shut every memory of her behind a door in his mind, and he did not want to open it now.

But George was right: She ought to be told of Rusty's death. Her knowledge of the last few weeks before he'd broken with the rest of the family might be valuable. But did it have to be Peter who called her?

It would mean letting go of his anger and his stubborn pride. His deliberate isolation on a speck of land in the middle of the ocean.

A foghorn blew plaintively across the distant water, and he hesitated, listening. Then he mounted the stairs to his room, the old house creaking around him in the darkness. He lay sleepless, well into the long night.

*Chapter 12*

"IT'S NOT JUST the impact of the clothes, you know," Mayling said, as she settled into the curve of the chintz sofa and crossed one slim golden leg over the other, "it's me. I'm essentially alien to everything on this island. You should walk around Main Street with me sometime off-season and notice how people stare. Sometimes I think I'm the only Asian in town—barring the family that runs the Chinese restaurant. It turns them off my clothes—the islanders, I mean. Too foreign, too New York. I have to content myself with catering to the summer trade."

"But you like it enough to come back every year," Merry said.

Mayling's laugh held a note of self-mockery. "Well, it *is* one of the most beautiful places on earth, and I've never been one to deny myself beauty. And, too, I suppose I come for the peace. New York erupts in violence on a daily basis. On the island I can't imagine that kind of ugliness."

"How do you explain what happened to Rusty Mason, then?"

Distress clouded Mayling's black eyes for the barest instant. "I can't," she said. "It's utterly inexplicable. What do you make of it, Detective? Or aren't you telling?"

Merry said nothing. Mayling drew on her cigarette and then released the smoke in a long blue sigh, her gaze fixed on the distance over Merry's left shoulder.

"At a certain point every April I begin to crave the peace here, my drafting board overlooking the sea, the luxury of not having to see the same crowd of people at all the same shows—and then, around the end of August, I can't be gone quick enough. Sky and I were planning to leave this afternoon, in fact. But Peter Mason asked us to stay for a few more days. Sky is his lawyer as well as his friend, you see."

And Mason apparently thought he needed legal help. "Could you tell me what you were doing the night Rusty Mason died, Ms. Stern?" Merry said.

Mayling's gaze snapped back to meet her own, but her face remained immobile. "I assume I was in bed," she said.

"Alone?"

One of Mayling's nostrils flared as a thin trail of cigarette smoke wafted upward from her right hand. "In any other circumstances I wouldn't say. You police can be rather impertinent, can't you?"

Merry smiled faintly, but the warmth failed to reach her green eyes. "Be glad I'm a woman. These questions sound even worse when a man asks them. Were you alone?"

"No. Sky arrived earlier in the evening."

"By ferry?"

"Plane. From New York. A quick-turnaround trip, so he could say he'd had a Labor Day weekend. I picked him up at the airport at eight-thirty, or thereabouts. You can check his flight."

"And that evening the two of you—?"

"Stayed in. Like the dull married couple we're not."

Merry looked at Mayling over her reading glasses. The designer's voice had an ironic edge Merry knew she was not supposed to miss. She decided to ignore it for the moment.

"How long have you known Peter Mason, Ms. Stern?"

"As long as I've known Sky." She paused, and did some mental arithmetic. "That'd be eight years this past August. I met Peter my first summer on the island. He and Sky spent more time together then."

Merry lifted one black brow inquiringly, her fingers poised above her laptop. Mayling shifted on the sofa and uncrossed her legs.

"This was about two years after Rusty had broken with the family, of course, and Peter was just starting to pull his life back together. He'd come into some money when Max died, and he'd bought the land out on the moors. The bog was dredged and the runners set, but he wasn't living in the farmhouse. It was pretty much an unrenovated shell. He was camping in one wing of the old place on the Cliff Road, and we were renting in town, on Centre Street, so we just saw more of each other."

"You're one of the few people on this island who actually knew Peter Mason had a brother," Merry said. "Did he talk about him much?"

Mayling studied her for an instant, then looked down at her fingernails. "The first time he spoke of Rusty in my presence," she said, "was to tell me that he was dead."

"Does that strike you as odd?"

"No," Mayling said, and she smiled, half amused, half saddened. "It's completely typical. You don't know Peter Mason, Detective, so I'll try to be very fair to him.

"Peter is capable of great love, and thwarted in that, I think he has turned his energies inward. He can be very focused, very driven. That made him a *summa cum laude* graduate of Princeton once; it makes him a dedicated farmer and a good athlete now. But sometimes it gets in the way of his living. As much as he thrives on being alone, he seems to envy other people's togetherness. And envy makes him sound bitter, sometimes." She stubbed out her cigarette. "Yet, at base, he's one of the dearest people on earth. He possesses integrity—which is a vanishing quality, in my life, at least. I'd trust him with a great deal."

She paused.

"But I'd never trust him in the same room with his brother."

Merry stopped writing and looked up from her pad. A curious end to a glowing testimonial. "Is he capable of killing a man?"

Mayling glanced over one shoulder at the sea, a bright blue line capping the edge of the sunlit bluff behind the house. All of the designer's movements were abrupt, Merry reflected, in contrast to her carefully chosen words.

"I don't know," Mayling said. "I think both Sky and I have been wondering. But neither of us has been willing to say it. He had the opportunity, surely, and probably the means. God knows he had the cause. I just can't decide if he had the will—not to commit the act, but to sustain the deception."

"You mean he'd crack under pressure?"

"I mean he's too honest. The way he's acted since the murder would be utterly uncharacteristic if he'd committed it himself. He'd be much more likely to kill Rusty in a fit of rage and then report himself to the police."

Merry's glasses were dangling speculatively from one corner of her mouth as she listened. "Rage. Why did Peter hate his brother?"

"He hasn't told you?" Mayling said, startled.

"I haven't asked."

"Because of a woman, of course."

"Before Rusty went to Brazil?"

"Six months before. Peter and the girl—Alison Miller—had just graduated from Princeton. They'd been dating since freshman year, and Peter asked her to marry him at a big Fourth of July party the Masons threw at the Cliff Road house. Sky was invited; he's the one who told me all this."

Merry had graduated ten years ago, too, from Cape Cod Community College. She realized, with a start, that she was the probably the same age as Peter Mason. A slight chill ran up her back. All these unknown lives, progressing for years in parallel to her own, intersecting suddenly with a death in the dark and fog. She had passed the Masons a thousand times on the island's streets in the past three decades and never known whether they were islanders or summer people. Or cared.

She usually spent Fourth of July on a blanket in the back of a truck, a beer in her hand, watching the fireworks off Jetties Beach. Up above her on the Cliff Road, the Masons would have watched the same thing from the terrace of their perfectly mown back yard, hidden behind ten-foot boxwood hedges, the women in brightly flowered sundresses with enamel bracelets on their tanned arms. The men would be in open-collared pastel madras shirts and vivid blazers, and their white teeth would flash in the glow of the colored sparks falling from the sky. They would drink Tanqueray and tonic. The night breeze off the sound would ruffle hair still wet from a last shower before dinner. Perhaps there had been a tent, a striped and poled affair with potted hydrangeas ranged around the tables.

Maybe, as she'd tipped back a longneck that night for another swig of beer, she'd even heard the distant strains of music, a phrase from a life that had nothing to do with hers. She had been twenty-two, and this summer she'd had her thirty-second birthday. She had worked straight through this past July Fourth.

"That was when Peter's mother still spent every summer here, and the kids all came home for three months, except Rusty, who was working in New York." Mayling was studying her as she spoke, conscious Merry had only half heard her. "They'd fly up on weekends."

"Pretty tight-knit family."

"Or maybe wealth just has its routines, like everything else."

"What happened at the party?"

"Rusty met Alison. And then he came back to Nantucket for two weeks in August. He told Sky he needed a vacation, but it's clear, looking back, that it was Alison he was after."

"She was living at the house?"

"Yes."

"What was she like?"

"From what Sky remembers, pretty unexpected," Mayling said. "Anything but the New York debutante who'd hooked a good Establishment boy. She was solidly middle-class. Probably a lot like me," she added, to Merry's surprise.

"I think we might define 'middle-class' differently, Ms. Stern," she said. "Could you explain what you mean?"

Mayling looked slightly nettled. "I grew up in the garment district of New York, Detective. I went to public schools. My father was a wholesaler, a Jew raised in Queens, and my mother was a Chinese immigrant who worked as a seamstress in his back room. They killed themselves just to get by. That's what I mean by middle-class. Alison went to Princeton for the degree, not for the deb balls. She came up to the island and got a job waitressing while she figured out what she wanted to do next—apply to grad school, or work for a few years first."

"Thank you," Merry said. "That helps. And Peter?"

"He was pretty aimless that summer, too," Sky said. "Good at knowing what he didn't want to do—work in the family business—but unable to hit on an alternative. He took a job as a lifeguard at Jetties Beach and spent his off hours browsing job websites."

Merry searched her memory for a youthful Peter Mason lifesaving on Jetties Beach, and gave up. She found it hard to picture him young. He seemed incapable of its essential silliness.

"So the farm wasn't even a thought at that point?"

"No. I think he was toying with law school. Sky's influence, probably—he was approaching his third year at Harvard." Mayling broke off and rubbed her temples.

"You okay?" Merry asked.

"Fine," she said. "I've just had these splitting headaches lately. Allergies, probably. Or gluten. Anyway, over the winter, Peter had a lot of time to think about his future."

"Alison left him?"

"By Labor Day. To do her justice, she probably never stood a chance. The way Sky tells it, Rusty was a competitive bastard. He measured himself against every guy he came in contact with. Even his brother. Rusty set out to seduce Alison, and so of course he was successful."

"Was it just a game to him?"

"Hard to say. It might have lasted, who knows? She lived in his Manhattan apartment until he left for Brazil later that year. But she didn't go with him."

"Why did Rusty leave, Ms. Stern?"

Mayling avoided her eyes and bent toward the coffee table for her pack of Dunhills. She shook one into her palm with delicate fingers and held it to her mouth. Apparently tobacco was not one of her allergies.

"I don't know," she said. "I don't think Sky does, either. He told me the Masons never talk about Rusty or Alison."

Merry typed *Alison Miller* in her laptop notes. "So Peter's been nursing a grudge over a college romance for ten years?"

"He never let Alison go," Mayling said. "That's not particularly healthy, but I don't believe he has any control over it. Peter apparently adored Rusty—and Rusty betrayed him without a second thought. Peter couldn't forgive him. Masons are excellent haters."

"And now the object of his hatred is dead," Merry observed.

Mayling nodded. "If any good is likely to come of Rusty's murder, it's that Peter may finally move on."

Would he kill for that kind of closure? Merry wondered. "You said Sky met Alison. What did he think of her?"

Mayling considered her answer. "She was fairly young, but then, they all were. Sky said she was intelligent, highly verbal."

"Meaning?"

"An effortless vocabulary, the sort of wit that takes the form of puns and double entendres. Sky seemed to consider her good at drawing people out. He said the Masons—Julia, George, Max—were entirely charmed by her. And Max had been against Peter's engagement; he thought he was too young. As perhaps he was." She stopped abruptly, and thought further. "Sky said Alison and Peter just seemed to fit. He couldn't explain what he meant. But I understood. I have felt it myself, about Sky, that he's an extension of me. They were probably two people who completed each other."

"And yet she left him after two weeks of Rusty?"

"If Peter found Rusty irresistible, why wouldn't Alison?"

"Has Peter Mason had any relationships since?"

"You mean, has he been emotionally involved? I don't know, really. I can't say I'd be the first person he'd tell. He spends a lot of time with a schoolteacher here on the island, Lucy Jacoby. But there never seems to be much between them. It's too bad, really. Peter has so much to offer. He just doesn't seem capable of feeling, anymore."

Merry closed her laptop. "Thank you, Ms. Stern. You've been very helpful."

"Not at all."

Merry assessed her for an instant, liking her more as she left than she had when she arrived. "I must say, as an islander, that I love your clothes," she said. "I just can't afford them. The other day I was glued to your window by some incredible sweaters you've got there."

"The Chinese New Year sweaters," Mayling said. "I'm glad you like them." When Merry looked puzzled, she added, "It's the animal buttons. The Chinese lunar calendar—the zodiac, if you will—runs according to a twelve-year cycle, each year represented by an animal."

Comprehension flooded Merry's mind. "The Year of the Dragon," she said.

"For instance. Yes. Or the Horse. Or the Rat, to take a less exalted example."

Her expression must have changed. Mayling laughed.

"It's not that bad, really," she said. "You aren't meant to *look* like the animal of your year."

"I didn't happen to notice whether you had a rat sweater in the window," Merry said. "Did you make many of them?"

"Oh, I could find you one, don't worry. They've met with varying degrees of success. So few people know the sign of their birth year; they scooped up the ones with the rabbits and dragons, and left those with the rats and pigs. Unfortunate. I'll have to give them away."

"Do you happen to know if anyone on the island bought one?"

"A sweater? Of course. Scads. Although they sell better in New York. Everything does." Mayling stubbed out her cigarette and gave Merry a long look. "What's going on? Was Rusty wearing one?"

Merry reached into her pocket and withdrew the plastic evidence bag that held the button she'd lifted from the grass by Peter Mason's driveway. "No, but his murderer was," she said. "There were some prints on it. We haven't identified them."

Mayling reached for the bag and turned it over in her palm. "It's from a rat sweater, all right," she said. "I should know; I wear one myself."

"Could I see it?" Merry asked, her voice carefully neutral.

Mayling looked at her swiftly. There was a moment's pause. "Of course," she said, and rose to go upstairs.

She returned in a matter of seconds with a cardigan made of heathered alpaca in the shifting colors of the sea, and handed it wordlessly to Merry. A solid row of rats marched up the left edge.

"Looks like the real thing," Merry said. "Does any other manufacturer use this type of button?"

Mayling shook her head. "They're handmade for me."

The sweater formed a soft weight in Merry's lap, like a sleeping cat. She shook it out and held it above her head, noticing the creases remained, as though it had been folded some time. A faint odor of plastic clung to the wool. Either this sweater had been stored, or it was fresh from the manufacturer's carton. She doubted it had come from Mayling's drawer. "It's terrific," she said. "When did it come into the store?"

"About mid-July. The color would be wonderful with your hair, you know."

"Is there any way you could trace the sale of specific sweaters?"

"I could try, I suppose," Mayling said slowly. "But I'll be honest. It's highly improbable that either the New York or the island store noted the type of sweater sold in most cases, if they did at all. And with the number of New Yorkers who come to Nantucket, the button lost at Peter's could have been owned by almost anyone." She folded her arms under her breasts protectively, as though feeling a chill. "Detective—this probably is irrelevant, but—"

"But what?"

"I sold one to Peter, you know, rather early on."

"To Peter? For himself?"

She shook her head. "It was a birthday gift. To Lucy Jacoby."

WHEN MAYLING STERN had shut the door of the house on the bluff, Merry walked to the Explorer without looking back. She imagined the designer standing just to one side of a window, too intelligent to pull back a blind and betray her watchful gaze, but following her progress down the hydrangea-lined path just the same. Merry glanced at the passenger side of the car and saw with relief that Seitz was inside, his head rocking to inaudible music. She yanked open the driver's side door and jumped in. Seitz's head hit the Explorer's roof with a little jolt of surprise.

"Find anything in the garage?" she said, as she started the car.

"Just a mangled front end," he said. "Got some great pictures. Some soil and paint samples, too."

## Chapter 13

THE BOYS—PERHAPS TWENTY of them—faced off in two lines on the muddy field of Vito Capizzo stadium and tackled each other on the coach's command. Their bodies, some gawky, some newly powerful, collided in a shuddering of bone and curses that was audible across the field where Will Starbuck stood. He had been poised on the slight rise between the high school parking lot and the football field for an hour, an oversized T-shirt rucked up around the hands he'd shoved in the pockets of his jeans, waiting for something. He did not know exactly what.

The coach blew piercingly on his whistle, and the grappling bodies fell apart. "Okay, okay, work it out, work it out," he shouted. The crowd of muddied uniforms, with their bulging pads incongruously large for the breadth of the players' bodies, turned toward the far goalpost in unison and began to lap the field. One boy cast a glance over his shoulder and, it seemed to Will, saw him for an instant. Then he turned back and trotted on. Sandy Stewart, who had been his best friend. Will stood still, the familiar shame and nausea burning in his gut.

The coach was walking toward him, whistling under

his breath. He was fit and powerful, a graduate of Nantucket High who'd once played for the NFL. He'd known the glory years of Whaler football under Capizzo, when the team had been a powerhouse in the Mayflower League and the annual game between Nantucket and Martha's Vineyard was the stuff of legend. In recent years, worry about head injuries and the increasing popularity of lacrosse and soccer had eroded some of the local support for football. Fewer people showed up for the Saturday afternoon games. The team was technically coed, although it was rare for a girl to play. The coach made the most of the few kids he had.

He grunted as he took the slight rise toward the school, throwing his back into it. He seemed unaware of Will standing motionless above him.

"Hey, Coach," Will said.

He glanced up as he crested the rise, and nodded coolly. "Hello, Starbuck."

"Listen, Coach—" Will began, somewhat desperately.

"You want to play football, right, Starbuck?"

Will nodded.

"Then where were you all summer? You know I run an offseason training program. Every other kid out there managed to show up."

He met the coach's eyes, unable to explain. How he'd played football for years with his dad and couldn't bear to touch the ball for months after he'd found the rotting corpse on the beach. How he'd lost too much time to grief and medication, counseling and his mother's watchful eyes, until all he wanted was to be *normal* again. Normal and far below the radar, like every other fifteen-year-old kid.

"Look, I've got to see some commitment before I can make a place for you on the team," the coach said. "There's no freeloaders on the Whalers, you understand? You don't win games with a short attention span."

"I know," Will said. "I'd commit. Football's important to me."

The coach assessed his lanky frame. "You played Boys and Girls Club at Cyrus Pierce, right? What's your position?"

"Receiver."

"Sprint time?"

"Five-point-three, but I was shorter last year." Will flinched as a horn blared at his elbow. He turned and saw a Nantucket police Explorer pulling up behind him. Meredith Folger rolled down the window, leaned out, and waved.

"You in trouble?" the coach asked.

Will shook his head. "She's . . . sort of a friend."

"Better get going then. And Starbuck—"

"Yes, Coach?"

"Come by tomorrow. We'll see what you can do."

He waited until the coach left before he approached Meredith Folger. She turned off the ignition and opened the car door.

"Hey. How was the first day?" she said.

He thought of the frozen faces of his home room, the guys who'd looked past him. Thought of the word "whackjob" that had been scrawled on his locker door in pink highlighter, faint but unmistakable, the period before lunch. Thought of how he'd eaten alone, nearly choking on the peanut butter and jelly Tess had packed for him, while a table of girls tittered and giggled across the aisle, pretending they weren't talking about him when he met their eyes. Thought of Sandy Stewart slouched in front of his buddies, stone-faced and remote, saying, "Yo, Starbuck. You're back," and then walking past him to sit somewhere else. He was a pariah. A refugee from the funny farm. A kid with a padded cell.

"Couldn't be better," he said to Merry Folger. "It's gonna be a great year."

She smiled brightly and then looked past him to the football team, now finished its laps and laboring wearily up the rise to the parking lot. The guys surveyed the squad car and Will standing uneasily next to it, and nudged one another. Sandy Stewart met Merry's eyes and nodded once, curtly, then looked away. The entire group fell silent as they passed her, until one kid in the back started humming the "do-do-do-do, do-do-do-do" of *The Twilight Zone* theme and the rest of them burst out in snickers. She turned back to Will, her smile gone and a slight furrow between her green eyes. "Not a group with triple-digit IQs, huh?"

"They're okay," he said defensively. "What do you want?"

"Nothing much," Merry said. "I just came over because I saw you. I'm looking for Lucy Jacoby."

"Miss Jacoby? The English teacher?"

"Yep."

"She's not here."

"Darn, I thought I'd catch her," Merry said, and pulled out her keys. "You don't happen to know where she lives, do you?"

"Actually, yeah, I do," Will said. "Out at Tom Nevers.

Off the Chuck Hollow Road, right around where it intersects Jonathan Lane. She's got a pink door. But I think she's sick."

Merry stopped in the act of opening her car door. "Didn't she come in today?"

Will shook his head. "It didn't really matter, since all they do the first day is pass out books and stuff," he said. "But it was weird. She didn't even get a substitute—they usually do if they know they're going to be out."

Merry nodded thoughtfully, one foot on the car's doorsill. Then she looked at Will. As usual his fine-boned face was pale, and the dark circles under his beautiful eyes seemed, unbelievably, to have deepened. He must not have slept the previous night. "Want me to run you home?"

He shook his head. "I've got the bike. I thought I'd drop by Peter's and see how the harvest is going."

THE DOOR WAS closer to old rose than pink. The cottage nestled between two big-shouldered, obviously new houses thrust forward on the Chuck Hollow Road, windows looking blankly south into the Atlantic. Summer people, Merry decided, gone back to the mainland for the winter. Lucy Jacoby's house would be the only one with lights on these fall evenings, but come spring, the bulk of her absent neighbors' houses would shield her somewhat from the ceaseless winds. The place looked cozy for a woman living alone.

For a moment, Merry imagined what it would be like to have her own house, an ordered refuge from work, instead of living amid the jumble on Tattle Court. Then she stifled the impulse. She was lucky even to be able to live on the island. Most of the kids she'd grown up with had been priced out of the housing market and had moved to the Cape or Boston suburbs. It was the single ones like her who could stay, taking rooms with aging relatives and clinging to a life that was swiftly vanishing.

She parked the car in front of the house and walked up the drive. A knockoff of a Nantucket lightship basket hung from the door, a few uncollected letters still sitting inside it. She pushed the bell and waited. After about thirty seconds, she pushed the bell again. Perhaps it was out of order. She knocked firmly on the door and listened, holding her breath, for some movement inside. Where was Lucy Jacoby, if not home sick in bed?

She turned and walked back down the path, then stopped and scanned the house, her hands shielding her eyes. No lights shone from the windows on either side of the door. The eaves of the roof sloped down to the first floor; a skylight was cut in the loft space above. The house looked blank and unoccupied. Merry took the path leading around the left side of the house to the yard, hesitated in front of the gate, and then opened it.

The garden was carefully plotted and groomed, with semicircular beds ranged around a center square of roses in riotous bloom. Merry stopped in respect. Roses like these—hybrid teas rather than the hardy island ramblers that covered fences and cottage roofs—were extraordinarily difficult to grow. The damp climate encouraged black spot. She walked over to them slowly and reached out a finger to touch an enormous Peace rose, pink and yellow and cream, awed that something so beautiful could be hidden away behind the house. Lucy Jacoby was either a pro or engaged in a labor of love.

Merry started as a patchwork cat made a four-point landing on the large sundial in the middle of the rose bed, curled its tail around its body, and gazed at her soberly.

"I don't belong here, do I, but you're too well-bred to say so."

The cat flicked one ear and looked away.

"No, you don't," a woman replied.

Merry turned. The slight figure standing under the loggia that ran the length of the house took a step backward into the shadows beneath the vines. Merry strained to make out her face. "Miss Jacoby?"

"Of course," the woman said impatiently. "Who are you?"

"Detective Meredith Folger," Merry said, walking toward her, "of the Nantucket police."

Lucy Jacoby turned to the steps leading up to her back door and sat down abruptly. She put her head in her hands.

Merry stopped short. "They said you called in sick today at school," she said. "You okay?"

"Yes, yes, I'm fine," Lucy said. She pressed her hands against her head once, briefly, as if adjusting a hat, and then looked up at Merry. "I was—expecting someone else."

Merry stared at her wordlessly. Expecting? Or avoiding? She had imagined Peter Mason's sometime girlfriend would reek of off-island elegance—the sort who knew how to assess wine and hoist herself out of a limo without her dress hiking up for the camera; the kind who could attend auctions and bid without anyone knowing she was there. Lucy had all the elements of a beauty, but she was crumpled on her doorstep like an emptied sack.

"I only wanted to talk to you for a few minutes," she said, "but if now's not a good time—"

"You'll come back?" Lucy said, a note of panic in her voice. "No! Just say what you have to say now."

Merry shifted awkwardly in her Sperrys and glanced around the yard. The crash of surf at Tom Nevers Head came faintly up from the shore, and shades of crimson and orange crept along the horizon to the west. The calico cat arched its back against her bare knees and slid around her leg, meowing soundlessly. Lucy reached for her and pulled her into a huddled lump against her cheek.

"Can we go inside?" Merry asked.

Lucy hesitated, then nodded and stood up. She turned toward the house, holding the screen door open behind her.

The cottage held only two rooms, a small kitchen and an open area that served as living room, dining room, and study. A large easy chair and ottoman facing the fireplace still held the imprint of Lucy's body. An open bottle of wine and a half-filled glass stood on the end table next to the chair. Against the front wall was a desk cluttered with papers and a computer, and next to it was a wine rack holding about thirty bottles, Merry guessed. She glanced up at the open vault of the ceiling, clear to the second story, and saw skylights cut in the roof on the garden side. The railing of a loft topped the partition to the kitchen: Lucy's sleeping area, probably. The walls—as in Peter Mason's study—held shelves of books from floor to ceiling. Merry wandered over to them and scanned the titles while Lucy Jacoby ran a glass under the tap. *The Perpetual Orgy: Flaubert and Madame Bovary,* she read. *Becoming a Heroine*. *Gilgamesh*. *In Search of Lost Roses*.

"Why'd they send a woman?" Lucy said, as she walked into the room. "Did they think I'd talk to you more easily?"

Merry turned. "Talk about what?"

"Whatever it is you want to know."

"This is a great house," Merry said. "Somebody did a terrific job of gutting and renovating the space."

"Thank you," Lucy said. She set her glass down on an end table. "Call it therapy. I spent the winter after my divorce tearing out walls. A fitting metaphor, I thought."

"You did this? Wow." She scanned the room with respect.

"There's no end to my ingenuity, Detective. I surprise even myself with what I get away with."

Merry turned and looked at her.

"Have a seat," Lucy said. "And say what you came to say." She remained standing, braced for some onslaught, in the middle of the room.

Merry sat down on the ottoman a trifle gingerly, feeling as though she were perched on someone's unmade bed. For all its simplicity, the room was a place of richness and wealth. The wool throw on the back of the chair was from Nantucket Looms, as was the deep purple rag rug, and both had cost more than Merry would spend. "I'm told you're a friend of Peter Mason's, and I'd like some information about him, if you're willing to offer it."

Lucy stood still for an instant, as if the words she had been waiting for had yet to come. Then she seemed to crumple slightly, and reached for her glass. She took a long drink. "That's it?" she said. "That's why you're here?"

Merry nodded. Lucy closed her eyes, and Merry could almost feel the relief that suffused her body.

"You were expecting something else," Merry said.

Lucy's eyes flew open, and a warning flashed for an instant in her face. Then she shrugged and turned to sit in a chair. "I'm sorry, Detective," she said, "but when you've lived with someone as violent as my ex-husband you stop expecting trouble to be somebody else's problem. Even after five years, I'm afraid of what I'll hear. Now, what's happened to Peter?"

"His brother was found dead over at the farm," Merry said, "and we're making some routine inquiries of his friends."

Lucy sat very still, and all expression left her face. "How awful. I must call him right away."

"He hasn't told you?" Merry asked.

"Why should he?" Lucy looked as if she were challenging Meredith to say what she was thinking—that it was odd Peter Mason hadn't sought her out for comfort at his brother's death. "He must be terribly upset. And death is a family matter first, not something you share with friends." She smoothed her wild curls; Merry noticed her hands were shaking.

"How long have you known Mr. Mason?"

"Why does it matter?"

"Let's just say that anything could matter. In fact, it might keep Peter from being murdered."

"Murdered? But that's ridiculous. Why would anyone want to kill Peter? And the brother's death was an accident, surely?"

Merry hesitated. "Rusty Mason—that was his name—was murdered, Miss Jacoby. You can trust me on that. The problem is, he hadn't been on this island in ten years or so, and there's a chance he was killed by mistake. We have to work to some extent on the assumption that the intended victim was Peter Mason. That's why I'm talking to you."

Lucy took a deep breath and then expelled it, slowly. "All right," she said. "Shoot."

Merry pulled her laptop and her half-glasses out of her purse. "Start with when you met," she suggested.

"Five years ago, the first winter I came to the island."

Merry looked up, fingers poised to type, and waited. Lucy looked at her steadily and said nothing. Finally she looked away, at the fire, and capitulated.

"We met in the Nantucket Bookworks one dreary February evening, when the light was gone by five o'clock and I was certain I wouldn't last out the day if I didn't talk to someone. I threw on something and drove into town, drove anywhere, half-mad because it was an island and I couldn't get off. If there'd been a ferry running at that hour I'd probably have left everything and never come back. But there was a light coming out of the bookshop. Peter was reading."

She stopped. Merry hesitated. "And you asked him about the book?" she said.

"The book? What book?"

"The one he was reading. You know, like, 'Would it appeal to a fan of *Gone Girl*?' or something like that."

Lucy Jacoby smiled faintly. "He was *giving* a reading, Detective. Of his poems. For an audience. You didn't know he was a poet?"

"Of course not," Merry said. "I don't know anything about him. That's why I'm here."

"He's quite a talent, in fact. Lyric, tortured, very dark; and always—*always*—impassioned with words. I keep trying to get him for my senior class, but he's so damnably shy about his work." She twirled the stem of her glass, an impatient gesture that covered her rapidity of thought. "He only reads during the winter, when the off-islanders have gone home, you know. And as for getting him to publish . . ."

"And so you struck up a conversation?"

Lucy looked down at her hands. "I don't know if you can understand what I was like that winter," she said. "I thought nothing could make me whole again. I swung between a giddy euphoria and the blackest gloom. I used to lie awake nights and either thank God I was free—or imagine ways I could kill myself. And then there was Peter, reading, and every word he spoke was a lifeline thrown out to me. I clung to it. I stood by a bookshelf and listened to poem after poem, struck dumb, incapable even of clapping when he finished. Everyone left, in the dribs and drabs of people who really don't want to go home again, out into the wet. I was more honest. I stayed. He looked up from the papers he was gathering together so carefully with those strong hands of his, and saw my face." Lucy smiled faintly. "He said, 'You were *listening*, weren't you?' We've been friends ever since."

Merry shifted uncomfortably, aware that she was out of her depth. "And he never mentioned his brother?"

Lucy started, and shook her head. "I've met his sister, George, and the children; but other than his mother he never mentions family. He doesn't seem to be involved with anyone, either."

"Involved?"

"Emotionally. Sexually. What you will. There are no women in his life." Her head was up, daring Merry to ask her why she wasn't.

"How often do you see Mr. Mason, Miss Jacoby?"

She didn't hesitate. "Three times a week."

"Every week?"

"Absolutely. We do interval training together at the high school track on Mondays, Wednesdays, and Fridays. Five o'clock. He rarely misses."

"Intervals?" said Merry, bewildered. Peter Mason did altogether too much with his time.

"Wind sprints. A quarter mile fast, a quarter mile slow," Lucy said. "Increases your speed and your distance. Not that I can keep up with him; he just likes the company. And lapping me, of course."

"I see. Did you run yesterday?"

Lucy Jacoby dropped her eyes and then looked away. She swallowed. "No," she said. "I couldn't make it. I left a message to that effect with Rebecca." Her eyes drifted toward her wineglass and Merry thought she would take a drink, but she restrained herself and leaned forward. "How is any of this likely to help Peter, Detective?"

"His friends might know if he'd been threatened, even if he couldn't admit it to himself," she said. "Is there anyone on the island likely to gain from Peter Mason's death? Anyone who'd be happy if he were injured?"

Lucy pondered the question for several seconds. "I'd be willing to bet there are a number."

Merry had not expected this. "Really?"

"He's a Mason, Detective. When you're as powerful and driving and hungry as that family has been, you breed violence and you attract it in return. If Rusty's the first to die, they've been lucky."

Merry reflected that the English teacher had a flair for the dramatic. Her gloom probably made for difficult living as well. The cloud of auburn hair curling around Lucy's face and the lines running from nose to mouth gave her the look of a terrible angel.

"Ms. Jacoby," Merry said, "where were you Sunday night?"

"What time?"

"Oh, between, say, dinner and breakfast."

Lucy said nothing for several seconds. "So you think I killed Rusty? Why in God's name *would* I?"

"I'm asking where you were that night purely as a matter of routine, Ms. Jacoby. In case you saw or heard something that might help us out."

"Well, I didn't," Lucy said angrily. "If you want to know, I wasn't even here. I was over on the Cape shopping for clothes at the Labor Day sales."

"When did you get back?"

"I had dinner, saw a movie, and then caught the Fast Ferry home."

"The one that gets in around ten P.M.?"

"Yes."

"Had you parked your car in the day lot?"

"Why does it matter?"

"If you took a taxi, you'd have a witness," Merry said evenly. Lucy Jacoby's discomfort made her uneasy.

"My car's been in the shop for a week," the woman

said. "I rode my bike to Town and I rode it back. I'm sorry that doesn't suit your purposes."

"I have no purposes," Merry said, "only procedures. I'm sorry you've been having car trouble. A week sounds serious."

"The clutch died. No surprise in an eight-year-old American car."

"One last question," Merry said. "Peter Mason gave you a birthday gift, I understand. A sweater from Mayling Stern."

Lucy looked puzzled. "What business is it of yours?"

"Have you lost one of the buttons, by any chance? Perhaps after visiting Mason Farms?"

"I've never worn the sweater, Detective."

"Really." Merry was startled, and showed it. If she'd owned one, she'd never have taken it off.

"It was the buttons, actually. I have a phobia about rats. I can't stand them—I never could, even as a child. I gave the sweater away to a clothing drive and didn't tell Peter. Why are you interested in his sweater?"

"It's not important. You wouldn't happen to remember which clothing drive?"

Lucy reached for her wineglass. "Our Lady of the Island," she said. "For their bazaar. Sometime around the first of August, I think it was. My birthday is July fifteenth."

Merry took off her glasses and stood up. "Thanks for your time."

"Not at all," Lucy said automatically. She looked, however, like a wounded animal. Merry felt vaguely guilty. Lucy led her to the door, and turned, one hand on the knob. "If I can help in any way, don't hesitate to ask. But do call first before you come out," she said. "I won my sanctuary, Detective, and I guard it jealously."

AS SHE DROVE away, Merry wondered why Lucy Jacoby had no interest in knowing how Rusty Mason died. And what had compelled her to drink so heavily that she had missed the first day of school.

*Chapter 14*

PETER HOOKED ONE hip-booted leg over the side of the flatbed truck, reached his hand into the shifting mass of cranberries, and let the wet beads run through his fingers. A day's harvest, he thought, a piling up of summer's wealth, and with it a certain sadness. The crop was a good one, a relief after the tough winter, and he felt lucky. But the flatbed truck, bound for the ferry and an Ocean Spray depot, represented the end of the growing season. It was a need for rebirth that had driven him into farming in the first place; now the promise of spring, the chance to witness a yearly renewal, kept him in the business. In a few months, the tight mat of red-black vines running over acre after acre of his land would settle into a protective layer of ice; he and the farm would endure a winter vigil that always seemed to last too long. He shook off his hands and jumped down to the ground.

Rafe sat on the running board of the truck's cab, a beer resting on one bent knee. A spreading map of sweat stained the shirt under his heavy overalls. The dog Ney was sprawled on the wet turf next to him, muzzle on forepaws, his clear, light eyes following every movement the two men made. A yellow metal wet-harvesting machine—called a beater because of the egg-beating effect of its blades in the water—was propped at rest where the waterlogged vines began, just beyond the truck. When propelled through the flooded fields, the whirling blades knocked the berries off their vines and sent them bobbing in a blood-red tide to the surface. The beaters were large and awkward, like early forms of the velocipede, or nightmarish insects; but they were simple improvements on a harvesting process that had changed little through the first century of cranberry cultivation.

That morning, Peter had summoned the crew of harvesters and, avoiding the acreage where Rusty had died, moved to the land on the other side of the driveway. They had opened the sluice gates of the channels that ran from Gibbs Pond to the farm and flooded the bog for a wet harvest. Peter liked to start the season that way: taking the fruit intended for processing first, and leaving berries bound for the grocer to be dry-harvested last. Striding with the beaters through thigh-high water had given them all a sense of purpose and shifted some of the weight of Monday's violence.

"I think we've made us some money, Pete," Rafe said.

"Yeah, we'll survive the winter." He sat down next to Rafe and reached for the foreman's beer. It cost roughly twenty dollars to produce a one-hundred pound barrel of cranberries. In recent years, Ocean Spray had paid him up to fifty dollars per barrel, but oversupply in the market was driving prices down. The Ocean Spray cooperative had been sued in recent years for price-fixing. Peter's lawyer, Sky Tate-Jackson, kept an eye on the litigation so Peter could harvest his berries, a luxury other growers didn't always have. Mason Farms yielded an average of 190 barrels per acre. They had harvested five acres to date, and had forty-five more to go. The revenues for the year might be several hundred thousand dollars.

Peter tipped back Rafe's bottle and took a long draft, then wiped his face with his T-shirt and sighed deeply. The suspenders of his hip boots hung down to his knees. "I understand why nobody ran triathlons fifty years ago," he said, fondling Ney's ruff. "No farmhand in his right mind would move if he had the option of sitting for an hour. Much less taking a nap. I feel like an old man."

"You *are* an old man" Rafe said, and slapped him on the shoulder. "Just can't face it. All that training of yours is one pathetic denial. You'll run tonight and you won't be able to move tomorrow. But I'll be out here working."

"It's Wednesday, Rafe. Can't disappoint Lucy."

Rafe snorted and took back his beer. "Yeah, well, don't come whining when you can't pedal home, you hear? Because I'm already gone. Taking the Rover with me."

"No ride, no sympathy. Got it. How's Tess?"

"Same as always, pretty much. She won't relax until the kid starts to look normal and acts more like it. He's too peaky, too quiet, keeps too much to himself. He's lost that kid look."

"The unself-conscious immersion in his world."

"I s'pose."

Peter braced himself on Rafe's knee and stood up. As if on cue, Ney sprang up and waited, tail wagging, for his master to choose a direction. "Should Will be coming out here all the time after what happened Monday?"

"Can't keep avoiding places. Rate the kid's going, he won't be able to leave the house." Rafe shielded his eyes with his hand. Peter was backlit in the slanting rays of late afternoon, his dark hair a bright helmet. "Besides, he's happy when he's here. Doesn't matter if he's harvesting, like yesterday, or sitting with a book in the house, he's doing something other than moping, and that's all to the good."

"If Tess thinks there's anything that might help . . ."

"She'll tell you. The woman's proud, but where her kid's concerned, she isn't shy."

LUCY JACOBY STOOD with her hands braced against the goalpost, one Lycra-clad leg bent and the other stretched firmly behind her. She was lost in thought. Occasionally a passing member of the track team would wave and smile at the English teacher, but she didn't notice. Shifting from one leg to the other, she went through her pre-run warm-up with the mechanical precision of long familiarity. She was thinking of Will Starbuck. There was something too casual and studied in his questions about *Madame Bovary*, the book she had assigned the advanced sophomores. He was intensely interested in Emma's suicide, and doing a poor job of hiding it.

A sixth sense compelled Lucy to scan the high school parking lot. She was rewarded with the sight of Peter turning his racing bike in from the Surfside Road. As he rolled to a halt, he clicked his right shoe out of the bike's clip and swung off the saddle. Lucy raised one arm in greeting.

She set off at a slow trot toward the parking lot, cutting across the track and the field, while Peter changed from bike to running shoes. Her sweatshirt would be too warm, she decided. The day had started cool, with a hint of fog, but the sun had burned through by noon.

"Hey," she said. "I wasn't sure you'd come."

Peter looked up from locking his bike and smiled at her. "Training. My substitute for God."

"I thought that was me."

"You just keep me honest." He stood up and bounced from one leg to the other, unaware that her face had drained of color. "I wouldn't be here today if you weren't waiting. Turn around."

Lucy obediently presented her back. Peter braced himself against her shoulders and stretched his calves. "Thanks for the flowers, by the way."

Lucy was thankful he couldn't see her. "Not at all."

Peter released her and stood up. "Ready?"

"I mean, no, forget *not at all*." Lucy faced him. "That's a stupid convention. I've been feeling so inadequate. Your brother dies—is *murdered*—and I don't even hear about it for two days. And then I send flowers. It's so ridiculous! I feel like such an idiot! I've never known how to deal with death."

"It's okay," Peter said. "The flowers were nice."

"*Nice*. Nice is not what you need when you're facing a funeral. Why do we do these things? Why couldn't I just come over to your house and talk to you?"

"Because the car was in the shop?"

"I was even afraid to call you, Peter. I'm such a jerk."

"You're not a jerk," he said, awkwardly reaching one hand to her elbow. She stiffened at his touch, and he remembered they were at the school. He looked around. No one seemed remotely interested in them.

"I should have called you," he said. "I'm sorry. You said Friday you were going to the Cape to shop, and then when everything happened Monday I completely forgot about running. Yesterday I wanted to get the harvest started—"

"I've just been wondering why it's so hard for us to convey emotion to each another. We're both so bad at it."

"Are we?" Peter said, surprised. "I suppose we are."

Lucy looked down at her shoes. "Anyway, I'm sorry it had to be something as trite as flowers. I could have called and asked if you were okay."

"I'm okay," Peter said. "Really. There's no question that something as brutal and unexpected as a drowning in the front yard is disturbing. But it's over."

"I am a rock, huh?"

"I am an island," he agreed. "And as the man said, an island feels no pain."

Lucy sighed. "Look, could we skip the sprints today and just take a long, slow run? I've been cooped up for a couple of days and I'd really like to get off this track."

Peter studied her for an instant. Her cheekbones stood out prominently under the cloud of auburn curls. "Are you eating enough?"

She nodded impatiently. "I was out sick yesterday, that's all."

"Sick?"

"Under the weather."

It was unusual for Lucy to indulge her moods on a weekday. She rarely missed school. "What happened on the Cape?" he asked.

"Nothing." She stirred the asphalt dust with her toe. "Really. The Cape was fine. Got a terrific dress, saw a movie, bought four boxes of seconds at the Cape Cod Candle factory—"

"Lucy," Peter said, reaching for her shoulders and shaking her slightly. "Don't do this. What happened?"

"I saw someone I used to know," she said, straining away from him. "On the ferry."

"From Italy? From the old days?"

She nodded.

"Did he speak to you?"

"What do you think? It's a goddamn ferry, you can't get off!" she burst out. "I thought I'd go insane. I kept moving, I kept changing my seat, but he kept following me around the boat. I swear, Peter, I was this close to jumping over the side."

"What did you do?"

"I ducked into the women's room and stayed there until the boat docked."

"For forty-five minutes? Is this guy on the island?"

"I guess so. I didn't see him when I got off. But I've wanted to hide ever since. I keep thinking I'll run into him in town. What's he doing here, Peter? What else could he be doing but looking for me? I keep waiting for something to happen. I keep expecting a knock on the door."

"Why didn't you tell me?"

Lucy did not reply. Peter pulled her into a rough embrace. Lucy's demons were too real, and even an island couldn't protect her.

"I think we should tell the police," he said. "Call it harassment, call it anything you like, and get the guy picked up for questioning. If he's who you think he is, he won't be able to get off the island fast enough."

"No!" Lucy said, rearing back. "Promise me you won't talk to that woman!"

"Meredith Folger?" he frowned. "What's wrong with her?"

"Nothing. Just don't tell her anything about me, do you understand? I'll deal with this myself. I've got to, sooner or later."

Peter made as if to speak, then nodded. "Okay. Just do me a favor. If anything comes up, call me. Promise?"

Lucy gave him a watery smile. "I really am a head-case, aren't I?"

"Yeah. But it's a nice head," Peter said. "Now. Can we run?"

IT WAS A relatively quiet afternoon at the station. John Folger's tanned forehead had a slight wrinkle in it, and his left thumb moved backward and forward across his salt-and-pepper mustache. He was reviewing the Mason murder scene summary for the third time. His eyes flicked up from the folder on his desk and focused on Merry, seated beyond the glass wall of his office in her cubicle, engrossed in an online legal database. She was reviewing federal securities regulations and case law. His daughter's expression was obscured by the fall of tow-colored hair down one cheekbone, but from the set of her head he knew she was confused and near exhaustion. The chief sighed and slapped the folder shut. Time for him to go home. Much as he wanted to help, the last thing she needed was her dad looking over her shoulder. He would wait another few days before he asked his questions.

MERRY PULLED OFF her reading glasses and thrust her arms up over her head, stretching painfully. She had been plowing through the database and found none of it riveting. She was convinced that somewhere in the legalese lay the clue to Rusty Mason's sealed indictment, but she was beginning to feel intimidated by the mass of material on securities convictions. A quiet cloud of gloom, familiar from her days at Cape Cod Community, had settled over her desk. "There's got to be a video somewhere that explains this stuff," she muttered out loud. "Too many white-collar types have made too much money for it to be this dull."

"Hey, just what the world needs. Another lawyer. You looking for a new career, hotshot?"

She looked up and met Matt Bailey's eyes, cold and hard above an unfriendly grin. He was leaning on the edge of her desk, his face thrust forward, challenging her. No forgiveness or goodwill there; he was gunning for her to blow the case. She resisted the impulse to slam a reply down his throat and smiled at him. "It never hurts to have a fallback."

"Or Daddy looking out for you," he said. He pushed himself away from her desk before she could answer, and she felt the anger in the trembling wood. Bailey was vicious. She should never have refused a date with him six months back; he'd taken it too personally. Then again, she hadn't been groped and bored, which gave her a slight sense of victory.

Bailey turned and stopped dead as he found himself face to face with Chief Folger, on the point of exiting his office.

"Do I pay you to work, Bailey?" John asked, "or run your mouth?"

Matt turned toward his cubicle without a word.

The chief looked around. The few heads still present bent immediately to their paperwork. He nodded, to no one in particular, and turned out the light in his office.

He said nothing to Merry as he left the station. But she smiled at his disappearing back.

HALF AN HOUR later, she was the only one still at her desk. The quiet in the station was so absolute, and her concentration so deep, that she jumped several inches off her chair when the phone rang. The receiver clattered out of her hand and over the end of the desk. She could hear the caller squawking incomprehensibly from his disembodied position on the floor, and for an instant she thought about leaving him there. Then she reached over the sickly Sansevieria plant dying slowly under the lamp and put the receiver to her ear.

"Meredith Folger."

"Ah, Detective Folger. Just the woman I need. You seem to have dropped me."

"Yeah, well, people were beginning to talk," Merry said.

A puzzled silence filled her ear. She thrust her forehead into her free hand and closed her eyes. "What can I do for you?"

Her caller seized on normalcy with relief. "Dr. Whitlow, state crime lab. Your medical examiner sent over a body two days ago. Number 37552."

Whitlow. She imagined a balding, pasty-faced guy with a nose that twitched like a rabbit's and a white lab coat smelling perpetually of formaldehyde. "Yes, that's right. Rusty Mason."

There was another pained silence. Apparently the coroner's office preferred to avoid names. "The autopsy was witnessed by Clarence Strangerfield," he said, "but I'm emailing a copy of the report for your files. Mr.

Strangerfield was exceedingly unhelpful in the matter of the body's disposition. What do you want done with it?"

"I'll have to get back to you on that after I talk to the next of kin."

"So Mr. Strangerfield said. It's so much more helpful if the final disposition of the corpse is noted on the committal form."

"I thought the state crime lab felt fortunate when it *had* a next of kin, Dr. Whitlow," Merry said briskly. "Is there anything unusual in the report I should know before you send it?"

Another silence. A rustling sound came over the line, as though Whitlow were fumbling in a paper hospital gown. She shut out the image and decided he was flipping the pages on a clipboard chart. "Rigor was just coming on at the time of the body's discovery, according to the medical examiner at the scene, making it likely that death occurred six to twelve hours previous. There were abrasions on the rear of the calves—bruising occurred prior to death, of course—suggesting a forceful blow; further bruising on back of head and shoulders indicating victim somersaulted when struck. Cranium fractured, presumably when victim fell backward following the blow from the lower rear, but inadequate to cause death. Grains of sand driven into the back of the skull and surface clotting of blood, somewhat reduced because of the water in which victim was immersed. Death was by drowning. Impossible to set the exact hour due to the immersion of the body, which would affect the onset of rigor; probably within eight hours of discovery. Tissues of the nasal passages inflamed and cartilage partially eroded from repeated exposure to a chemical agent, presumably cocaine. Traces of cocaine found in the follicles of deceased's hair and in the sinus passages. Deceased carried antibodies for the hepatitis C and HIV viruses—"

"What?" Merry said, startled.

Silence. Whitlow disliked interruptions. "I'm sending you the report," he said.

"Whoa, whoa—just a minute, here. You're telling me Rusty Mason was HIV-positive?"

"Over a million Americans are, Detective."

"Yeah, well, they're not getting killed in my backyard. How advanced was he?"

Whitlow cleared his throat. "It's hard to say. The effects of autoimmune deficiency vary from case to case, you know."

"I'm sure you can do better than that."

"His T-cell count suggests he was in the early to middle stages of the disease," the coroner said grudgingly.

"Think he knew he had it?"

"Absolutely. He was treating it. Lab sampling turned up antiretrovirals in his system."

"Dr. Whitlow," Merry said, "there's no way this guy could have bonked his head, gotten a little confused, and dragged himself to the bog, is there?"

"Are you asking if he committed suicide?" Whitlow was unenthused.

"Intentionally or no."

"Highly unlikely. The force of the blow to the back of the legs was strong enough to send him head over heels, fracturing his skull at impact. He would have lost consciousness immediately. And the presence of treatment drugs indicates a desire to live—they don't come cheap."

## Chapter 15

PETER MARKED HIS place in *War and Peace* with a forefinger and threw his head back against his chair. The sweeping strains of Rachmaninoff's Second Piano Concerto filled the room, a faint breeze stirred in the darkness beyond the open window, and Ney lay at his feet, warm and relaxed, whiffling softly in his sleep. Usually Peter required nothing more than these—good books, good music, a day of hard work followed by an evening of solitude—to feel complete contentment. But tonight he was restless and uneasy, his concentration broken by the slightest sound. He pressed the palms of his hands against his eyes. There would be no peace until Rusty's killer was flushed out of hiding and the past could return to dust.

The night had been broken more than once by the insistent buzz of his cell phone, bringing Ney to his feet with his tags clinking. The first caller was Merry Folger, telling him the state crime lab was done with Rusty's body, and what did he intend to do with it? He'd thought for a moment and told her he'd call her back. The second call, from Georgiana, came through with exquisite timing a mere ten minutes later. She had reached their mother in Rome, listened with forbearance while Julia Mason screamed and moaned, then agreed to meet her plane at JFK the following afternoon.

"When's the funeral, Peter?" she had asked.

"Whenever we like. The autopsy's over."

"What did they find?"

"The woman handling the case said she'd talk to me when I got back from Greenwich."

"So you're coming here?"

"It's easy for everybody to reach, and it seems like the only place Rusty really thought of as home. I wouldn't ask all of you to fly here."

There was a small silence, then an equally small sigh. "It's just that I'm dreading this so much," George said.

"All the more reason to be close to the kids and Hale. We got through living with Rusty, and we'll get through burying him."

"It will rain. You *know* it will rain. We'll be gathered around a sodden hole in the ground some idiot has attempted to disguise with Astroturf. The flowers will be hideous. Mother will make a scene. People will ask repeatedly where he's been all these years, and how he died. I can't bear it."

"I've been thinking, Georgiana," Peter said. "What if we have the body cremated? Take the *Seventh Wave* out into the sound and commit him to the deep. It seems cleaner, somehow. And you know that boat was the only thing he really loved."

"It's an idea," she said slowly. "We'd have to persuade Mother. I can call Dr. Pritchett—he's the yacht club chaplain—and ask for something private, a bit simpler than the usual solemn public ceremony he stages. A burial at sea might be just the thing. We could have a quiet memorial service, just the family, and skip the graveside horrors. I'll never be able to swim in the sound again, of course."

"To my knowledge, you haven't dropped a toe in Long Island Sound in fourteen years."

"Barring the occasional capsizing," Georgiana said, "not if I can help it. Peter, it's horrible that we can discuss this so casually. I have to remind myself that Rusty was murdered. I suppose it's because I'm not there that it doesn't seem real to me."

"No," Peter said. "It's because Rusty has seemed dead for years. And we've been just as glad. There's a vacuum of feeling where his life used to be. That's what's so horrible. And there's nothing we can do about it, now."

"It's been pretty shitty for you, hasn't it?"

"Yes. But I'm hoping it won't get any worse."

Georgiana was silent a moment. Then, "Do they know who?" she asked.

"I don't think so."

HE HAD CALLED the station and only then realized Merry wasn't on duty. The idea that she had a home—a life separate from her official capacity—was a revelation. He found himself wondering idly whether she lived alone, or knew how to cook, and if she had bookshelves, what she kept on them. It occurred to him that his tendency to see only pieces of people—the pieces that related to himself—was one more sign of how detached he'd become in the isolation of the farm. He failed to connect. He debated calling her cell. Then he redialed the station number and left a message that he would reach her in the morning.

The final call was from Sky Tate-Jackson.

"Have they come up with anything?" he asked, by way of greeting. He sounded nervous and tired. Peter knew he'd wanted to leave the island and felt a twinge of guilt for making him stay.

"Malcolm Scott," Peter said. "Name mean anything to you?"

"Men's clothing designer?"

Peter snorted.

"Golf pro?"

"He was ME's chief financial officer in Max's time. Retired now, splits his year between Chappaqua and Boca Raton. I caught him just before he left town for the winter."

There was a pause as Sky digested this information. "The point being?"

"Scott will see us Friday afternoon, if you can make time. I think he knows every dollar Mason Enterprises spent, and amazingly, he remembers why. He's our key to the M&A fiasco Rusty tried to pull off."

"Peter—" Sky began, and then stopped. "Digging up the past isn't going to do squat to help this investigation. You're wasting your time. Concentrate on getting the harvest in and let the police do their job."

"I'm picking up Rusty's ashes in Boston Friday morning," Peter said. "I can catch a shuttle and meet you in New York by one o'clock, if that suits."

"Who decided on cremation?"

"I did. Ashes to ashes, dust to dust. We'd love to have you and Mayling at George's Saturday for the memorial service."

Another pause. Then, "You're a cold bastard," Sky said, and hung up.

THE LAST NOTES of the concerto reverberated in the air. He closed his eyes in the silence for an instant and then reached down to restart the piece, wanting to hear again the opening chords. The last measured steps of a man on the verge of passion, he thought. He hadn't listened to Rachmaninoff in years. He told himself it was because the Romantic composers wore poorly with time; that intellectually, he had outstripped the music he had lived for in college; but the real reason was that Rachmaninoff was indelibly linked to Alison. In his mind he saw her outlined against a moonlit window, her lithe frame impossibly graceful in the darkness, her eyes picking up the faint glow slanting through the leaded panes. She was listening to the music, head up and thoughts far away, her dancer's body unconsciously swaying in time. The opening chords drew him toward her, step by step, until he stopped, poised on the edge of the sonorous plunge.

"All the dark, impassioned, Russian night," she said, turning toward him. "Do you feel it, Peter?" And then the music swept him into her arms.

Ney thrust his cold nose into Peter's ear and whined softly.

"What, you want to hear the rest, too?" Peter said, fondling the bristling dome of the dog's head. "Or do you find Bartók more challenging?"

He stood up and stretched. His legs ached with the pleasant memory of that afternoon's long, slow run through the moors. A low growl came from his feet, and he looked down in surprise. Ney's ears were pointed toward the open window, and the hair on his back stood up in a vicious ridge. Suddenly he barked and shot over to the screen.

The dog loved to chase a pair of nocturnal cats that lived wild on the moors. Peter reached for Ney's leash and snapped it on, something he rarely did at night, but he had no desire to race after the dog while he tracked a mangy animal through the heath. Ney whined feverishly.

"Hey, pup," he said, opening the screen, "don't get your hopes up. You're headed for the hayloft."

The breeze had picked up and blew freshly from the northwest, sending the scent of scrub pine and bayberry off the cooling countryside. He glanced up at the sky, where a new September moon shot in and out of swiftly moving clouds. "Might get some weather tomorrow."

Ney trotted in front of him, conscious of the indignity of the lead, his ears up and his bark caught in his throat. The cat he'd scented must have gone downwind. Peter's shoes were slick with dew from the stubby ends of the grass, left high all summer, then mown and baled a few weeks before the cranberry harvest. A few crickets sounded, already marked with the lethargy of cooler nights, the most mournful note of late summer; and Peter shivered suddenly. Ney reached the barn door and turned to look at him, tail wagging.

Rafe was gone, probably to the Greengage, but his light was on and a magazine left open on the desk. Ney trotted over to the dog bed in one corner of the room and flopped down, secure in the comfort of his routines. Peter unhooked the dog's leash and smoothed his ears once before turning to go. As he did, he glanced at the magazine on the desk and his eye was caught by the face of a famous baseball player, endorsing a mutual fund. Peter bent closer, a line between his brows, and flipped over the cover. An investment monthly. What did Rafe have to invest?

He shook away his curiosity and reflected that Merry Folger had shown him two nights ago how little he knew about Rafe. The man could have a personal investment analyst on retainer at Morgan Stanley for all Peter knew. Or cared to ask.

He pulled shut the door and clattered down the stairs. The wind had grown stronger, and the barn door he'd left ajar was shuddering in the sporadic gusts. He considered leaving it open for Rafe and the Rover, then heaved it closed and made for the house, head down and hands in his pockets. He felt completely alone tonight and tired to his bones. Perhaps he should have gone with Rafe to the Greengage. But the funeral and family he faced during the next few days would exact an emotional toll, and he knew he'd better get his sleep.

George was right; his mother would make a scene. She was a strong-willed and self-blinding woman who had never accepted her son's flight, just as she'd never forgiven his father for driving Rusty to it. That last Christmas had torn open the abyss between his parents. Julia was white and silent at Max's funeral, her unvented fury leaving her impotent and speechless; at Rusty's memorial, she would be terrible in her rage and unappeased in her loss.

A twig cracked somewhere in front of him. Peter looked up, pulled out of his thoughts, and stopped. A dim figure in a coat and a shapeless hat, pulled low on the brow, stood in the darkness just beyond the kitchen doorway. He was reminded suddenly of the detective, as she had stood by his fire two nights ago. Perhaps she'd come to talk about the autopsy. To his surprise, the thought of her made his pulse quicken.

"Detective Folger?" he said, walking forward. "Merry?"

He saw the brief candle's flare of the gun as it went off and instinctively jumped aside, conscious of the shot's report coming a second after the stinging pain. The blood was on his hands and he had touched them to his face. He had never been able to stand the sight or smell of blood. As he crumpled to the ground he heard Ney, barking wildly in the barn, and knew that his assailant was running towards him.

THE HEADLIGHTS OF the Explorer pulled up on the shoulder of Codfish Park Road threw Merry's shadow across the night sand almost to the waterline of Siasconset beach. She stood with her hands on her hips and her back to the light, staring at a waterlogged leather gym bag that sat like a grotesque jellyfish on the sand just above the high-water mark. Howie Seitz, his arm around a girl and his feet planted firmly next to the bag, was grinning triumphantly, and, Merry thought, with reason. He was out of uniform, and his eyes, caught in the headlights when he looked up at her, glittered like agates. His success and the rightness of his air of virtue annoyed her, and she scowled until her face was all black eyebrow.

"Tell me you haven't destroyed the evidence, Seitz," she said.

"Hey, you trained me, Detective. No way I'd screw up evidence. I just opened the thing to see if there was an ID inside, and that's when I saw the passport. I stayed with the bag while Deanna ran up to call you."

"Good of you," Merry said shortly, nodding toward the girl. She was a lithe summer kid, maybe all of seventeen, with the requisite mass of hair and buttery dark skin. She was clearly undecided whether this hiatus in an evening's grope on the beach was an excitement or a bore. She flicked her hair over one shoulder impatiently and huddled closer to Howie.

Merry walked over to them and squatted down next to the bag. It smelled vividly of rotten fish. She pulled on a pair of latex gloves and unzipped the bag. A large clump of seaweed wrapped around the gills of something indeterminate was decaying quietly under her nose. Just like Howie to leave it there for her. He'd probably been hoping she'd retch. She carefully scooped out the stinking mass and laid it on the sand at his feet, then extended her hand. He slapped her palm with his flashlight. The bleached white shape of a rat gleamed suddenly at her feet, and she jumped, dropping the light.

"A Mayling Stern sweater," she said through bitten lips. "I'll be damned." She lifted the sodden mass of sea-blue wool and scanned the button edge. Sure enough, one of them was missing. Her heart pounding, she dove back into the bag and shone the flashlight on its contents. Howie uncharacteristically said nothing, but waited to be released, his hand running up and down the girl's shoulder. The wind off the Atlantic was brisk, and she was probably freezing.

"Looks like a change of clothes, some bottles—shampoo and prescription drugs—in a plastic baggie, and some papers. There's his passport. Brazilian. That explains the FBI's failure to pick him up at the border. No doubt it's waterlogged and indecipherable by now. Let's hope Clarence can pull some prints." She flicked the passport cover open under the light for Howie to see, revealing an evil-looking photograph of Rusty Mason. "Jorge Luis Ribeiro.

Not the name we ran by the rental car agencies or ticket sellers. We'll have to redo those queries, Seitz."

One more piece of paper lay at the bottom of the bag. Merry reached in and extracted a blurred black-and-white photograph. She passed it under the light curiously, brushing away some grains of sand that clung to its surface. "Now what's so important about this, I wonder," she said.

The snapshot had been old and worn well before its submersion in seawater. A sepia haze had leached through the photographic paper, clouding the image. A woman stood on a city sidewalk, leaning toward the open window of a limousine, apparently taking leave of its occupant, whose face was clearly visible in the center of the frame. A dark-haired man well past middle age, but distinguished and arresting; the sort of face that commanded attention. The woman's face was half hidden by sunglasses, but her carriage and clothing suggested elegance, and from the length of toned leg braced on the sidewalk, Merry concluded she was rather young.

"What's so important about this picture that you bring it six thousand miles in a bag with a change of clothing?"

"Maybe it had some sentimental value?" Seitz said.

"Thank you, Howie. Advance to senior year." She shoved her hair behind her ears. "When do you get off this island, anyway?"

"Saturday morning. And man, it won't be fast enough," Howie said joyfully. Deanna stiffened and shot him a look. Too late, he caught himself. She wriggled out from under his arm.

"Yeah, well, like I've got a life here in high school too, you know, and I've got better things to do on a weeknight

than freeze my ass off out here on the beach," she said.
"Later, Howie. Call me when you know what it's worth."
She shot off across the sand, hair streaming furiously in
her wake.

"Car thirty-four," the Explorer's police radio squawked
suddenly in the darkness, and Merry jumped, sitting back
on the cold sand. That was *her* car. She looked at the
swiftly vanishing teenager. "You can go catch up with
her," she said to Howie. "You're not on duty. I'll handle
this." She stood up and brushed off her pants.

"You're not on duty, either," Howie said.

Merry hoisted the water-soaked bag, crossed to the
Explorer, and picked up the handset. "When has that
ever mattered? Get out of here. And Seitz . . ." She leaned
back around the doorframe to thank him, heard another
burst of static over the line, and thought better of it. "Car
thirty-four," she said, clicking on the radio. "Over."

Howie thrust his hands in his jeans and shrugged off in
the direction Deanna had taken.

Merry began to swear. Her voice stopped Howie in his
tracks. She caught a last glimpse of his bewildered face in
the headlights as she roared past him, hell-bent for the
Milestone Road and town.

THEY HAD PETER on a gurney behind a hanging plastic curtain at the Nantucket Cottage Hospital. His arrival
by ambulance had caused a sensation. Gunshot wounds,
however common to urban emergency rooms, were a rar-
ity on the island. Only two of the seats in the waiting
area held patients—an elderly gentleman who propped
a swollen wrist on his knee and a small girl with a candy
wrapper stuck high in her right nostril. The television

screen, suspended from the ceiling, ran baseball scores unattended. The two patients looked up at Merry hopefully when she tore through the emergency room's swinging doors, sensing the arrival of Chapter Two in the unfolding drama.

"They're taping him up, Detective," said Peter's housekeeper, Rebecca.

She was standing in front of the reception desk, her gaunt frame hunched like a question mark over a sheaf of papers. She wore no makeup, and her iron-gray hair was clipped short all over her head like a man's. She chewed her inner cheek as she filled out the forms and her bony right hand shook.

"Where was he hit?" Merry asked.

"Left arm. Bullet went in and out, took a nick of bone with it. If the poor fool weren't so skittish around blood, he'd have walked here, maybe. He'll be fine." Rebecca's head came up, and her eyes were angry. "What I want to know is, how are folks supposed to sleep nights when you cops can't keep 'em safe, hey? Enough to make even me pack a gun."

Merry went past her into the ER's examining bays.

She found Peter, naked to the waist under a white sheet, staring at the acoustic tiles of the ceiling. The yellow fluorescence of the room was not kind to his face, which had turned gray under his tan. The skin seemed to have shrunk over the jutting bone of his nose and the planes of his forehead, throwing his skull into sharp relief. His light eyes were not so much unfocused as too focused, Merry thought, as if the tiles mattered to the exclusion of everything. He seemed oblivious to her presence at the foot of the gurney.

The doctor bending over Peter's left shoulder ignored her as well. His fine, long-fingered hands were engaged in pressing white adhesive tape onto the ends of a bandage that encircled Peter's deltoid muscle.

"Hey, Peter," Merry said, unconsciously using his first name, something she had never done.

He lifted his head slightly, a gleam of welcome flashing for an instant across his face. The doctor straightened up and nodded to the nurse positioned at Peter's head. She smiled cheerfully down at him as though he were a child and said, "Just a short roll, Mr. Mason, to your room, and then we'll give you something to sleep."

"You're keeping him here tonight?" Merry said to the doctor. She felt oddly relieved.

"Normally I'd send him home. But he's lost a bit of blood. Wouldn't want him fainting again." He studied her an instant and said, "You the girlfriend?"

Merry flushed, felt annoyed because she did, and pulled out her badge a trifle belligerently. The doctor's face cleared and he said, "Detective Folger. A Clarence Strangerfield, from your station, wants you to call him."

"Thanks. Listen, is Mason able to talk?"

"I think so. Nurse?"

The woman turned in the act of rotating the gurney toward the hallway's swinging doors and looked inquiringly at the doctor.

"Hold up a minute. Ms. Folger? I mean—Detective?"

Merry went to Peter's side and flashed him a quick smile. She restrained an impulse, surprising in the extreme, to smooth his forehead. She noticed again how deeply set his gray eyes were, how the jutting brow gave his face the look of a hawk. "Did you see anything?"

He frowned. "Not enough. A woman and the flash of a gun. No face. Just a coat and hat."

"But you thought it was a woman."

His eyes flicked upward and held her own. "I thought it was you," he said.

## Chapter 17

"WHAT HAVE YOU got for me, Clarence?"

"Looks like a nine-millimetah, prob'ly from a Browning," Clarence said. After an hour of combing the grass, he had just managed to retrieve the casing under a pine tree some thirty feet from where Peter had fallen. Now he was crouched near the barn's double doors, holding a bit of wood between thumb and forefinger. The slug had entered the barn door, and Nathaniel Coffin was busy extracting what remained of it. Clarence pulled the plastic bag that contained the casing out of his evidence case and offered it to Merry. "No prints on the casing—the fellah was wearin' gloves, ah believe. Nice set of footprints ovah there, howevah. Nice set. Not that you can see them at the moment."

Another of Clarence's team was pouring plaster of paris into a wooden frame set over the prints, near a clump of pines just beyond the far side of the house. Merry picked her way carefully to the spot, hating to disturb the grass and hoping that Clarence had studied it. She crouched down. Under the floodlights the crime scene unit had rigged up, dew glittered on every blade of freshly mown stubble. She reached for her half-glasses and allowed herself an instant to inhale the comforting scent of wet earth. Then she studied the ground. Slight indentations showed where the shooter's heel and toe had sunk into the sandy soil as he waited for Peter to walk toward the barn, leave the dog, and walk back into firing range.

Merry's eyes narrowed. Peter might be right. The prints—narrow and long, with a pointed toe and shallow heel—suggested a woman's shoe rather than a man's. Something turned in the back of Merry's brain. What did the print remind her of? She shook her head and closed her eyes, concentrating. Boots. Low-slung, cuffed suede boots worn with skinny jeans.

"Ah've only found the one casing. No sign of the weapon, eithah."

"Clarence, I want you to send somebody up into the barn loft."

"Thaht Woman got the dahg, Marradith."

Thaht Woman was Rebecca. Clarence had borne the brunt of her tongue.

"It's not the dog I'm thinking of. Find out what's missing from the gun rack."

Clarence turned and shouted for Coffin. He came at a trot. Clarence sent him to the loft.

Merry hunkered on her heels in the grass, trying not to touch the ground surrounding the prints. "I almost forgot. Mason's bag is in the back of the car."

"So now yahr haulin' his luggage?"

"Not Peter's, Rusty's. Howie Seitz found it washed up on the beach at Siasconset."

Clarence rolled his eyes. "Ah'm thaht wahrn out, Marradith, I wish he'd thrown it back into the surf."

"There's papers, a passport, some clothes and stuff in the bag. You'll want to take a look at all of it."

Clarence's bulk loomed over her. "And they call this the off-season." He snorted. "If the bag washed up at 'Sconset, Marradith, ah've got a good idea where it went into the watah."

"You do?"

"Ayah. And thaht means somebody screwed up."

"It does?"

"Carhse it does," he said impatiently. "Yah don't think they wanted it found, do yah? They consigned it for burial to the deep, and that's wharh it was intended to stay. The ocean's a hahndy place to dump evidence, but it doesn't always behave prop'rly." He looked at her with pity. "Yah don't sail, do yah?"

Merry shook her head.

"No college geology, eithah?" Clarence summoned his patience. "Most of 'Sconset beach owes its existence to the teeth of the Atlantic gnawin' on the south shore— it's been shoving sand left and right for years, dumpin' it on Smith Point to the west and on 'Sconset to the east. If something washed up there, it was prob'ly thrown in the watah somewhere below Surfside. It looks as though things should drift out to sea around there, but they don't do it directly."

"Surfside," Merry said thoughtfully. "Not exactly near the scene of the crime, but not very far away, either."

"It was done with a cah, remembah," Clarence said gently. "With a cah, yah can get the evidence wherever yah want it, and fast."

"The car, again. Whose car?" Merry said with exasperation.

There was a delicate silence. Clarence was aware that one car, at least, had a damaged fender; and he was itching to go over that car for fibers and other forensic samples, but Merry wouldn't permit him to invade Mayling Stern's garage without a warrant—and serving a warrant without enough evidence to charge her might only startle her into flight. For now, they had paid one of Clarence's numerous 'Sconset cousins to keep an eye on the garage, with strict instructions to report immediately if the car was moved or the garage was the site of inordinate activity. Thus far he had witnessed frequent comings and goings on the part of the house cook, usually in pursuit of armloads of groceries, bouquets of flowers, and *The New York Times*; but she drove a battered station wagon, and never remained in the garage longer than was necessary to start or park the car. Clarence's cousin Aubrey said the Stern woman must be keeping a low profile; she hadn't poked her head around the front of the house in days.

"Shahrt of doin' a house-to-house search, I doubt yah'll find it," Clarence said.

"Thanks, Clare," said Merry shortly. "I hadn't realized that." She looked down at the prints. "I guess you've got an idea about these, too."

"Ayeh. The gunman is standing half hidden under the tree here, and he watches Mason leave with the dahg and walk tawrd the bahn. He waits till the dahg's shut up and Mason is walkin' tawrd him, and then he shoots. He doesn't know Mason's going to faint when he sees blood, so he thinks the guy's dead when he crumples to the ground. He takes off."

Merry nodded. Then she shook her head. "It's all wrong."

Clarence waited.

"I came over here a couple of days ago and the dog

came around the house, heading for the barn, like the Hound of the Baskervilles. He all but lunged for my throat. Tonight, the dog trots to the barn without a peep. Rebecca says so. It was the dog's barking after the shots were fired that caused her to come running."

"Which means no one was here when Mason walked to the bahn?"

"Possibly, but I doubt it. It's more likely that the dog didn't bark because it recognized the shooter's scent. He or she—I'm betting on she—stood here, sure that neither the dog nor anyone else would disturb her. She knows Rafe goes into town most evenings and the dog gets locked in the loft at night. Even if the dog decided to pick up on her existence, she's a friend, right? So she greets the dog and skips the shooting this time around. But if Ney gives her a miss—this is the one time of day she's got a clear shot at Peter Mason without Rafe coming at a run. She knows the routines of the place, Clarence. Just as she knew a few days ago that the bog would be flooded for the first time in months."

She stopped. Clarence was silent. Merry stood up creakily and pulled off her glasses, fumbling for the pocket of her coat as she stared toward the spot where Peter Mason had fallen. "Another thing. Look closely at the marks on the grass. She ran over toward the body, stood there an instant, and then veered back into the moors. Why? Why walk up to Peter and then leave without firing another shot? She must have seen that he wasn't dead. Why not kill him while he was passed out? Doesn't make sense, Clare."

"Maybe Thaht Woman scared her off," he said.

"Maybe. For lack of a better answer—"

A long shadow, grotesque under the stark lighting, advanced across the dew toward them. Coffin was done with the loft.

"No pistol on the rack, sir, no handgun of any kind, for that matter," he said. "Just a rifle—not that that's unusual for a farm—and it's registered."

"Thanks," Clarence said. "Yah dusted the rack faw fingerprints?"

"You won't find anything," Merry said sourly. "We're not dealing with a bonehead. Inexperienced, perhaps. Stupid, no. Coffin, there's a soggy piece of luggage staining the backseat of my car. Haul it out and take it to the station with you. Everything in there should be tagged as evidence in Rusty Mason's murder."

When he had trotted back toward the front door of the saltbox, she looked at Clarence. The crime scene chief was down on his hands and knees, studying the faint marks leading from the clear set of prints to the body. "Ayeh. I missed it, Detective," he said regretfully. "My sincere apologies."

"They're pretty faint," she said absently. "Forget it. Listen, Clare—there was a pistol on that rack the last time I saw it."

"What type?"

"Oh, it was a Browning. Nine-millimeter. In fact, it was the weapon used tonight, I'm sure of it. The killer knew what he—or she—was dealing with. She knew where to find the gun. She must have entered the loft tonight after Rafe left. She took the Browning and waited for Peter to wrap up his evening. Pretty cool stuff."

"Why do you think it was a woman?" Clarence heaved himself to his feet and brushed off his knees. "The prints are narrah. But they're still within a fair range of shoe size—it could be a flaht oxford type with a slight heel and a pointed toe, or a kid's bucks, faw instance. Or cowboy boots—like the ones that Rafe da Silva wahrs when he's paintin' the town red."

He peered warily at Merry from under his brows, as though he expected her to take a swing at him.

"What're you saying, Clarence?"

"I'm just wonderin' why Rafe's always fah from home when the trouble hits, that's all." He stomped off toward his forensics team without waiting for her reply.

THE GREENGAGE WAS closing down for the evening when Merry walked in. A few diners were still sitting at two tables near the Federal-style mantelpiece, where the last embers of an early-fall fire fell quietly into ash. The honey-colored wood floors and muted bayberry walls, hung with framed prints of whaling ships, gave the room intimacy and peace. The restaurant looked like a sure thing, Merry thought—a tribute to Tess's will and instinct, a measure of her canny perseverance. There was an air of bravery about the Greengage nonetheless: financing this first year could not have been easy. The reconstruction of the rooms alone represented a capital outlay Tess Starbuck must still be struggling to recoup. And what would the winter, and its loss of tourist revenue, mean for her and Will? Merry hardened her heart, and looked around for Rafe.

He was in the bar, an inviting room adjacent to the dining area where local fisherman—Dan's old friends—held pride of place. They were pulled up to tables near a second fire, legs stretched out in front of them, heavy boots quickly taking the shine from the recently sanded and refinished floors. Merry recognized a group of three men who sat with Rafe, arms carelessly draped across the backs of their wives' chairs, and understood with a shock why he spent so much time at the Greengage: these were his people, the friends of a lifetime, kids who'd gone to school with him and her brother, Billy. A world his father had cut out from under him when he threw him off the da Silva boat.

The group turned to look at her as she stood in the doorway, and abruptly fell silent. Rafe thrust himself back from the table and stood up, his chair scraping across the floor harshly in the quiet. "Hey, Merry," he said.

Merry nodded toward the table of inquiring faces and wished for a heart that beat less fast. "Can I talk to you for a second?"

Rafe glanced at his buddies. "Sure. Sure. Everybody was taking off, anyway." He slid past the gathered chairs and shoved his hands in his jeans, rocking slightly on the heels of his dress boots. Clarence was right. They weren't far off the prints in the Mason Farms front yard.

The assembled fishermen eased out of their seats and threw on light jackets, clapping Rafe on the back as they passed him, the women reaching on tiptoe to peck his cheek. Rafe belonged. Merry felt curiously relieved as she watched the unconscious display of brotherhood, and knew that her anxiety for Rafe was broader than she admitted; she was concerned about the fabric of his life, not just that part of it that might have included her.

He motioned her toward a chair. She shook her head. "I stopped by to tell you Peter's in Cottage Hospital. Somebody took a potshot at him tonight."

Rafe slammed his palm down on the table and shoved a chair over on its side. Conversation at the last table of diners in the neighboring room ceased abruptly. After an agonizingly speechless instant, he bent to pick up the chair and looked at her. "He okay?"

"Just nicked. Left biceps." She almost reached out a hand to Rafe and stopped herself just in time. "The doc kept him there overnight anyway. Seems he faints at the sight of blood."

Rafe slumped against the edge of the table. "I knew they were after Pete, not his brother. Why the hell didn't I stick close to him?"

"So you'd have an ironclad alibi, maybe?" Merry said quietly. She steeled herself for his reaction.

"I'm gonna ignore that asinine remark," he said.

Sometimes she hated this job. "Where were you about an hour ago?"

"Here."

"And half a dozen people can back you up. Okay. Where was Tess?"

That brought him around to face her. "Why would it matter?"

"Please answer the question, Rafe."

"She was in the kitchen cooking. Same as she is every night."

"Who's the chief waiter around here?"

Rafe nodded toward the outer room. "Sammy. Sammy and Regina. Sometimes Will fills in as busboy, but not tonight. Had homework."

Merry turned on her heel and walked into the dining room, seeing the man who had to be Sammy almost immediately. He wore a crisp white shirt and black jeans.

He was propped against the far wall, a napkin in his hand, alert to the whim of the last diners.

"You're Sammy?" Merry said.

"I am. How can I help you?"

"Detective Folger, Nantucket police. About when would you say the last food order went back to the kitchen?"

His eyes flicked from the badge to her face. "Geez, it was a while ago. These guys have been sitting here all night, talking and drinking single-malts. But they were the last table I sat. Must have sent the order back around nine."

"And you brought it to the table when?"

He shut his eyes and wrinkled his face, seeing the meals in his mind's eye. "The pork loin took a little while, and so did the bluefish in parchment. Tess held up the scampi. Say, nine twenty-five, maybe."

"Who's normally staffing the kitchen?"

"Tess. She runs the place herself. During the summer she had Otis Carmichael helping her—sous-chef, she called him—but he just comes in on weekends now. Weeknights she handles it alone, and Regina and I help her assemble the plates. It's still kind of a shoestring place—that's why we've only got twenty tables."

Merry glanced at her watch. Eleven-thirty. It was just enough: Tess could have sent out the last meals, hopped in the Rover parked outside, and made it to Mason Farms by nine forty-five. On the off chance that someone from the farm noticed the car's arrival, she would look like Rafe heading for bed. A quick trip into the barn for the gun and then a brief wait in darkness, alone under the pine trees, as Peter and Ney took their bedtime walk. She could have been back in the kitchen by ten-fifteen.

"Did they order anything else?" she asked, nodding toward the last table.

Sammy looked at her curiously. "Yeah, they had dessert," he said. "And coffee. Why?"

"So you'd have gone back into the kitchen around what time?"

"Geez, I dunno."

"Try to think."

"Nine forty-five, or thereabouts," a voice said behind them. Merry turned and saw a girl in her late teens, her long blonde hair braided into a coil around her head.

"You're Regina?"

The waitress nodded. "I know it was nine forty-five because my boyfriend stopped by to see if I was ready to go. The kitchen technically stays open until ten, but weeknights after Labor Day we're usually cleaning up by nine-thirty. Tonight there were still two tables—remember, Sammy? You called me in to help with the dessert plates. You couldn't find the rum cheesecake."

"That's right, I did," he said. "Tess had stepped upstairs."

"You know she was upstairs?" Merry said swiftly.

Sammy shrugged. "Where else would she be? Probably took Will some pie. Hey, you're not moonlighting for the Board of Health, are you? The place is clean as a whistle, believe me."

"Could I say hello to Tess?" Merry asked.

"Come on back."

"I'll take her, Sammy," Regina said. "You clear the last table." For a girl of her age, she had a commanding air. Sammy didn't argue.

Regina led Merry back through the bar to the kitchen. Rafe had left his seat by the fire.

"You're Chief Folger's daughter, aren't you?" Regina said.

"That's right."

"Must be nice to have your dad for a boss."

"That's not the first word that comes to mind."

"You working on the Mason murder?"

"You guessed it."

"It's not a guess. My boyfriend's a cop, too." Regina turned and held open the kitchen's swinging door, waiting for Merry to pass in front of her. "Matt Bailey. You know him?"

The malice in the girl's eyes was so blatant that Merry shivered slightly as she walked past her. "Yeah. He strikes out with women his age," she said.

TESS WAS ALONE in the kitchen, a slim figure struggling with a towering mass of dirty pots and empty plates. She wore heavy pink rubber gloves, and her auburn hair was beaded from the cloud of steam sent up by her spray nozzle. She brushed back a wisp from her face with one gloved hand, and her shoulders slumped. Any twinge of jealousy Merry felt died away. It was clear that the elegant rooms beyond the kitchen were purchased at great cost: Tess Starbuck was bone-tired. At that moment she turned to place a cleaned pan on a dish rack and saw Merry. She smiled. The lines of weariness disappeared suddenly and she looked as she must have when Dan Starbuck married her—as Rafe must see her, Merry thought. Then the smile faded and with it the illusion of youth.

"Should I grab a towel?"

"Nah, don't bother. These can drain. We use them too

often to bother putting them away. How're you doing, Detective? Making any headway?"

"Only backwards," Merry said. "I stopped in to tell you Peter Mason was shot tonight. Don't worry," she added quickly, as Tess's face went white, "he's fine. Just nicked in the arm. But I didn't want Will to hear about it in school."

"That's very kind of you," Tess said. Her words were barely audible over the running water. She shut off the tap, pulled her hands out of the gloves, and reached for a towel. But instead of drying her hands she rested them on the edge of the sink, staring at the tile wall in front of her. "This gets worse and worse, doesn't it?"

"Seems like it," Merry said. "Did you do a lot of business tonight?"

Tess seemed to hear her from a great distance. She sat down in a chair and put her head in her hands. Merry thought of Will, and knew where he got his brittle strength, his intelligence—and his vulnerability. His mother raised her head and met Merry's eyes. "Yes, thank God. But I'll be glad to get to bed. I've been standing in this ten-foot-square area for eight hours."

"Where's Will?"

Tess motioned toward the back stairs that led from one corner of the kitchen to the second and third floors. "Homework. Rafe's with him now."

So Rafe would break the news. He was becoming the boy's surrogate father "Well, at least you got out to see the moon," Merry said. "You've got some sand on your shoes."

Tess stared at her as if she had spoken gibberish. Then she looked down at her cuffed, narrow-heeled ankle boots and ran one finger over the clay-colored smears just above the sole. "I've got to stop smoking," she said, and laughed. "I've tried and tried and can't quit. I have a no-cigarettes rule in the kitchen—think it's dirty. So I duck out every half hour to take a drag by the back door. Stupid, isn't it? For a woman my age. I'd almost kicked it. And then Dan died."

"Some habits are hard to break, Tess," Merry said gently. "Say hello to Will."

As she backed down the drive, Merry could see Rafe's shaggy head silhouetted in the window of a third-floor room. Standing guard until she was safely gone. Will's was the only window lit that high up in the house. She imagined the yellow light spilling over the desk, and the boy with the long, dark bangs pretending to study, while he stared at nothing. Not even Rafe's strong presence could keep fear from that room tonight. She wished, very hard, for evidence that would clear Rafe and Tess completely. And wondered how much money they could expect from Peter Mason's death.

## Chapter 18

"So the name Jose Luis Ribeiro doesn't mean anything to you?" Merry asked. She was sitting in Peter Mason's brightly lit study, the hum of an overactive bee slightly distracting from beyond the open window.

"I think in Portuguese it's about as common as Joe Smith, Detective. Sorry."

"Your brother was traveling under that name on a Brazilian passport. Or so we assume. His picture's in it, and there's no other travel document in the bag, so we're fairly confident it's the passport he used. I suppose that's why his border entry—there's a Miami control stamp in the passport—didn't ring any bells in the federal computer system. The sealed indictment would have guaranteed him a welcoming party if he'd used his real name and documentation."

"You're very chatty today," Peter said. He was stretched out on the sofa in a patch of morning sunlight, and looked as though he were feeling a lazy sense of well-being, probably born of light-headedness and a good breakfast. Unlike Rusty, he had escaped death.

She studied him. "Is that a polite way of saying your arm is throbbing and you wish I'd shut up?"

"No. It's merely an aside."

"I see. I talk a lot when I've got a lot on my mind. Or when I'm nervous. I'm both, today."

"I fall deathly silent when I'm nervous. Habit of child-hood—I hoped I'd turn invisible before my mother found out."

"Found out what?"

"Whatever evil I'd done that day. Do you live alone, Detective?" Peter asked suddenly.

"No," she said. "I live with my family. And if you're going to ask whether I've had it easy because my dad is my boss, don't bother. I've answered that question *ad nau-seam*. You didn't know I knew that term, did you?"

"What an interesting pronunciation," Peter replied. "Do you have bookshelves?"

"Last time I checked."

"What do they have on them?" Peter persisted.

"Potted plants. Among other things. At my house, everything from Great-Aunt Mitchell's underwear to back issues of nineteenth-century feed catalogues are piled on the shelves." She gave up discussing the case. "You're pretty chatty yourself."

"And I've got nothing on my mind at all, as it happens. Too little blood has gone to the brain in the past twelve hours. What exactly is making you jumpy? Afraid they won't miss, next time? Concerned for your career? Won-dering whether Dad's beginning to think you take after Mom's side of the—" He broke off at the sight of her face, which had frozen, gone white, and then red. "Whoa, I'm sorry," he said, sitting upright. "What did I say?"

"What have you heard about my mother?"

"Nothing!"

"Has Rafe talked about her?"

"Why would he? It was just—"

"—an aside. Right. Please keep your asides to yourself, Mr. Mason."

"From now on, I will." The laziness had vanished. "If I trespassed on private ground, I'm sorry."

Merry could not immediately answer him. She was fighting an unexpected urge to cry and a desire to run far away from Mason Farms. She had lost sleep the past few nights—tossing and turning with a cloud of bickering voices in her brain. She had intended to be at her most rational this morning, and instead she was a morass of feeling—fear that Peter Mason might be killed, and that it would be her fault; anxiety about whether she could solve this case; foreboding about Rafe's involvement in it; and a longing for his lost warmth and affection that had become acute since their encounter in the barn. Near-exhaustion and tension had her close to snapping.

"My mother killed herself, Mr. Mason," she said. "After my brother came home from Iraq in a body bag."

"I'm sorry."

"*Don't say that*," she burst out furiously. "It always sounds so inadequate. She was an artist, you know—painted portraits. One night after dinner—she wouldn't have left us without a meal on the table for anything in the world—she filled my grandfather's waders with stones and walked into Madaket Harbor. With my dad being police chief, he basically organized the hunt for the body. It was pretty public when they found her the next day. He handled it really well, actually. I probably didn't."

"Why is that a failing?"

"I'm over thirty years old and I'm still trying to show my father that I'm not going to crack under pressure."

"Again, I'm sorry. And as you said, that always sounds inadequate. But I know something about trying to please fathers. It's a useless exercise."

"You know nothing about my dad. Could we just deal with the evidence, please, and leave each other's personal life out of this?"

"Absolutely," he said.

Merry turned to a pile of evidence sealed in plastic that she had brought with her. She set her face in an efficient mask.

"These are some of the contents of your brother's luggage, which was found last night near Siasconset."

"'Sconset?"

"On Low Beach. I had to sign out these items from our Evidence department because of your injury—I didn't want to ask you to come over to the station."

"Thanks. I was in no shape to get there."

"We found this picture," Meredith said, "along with several letters we think were signed by Rusty—the handwriting seems to match the signature on his fake passport. All of them are pretty water-damaged and they have to remain in the plastic, I'm afraid. Please look at the photograph first. Do you recognize anyone?"

Peter studied the faded black-and-white figures. "The man in the car is my father."

"And the woman?"

"Is *not* my mother."

"You're sure? She's wearing shades, after all."

"I can pick out my mother at five hundred feet by the way she carries her head," he said. "I'm certain this isn't her."

"No idea who it might be?"

"None."

Merry nodded briefly. "We think it may be important, since Rusty chose to bring it with him." She flipped through some sealed sheets of paper. "These letters may be copies, or drafts he never sent. Or maybe he was waiting until he got to the US to deliver them. Regardless, they're all remarkably similar. I'd say they represent blackmail."

Peter looked up from the photograph with sudden interest. "You think Rusty came back here to extort some cash?"

"Maybe. Maybe he's been doing that for a while. Who knows? He had a very good reason for needing it, Mr. Mason." She paused, debating how to tell him, and decided that to be blunt was best. "According to the coroner, your brother had both hepatitis C and HIV. He had a lot of pretty pricey health care ahead of him, the kind that's harder to get in Brazil. Probably the kind he couldn't pay for, although we can't swear to that yet. We've cabled the Brazilian police to search for bank accounts under this name, or under his own, using the address on the passport."

Peter picked up Rusty's passport and stared at the face. "Jesus," he muttered. "How far along was he?"

"Not very," Merry said. "He had the virus but not the disease. And having learned a bit about your brother, I'd say he intended to fight it every step of the way." She passed him the letters.

Peter scanned the first sheet. "This is to Sky."

Merry nodded. "We figured that meant Tate-Jackson. Nobody else with that name. You should see the next one."

Peter flipped to the second page. "Sundance?"

"Sounds like a Woodstock reunion, doesn't it? All we need is an Aragorn or a Galadriel. Or somebody named Love. The third one could be anyone—a guy named George."

"That's my sister."

"We've typed up copies of all three for you to keep. The actual letters I'll have to return to Evidence. I want you to read through them, think about what they mean, and get back to me if you've any ideas. With you getting shot last night, it looks like Rusty's death was an accident. But blackmail is a pretty strong motive for knocking him off. Money in any form, if it comes to that. Much more solid motive than love."

"How sad."

"Is it? You'd rather be killed by someone you love? Or loved once? I don't know. If it's going to be ugly, I'd rather it be about dollars and cents than about my place in the universe. Which reminds me: I've got to ask you a nasty question."

"Shoot."

She paused in mid-speech, and looked at him. "You've got a weird sense of humor, Mr. Mason."

"Chalk it up to the loss of blood."

"Or that heady feeling of having beaten death."

"That too."

"What are the terms of your will?"

The question brought Peter up short. Sky had asked nearly the same thing, and he'd dismissed the thought as irrelevant, so convinced was he that Rusty had been the intended victim. He leaned back in the sofa cushions and raised one hand to his brow. Merry watched him closely.

"I leave my books and belongings to George, for her

four kids; except for the collection of nautical architectural drawings—they go to Sky." He paused. "It felt morbid to write a will. Talking about it is fucking awful."

"Go on."

"I leave Mason Farms to the Nantucket Conservation Foundation—I'm hoping they'll run it in conjunction with the neighboring co-op. At the very least, it won't be developed, and that's something."

Merry walked over to the study window and gazed out at the bog. Still flooded for harvesting, it stretched like red porridge to the edge of the moor. Fifty acres in the middle of Nantucket—even if part of it was classified as wetlands—represented a fortune in real estate. "What's this place worth, anyway?"

He smiled faintly. "More than it looks. The land is obviously highly valuable, but it was expensive to establish the cranberry bogs. I've sunk about five million into the farm's infrastructure. The place didn't make a nickel for four years—it takes that long for the vines to bear. Then there's the routine maintenance, Rafe's salary, the seasonal workers, the equipment—it adds up. Technically, I haven't even earned back the cost of my initial investment. But I'm in it for the long term."

"And you've left all this to the NCF," she said woodenly.

"I hate the thought of these moors being bulldozed."

"You realize the scarcity of buildable lots on Nantucket means that housing prices just get higher, right?" Merry sat down in the chair opposite Peter. "Most of the families I grew up with have left for the mainland because they can't afford to live here. People like firemen, and teachers, and . . ."

"Cops," Peter agreed. "I know. The island is a privileged enclave. A gated community whose gate is the sea. Conservation isn't perfect. But would you rather this became a golf course when I die?"

The conversation was getting personal again. She picked up her laptop and tried to focus. "So much for the land. What about money?"

Peter shifted, and jarred his arm uncomfortably. "You want to see my assets?"

"I want to know what your life is worth to somebody who's desperate," she said.

"I didn't leave anything to Rusty, if that's what you're asking. I'd written him out of my life—and my death. The bulk of the fortune—what a grandiose word for stock and trust-fund income—goes to George's children, in trust once again. The Mason family trusts have always been handled by our New York lawyers and bankers. That part of it was pretty automatic."

"I'm going to have to ask you for a ballpark figure."

"My net worth?"

"If you like."

Peter was looking increasingly uncomfortable. "I have about fifty million to play with. Does that give you an idea?"

"Yeah." Merry adjusted her glasses and typed the figure into her notes. All because some early Mason figured out whale oil wouldn't last forever and opened a department store in Manhattan. History sucked. She looked up. "How's your sister doing for cash?"

Peter probably didn't intend to patronize her, but the expression of amusement on his face felt like condescension, and she stiffened.

"These are routine questions, you understand?" she said.

"Completely. George inherited about the same amount as I did. My father disinherited Rusty. Everything else went to Mother."

"Your sister hasn't gone through it all, or anything like that?"

"I don't think so. Her husband, Hale, would hardly let her. He's a director at Salomon Brothers, the New York investment banking firm."

"Where Rusty worked."

"Yes—Hale probably got him his job when he was first out of college. They worked in separate sides of the house, however—Hale does corporate finance. Rusty is—was—a bond trader."

"Your sister work?"

"She blogs. Lifestyle stuff."

"And the kids? They know you left them your money?"

"I doubt it. And the oldest is only nine. I think we can rule them out."

"Have you left anyone anything else?"

"Odds and ends. I gave Rafe the price of a boat and Will Starbuck the cost of his college tuition. He's pretty bright. I don't know if Tess realizes what he could do in the proper environment in a couple of years. Call it about four hundred thousand altogether."

"So, if you died, would the money go to Will immediately?"

"No. It would be invested in a tax-free education account, and Tess could draw down funds as the need arose."

"And if you're alive, you'll just pay the school bills as

they come in, is that it? The trust only happens if you're dead?"

"Of course."

So Peter Mason dead was worth a great deal. Peter Mason alive wasn't worth the shorts he was wearing. "Does Tess know about this?"

Peter shook his head. "She's very proud. I don't want her to know about it until Will's college-bound. I may even figure out a way for it to look like financial aid from the university. Whatever university he chooses. I haven't worked that out yet."

The spark of an idea flared in Merry's brain. "Who witnessed the will for you, Mr. Mason?"

"Two of the family attorneys in New York."

The spark flared and died.

"Rafe is the one who suggested I keep Tess in the dark originally," Peter offered. "He came up with the idea of paying Will a fixed wage for his work on the farm, too, because she was so upset when I gave him my old bike."

"Rafe," Merry said. "He knows about your will?"

"The tuition bequest. Yes. He could be Will's stepfather someday. I didn't want Rafe to worry about college. He doesn't make much, Detective. Tess's restaurant, Will's education—it can all look like a financial nightmare. It would be sad if fear of debt kept him from following his heart."

Merry's breathing was suspended, and the circulation in her legs seemed to have stopped. She was numb from her waist to her toes. *Good God*, she thought, *he doesn't even realize that he's giving Rafe a motive for murder.*

To her surprise, Peter grinned. "So it's not much in the end. And if you go looking for love as a motive, you'll come up even more empty-handed."

"On that note," Merry said, "we need to talk about your friends, Mr. Mason."

"My friends?"

"Yeah. Mayling Stern, the clothing designer, and the guy she lives with."

"Schuyler Tate-Jackson."

"What a mouthful that is."

"Why do you think we call him Sky?"

"What's the problem between him and Ms. Stern?"

"Is there one?"

"I'd lay even money on it. She was fishing for me to ask her why they're not married. Any ideas?"

"Not really," he said. "I consider that their business, and not something I'd ask them."

"So your friendship doesn't include trading secrets? No feelings, no personal stuff?"

Peter looked perplexed. "Why do you care?"

"Just wondering if you know enough about either of them to judge their characters, that's all."

"I'm an excellent judge, Detective."

Merry felt a flicker of amusement. "Yeah, well, whether you're accurate or not is another question. Let me ask you this: does Ms. Stern lie?"

"Does she lie?" Peter closed his eyes. Her questions were tiring him. "I suppose we all do, if the reasons are compelling enough. Why?"

"Mayling Stern's Mercedes has a damaged front end. It's pretty recent. Anything older than a week would rust in this humidity. But she doesn't mention it when I ask her what she did this weekend, and there's no accident report on file at the station."

"A lot of people don't report accidents."

"But when your partner is being blackmailed by an old friend, who just happens to be run over . . . it doesn't inspire confidence."

"Mayling never knew Rusty."

"And another thing." Merry fished in her purse and pulled out a plastic evidence bag. It held the rat button. "I've been carrying this around so long it's started to feel like a good-luck charm."

"What is it?" Peter turned the bag curiously in his fingers.

"A button from one of Stern's sweaters."

"The Chinese New Year ones," he said. "I bought one for a friend's birthday."

"Lucy Jacoby. The English teacher. Did she like it?"

"She said so."

"I found that button near your brother's body. I also found a Stern sweater with a missing rat in Rusty's luggage we recovered from Low Beach. I figure whoever murdered him got blood on her clothes when she dragged Rusty to the bog, and so dumped the sweater with your brother's stuff. I don't know whether he—or she—knew one of the buttons had been lost."

"And you think the sweater you found is Lucy's?"

Merry shrugged. "Mayling Stern owns one exactly like it. And if I believe Lucy, she hates rats, and gave your gift away to a clothing drive a little while after she got it. Which means anybody who went to Our Lady of the Island's bazaar might have picked it up, worn it to murder Rusty, and dumped it in the ocean. *If* we believe Lucy.

The people who ran the bazaar have no record of individual items or purchasers. I checked. But you know her best. Does the story make sense?"

"Yes and no. I thought she liked the gift, but if she hated rats, she'd never tell me in a million years, and it would be like her to get rid of the sweater quietly—and charitably—behind my back. Mayling's sold a lot of these sweaters, Detective. Any kind of killer could have worn one."

"True enough," Merry said. "Tell me about Lucy Jacoby, Mr. Mason. Why's she so paranoid about strangers? I spoke to her the day after the murder, and she was constantly looking over her shoulder. You'd think she'd killed Rusty herself."

"You can rule out that possibility, Detective. Lucy never knew my brother, nor did anyone she cares about."

"Except you."

He looked up at her quickly, a fleeting expression of pain crossing his features, and Merry realized that he knew Lucy Jacoby was in love with him, and that the fact didn't make him happy.

"She's not the sort of person who resorts to violence," he said. "She takes her suffering as though it were expected, and fades away."

"Any idea why she skipped the first day of school?"

"One or two," Peter said warily. "Why?"

"I think she'd tied one on the night before."

There was a brief silence. "How to explain this?" Peter said. "Lucy came to Nantucket to escape an unhappy marriage. Her husband—a man she met in Europe during a junior year abroad—is what is known as a gray arms dealer."

"A *what?*"

"He brokers the sale of components for deadly weapons. He lives two lives—one, that of an Italian aristocrat with estates in Portofino and Milano; the other, surrounded by dangerous people. Lucy lives in fear of them. Her husband wants her dead."

"Why?"

"Because she left." Peter gave Merry an appraising look. "Have you ever been beaten by a man, Detective?"

Her face flooded with color. "I take it you don't mean that spanking I got when I was four?"

"I mean blows strong enough to raise bruises—but never on the face, or the arm, or the leg, where they might be visible. Lucy says she was beaten daily. The bruises never healed."

"Why'd she marry him?"

"For the reason most women marry men. She thought she could save him."

"So she drinks?"

"Not usually. She handles stress with exercise—running sprints with me, for instance," Peter said. "But on Labor Day, Lucy thought she recognized a guy on the ferry. One of Marcello's thugs. She's terrified—waiting for her ex-husband to appear on her doorstep. I offered to put her up in my old family house on Cliff Road, I even suggested she head for the mainland. She thought that running was pointless."

"I've got a better idea," Merry said. "She could go to the police."

Peter shook his head. "I suggested that, too. She seemed more afraid of police involvement than of anything else."

Merry thought of Lucy Jacoby, half-hidden in the vines of her loggia like a nesting bird, and felt a spark of pity for her. Peter was right. There was no way he could explain the circumstances of that life to Merry. It was as alien as a foreign tongue—as alien as Peter Mason, if she was honest with herself. Over the past few days she'd viewed his life more closely, and had almost come to believe it was little different from her own. But she was wrong. They existed on two separate planes, thrust into sharp contact by violence and death. Once she found the murderer—once the violence ended—the planes would part again.

Worry was alive in his face. Merry knew that she had called Lucy's danger to his mind at a time when he was physically ill-equipped to help her. *Give him something else to think about*, she advised herself grimly.

"There's one more thing," she said. "Tess Starbuck."

"What about her?"

"If you're alive, the tuition money goes to Will. If you die, she takes control. Do you have any idea how well the Greengage is doing? Can Tess make it until next season?"

"I don't know." Peter passed his good hand over his eyes. "God, this is awful, isn't it? Looking closely at everyone you know, wondering what price they've placed on your life."

"As I said, I'd rather it were about dollars and cents than about the people I love," Merry said dryly. "Unfortunately, you're stuck with both."

"That's always been true," Peter said. "I thought it might be different, here on the island, if I called myself a farmer. I thought I could stop wondering if my friends were really my friends, if a woman loved me for myself instead of what I could buy."

Merry was silent.

"But tell me something, Detective: If I'm the one this murderer wants—for love or money—why am I still alive? A real killer would have finished the job."

*Chapter 19*

WHEN MERRY HAD gone, Peter lay back on the sofa cushions and closed his eyes. Rusty's face as he had last seen it in death—lined, emptied, and forever unreachable—hung in his mind. He had felt no sense of loss at the murder, and no rage toward the killer; those had been felt long ago, in the presence of another form of death. But in the void left by his brother, a simple conviction remained: that in the world he valued, justice must be done. *How dispassionate*, he thought, *how like a man of my class. I am doing the decent thing, to keep me from feeling the unthinkable—relief that a door has closed.*

He allowed himself to consider his brother's disease. He had never personally known someone with AIDS before, and he realized, suddenly, that this is what it meant to live on an island. Rusty brought the illness into his study, as he lay caught in a shaft of sunlight, and forced him to look at it. Rusty, who had played rugby like a god, who had loved too many women to remember, who had burnished his strength like a bright shield held before the eyes of everyone—Rusty was incurably sick. Peter felt a strange pity. His fingers clenched and the movement of his sore left arm caused him to curse in pain.

Footsteps clattered down the hallway from the kitchen

and Rebecca pushed the door open. "What happened?" she said hoarsely.

He cradled his arm in the least painful position and grimaced at her. "Sorry. Just jogged it a bit."

She rolled her eyes and turned on her heel, annoyance in every line of her body. Poor Rebecca. Alone in her room in the converted icehouse the previous night, she hadn't slept, and despite her obvious relief at his return from the hospital, she would probably be up again tonight worrying the gunman would come back.

Peter glanced down at the copies of the letters Merry Folger had left on the sofa next to him—Rusty's letters. He picked up the first, addressed to Sky. It was undated.

> *Barra da Tijuca*
> *Rio de Janeiro,*
> *Brasil*
>
> *Dear Sky:*
> *I know it's been a while, and I'd apologize, only why bother? We've both got our lives, and I'm sure you haven't spared much thought for mine.*
> *Maybe I'd better start over. The bitterness is some-thing I can't control anymore, even if I'd like to, and it invades even this attempt at writing a letter to an old friend.*
> *I've heard about you from time to time, from chance encounters in Rio bars with people you know, or have once known. I've liked getting the occasional email you send out, even though I've never answered them. You've been a sort of lifeline to the past. It's good to*

*know you're doing so well. As for me—what is there to say after ten years?*

*Maybe spending a few years in a minimum-security country club would have been better than rotting in this beautiful hell. Was I a fool to run? The only difference between wisdom and idiocy is how it looks in retrospect. I've wasted a third of my life here, figuring out what paradise really means: a dream come true has the profile of nightmare.*

*It's time to wake up. For both of us.*

*I'm going through rough times—you have no idea how bad—and while money can't solve everything, sometimes it helps pretend. We both know I could end your career by informing certain people how it began. I wouldn't be above keeping silent, however, for a price.*

*Pretty bald, isn't it? Pretty brutal? But then, so am I. How much is your life worth, Sky? Add it all up, like the honest broker you are—the houses, the partnership, the professional esteem, the reputation you've spent a decade building. The love of that woman who keeps you sane. Think about it long and hard. If you talk to the police I'll go public.*

*Contact me at Peter's on Labor Day. You know where he lives; I don't.*

*Yet.*

*But I will.*

There was, of course, no signature. Someone from Merry's forensics team had dutifully typed the word "Socks" at the bottom, Rusty's nickname from college. He had rarely done his laundry on a regular basis, and his roommates had gone from calling him Rusty to Musty and finally to

Socks. The innocence of the moniker placed at the end of such a letter, filled as it was with the perversion of Rusty's history with Sky, jarred Peter. Or perhaps it was the vividness of memory that it brought, and the sense of lost youth. He shrugged off his thoughts and turned to the body of the letter itself. Sky, contrary to his words, knew why Rusty had left, and that knowledge somehow incriminated him. Or so Rusty believed— enough to think Sky would be willing to pay him not to talk. What could Sky know? He was supposed to meet the lawyer in New York tomorrow and interview his father's former CFO, Malcolm Scott. But should he confront Sky with this letter now, while they were both still on the island?

This letter. He stopped, his gaze suspended in midair, and saw once again the interior of Mayling's studio, the dim light of a foggy Labor Day, and her fingers scrabbling desperately at scattered sheets of paper. She had been angry and afraid. Was the piece of paper he'd just read only a copy? Had Rusty actually sent his blackmail note to Sky—and Mayling knew it?

Peter turned to the second letter, hoping for some answers. Like the first, it had been written in Rio; but this one was dated August 20. He scanned it quickly, and stopped short at the sight of his own name. He went back to the top and read it more slowly, trying to understand what it meant.

> *Dear Sundance—*
> *Bad pennies, like bad drugs, always come back to haunt you. Don't ask how I found out where you are; we'll have hours to catch up with each other when I get*

*to Nantucket. I'm coming home. I don't expect you to
greet me at the dock.*

*I need money; I'm sure you must have some. Sud-
den death has a way of making people wealthy. On the
other hand, if you're unwilling to part with cash, I can
offer you the destruction of that safe little world you're
in the process of building. You realize that all I have to
do is say a word to my brother Peter. So I think we'll
have a lot to discuss.*

*I'll be in touch.*

There was infuriatingly little to suggest what sort of
hold Rusty had on Sundance, or who he—or she—was.
Only that Sundance lived on Nantucket, had known
Rusty at some point in the past, and possibly now knew
Peter. That could be anyone, he thought impatiently.
It was as though Rusty was afraid that Sundance, whoever he was, might decide to expose him to the law;
and his letter, as a result, revealed nothing that could
be taken as blackmail. Rusty had become careful in his
final years.

Peter read the letter again quickly and pondered the
final paragraph. "Sudden death has a way of making people wealthy." He shook his head. Will and Tess Starbuck
were his only friends in mourning, but Dan's death had
brought them more debt than wealth.

He shuffled the sheets and found the final letter, the
one to George. He liked reading this the least, afraid
he would discover something about the Whitneys'
lives he'd rather not know. This was the worst of it,
he thought; Rusty had brought ugliness back into his
world. He read on.

*My dearest George—*

*Lo, and the prodigal brother returneth.*

*Biblical words for catastrophic events. I assume that you, of anyone, have fatted calves to kill—a room, for instance, up in the eaves of that palatial house you call home. I can see it now—done up in Mario Buatta, probably, reeking of nouveau wealth and Hale's unfortunate conservatism. I'm counting on the conservatism, by the way, to keep me healthy: make sure you tell him I'm coming home around Labor Day. He needn't leave the country, either—I have no intention of bringing up our unfortunate mutual past. Provided I'm well looked after.*

*I won't bother to lull you into thinking I'm a changed man—for the better, that is—with false interest in your brats or sweet inquiries about your marital happiness. I never liked kids, I have no hope for Hale's, and I wrote off your marriage the day it occurred. You were always one to go for security over risk, George; something you inherited with Peter. Much good may it do you. You'll die well and fat and without a single live emotion in your body, your only satisfaction the knowledge you've lived a life as empty as your mother's. And Peter—Peter, who actually thought his outraged integrity might shame me—you're hypocrites, both of you.*

*So I've had a bit too much cachaça. I'm sober enough to know you can't turn me away, George, not if you want your home intact and your children safe in the illusions you've given them. Make sure Hale knows I'm coming. He doesn't have to throw himself off the Greenwich train or lock himself in the*

*library with a gun. He just needs to negotiate. Man*
*to man.*
R.

Peter read the letter three times. Then he folded it
carefully with his one good hand, eased himself to a standing position, and reached for a buff leather briefcase that
rested on the floor next to his desk. On second thought,
he turned and folded the letter to Sky and placed it with
George's. He would take them both to New York.

Hale Whitney was a shy, introspective, cherubic-faced
forty-five-year-old who had entered a new world when
he met Georgiana. He exuded confidentiality, trustwor-
thiness, and respectability. He had a wicked instinct for
making money. But he was no street fighter—threatened
with the loss of his reputation, or his home, suicide
might seem like a reasonable option. Rusty had hit
George first, to make sure Hale didn't bolt. He had been
very clever.

Peter snapped the tabs on the briefcase and stood up.
Then he reached for his cell phone and called the Nantucket police station. He was put through to Merry Folger
within seconds.

"You read the letters?" she said.

"Yes. Detective—this has everything to do with my
family history and Rusty's past. I may be in a position to
clear it up for you when I get back from New York."

"New York?"

"Well, the suburbs, actually. I'm interviewing my
father's former CFO in Westchester. Then I have Rusty's
funeral, and some conversations with family and friends
that may lead somewhere."

There was a short silence on the line. "Would the CFO know about that sealed indictment from ten years ago?"

"I hope so."

"I think I should come with you," she said.

Peter opened his mouth to dissuade her, then stopped in mid-thought. He had a sudden vision of her intelligent green eyes and the way her jaw clenched when she asked her unswervingly tough questions.

"We'll catch the eight-thirty flight," he said. "Pack light."

*Chapter 20*

FRIDAY MORNING OF a short week after Labor Day, and still she felt exhausted. Lucy Jacoby struggled to open her eyes at the insistent ringing of her alarm, sensing the dim light of five-thirty beyond the skylight of her loft bedroom. She sighed deeply and threw her arms over her head, reaching for the coolness of the empty white linen pillowcase next to her own, resisting the day and its rush of duties, tensions, and memories. She felt a profound desire for sleep, an almost overwhelming compulsion. Should she call in sick again today? Have coffee over her morning paper and then catch a ferry for the mainland? Unbidden, the face of a familiar stranger rose in her drowsing mind. Her last encounter on the ferry had been a horrible one. There was no escape in that direction.

She swung her stiff limbs out of bed in the dim, fog-laden light and padded to the small window cut in the peak of the gable. From here she could see the Atlantic off Tom Nevers Head. It stretched like a sheet of iron to the horizon, and she shivered. She had never found charm in the sight of limitless distance. Time for a warm shower, coffee, the intimacy of her garden.

SHE WAS HUDDLED over the dew-laden rose bed with a pair of secateurs in her hand when Peter pushed open her garden gate. The fall of auburn curls flashed around her shoulders as she turned, and fear suffused her face at the sight of the neat sling supporting his arm.

His heart turned over. She was like a burdened child, playing in the dirt to keep her mind off her worries. The mingled scents of her flowers drifted to his nose on the shifting damp.

"Peter! What happened?" She stood up quickly, dropping her shears at her feet.

"Somebody took a shot at me Wednesday night," he said. "Nothing serious. I'm fine."

No one would ever know what it had cost him in pain and swearing to get dressed that morning.

"Who would do such a thing?"

He walked toward her slowly in his business suit. The dew spattered the polished leather of his shoes and left raindrop-sized stains on their tips. "The roses are still blooming."

"Not for long," she said, glancing back over her shoulder. The words were laced with regret. "I can keep them going until mid-September, but after that, I admit defeat and leave the heads on to wither. It triggers their dormancy. The drop in temperature at night is doing it for me, anyway. You've probably seen the last flowering."

Peter stopped at the edge of the bed and, with his good arm, reached toward a coppery pink bloom. "This one reminds me of you," he said. "It has your fiery head."

He glanced at Lucy and saw her pallor and widened eyes. She was staring fixedly at the sling. "Whoever killed

Rusty must have come back for me, but he failed. That's a good thing, Lucy, not a reason to worry."

"Unless he was hunting for you all along," she whispered, "and got Rusty by mistake. Oh, Peter, I'm so afraid."

"Don't be. I can take care of myself."

"What does—the detective think?"

"I don't know."

Lucy stared at him, her lips compressed. "That's a lie."

Peter thrust his good right hand into his pocket, turning over his keys with his fingers. He came to a decision. "I think she's always believed the killer was after me, and this has just confirmed her hunch. But I don't agree with her. And I don't want you worrying for no good reason."

Lucy dusted the dirt from her knees. "That sling is as good a reason as any. Be careful, Peter, or I'll never forgive you. Where are you going in that suit?"

"Boston first, then New York. I have to collect my brother's ashes and see a colleague of my father's."

"Gone long?" Her voice was trembling again, and Peter thought he knew why. He hesitated, then placed one hand lightly on her shoulder.

"You'll never know I've been away. How are you feeling, alone in this house? You can move to the farm while I'm gone—Rebecca and Rafe would be some company. Not to mention Ney."

Lucy smiled a watery smile and shook her head. "I'll stay here," she said. "I've got to face things sooner or later." She jumped suddenly and glanced around for her watch. "What time is it? I should change for school."

"Seven-thirty."

"I'll be late. I always am." She reached for her garden shears and snipped off the coppery-pink rose Peter had admired. "Here," she said, "take this with you. Roses are good luck."

Peter breathed in its scent. "You know, this is the one thing the farm still lacks. We should plan a rose garden this winter. What's the name of this?"

Lucy's eyes shifted away, and she shrugged. "I don't know. I got it from a friend." She made for her back door with her characteristic furtiveness, a small animal bolting for protective cover. At the screen she paused and looked at him sharply. "Call when you get back."

"Because you'll never call me," he said to the empty doorway.

PETER PLACED THE rose carefully on the Rover's passenger seat and gingerly threw the car into first with his good hand. He could just manage to steer and shift single-handedly if he did it slowly and had plenty of warning; but he wouldn't mind letting Merry Folger drive the rental car once they got to New York. He glanced down at the rose as he bumped over the ruts of the Chuck Hollow Road and turned the car toward Milestone. It was an extraordinary color, the orange-fuchsia of each petal's tip deepening at the base to a glorious, tropical copper. It smelled of cinnamon and citrus and the deep woodsiness of tea. He had never seen anything like it. Not that he was an expert on roses—his mother had grown them, but as a child, he'd ignored everything that wasn't a ball or a book. He glanced at it again and had a sudden, vivid image of his study at night, with Rachmaninoff playing and the heady scent of this flower drifting in through the screened windows—and made a decision on impulse. Instead of heading for the airport, he turned toward the Rotary and Maplethorne's Nursery.

When the Rover crunched over the gravel and pulled to a stop near the railroad ties that served as markers for the garden center's parking, Buck Maplethorne was in the midst of hauling a hose down an avenue of fall chrysanthemums, set out on trestle tables to brighten the foggy morning. He looked over his shoulder at Peter, gave him a swift grin, and shoved the hose nozzle into the outdoor spigot.

"Peter. You look like Summer People in that getup."

"Blood will out, Buck, blood will out. You can buy land here, but you can't buy history."

Real islanders still called Buck "that fellah from Vermont," although he'd come around the Point, as Nantucketers referred to a permanent move on-island, eighteen years earlier. He glanced at Peter's arm. "What happened?"

"Nicked my biceps."

"Harvesting?"

"Sort of."

"I heard about your brother on the news." Buck attached a spray wand to his hose. "I'm sorry for your loss."

"Thanks. It was a shock."

"They any closer to finding out who did it?"

Peter shook his head. "It's early days, yet."

"Can't remember when there was a murder here. But you didn't come to talk about that. What can I do for you? I'm placing orders this afternoon."

"Could you rent me another beater in time for harvesting Monday?"

"You're wet harvesting with that arm?"

"You'll notice I have two."

"I'll put in the order and call you when the delivery arrives. You can return it, end of next week, and that way you're only paying for five days."

Peter pulled the rose out of the car's interior and handed it to the nurseryman. "What can you tell me about this?"

Buck Maplethorne let out a low whistle. "Now *that's* a beaut," he said. "Where'd you find it?"

"A friend's garden. I was hoping you'd know the name and how to order it."

"I can find anything online," Buck said, "if it's grown in the U.S. Give me a couple of hours."

"You can have several days," Peter told him. "I'll stop by Sunday when I get back."

JOHN FOLGER HAD his coffee mug and his morning copy of the *Inquirer and Mirror* spread out on the scarred oak table in the kitchen. The screen door was open and the morning sounds of the island—birds, distant foghorns, and the whoosh of bicycle tires—filtered into the room. Ralph Waldo, humming over his tomato plants, was just audible.

The chief took a long draft of coffee and grimaced; he had never really acquired the taste for it. He'd given up a lifelong smoking habit three years earlier. Caffeine was a poor substitute.

A loud thump reverberated through the house, and John glanced up at the ceiling. Merry was tossing shoes around again. He snapped a sheet of newsprint irritably between his fingers. John was uneasy about the progress of the Mason case, or lack thereof. But second-guessing Merry's work felt like helicopter parenting, and he was trying to reform.

The thumping made its way down the uncarpeted steps and his daughter swung into the kitchen with her hair gathered in one hand. She was wearing a simple black dress and casting about the kitchen distractedly.

"Lose something?" John asked.

"Laptop," she said. "Hairband. I've got ten minutes to get to the airport, dammit. And can I find my laptop? Can I have a good-hair day? Not a chance."

"Check your car. And safe travels."

"Thanks." She fished a plastic clip out of a drawer full of rubber bands and plastic-bag twizzles, snapped it into her hair, and dashed for the driveway. John heard the Explorer's door jerk open and shut. Two seconds later she was back.

"Not there," she said. "I think I was using it somewhere around here last night."

A slight thrill of self-conscious guilt rose in the pit of John Folger's stomach. He remembered where her laptop was: on his bedside table. He had opened it after she'd gone to bed and read through her case file himself. He took a quick sip of coffee to hide his confusion.

Merry turned at the sound of Ralph Waldo's wheelbarrow, its unoiled wheels complaining and burdened, as he trundled a load of compost toward the tomato bed. "Ralph! Hey, Ralph!" She shot through the screen door.

John Folger hurried up to his bedroom, retrieved the laptop, and sauntered into the kitchen just as Merry reentered the house.

"Dining room table," he said. "Beneath yesterday's paper."

"I must be losing my mind," Merry said. "Thanks. I've got to go."

"Meredith—"

She paused in the open doorway.

"Why are you letting Peter Mason off scot-free?"

"Because he didn't kill his brother. Nobody leaves a body in his own front yard and tells the police he hated the victim's guts."

"Unless he figures the best cover is to look like a knucklehead," John said mildly. "He has no alibi, remember; he's got the motive; and he's definitely got the opportunity."

"Are you suggesting he shot himself Wednesday night?"

"More than one suspect in a murder investigation has pulled the self-inflicted-wound number on a rookie detective."

"It's incompatible with the evidence," Merry said.

"The footprints near the body?"

"How'd you know about the footprints near the body?" Her eyes narrowed and she glanced down at the laptop in her hand. "Oh, Dad, couldn't you just have asked?"

"I should have. I'm sorry."

"You don't trust me, do you?"

"I do. I'm just . . . making sure you're not on the wrong page."

She sighed in exasperation. "The footprints are the clearest indication that Peter Mason didn't kill his brother. Someone else did—and wants us to think that Peter was the intended target."

"I'm not following you," John said.

Merry glanced at her watch. "I'll have to throw on the siren to get to the plane in time. But here's my theory. The prints walk up to Peter's body and stop. Whoever shot him took the time—despite a frantic dog willing to eat its way out of the barn and a housekeeper running to the scene in her nightie—to check whether Peter was dead. A real killer would have noticed he'd simply fainted and would have shot him at point-blank range in the head or chest. This shooter turned and walked away. Then there's the shot itself."

"What about it?"

"Peter told me yesterday that he saw the muzzle flare and instinctively dodged left, trying to get out of the way. If the shooter was aiming at his chest the bullet ought to have hit his right side. But it went into Peter's *left* arm. He dodged *into* the bullet's path."

"So the perp was a lousy shot."

"Maybe."

"But you don't think so."

"I think he—or she—never intended to hit Peter at all. I think the attack was a red herring—to make us think Peter was supposed to die, not his brother. When Peter went down in a dead faint, for one awful moment the gunman thought he'd killed him. So he walked over to see. Then he hightailed it out of there."

John Folger sat back in his seat, mulling it over.

"Do me a favor this morning?"

"Of course," he said.

"Put through a request for a search warrant of Mayling Stern's garage. And then send Clarence over to work on the Mercedes."

"You think you've got enough to charge her?"

"I might, by tonight. And Dad—next time you want a report on my investigation, *ask* to see my notes first, okay? I'm going to passcode my computer."

She was out the screen door before he could answer.

## Chapter 21

"How do you think Flaubert feels about Emma?" Lucy Jacoby asked the room in general. She was pacing slowly back and forth in front of the rows of desks that ran from the front of the advanced sophomore English class to the back, one hand propping up the elbow of the arm that held her copy of *Madame Bovary*.

"I think he feels bad for her," a girl ventured. "I mean, like, she's got such a boring life. It's like she lives *here*."

A wave of self-conscious tittering rippled through the room and a wad of paper, tossed with precision, struck the girl on the back of the neck. She grinned, delighted with the attention. Will raised his hand. Lucy nodded to him, and he felt a slow flush mount in his cheeks as a few hostile eyes turned in his direction.

"I think he hates her," he said.

The room fell silent. "Go on," Lucy said.

"I think he likes watching her sink further and further into her mess, regardless of the stuff she does to distract herself—all the guys, the fantasies of having money and buying things—because he knows she can't escape the way she is. He takes away everything she cares about until she's left with just herself. Which is so terrifying that suicide is the only way out."

"—Of what, Will?"

"Well—out of the loneliness—of living, I guess. Out of knowing that dreams never come true, they're just life's way of screwing you for believing things could be different or better. I think Flaubert hated the fact that people like Emma kid themselves into thinking that certain things matter—the clothes they wear, the things they own—to get through the day. He probably did it himself and knew it was pointless. So he took it out on Emma. He made her pay for being human."

Lucy stared at him as though frozen, her thoughts far away. "Well, that's one view. A lot of scholars would agree with you. Any other thoughts?" She looked around the room at the group of blank faces. "I'd like you to think about the author's perspective for tomorrow and be prepared to discuss it at some length. Consider the fact that Flaubert, like all writers, created his character out of thin air, and he made choices when he chose to depict Emma as he did. He chose to subject her to loss after loss—the particularly brutal ones being those of her own making." She snapped the book shut. There was the sudden sound of chairs scraping the floor as twenty kids shoved themselves away from their desks and made for the door. As his classmates passed him, Will stood up and collected his books into a symmetrical pile, his eyes fixed on them as if they were the only significant thing in his life.

"Will."

Lucy Jacoby was holding out a paperback. *Thirteen Reasons Why*, by Jay Asher.

"You might try this, if you're looking for a good read," she said. "It's kind of a contemporary riff on Emma, but with American kids your age."

Will turned the book over in his hands. It was about a girl's suicide and the friends she left behind. Did his English teacher think he was planning to kill himself? "You want me to write a report on it or something?"

"Just think about it," she said. "That's all."

HE WAS STUDYING the book's back cover as he stood by his locker later that day, figuring out what he needed for the weekend.

"What'd she give you, Starbuck?"

Sandy Stewart, who had been his friend once, before his life had turned so weird.

Will shrugged. "Thing she wants me to read." He started to shove the book into his backpack.

"Can I see it?"

He assessed the situation. Sandy's face wore the closed, wary look he usually adopted with him these days, but it wasn't obviously hostile. He'd left his football buddies somewhere else. None of them had said a word to Will when he'd shown up at practice Wednesday. Coach had liked his sprint times. Will was trying not to think about the game tomorrow, and whether he'd be allowed to play.

"Sure," he said.

Sandy flipped through the pages. His dad was an ex-newspaper reporter from Washington who'd moved his family to the island five years ago to write a novel. When Will first met Sandy in middle school, he usually had his nose in a book. Steampunk, fantasy, World War II survival stories. But that was so uncool now. Will waited for him to say something snarky.

A few scraps of paper fluttered out of the paperback and

fell to the ground. Sandy stooped to pick them up and tucked them carefully back into the book.

"Can I borrow it when you're done?"

"Seriously?"

"Yeah, dude. I'm bored as shit with the stuff we're reading."

"Take it now," Will said.

"K. I'll drop it by your house Sunday. See you at the game tomorrow."

Sandy sauntered off and Will cinched his backpack as though nothing momentous had just happened. But for an instant, a crooked smile flickered over his face.

*Chapter 22*

THE RENTED TOYOTA was British racing green, a color the Japanese never got right, Peter reflected. It felt like a toy after the solid bulk of the Rover, but it took the steep curve of Hamilton Road responsively under Merry's surprisingly aggressive driving. He had relaxed once he realized she was competent, and kept one eye on the windshield and the other on the ragged bank to his right. Lined with old Westchester houses set amid trees and well-tended gardens, The Hill, as it was known, seemed exhausted after a summer of heat and bloom and braced for the onslaught of falling leaves. He had immediately warmed to this town, to its echoes of his Greenwich boyhood and its train whistle piercing the air with scheduled chaos. The conviction that in Chappaqua he would find the key to the past strengthened with every switchback in the road.

He had collected Rusty's ashes from a mortuary in Boston three hours before. Then he and Meredith Folger had caught their second flight of the day, to White Plains. Sky Tate-Jackson had gone straight from Nantucket to New York.

"We need to talk about those letters, Peter," she said now. Somewhere over Rhode Island, while he'd filled her in on his theory about Rusty's insider trading with ME stock, she'd finally dropped the formality of "Mr. Mason."

"I wondered when you'd get around to that."

"The one to Sundance—an unknown—I think we can ignore for the moment. The ones to Sky Tate-Jackson and your sister have me worried."

He said nothing, wincing slightly as the car cornered sharply and his weight shifted onto his left side.

She gave him a quick sidelong glance from under her dark brows. "Am I going to have to draw you out in my celebrated fashion?"

"It would seem Sky stepped over the boundary of the law. I'm counting on your celebrated fashion to discover exactly how this afternoon. Rusty seemed to think it was capable of ending his career. I'll bet it involved helping Rusty on his way out of the country—but who knows?"

So they'd leave George aside for the moment. That was okay. She had all afternoon. "That'd be around the time of the indictment. Sky was where ten years ago?"

"Clerking for an appellate court judge."

"Guy can get disbarred just for withholding evidence," Merry said conversationally.

"I didn't know that."

"Betcha Sky does."


MALCOLM SCOTT LIVED just at the apex of The Hill where the road circled and dove back down to the train tracks below. Built in an era when ostentation was considered in poor taste, the house, although huge, had been cast as a modest country cottage with peasant shutters and used brick. When Merry and Peter drove into the gravel drive, an aged golden retriever struggled to its feet and woofed woollily in its throat.

The sound summoned Scott to the apple-green front door. Peter waved to him as they pulled to a halt, struck immediately by the change in the man's appearance. He stood upright and alone by the lintel, but his once-powerful frame had shrunk, and the sharp-featured head with its flowing mane of hair was withered and frail.

"Had lunch?" he asked testily, by way of greeting.

"Unfortunately, yes." Peter had last seen Scott at Max's funeral, when he had just hit seventy; he must be eighty now. "This is Detective Meredith Folger of the Nantucket police," he added, as he shook the man's hand. "It's good to see you, Mr. Scott. It's been some time."

"You've grown up. I've grown old." Scott opened the screen door.

Peter motioned Merry ahead of him. She hesitated just inside the doorway, relishing the cool dimness that immediately descended on her sun-struck eyes. The hall smelled vaguely of mothballs and cleanliness. She peered up into second-story rafters, feeling Peter's height blocking the light behind her.

"In here," Scott said. The testiness was habitual rather than personal, Merry decided. Scott had moved into a small sitting room, done in yellow-flowered chintz, with wide windows that caught the afternoon sunlight. A woman in a bright orange skirt and a broad straw sun hat stood in the garden. There was a paintbrush in her hand and an easel set up nearby. Merry saw a sharp flash of her late mother.

"Betty," Scott said, waving vaguely toward his wife. "Sit down."

Merry settled herself on a couch with her back to the view of Betty Scott and her roses, while Peter took a wing chair facing Malcolm, who sat rigidly at his desk. He had a closed manila file in front of him, and he adjusted the edges restlessly with his thumb and forefinger as he peered at Peter.

"You've turned out a fine boy," he said. "It's been a while."

"Yes, it has."

"You must take after Julia."

"Her father, actually."

"Isn't Max, that's for sure."

"I'm supposed to have some of his expressions."

"Haven't seen any yet."

"You'd probably have to make me angry."

"Well, I might, at that. Not like your brother. Now, he was the *image* of Maxwell Mason," Scott said, turning his fierce gaze on Merry. "Didn't wait for somebody else to make him angry, either. Had the temper of a bull in rut."

Merry pulled out her laptop and opened it. "Rusty, however, is dead, Mr. Scott," she said. "His temper—or something else—got him killed."

"Not surprising." Scott leaned back in his chair. "That boy lived too long."

"Maybe." Merry looked at him severely over her frames. "But I imagine dying isn't easy at any age."

"I'm finding it difficult to do myself, and you'd think with eight decades of practice I'd have a little more grace. Doctors say I've got a few months yet to learn."

He opened the manila folder and raised a pair of gold-rimmed spectacles to his nose. He peered at a document carefully, as though seeing it for the first time, and lifted it closer to his face. Then his eyes shifted back to Peter. "You're here to find out why your father gave up on living, aren't you? Your brother's just a side issue."

Peter considered the old man's words. "That could be true. I've got a gut feeling that whatever happened between the two of them ten years ago ended on my farm this week. That may seem crazy—"

"Seems like common sense. Your brother left town with his business at loose ends; he came back, and some loose ends snared him."

"You know why he was here?" Merry broke in.

"Haven't the foggiest. Nosir."

Merry's hands hovered over her keyboard. "We had hoped you could tell us about the family rift before Mr. Max Mason's death," she said.

"Now, let's see, that would be—oh, close to ten years ago now, wouldn't it?" He shifted the papers in the folder as though Max's death certificate were among them. "How far back in family history do you want me to go? I knew Max Mason thirty-five years."

"As you know, Mr. Scott, my father died a month after disowning my brother," Peter said. "A grand jury investigated Rusty for securities fraud, but because of his status as a fugitive from US law—he'd gone to Brazil, and they're notoriously unresponsive to extradition requests—the indictment was sealed. My father never told us why he broke with my brother, and we never knew exactly what he had done. But when Rusty turned up dead a few days ago, I started to wonder if the past might not have something to do with it."

"Why?" Scott asked.

"Because of the things Rusty brought with him," Merry

said. "Letters, a photograph, all of them references to the past. It was very much alive for him; we think it's possible he wanted to reawaken it in a certain group of people. That may be why he was killed."

"If someone wants the past to remain dead," Peter said, "you may know why. You were intimately involved in my father's business. Was it insider trading?"

"For starters," Scott replied.

"In the stock of a company my father intended to acquire?"

"If you know all about it, why are you here?"

"That's the extent of my knowledge, Mr. Scott, and to be frank, it's all speculation on my part."

"What else have you guessed?"

"That a brush with insider trading wouldn't be enough for Max to cut off his son."

"Go on."

Peter focused on the line where the white ceiling met a butter-yellow wall. "If I think like Rusty, then making money isn't the point. I go for the bigger prize: power over Max, whom I've loved and hated and striven to beat for most of my life."

"You've got that right."

"I take my knowledge of Max's plans—the time, the target, the extent of debt-to-asset leverage—to someone else. A White Knight." He looked at Merry.

"One of Max's competitors?" she asked.

"Yes. A White Knight can step in with a higher offering price per share than the initial acquirer of a target company—in this case, Mason Enterprises—and foil the takeover attempt."

"And if Rusty had bought a bunch of the target

company's stock before your father's takeover bid, he'd ultimately get a higher price for it from the competitor," Merry suggested.

"Right. Rusty probably laughed all the way to the bank. Until the feds showed up."

Malcolm Scott gave vent to a high cackle and slapped the file on his desk. "Ten years," he said. "Ten years I've been waiting for one of you idiots to ask me about it. It's all right here." He opened the manila folder. "Max's target was Ultracom, an aerospace firm that was developing unmanned aerial vehicles for combat."

"Drones," Peter said.

"He was leveraging everything he'd got," Scott continued, "banking on the idea that public distaste for the Iraq war would spur the military to risk machines instead of men. He was right, of course. He'd have made a fortune."

"Enter Rusty," Merry said. "Do you know where he got his inside information?"

Malcolm Scott leaned back in his chair and dropped heavy lids over the furious blue eyes. "Max didn't tell him, that's for sure. At the time, Max didn't even tell me."

"But we can assume Rusty's information was good?" Peter said.

"Good enough to screw matters up royally. That brother of yours was the devil's own. I say that knowing full well he was Max's son. Ever hear of Mitch Hazlitt?"

Peter shook his head. He glanced at Merry.

"The corporate raider," she said. "He's doing time in some minimum-security country club upstate." Reading through the case-law database had paid off.

Scott nodded. "Rusty chose Hazlitt to take on Max. Only Hazlitt had an even better idea. He decided to skip Ultracom and go after Mason Enterprises. Max would be at his most vulnerable, because his liquidity would be sunk in Ultracom. He wouldn't have the resources to fight Hazlitt off."

"And suddenly, Rusty was in way over his head," Merry said slowly.

"If he'd been a little older or wiser, he'd have seen it coming. You give a shark your finger, and he'll take your arm. He'd handed his father to Mitch Hazlitt, something I doubt even *he* intended to do."

"Knowing Rusty, he'd try to ride it out somehow, anyhow," Peter said.

"Don't think he had any other option, myself. Other than looking the fool in front of your dad. Probably Hazlitt anticipated that. He made Rusty an offer he couldn't refuse."

"Meaning?"

Malcolm Scott looked through the bay window, beyond his wife painting in the garden, at something that had died long ago.

"If Hazlitt succeeded—and he would have—Rusty was to have Max's job."

Peter whistled—a low, bated breath. *The thing Max couldn't forgive. The reason Rusty ran.*

Scott was still talking. "Not that your brother would have survived very long. The Hazlitts of this world eat the Rusty Masons alive."

There was a small silence. "To my father, Mason Enterprises was a sacred family stewardship," Peter said. "It was the core of his identity. He would have fought to the death to keep it."

"So what happened?" Merry asked.

For once, Malcolm Scott was silent.

"Max discovered what Rusty intended, called off the Ultracom takeover, informed the SEC that inside information had been traded, and disowned his son," Peter ventured.

"How'd Max find out?" Merry persisted.

Scott's fierce gaze faltered. "I couldn't say, Detective, any more than I can tell you how Rusty got the information in the first place. But I know the day it happened. December seventeenth. Max called me into his office and sat me down. I was the one dealing with Salomon's corporate finance side, leveraging Mason Enterprises beyond anything I thought possible, and I was the one who'd have to explain to them that the whole venture was called off. Max had that look of his—like he'd swallowed a frying pan hot off the fire—and he was dead quiet." Malcolm shot a blue glance at Peter. "Your father had a habit of holding in his rage, as no doubt you know. Made it all the more terrifying."

"You're right."

"He saved ME. But everything we'd planned, the months of work, went in the wastebasket."

"Rusty went to Brazil—" Merry said.

"My father went to Greenwich for Christmas," Peter added. "The SEC launched an investigation into Rusty's activities—"

"—and a month later, I went to Max Mason's funeral," Scott concluded. "I have never felt so heavy-hearted and lost in my life as I did on that day. Nosir."

The September sunlight faded early, and in the space of their conversation Betty Scott's easel had moved into shadow. Peter drifted over to the window in the silence that followed Scott's final comment. Betty was painting her roses. Her carriage was erect, and her grace, like the house's, was built into the bone. As he watched, she reached for a copper-pink bud and touched it to her nose; the color glowed on her porcelain skin like sunlight on clear water. Betty must have felt his eyes upon her, because she waved at the window, with a smile meant for Malcolm that included him in its compass.

He felt a twinge of loneliness. These two had grown old together through the decades, in the certainty that their last years would be spent on these lawns, under the spreading trees and the lengthening shadows. And he had no one.

"That's the hardest thing about learning to die," Scott said, and his voice cracked. He had left the desk and was standing at Peter's right elbow. "I don't know what will become of her after I'm gone." Abruptly, he abandoned them for the front hall.

"I guess we're done." Merry flipped closed her laptop.

At the front door, she offered her hand to Malcolm Scott. "Thank you for being so forthright. I'll let you know what I learn about Rusty's death."

"And my apologies for taking so many years to ask," Peter said.

Scott's face wore a listening expression, but it wasn't for them. There was the sudden sound of many wheels rolling on iron, and an instant later, a train's plaintive blast rent the twilight air. Scott smiled the delighted smile of the very young.

"The evening train. I listen for it, any time of day. Can't get to sleep the first week we're in Florida, I'm so used to waiting for the whistle. Used to take the New

Haven line into Manhattan in my foolish Yale youth, went to the debutante balls. Met Betty at one of those things, matter of fact."

He took Merry's elbow and shook it gently. "Walked down to that train every morning for forty-five years until I didn't have to anymore. First day of the rest of my life, I walked down anyway. Bought a paper from Reggie, the station newsboy, and watched the rest of 'em getting off to Gotham. Hah! Newsboy. He's seventy if he's a day."

He started to push open the screen door for them and then stopped. "You said you found some pictures and letters in Rusty's things," he said. "What'd they say?"

Merry hesitated an instant. "I'd like to talk to the people who received them before I discuss them," she said.

"Blackmail, huh?" Scott said, an edge of satisfaction in his voice. "Figures. He knew how to turn a trick, that boy."

Merry reached into her briefcase and pulled out the photograph that had washed up on the beach. "There's no reason you can't see this," she said.

Malcolm Scott took the snapshot in a hand that shook slightly with age, and adjusted his spectacles. Then a curiously set expression came across his drawn features. He thrust the photograph back at Merry without a word.

"Any idea who she is, sir?"

"None at all," Scott said. "It's time you were going."

MERRY SIGHED AS she steered the Toyota toward Manhattan and Sky Tate-Jackson. "My mother was painting a portrait of Billy when she killed herself. It's still on her easel, in the middle of our hallway, unfinished. No one seems to know what to do with it. So we leave it there, like a postcard from the grave." She looked over her shoulder and waved at Malcolm Scott. "He's a canny old bastard."

"He told us everything he knew."

"You don't really believe that."

"Don't you?"

"The most important thing is missing—the name of the person who told Rusty about Max's merger plans, and the one who told Max that Rusty was doing him dirty behind his back."

"The source," Peter said. "My father would have punished that kind of betrayal. You think Malcolm Scott is protecting him?"

"Could be. You can check my notes, but I believe his exact words were that he *couldn't* tell us, not that he didn't actually know."

Peter looked at her soberly. "Whoever it is has a hell of a motive for murder."

## Chapter 23

NIGHT WAS FALLING over New York City, and pin-points of light sprang into life behind a thousand office windows. The lawyers and the bankers and the raiders and their secretaries were getting their second wind before plunging on into the evening hours; in their minds, the day was still young. Peter had told Merry he'd never taken a train out of the city before midnight without seeing an endless tide of workers borne late into suburban homes. There was no meaning to rush hour in this place. Sky understood that, and lived by the same code. He would still be at his firm this evening.

They were sitting in the trim, modern, graphite-colored chairs that Mayling probably had chosen for Sky's office. Peter was familiar enough with the place to enter it unannounced. Merry could barely make out his features: they hadn't bothered to turn on the lights. Merry saw a city skyline too rarely to miss this dazzling Manhattan view.

"Peter." Sky shut his office door firmly and crossed the room with his lanky stride. He was admirably in command of himself. Perhaps, Merry thought, he's known that he must face this sooner or later.

"I've brought Detective Folger with me."

Merry rose and straightened her skirt, impossibly wrinkled after the long day of travel. Sky Tate-Jackson took her hand in his—a light, dry shake. He was like a character actor from a BBC production, she thought: fine features and height held together by good manners.

"You've seen Malcolm Scott?" He threw his suit jacket over the back of his desk chair and stood by the floor-to-ceiling glass that served as both wall and window, his hands in his pockets, surveying the city fifty-eight floors below. He had not bothered to turn on a light either.

"We have." Merry reached into her briefcase and withdrew a piece of paper. "I'd appreciate it if you'd look this over, Mr. Tate-Jackson."

"What is it?"

"A letter from Rusty Mason. The one he probably sent you sometime last week."

"Did Mayling give it to you?"

"So he *did* send it," Peter broke in. "I'll be damned. When I told you he'd been killed, you let me think that you didn't know he was coming to the island."

Sky ignored Merry's outstretched hand. She dropped the paper on his desk.

"No, Mayling didn't give it to me," she said. "Actually, this one's a copy. It was found when Rusty's things washed up on Siasconset beach, a few hundred feet from your door."

"It's like him to make a copy," Sky said bitterly. "But you're wrong about the timing. I didn't read that letter until the morning after he died."

"Labor Day."

"I flew up to Nantucket on Sunday evening, if you

remember. I didn't bother to look at my few pieces of mail until the next day."

"That's a little hard to believe."

"The truth sometimes is. Especially where Rusty's concerned."

"It's far easier, for instance," Merry said, "to envision you receiving this letter in New York instead of on the island, flying back to Nantucket to meet—and kill—him, then putting on a good face the next day when Peter found you fishing for blues in the fog. I have to take that scenario seriously."

"I'm sure you do," Sky said. He jingled some loose change in one pocket, then turned to face them. "I certainly wasn't going to mention the letter's existence once I knew he was dead. On advice of my own counsel, I pled the Fifth."

"What did he have on you, Sky?" Peter asked.

"What did Rusty have on anybody? Our collective stupidity, the fact that we were naive enough to care about someone who cared only about himself."

"I assume it was your life at stake," Merry said, "or at least, life as you know it."

"That's a good start." He laughed. "Christ, it was brilliant. If you've met with Scott, you know what Rusty did. Or attempted to do. He shot the moon and got himself fucked."

"Do you know where he got his inside information?" Merry asked.

"He had some sort of source within ME, that's all I know." Sky paused. "It wouldn't surprise me if it was Scott himself. I've wondered for years if Malcolm got antsy in his old age and used Rusty to move against Max. It wouldn't be the first time in corporate history."

"I don't think so," Peter said. "Not after talking to Scott. He's sick and he hasn't much time left. I think he'd have told us if he had something that serious to get off his chest."

"Whoever it was panicked when Hazlitt got involved. The source went to Max with the story. Max scrapped his takeover plans. No surprise. But it left your brother with nowhere to hide. That's when he came to me."

They waited. After a moment, Sky went on, his words coming more slowly now.

"I was clerking on the First Circuit. He showed up in Boston in the middle of the night, without a coat, in the middle of a snowstorm, looking crazed. He'd gotten himself in too deep. Hazlitt had 'lent' him the funds to buy a huge block of stock—"

"ME stock?" Peter broke in.

Sky shook his head. "The target of the takeover. I've forgotten the name."

"Ultracom," Merry said.

"A takeover bid drives up the price of the target company's stock, as you know. It usually drives down the stock of the raider company—in this case, ME. Rusty bought his block before Max published his offer to Ultracom stockholders, and waited for the price per share to rise. He knew that when Hazlitt challenged Max's offer, the stock would soar even higher. He figured he'd sell his block a few days later, at a huge profit, and repay Hazlitt's 'loan.'"

"But then Hazlitt went after ME and Max pulled out of the bid," Merry said. "The Ultracom stock must have plummeted. No profit for Rusty, no payment for Hazlitt. I wonder if the creep called in the loan."

"Why do you think he made it in the first place?"

"Sorry?"

"*The loan,*" Sky said impatiently. "Hazlitt gave Rusty that money for leverage. He wanted a way to get Rusty's stock."

"His ME stock," Peter said, comprehension dawning.

"Exactly. The seven percent of voting shares held by each of Max's children. Max had—what, thirty percent?—and he voted your shares with his own until you reached the age of twenty-five. Is that right?"

Peter nodded. "We inherited the stock from my grandmother, split three ways. A trust. I never thought about it until Max died."

"So Max controlled fifty-one percent of the stock, with the rest held publicly. Even if Hazlitt was able to buy up the other forty-nine percent, he needed part of Max's voting power. Otherwise the whole gamble was for naught."

"He needed Rusty's part," Merry said.

"Rusty turned twenty-five that year." Peter was thinking out loud. "Hazlitt gets him in debt, and then forces him to sell his shares."

"Rusty refused, apparently," Sky said.

"You're kidding."

"It was the only bargaining chip he had. He told Hazlitt he'd vote with him in return for Max's job."

"Jesus." Peter's voice held shock. "There wouldn't have been a job. Hazlitt would have cut the company into bits and sold off the pieces."

"None of that really mattered anyway," Sky said. "The stock, the debt—they were the least of Rusty's problems."

"Max discovered he'd leaked the takeover information to Hazlitt," Merry said smoothly.

"And turned his son in," Sky concluded. "Rusty came to me for advice. As if an appellate clerk could help him."

"You told him to leave the country?" Merry asked.

"I told him if Hazlitt didn't get him, the SEC would. I told him to make a clean breast of it and take the consequences. I remember what he said to me: 'I'll be damned if I graduated from Princeton to rot in a federal jail. I'll die first.'"

"And so he did," Peter murmured. "On my doorstep."

"A lot of twenty-five-year-olds have been made idiots by a love of money and power," Sky said. "But none so completely as your brother."

*That horrible year*, Merry thought. *The year Peter lost Alison. And his brother. And finally, Max. He must have lost a bit of himself as well.*

"Why didn't Rusty come to me then, Sky?" Peter said.

"I should think that was obvious. Because he'd failed."

THE ROOM WAS now wholly dark, the floor checkered with bars of reflected light from the office windows opposite and the glow of Merry's computer. They had all fallen silent—Sky seemed lost in thought; Merry watchful; Peter oppressed by the weight of old disaster. The wind whined around the building's height. Sky switched on a black metal desk lamp, flooding the lacquered wood with a disk of light.

"He called when he got to Rio," he said. "I'd email once in a while, although less and less frequently as the years passed. He never answered me—I think he was afraid of cyber traces. It wasn't until about two years ago that he started to rehash the past. Some business deals hadn't worked out as he'd planned, and the tone of his letters changed; he seemed to have grown bitter. I don't know. Maybe he realized this exile was endless."

Merry glanced at Peter and mouthed the word "AIDS." Peter nodded.

"He wrote and asked what the statute of limitations was for prosecuting insider trading, and God help me, I told him the truth," Sky said. "I told him that when the subject flees the country, and a sealed indictment is handed down by a grand jury, there is no limit on the duration of liability. He'd be picked up at any border the minute he tried to reenter the US."

"You wanted him to stay away, didn't you, Mr. Tate-Jackson?" Merry said.

"Didn't everybody?"

She ignored him and went on. "Because whether he was picked up or not, he was dangerous. He knew you'd lied to the SEC investigators who pursued the case, and then to a grand jury. You told no one what Rusty had done or where he was living. Withholding information from federal officials is not only a punishable offense; if you're a lawyer, it's grounds for disbarment."

"I don't know why he had to ruin my life, too," Sky said quietly. "I'd tried to help him. It isn't fair, dammit. It isn't fair."

"No, it's not," Peter said. "For what it's worth, Sky, I'm sorry."

"Do you believe me when I say I didn't kill him?"

"I find it hard to believe that anyone I know killed Rusty. But Detective Folger doesn't have that problem. And her mind is turning over a lot of facts about you and Mayling."

"Mayling?" Sky was startled, and, Merry thought,

really afraid for the first time. "She's got nothing to do with this."

"How did she damage the front end of her Mercedes, Mr. Tate-Jackson?" Merry asked. "There's no accident report. She told me she picked you up at the airport around eight—but the attendant at Cape Air says you waited for almost an hour, then took a taxi. Is that right?"

Sky's face had frozen.

Merry and Peter waited.

"Okay, *yes*, she damaged the car that night," he muttered furiously. "The night Rusty died. I have no idea how it happened."

"You weren't in the car, then."

"No. No—as you said, Mayling was supposed to meet me the airport. I'd texted her my ETA, which was a few minutes after eight o'clock, and when she hadn't shown by eight forty-five, I called a taxi. I got to the house—it's only about a seven-minute drive—and neither she nor the car was there. I figured she'd somehow missed the message and had gone into town for dinner with friends. But when she came back at midnight, she was incoherent."

His voice faltered, and he looked down at his clenched hands. "I don't know how to explain this—she's been having something like blackouts for some time, now. She functions normally, but she doesn't remember where she's been, who she's met, or what she's done."

"Drinking?" Merry asked.

"I don't think so. We ran her through a series of tests in the spring. The doctors were looking for a brain tumor. They've decided it's stress." He laughed hollowly. "*Stress.* She's been on the island doodling in the sun for three months now.

"That night, she couldn't tell me what she'd been doing or where she'd gone—she just fell into bed. The next morning, when I'd seen the damage and asked her about it, she couldn't remember a thing. She said vaguely she'd probably hit a deer. Labor Day weekend, with no warning, and Rusty dead on the road. I don't know what to think, I really don't."

Merry hesitated. She had bided her time to confront Mayling Stern with the evidence she was slowly, inexorably gathering. She had deliberately withheld her knowledge of the damaged car, so carefully hidden in the garage. By probing Sky, she could be sending his companion to New York on the next plane, and from there, anywhere on the globe. It was a risk she'd have to take.

"If she thought Rusty could destroy your life, would Mayling try to protect you, Mr. Tate-Jackson?"

"But she didn't know he was blackmailing me!"

"Are you sure?" Peter countered. "When I went to your house to tell you about Rusty, I walked in on Mayling reading a letter. She was so surprised she dropped the pages, and when I tried to help her gather them up, she lashed out at me pretty viciously."

Merry shot a look at Peter. He hadn't told her this.

"A letter?" Sky repeated. "But even if it were *the* letter, Rusty was already dead."

"Maybe she was rereading it," Merry said. "Before putting it back."

"Reassuring herself that she'd done the right thing in running him over—is that what you're saying?"

"People do strange things out of guilt."

Sky gave a short bark of laughter, derisive and angry. "Listen, for the last time: *I read Rusty's letter the day after he died, and I'll swear it had never been opened.*"

"You'd say that in order to protect yourself—or May-ling," Merry said. "Do you have any proof? The envelope with its postmark, for instance?"

Sky shook his head. "You'll have to take my word. But that seems to be something no one does anymore."

"As a police officer on a murder investigation, Mr. Tate-Jackson, I have to weigh abstractions like honor and trust—a man's word—against the instinct to protect yourself or someone you love." *Or frame your girlfriend by borrowing her car and sweater to murder somebody*, Merry added mentally. Everything Sky Tate-Jackson had told her could be a complete crock.

"How much of this will have to come out?" he asked. "About my—career, I mean?"

Merry shrugged. "Rusty's dead. The sealed indictment is pointless, now. I'm guessing you're safe from further prosecution and disbarment—unless, of course, you killed him to avoid just those things."

"I didn't." Sky sighed. "I can face whatever I have to face. But I don't want Mayling hurt."

"Make sure she doesn't skip town, okay?"

He hesitated, and Merry felt her hackles rise. She wished he was still on-island, under the casual surveillance of the extended Strangerfield clan.

"Okay," he conceded. "I'll call Mayling tonight and explain the situation. She wants to get back here to work, but I'm heading to Nantucket after Rusty's funeral tomorrow, anyway."

"Good."

Some of the tension seemed to leave Sky's body, as though they had reached an understanding. "What do you plan to do next?"

"Keep hunting. I should tell you we're taking out a warrant to get access to Mayling's car."

"I suppose it was inevitable." He was resigned but annoyed. "Don't you think you've overlooked something, however?"

"What?" Merry held his gaze.

"The source. Whoever gave Rusty his information about Max's merger. It seems to me the source had the most to lose."

She glanced at Peter. "We've been thinking that, too. The source sold out Max, then sold out Rusty in turn. It must have cost him something."

"Maybe everything."

"The question is—would that still be a motive for murder ten years later?" Peter said.

"Depends who the source is," Sky replied.

"He's a needle in a haystack," Merry objected. "Even Malcolm Scott couldn't give us a name." No need to tell a suspect like Sky that she thought Scott knew more than he'd shared.

"There's one person who might help you." Sky avoided Peter's eyes, but Merry realized he was speaking to him. "Alison. She was living with Rusty at the time."

"Keep her out of this," Peter said softly.

"She should be told he's dead, don't you think?"

"She watches the news."

"You're afraid to see her, aren't you, Peter?"

"Yes."

"Then the detective needs to take the decision out of your hands." Sky's face was flushed and defiant. He was trading Alison for Mayling.

"I don't even know where she is," Peter attempted.

"The Princeton Alumni Office does," Sky said harshly. "I've already contacted them."

"You had no right." Peter's voice was almost inaudible.

"I had every right. What else could I do—wait for you and the police to see that my alibi is threadbare, my motives excellent, and my opportunity perfect? My job is damage control. If there's a chance Alison can save me—or Mayling, for God's sake—"

"You're right," Peter said with effort. "Send me Alison's email address. I'll start there."

He rose from his chair and Merry followed. She held out her hand to Sky Tate-Jackson.

He was too well-bred not to shake it.

PETER DROPPED HER at LaGuardia in time for the last shuttle to Boston.

"I hope the funeral goes—well. Or well enough. You know what I mean." She slid out of the rental car.

"Merry—"

"Yes?"

"Thanks for coming along. There's no easy way to tell a friend he's suspected of murder."

"It's even harder to tell your sister," she said carefully, but he saw the steel in her green eyes. "You've got to confront her with that letter, Peter. And her husband. Sure you don't want me around?"

*Chapter 24*

WILL WADED THROUGH water above his knees, the beater whirring merrily in front of him. He was completely happy. He had biked over to the farm after football practice, thrown on a pair of waterproof overalls, and plunged into the midst of the harvesting team Rafe had organized in Peter's absence. The flooded fields, stripped of their bobbing red berries, glistened under the setting sun.

"Will!" Rafe shouted from the flatbed truck. "Wrap it up, okay? You can come back another day."

Will waved in his direction and steered the beater toward the end of the row. Tomorrow was his first game, but he could probably come here early Sunday. A shadow passed over his mind as he remembered the last time he'd been to the farm in the early morning, but he shook it off. He was getting better at avoiding mental darkness. There had been a time when he could not fight it, and that had terrified him.

He cut the beater's motor and hauled it up onto the dry bank behind him, then shook himself like a wet puppy and grinned as he caught Rafe in the shower of drops. He yanked off his overalls, which smelled not unpleasantly of dampness, earth, and mold, and looked around. "Where's Ney?"

"Gone home," Rafe said. He was paying out the hired harvesters' wages in crisp bills, snapping each one to be certain they didn't stick to each other, and his lips moved soundlessly as he counted. "Knows it's suppertime, and Rebecca's dropping food left and right. Dog's as good as a vacuum cleaner."

"She drops stuff on purpose."

Rafe handed the last man his wad and clapped him on the back. "Probably right. School okay today? Got your homework?"

"I have two days to do it."

"Don't leave your backpack here."

"It's with my bike. Don't worry. I'm not totally clueless," Will said. He gathered up his gear and sauntered toward the house, pulling his beater in tow.

The foreman's eyes followed him speculatively. Whether it was the prospect of two free days at home, or better yet, football, Will looked happier tonight than he had in months. Rafe felt a curious thankfulness, as though a burden had lifted from his shoulders.

He turned the truck's ignition and drove off toward the barn.

WILL'S BACKPACK, HEAVY with books, pulled at his shoulders as he pedaled home. His young body shook off the strain of guiding the heavy beater through the bog more readily than those of the hired crew, worn out by years of hard labor, and he was still naive enough to find the ache of well-used muscles pleasant. He would sleep soundly tonight. He whistled slightly under his breath as the bike cut through the rough path that led across the moors to the Milestone Road; he was coming up on the radar tower and Altar Rock. Already in mid-September the days were shorter and the color faded early from the six-o'clock landscape; the twisting path was obscured by a gray light that turned the brilliance of the fall flowers to a mottled dimness. His eyes narrowed as he peered ahead.

He stood up on his pedals and leaned forward over the handlebars, hastening the bike toward town. His fall, when it came, was that much harder.

The bike shuddered violently as its throat met the taut wire stretched across the path, flipped over, and fired Will like a projectile fifteen feet through the air. The weight of the backpack pulled his upper body mercilessly to the ground as he fell. The back of his skull glanced off a rock, and he rolled over, his brain screaming in panic even as the darkness descended. He came to rest on his back.

A covey of bobwhite rose into the evening sky, leaving a listening stillness behind them. The front wheel of the bike spun merrily, uselessly, in the air.

## Chapter 25

"IT'S ABOUT TIME, Detective," Rafe said, spitting the words through clenched teeth. He stood like a commando next to Will's bike, legs spread and braced, arms folded over his powerful chest. The darkness was absolute out here on the moors at eleven o'clock at night, and a light rain was falling. Rafe was soaked. His dark hair was plastered to his scalp beneath his Red Sox cap.

Merry had a headache. She'd missed most of her meals between planes and rental cars. The pit in her stomach deepened when Howie Seitz met her at the airport with the news of Will's accident. His second bit of information—that Clarence's divers had found a rented Jeep at the bottom of Gibbs Pond—buoyed her momentarily. The implications ran through her head all the way out to Mason Farms.

Gibbs Pond sat between Peter Mason's cranberry bog and the cooperative on Nantucket Conservation Foundation land; it was the main source of water for both. Whoever had knocked Rusty over with the Jeep had simply disposed of it in the most likely spot. But why, an insistent interior voice asked her, hadn't the murderer left Rusty's body inside the Jeep when it went into the pond? Why leave the body at the scene of the crime?

*Because he wanted Rusty to be found*, Merry thought.

She forced herself to consider the worst. Whoever had thought of the pond knew the island and the immediate neighborhood well. Peter Mason was obvious, but as nobody had known Rusty was on-island, he would probably have left his brother's body in the car when he sank it. But perhaps he'd had doubts. Rusty had rented the Jeep from an airport kiosk, after all. He'd been seen. Peter might have panicked, disposed of the murder weapon, and left his brother to lie like a vagrant in the bog.

Her headache had begun at that moment.

Now she slammed the Explorer's door and looked at Rafe. Merry knew this mood. He was furious and hurt. He'd failed to protect Tess's son, a boy he'd begun to think of as his own. "I'm sorry, Rafe," she said. "Will didn't deserve this."

"Folks never get what they deserve, Merr. Good or bad."

She still wore her dress under the slicker she always kept in the car. She walked over to the bike, stumbling as her thin heels sank into the wet sand, and bent down to beam her flashlight on the throat of the handlebars. A faint mark of bruised paint, nothing more, and some lingering patches of torn grass from the impact with the heath. The rain on her head was chill. She thrust her hair behind her ears, pulled up the hood of her slicker, and played the beam around the trampled bit of earth.

The rain hadn't helped. The once-dusty path through the moors was a morass of wet sand and mud. Will had been taken away by the rescue squad; tire tracks and the movements of men lifting his body had obscured any other tracks that might have remained. She closed her eyes for an instant, willing the pounding in her temples to stop.

"I wish I'd gotten here earlier," she said.

"Nate Coffin answered the call. He got somebody from your crime scene division, and they worked over the whole place pretty good."

"Peter is in Greenwich if you want to reach him. The funeral's tomorrow."

"I know Pete's schedule better'n my own," Rafe said. "I'll call him as soon as you're done with this. Did you find anything in New York?" He couldn't keep the bitterness from his voice.

"Meaning, if I'd been around today, Will might not be in Cottage Hospital?"

"I just wonder if you know what you're doing, Merry. I'm starting to think I'll be the next one on a stretcher, and I don't like that one bit."

She turned the flashlight beam on his face. "Stop it, Rafe. I couldn't have saved Will. Neither could you. So quit blaming yourself and blaming me."

She shifted the beam to the ground, searching for the stakes Clarence had told her were there. The first one sprang up suddenly, like a hidden watcher, in the darkness at the side of the trail. She walked over to it and crouched as low as her narrow skirt would permit, shining the light on its base. The weathered wood suggested the stake had stood in the field for some time, but the earth around it was only recently disturbed. A smart move on the killer's part—a new stake might have caught too many eyes. The force of the bike's impact against the wire had thrust the stake forward, but it had held. She searched for its mate on the opposite side of the trail and inspected it. Then the line, taut and gleaming and deadly in the flashlight's beam. Ordinary, lead-colored wire, strong yet light, available in any hardware store.

She stood up and snapped off the light. "So much for that," she said. "Guess I've got to face Tess now."

"I think you should leave Tess for tonight," Rafe said, walking toward Merry. "She can't tell you anything about this business, and all she'll want is to be alone with Will."

"I wish it weren't my job to show up at hospitals and accident scenes. I'm always the last person anyone wants to see. That's why I have to be paid to do this."

"I know you don't do it for the money, Merr," Rafe said awkwardly. "And I'm sorry I've been such a dick." He pulled her toward him in a rough embrace.

She had to shut her eyes against the shock of it, thrilling through her body. His strength, the way his arms seemed to fit around her, the good smells of rain-wet skin and flannel shirt.

"You love him very much, don't you?" she whispered.

"I love 'em both. It's killing me to see Tess like this, and not be able to help. She's everything to me, Merry."

"I know," she said. And heard a door close somewhere in her mind.


GEORGE'S ARM TIGHTENED around Peter's waist as the *Seventh Wave* motored toward the channel beyond the Indian Harbor Yacht Club. Behind them, the club's officers stood at attention on the dock in their dress uniforms. Rusty Mason, an acknowledged master of wind and water, had embarked on his final voyage. Indian Harbor was speeding him to his rest. As the Mason boat slid past the vessels of friends and former crew members, their flags dipped to half-mast in silent farewell. At the channel buoy, the deep boom of the first cannon fired from the shore reverberated across the water.

Long Island Sound was a flat, oily gray this Saturday afternoon; it fit the mood of the Masons and Whitneys scattered around the deck. Hale was at the wheel, his eyes on the darkening horizon, his eldest son, Maxie, at his elbow. Little Casey, almost consumed by the bulk of her life preserver, sat primly swinging her legs in the cockpit. Near her stood Sky Tate-Jackson and Dr. Pritchett, the yacht club chaplain, who had agreed to officiate over the burial—more as a favor to George and the Whitneys than from any remembered love for Rusty. He was an avid sailor himself and had lost some hotly contested races to Rusty's skill; had Rusty been less obviously exultant in his victory, Dr. Pritchett might have viewed him more kindly.

Julia Mason was below deck. Peter imagined her sitting there, ramrod-straight and icy in her composure, a deep furrow of displeasure etched into her brow. That line of unhappiness had probably greeted him at his birth, he thought; it had accompanied his mother through life, that much was certain, growing deeper with age, regardless of whether she witnessed her daughter's marriage or her husband's death. Josh and Abi Whitney, George's twins, sat opposite their grandmother, waiting for her to notice them. Presently they would grow bored with her stubborn disregard and come up on deck.

The boat lurched as it hit the wake from a cigarette boat, and Peter braced himself with his good arm to ride out the swinging passage through crest and trough. They were motoring across the sound to Oyster Bay, Rusty's boyhood haunt. There was no wind to fill the furled sails, nor had there been for the past week. A muggy, humid stillness had come down over the New York suburbs like wet wool, trapping the smog from the city and turning the sound the color of olive oil. The odor that rose from the waves was of heat and fatigue that came straight from the streets of Manhattan.

The metal box holding Rusty's ashes sat below on the galley table, one reason for Julia's steadfast vigil in the cabin. She had not spoken to Peter since his arrival at the Round Hill house late the previous evening. It was clear she held him responsible for his brother's death.

He had driven straight from LaGuardia in the desperate tug-and-hurl that was Friday night commuter traffic, clinging to the wheel with his one good arm to steady it over the potholes that riddled I-95, and sighing with relief when the Arch Street exit came into view. If he could fly directly to George's door, he'd visit more often, he thought. Gone were the days—his late teens and early twenties—when he'd exulted in speed, driven like a demon, and scorned all cars with automatic transmission. A decade on the island had eroded his tolerance for blaring horns, shaking fists, vicious cuts and weaves among the lesser cars that chose a tortoise pace. The realization disconcerted him even as he recognized its sense. He might be growing wiser, but he was certainly growing older. Perhaps with time he'd become even more eccentric, the sort of uncle the Whitney children would speak of with affectionate understanding—unmarried, childless, cultivating his cranberries and his sheep during the day and reliving Napoleon's battles by night. They would visit him during the summer holidays as they would a quaint reconstruction of a vanished settlement, for its historic value.

"There's the Sultan's," George said, pointing, and Peter looked down into her eyes, which had gone suddenly merry, and for an instant he was thirteen. The Sultan was their private joke, one of the lost pieces of childhood, the imaginary owner of a vast white abomination of a house that stood on a peak overlooking Oyster Bay. As young children, they had sailed to the bay with Max and moored overnight, the Sultan's house a main part of the entertainment. They watched lights go on in various oddly shaped windows, strained to hear the music of a harem, and craned to see the colored candles flicker across invisible lawns. George, the storyteller, spun elaborate tales of the lives lived behind the Sultan's vast doors, and once, at the age of eleven, had even tried to run away to the palace in a dory, only to be rescued by the Coast Guard several hours later.

"You know, the awful thing is, it was sold to a Saudi oil magnate two years ago," she said. "Life imitating art."

"I find that somehow comforting," Peter said. "The Whitney clan's childhood need not be impoverished. Their mother can go on inventing lives for the Sultan, and their dreams will be filled with strange music and the heavy scent of hashish."

"Or four A.M. nightmares."

"I hope this doesn't cause any," Peter said with a nod toward Casey.

Georgiana's merriness faded abruptly, and her lips flattened into a thin line. "I have to believe that scattering dust is less disturbing than lowering a coffin into the earth. And it's not as though they even knew Rusty."

Peter kissed her hair briefly, once, and she looked up at him gratefully. "Thank God you're here, Packy," she said, using his childhood name. "I couldn't handle Mother alone."

"Of course you could," Peter said. "You're the one she still speaks to."

"There's one disadvantage to that," George said. "I'm also the one who has to listen to her." She dropped her arm from his waist and flapped the loose folds of her jacket, searching for a breath of coolness. "And she'll get over her silence, wait and see. Laying the whole Rusty thing to rest will help immediately."

"She'll never lay it to rest," Peter said, a trace of bitterness in his voice. "She might have to wake up and care about someone else in the family. Your kids, for instance. There's a luxury to obsession, you know. It justifies all sorts of selfish behavior."

George looked at him speculatively and said nothing. He felt himself coloring slightly, and he glanced away from her, back to little Casey. George was thinking of Alison, he knew; his own selfish obsession, his excuse for solitude. Perhaps he was too much Julia's son. He turned and looked out over the water, at the Sultan's house, as Hale slowed the motor.

"Okay," Hale shouted. "I'm going to idle here instead of throwing out the anchor. Doc Pritchett, would you ask Mrs. Mason to come above deck, please? With the— remains?"

"I'll go," George said. A brief, wistful smile, a smile that asked Peter's forgiveness, flickered across her tanned face as she turned toward the hatch. *As if honesty should have to be forgiven*, he thought. That was the essence of

George: her short, dark hair; the eyebrows arched like a gull's wings; the ready smile and constant desire to please. Where had she come from in this family?

The *Seventh Wave* slowed, the throttle's vibration thrumming dully through the fiberglass hull, and its forward momentum slackened almost to motionlessness. Peter looked toward the cockpit, studying Hale as he turned and backed the boat until it faced away from the Long Island shore. Hale was slight and trim, with a quiet, bespectacled face that suggested rock-solid predictability. His once-sandy hair was fading and thinning with each passing year, the only sign that he was facing forty-five. He seemed to bear the stress of his job and his large family with comforting steadiness. He inspired his children with confidence and respect, but not with fun. For that, they turned to Peter.

Hale's head swiveled to the cabin's hatch, and Peter followed his gaze. George, holding the box containing Rusty's ashes, was helping his mother as she stepped gingerly from the ladder to the deck. It was the way Julia Mason allowed her driver to assist her from her car, the way she had taken the hands of a hundred servants during the course of her life. Despite years of exposure to sailing, she had never acquired sea legs; Peter thought it a deliberate refusal, as though in her world ladies did not become too comfortable with anything outside their expected competence. Her head came up as she gained the deck, and she looked straight at him, then allowed her gaze to shift without expression beyond him to the water. This was what she termed "cutting someone dead." He had just been declared *persona non grata* by his mother.

"Josh—Abi—come here, we're ready," George said, her

head swiveling as she did her reflexive Whitney count. As the children scrambled across the deck, she looked for Peter, and he moved silently to join her. She took a deep, shaky breath, as though she were standing at the top of a steep ski run, bracing herself for the descent. Doc Pritchett was at her side, lifting her burden gently from her hands, and turning solemnly toward the leeward side of the boat.

"Almighty God of the vast and changing sea, take Rusty to the depths of your great heart and keep him in everlasting light. He was a child of these tides, he was tossed by these swells, he loved their terrible power and fierce gifts. He understood the blessings You gave to those who master the craft of the ocean. Most of all, he paid homage to Your power, with his understanding that no man ever truly holds dominion over the waves, as no man can rule the Lord; but each of us can aspire to chart a true course. Amen."

"Is the sea God's great heart, Mom?" Maxie asked.

"Uncle Rusty thought so," George said.

Dr. Pritchett held aloft the box Peter had brought with him from Boston, and the wind from the sea caught Rusty's ashes and carried them in a fine veil out over the sound. For the first time since Rusty's death, as he watched his brother's dust sift into the ocean, an aching knot of sorrow formed itself in Peter's throat and would not be ignored. *Peace to you, Rusty, of late, unhappy memory*, he thought. *I don't ask for forgetting. We'll none of us have that, the rest of our lives.* He stared at the roiling water an instant and then turned back to George. Two large tears were coursing down her tanned cheeks, and her eyes were swimming; tears not for these ashes, but for him, and for herself—for the rifts that went unhealed, for their vanished dream of childhood.

He looked at his mother. Her fists were clenched at her sides, her arms stiff, and as he watched she stumbled like an automaton to the rail and clutched at the slender steel cord. The boat rolled in the swell, and Julia Mason, disregarding her balance, leaned toward the water as if intent upon following her son into the sea. Dr. Pritchett reached for her swiftly, discreetly, as though she had stumbled and he had merely steadied her; and the moment passed. She turned toward Peter and George, her arms slack and her eyes glittering.

"From the day you were born, you couldn't stand it," she said. "That he was everything you're not. One of those the gods loved." She looked past Peter, but her words were meant for him all the same. "You had to destroy him, didn't you?"

"Mother!" George said.

"You burned his body. Burned!" At that, Julia Mason's face crumpled and she was wracked by a harsh, guttural sobbing that seemed to break her in half. "I never got to see him again."

"What did Nana say, Mommy? What did Nana say?" Casey's hand was in her father's free one, and her eyes were solemn.

"I said your uncle is a murderer," Julia said, and she struggled past them to the hatch.

George looked after her, uncertain whether to follow, then bent down to Casey. "Nan's not well," she said. "Don't worry about anything she said." She looked up at the ring of serious children's faces and smiled at them uncertainly.

*Chapter 26*

After dinner it rained. They laid a fire in Hale's library and sat before it, books forgotten on the leather chesterfield, gazing into the flames. Georgiana's legs, sheathed in bright red wool, were drawn up under her, and her face was pensive. Hale sat behind his desk, studying his laptop. Julia had gone to her room upon their return from the boat and had refused dinner. The children were scattered about the house, and the echoes of their voices drifted faintly through the old plaster walls.

"Poor old Malcolm," Georgiana said. "He must have been wild to see you. How awful to be so old, and sick, and alone."

"Not alone," Peter said. "He has Betty."

"Oh, yes, but Peter! It's so senseless."

"What is?"

"That he's estranged from his granddaughter! Don't you remember? The daughter of his only son, the naval fighter pilot. The one shot down in a training run."

"No, I don't remember."

"Well, it was years ago," George said, "and nothing important enough for you to remember, but they raised her from babyhood, and then broke with her over some stupid transgression. There Malcolm is, dying without a word to his last relative on earth. It makes me so angry."

"How like you, George," Hale said, looking up at her fondly over his glasses, "to worry about other people's families."

She stood up restlessly and walked to the window, pressing her face to the glass. Her breath left a pale fog of condensation against the darkness. "It's just that pride is so infuriating, don't you think? Like you and Mummy. It gets in the way of so much. But I suppose it's easier than feeling." She paused, and shivered. "This rain is awful. Peter—" She slid down next to him, her eyes fixed on the fire. "Do you remember how it snowed the day we buried Daddy? Relentless, so cold and still. I stood by the windows and watched it mount up on the hemlocks, thinking of him lying out there in the ground, in the cold. It broke my heart."

"I remember."

"I'd feel the same way about this rain, if we'd buried Rusty."

"It seems less heartless, doesn't it, releasing him into the ocean."

"Air, water, earth, and fire, all the elements. Yes, it seems right. I'd like that to happen to me. Remember, will you?"

Peter nodded. The logs, still green, were steaming gently, and the flames were blue to their edges. He felt drained and sluggish, as though he could remain before this fire indefinitely, unspeaking, unthinking, and beyond all emotion.

"How long will you stay, Peter?"

He roused himself. "Just until morning. There's too much to be done."

"I was almost forgetting, wasn't I? It's not over, even with him gone."

"No." Peter glanced at Hale, working in his contained circle of quiet, and felt his spirits sink. Why disturb this peace? Because Merry Folger's hard green eyes awaited him back on the island. "And if it's going to end, you have to tell me about the letter."

"The what?"

"The letter. The one Rusty sent you from Rio, the one you didn't mention when I called and told you about his death."

There was a silence. Georgiana's face had frozen. Hale still stared calmly at his screen.

"They found a copy in his luggage. Did George tell you about the letter, Hale?" Peter asked.

"Naturally. It concerned me," Hale said imperturbably. He looked up at Peter and waited.

"I suppose I should have mentioned it," George said in a rush, "but when you called with the news that Rusty was dead, it didn't seem important anymore. In fact, it seemed like . . ."

"A godsend," Peter finished.

George looked down at her fingers, which she'd locked together in her distress, and she nodded rapidly. "Yes. I didn't know what the letter was about, you see," she said. "And then I asked Hale."

Hale cleared his throat quietly and took off his glasses. He passed his hands across his eyelids and sighed.

"When did you get the letter, George?" Peter said.

"The Saturday of Labor Day weekend," she whispered. "But we didn't talk about it until after Rusty was dead."

"He was clever, sending it to George," Hale said. "He

knew I'd never pay him. He figured she'd just put up and shut up."

"How nice," George said bitterly. She unfolded her long legs and reached for the drinks tray. "Scotch, Peter?"

"Three fingers. What'd he have on you, Hale?"

"My career," Hale said comfortably. "And the belief I'd do anything to hang on to it. His mistake, of course. My one rule in life is that I must be able to walk away from anything. I've kept my resignation in every drawer of every desk I've ever used. That's the sort of freedom Rusty could never understand. The freedom from desire." He strolled over to the leather sofa and stood staring down at the fire, his hands in his pockets. "I suppose you'd like to hear about it."

"I've got no choice." Peter took the Scotch from George's hand. "If it has to do with the final days of Rusty's life, I have to know."

"It seems silly to go into stuff that happened ten years ago, and I suppose the details are irrelevant in the eyes of the law. But they make a more interesting story." He accepted a glass of Scotch from his wife and placed his hand on her glossy cap of hair. The gesture moved Peter. Hale was such a private man. "George and I were married the summer before your father died."

"I remember. You met at a Salomon party."

"ME was a major client of the corporate finance department; Max came to a Salomon dinner and brought Georgiana. Julia was in Capri, I think."

"Paris," George corrected automatically. "For the collections."

"Whatever. Max brought George. I fell in love with her then and there."

"Hale," George said softly.

"I talked to her a bit, but I've never been the most dynamic man at a party, and she was absolutely dazzling. Max Mason's only daughter, twenty-seven years old and utterly unaware how beautiful she was. I was thirty-five and beginning to lose my hair, I had survived three lousy love affairs, I'd made money and I'd had success, but I was just another guy in a dark-blue summer suit and expensive handmade shoes. I hadn't the slightest idea how I'd ever see her again."

"Enter Rusty," Peter said.

"The firm had essentially given Rusty his job three years before as a favor to Max."

"I thought you'd brought him on."

Hale shook his head. "Too junior, frankly. I didn't become a director until a few years later. No, Rusty was a bond trader—just the sort of job a Mason would take. I only ran into him occasionally, in the elevator, that sort of thing. But I tried to strike up a friendship with him because of George. At first he ignored me completely."

"Until I started working on him," George broke in. "What Hale hasn't told you is that I was utterly infatuated with him from day one, and kept pumping Rusty for information. He was so—urbane, so—sophisticated. He knew how to hold a conversation. I got Rusty to ask Hale for drinks a few times so I could see him, but he was so terribly shy. He would never ask me out."

"Then one day, Rusty came by my desk and invited me to your home in Greenwich. It may have been his one disinterested act of our entire acquaintance."

"And you came," George said, her voice thrilling. "I thought then there might be hope."

"That weekend was a glimpse of life as it could be," Hale said. "In the midst of a wonderful family, their happiness, that beautiful home—"

"You poor ass," Peter laughed.

George shot him a look of hurt and surprise.

"You're right, of course," Hale said. "But I didn't find that out until later."

"After you'd been married a year. When Rusty came and asked you for your stock. Or rather, George's."

Hale looked down at the brandy and swirled it thoughtfully in his glass. "Oh no," he said. "That was later. He offered me the money first—what I thought was his money. A loan to buy shares of a company called Ultracom. A company Rusty said was likely to be the target of a takeover. A sure thing. Make a profit and pay back the loan when you sell the shares, he said. What a crock." He looked up at Peter, and his eyes were flat.

"You, too," Peter said.

Hale nodded. "It seems you know what went wrong with the plan. The takeover company became the target and pulled out of its tender offer, and Ultracom's value fell. We lost our loan instead of doubling our money. That's when I found out the takeover company was ME. And that the raider was Mitch Hazlitt."

"Rusty hadn't told you?"

Hale shook his head. "He was still smart about some things. He knew I was shy of trading on his information in the first place—it's always a stupid risk—but if I'd known where the information came from, I'd have gone to Max and told him Hazlitt was sniffing around the deal. I was older than Rusty, remember. I dealt in equity. I knew what a man like Hazlitt was capable of. But when it all came out, it was too late. I was in up to my neck. And I'd dragged Georgiana with me."

"I only wish you had," George said softly. "None of this might have happened."

"You couldn't have changed anything," Hale said. Then he looked back at Peter. "When things went wrong, Rusty and I were in a hole. As you can imagine. First, there was the matter of the loan—it had to be repaid, and to Hazlitt, not Rusty; neither of us had the money. We'd already taken a loss in the stock we'd purchased with the loan. Then there was the broader consideration—Max. The fact that we'd traded on information leaked from ME. I spent a whole day out of work, walking the paths in Central Park, wrestling with the mess in my mind."

"You didn't go to Max," Peter said.

"Not then. I was searching for a way out that wouldn't involve George or her father. I'd already sold the bulk of my assets to buy a co-op on Central Park South—we'd moved into it six months before, if you remember. A second mortgage on the place was possible, but that would mean telling George why I needed the money. I couldn't ask my new father-in-law for funds so soon in my marriage. And as you know, my parents have very little." He paused. "And then Rusty asked for the stock."

"George's seven percent voting stock."

"Yes. He had a buyer, a source of funds to repay the loan. Hazlitt. I began to see why the loan had been made in the first place. And it was out of the question, of course. I could never sell George's stock without giving her full knowledge of why it was necessary. But beyond that, it was unthinkable. Hazlitt was using extortion, with George's birthright as his object. I think it was then that I ceased to be helpless and began to be angry."

"And so you went to Max."

"It was an interview the likes of which I hope I may never witness again the rest of my life. He was in a white rage. Cold, efficient, and absolutely deadly. He dealt with the matter at hand—my troubles, the loan—and advanced me the full sum so that I could repay Hazlitt. Then he went to the US attorney's office and told them about his son. Me, he kept out of the whole affair. I owe the sanity of the past ten years to Max Mason. Not that I deserved it."

"It worked," George said. "Even after Daddy died. Hale was transferred to corporate finance—"

"A department considered boring, but safe," he said.

"—and he did so well that they made him a director," George finished.

"Forgive me, Hale," Peter said, "but what I don't understand is why you accepted the loan in the first place. I can perfectly well see Rusty trading on inside information. But it's completely unlike you."

Hale smiled, a trifle wistfully. "Not like safe, sober Hale, is it? Hale, who can always be trusted to do the right thing." He looked at his wife. "Maybe I was caught up in the lure of the risk, Peter. Or maybe I wanted to impress George with my trading prowess. Maybe I just wanted to be more like Rusty. But I learned. The hard way."

George lifted the hand Hale still held tightly, and kissed his palm. "My darling," she said. "Never, never do anything illegal for me again."

"Like murder, for instance?" Peter said quietly.

At that moment the phone rang, and the three of

them froze, Hale and George locked together in front of the fire, Peter on the sofa, until the ringing ended. The quiet murmur of Mrs. Shallit, the housekeeper, came to them through the closed study door, and then her footsteps crossed the hall.

"For Mr. Peter, madam," she said. "A Rafe da Silva." She said the name suspiciously, its cadences strange to her, and waited for Peter. He stood up and followed her to the phone.

George looked imploringly at Hale. "Does he think you killed him to protect me, or that I killed him to protect you?"

"Probably that both of us killed him to protect everyone," Hale said fondly. "Don't worry about it, love. It didn't happen." He turned as Peter came back into the study, his face like death.

"I've got to leave tonight."

"What is it?"

"Will Starbuck. Someone's tried to kill him."

*Chapter 27*

RAFE TURNED HIS head at the sound in the door-way. Merry Folger stood there, an expression both solemn and awkward on her face. He knew that her presence meant Peter had returned, but he felt no relief. Even Peter Mason could not pierce the coma wrapping Will in silence. He glanced at his watch as he stood up to join Merry: three-thirty in the morning. Any other hospital would have kicked them out long ago.

Tess had not looked up from Will's motionless form. Her hand held his, maddeningly slack. *How much more*, her rigid neck seemed to ask, *must I take?* She did not allow herself to say anything—no word of reproach to Merry, no wail of despair to Rafe, not even a word of love to her boy lying prone and broken before her. The mus-cles of her face seemed likely to shatter if she attempted to speak.

Rafe placed a hand lightly on each of her shoulders as he moved around the bed to the doorway. She seemed not to notice. He pulled the door shut behind him and heaved a deep sigh as he looked at Merry. "Man, that's tough," he said.

The banality of the words struck him even as he said them, and he hung his head, hands groping over his brow.

Merry nodded lamely. "Mason's out in the emergency room, waiting. Guess they don't want more than two people at a time in there," she said, nodding in Will's direction. Her words seemed overly loud, a sacrilege. "He's pretty beat," she finished, in a whisper.

Peter stood up as they approached, the sockets of his eyes standing out sharply in his white face. It occurred to Rafe that he was probably still weakened from his own wound three days earlier.

"How is he?" Peter asked.

"The same. Tess won't go home in case he wakes up. But the doctor says he probably won't, for a while. Fractured skull. They're flying him to the mainland soon as it's light. Tess'll go in the chopper. I'll have to follow by plane."

Peter nodded and gripped Rafe's shoulder in what passed between the two men for an embrace. "You found him last night?"

"Pretty late. We didn't call you until we knew the funeral was over."

"Tell me again what happened."

Rafe looked questioningly at Merry, and she nodded slightly and turned to Peter. "Will was deliberately thrown from his bike on the path leading from your house, Peter, through the moors near Altar Rock."

"Thrown?"

"A length of wire was staked across the path, pretty hard to see, about waist-high. Designed to catch a bike across the throat and knock off the rider."

"Who found him?"

"Ney," Rafe said. "But not for a while after Will fell, we figure. Dog was inside until about eight o'clock, with Rebecca. I was over in the barn, looking at some figures, and got a call from Tess. She'd just realized the kid hadn't made it home—too busy before that, in the kitchen, you know. I guess she thought in the back of her mind he was still out at the farm, and then looked up from her dishes and saw it was dark. Anyway, I got in the Rover and started driving the roads; Rebecca let the dog out and he hightailed it down the path through the moors. She thought he'd found a cat when the howling started." He paused. "Poor kid lost some blood."

"Rafe called the police after he called the ambulance," Merry said.

"I didn't see the wire in the dark right off," he said, "or the stakes. Thought it was just a regular fall."

"I didn't show up until eleven," Merry continued. "The ground was pretty useless by the time I got there—all those rescue squad footprints, and tire tracks. Not much you can tell except that the wire's there, and it did what it was supposed to—"

"Wait a minute," Peter said. "Let's back up a bit. Why would anyone want to hurt Will?"

Rafe shot a look at Merry from under his eyebrows and said nothing.

"That's the question of the hour," Merry replied. "Why *would* anyone want to hurt Will? You tell me."

Peter hesitated. "I don't know. Any more than I know why someone would kill Rusty, or shoot me. But I know the three are connected."

"There's a chance somebody decided Will had seen or suspected something dangerous. We can't know that until he wakes up."

The phrase *If he wakes up* hung unspoken among them.

"Can I go in there now?"

"I guess," Merry said. "There's the other aspect, of course, that we can't forget."

Peter turned. "Meaning?"

"That this has nothing to do with Will." Merry's voice had sharpened, and the anger was obvious now. "Haven't you learned anything about anything? That wire was probably meant for you, Peter. It was at a height for tripping a bike like yours, and it was stretched across a path you take all the time. Just Will's bad luck he rides a bike you once owned and knows the quickest way through the moors to the road." She stopped and fixed him in an uncharacteristic glare. "All that education and no common sense. I'll stop by the farm tomorrow morning and talk to you, okay? I want to hear about Greenwich."

"I'll be up early," he said.

She hauled her purse higher on her shoulder and left without a backward glance. The two men followed her progress out the door in silence.

"The Terror of Tattle Court," Rafe said ruefully, and looked at Peter. "She thinks this is all her fault, and she's taking it hard. I made a fool of myself last night and told her she wasn't doing her job."

"She's doing it quite well," Peter said. "Let's see Will."

HE HAD HATED hospitals since Max's death, hated the tubes and the clinical light and the soft whirr of machines that should have made him thankful but instead made him afraid. In hospitals, death was a glaring light shining full in his eyes, driving him to blink, to tear, and to avert his gaze.

Tess turned as they entered the room. "They say he has to go to Mass Gen," she said, her hand reaching blindly toward them. "I don't know what it means. He's supposed to play football this afternoon."

Rafe caught hold of the groping hand and covered it in his own. His touch seemed to calm Tess. She dropped her head and crumpled against his chest.

Peter was studying Will's face, the dark, luxurious eyelashes trembling with unconscious dreams. Will was meant for better things than this. He was lying in a bed intended for Peter. "What's the doctor's name?"

"Westfall."

Peter nodded and ducked out of the room, making for the nurse's station.

"Dr. Westfall," he said. "Where might I find him?"

The nurse looked up, her eyes smudged with dark underlying circles. "Chief resident," she said. "He's on call tonight. I'll page him."

Peter nodded and turned to look aimlessly around the waiting area. He was exhausted and restless at once, unable to sit down and read one of the helpful pamphlets on back injuries, venereal disease, and salmonella poisoning that lay scattered on tables. He drifted slowly around the room, hands in his pockets, dimly aware of the throbbing in his bandaged shoulder. He could not blot Will's image from his mind.

"How's the bullet wound?"

Peter turned. The chief resident was the same doc who had treated his left arm. "Not bad, actually. You do good work."

"You wanted to speak to me?"

"The boy lying in there was injured on my property."

"I see," Westfall said, and his tone hardened. "Two almost fatal attacks in a row. Unusual on this island."

"Very," Peter said. "The police seem to think this one was intended, like the last, for me."

"I see," Westfall said again. "Or rather, I don't, but never mind. You're a friend of the patient?"

"Yes. His mother tells me you'd like to fly him to Boston. I wanted to ask you why."

"Because he has a fractured skull and he's in a coma. I took a CT scan of his skull, and the Mass Gen neurologist on call looked at it on our joint computer system. She has requested Will's transfer to her facility. It's fairly simple."

"What's the risk in moving him?"

"Next to none. The risk if he stays, on the other hand . . ."

"I understand. Doctor—" He paused. "Tess Starbuck is not well off. I doubt she has any kind of health insurance. I know that MedEvacking someone to the city is fairly expensive. I'd like to make arrangements for any bills to be sent to me."

"That's already been taken care of, " Westfall said. "Mr. da Silva has directed that the bills be sent to him."

*Chapter 28*

MERRY HAD REACHED what she thought of as the dry, bleached-white stage of her exhaustion, when nausea replaced sleepiness and her forehead held a permanent frown. Her body moved seconds after her mind conjured the impulse, her walk was a delicate balance between weaving and stumbling. She had never been so tired, she thought, and yet so beyond comprehending it; she progressed through the wee hours on will alone, unquestioningly. She had been awake for two full days, and still her bed hung like a mirage before the hood of her car, receding indefinitely.

She pulled the Explorer to the sandy verge in front of Lucy Jacoby's house and turned off the ignition. No lights behind the snug eaves. She checked her watch—only a little after four in the morning. Not surprising that Lucy was sound asleep. Still—for a woman in mortal terror of pursuit and the unnamed horrors wrought by Italian gray arms dealers, she was remarkably comfortable in her isolation.

Merry studied the houses on either side of Lucy's. Both were dark. As she had thought on her last visit to Tom Nevers: Summer People, probably gone for the next eight months. Anybody in her right mind, who'd seen the sort of ghost Lucy had talked about, would have cleared out long ago.

*An Italian count with a penchant for playing rough. I wonder where she came up with that one*, Merry thought. She scowled to herself as she thought of Peter Mason's worry, the lines deepening around his eyes as he talked about Lucy, his all too chivalrous decency in the face of the all too obvious torch Lucy carried.

"Men are such chumps," Merry said out loud, and to her surprise, the words sounded vicious.

She got out of the car and walked around the side of Lucy's house, searching for the garbage. There it was. A stack of wine bottles next to it. Perfect. She crouched down and eyed them, then pulled the handkerchief she'd brought for this purpose out of her pocket. She lifted one of the bottles by its rim and carried it, willing herself to be careful and steady, back to the Explorer. Prints should show up all over this baby.

She turned the key and shoved the car into gear, not caring whether a light came on in Lucy's house or not. She needed coffee and a nap, and she needed to talk to the only guy on the island with any sense.

RALPH WALDO WAS wrapped in the faded blue seersucker bathrobe that Merry's grandmother had bought in Hyannis twenty years ago. His mug of black coffee steamed on the wooden table, burning a heat mark into the scarred surface. He had not yet shaved at four-thirty A.M., and the white bristles on his chin made him look, Merry thought, like a cross between Santa and a drunken sailor.

"This case means too much to you, Meredith Abiah.

No surprise. The first one always does. So what we've got is Rusty Mason's best friend killing him, or the best friend's girlfriend, or his sister, or the sister's husband," Ralph said. "Or someone unknown. We'll call him X."

"Right," Merry said. Then, almost against her will, "Dad thinks Peter did it, Ralph."

Ralph Waldo snorted, all the answer he deemed necessary. He slathered some butter on a piece of toasted Portuguese bread and handed it to her. "Eat that. You look like walking death." She did as she was told. He set about toasting another piece.

"I'm stuck on Lucy Jacoby, Ralph."

"You're stuck on something else, too. Motives for killing Peter Mason. And people to pull the trigger."

Merry wrinkled her brow. "They're the same bunch, Ralph. Rafe da Silva and Tess Starbuck, the motive being money."

"How's that coffee?"

"Tastes like the inside of a trash can."

He nodded approvingly. "Good. Now let's think systematically about what you've done. You've decided Rusty was the target of the murder. You've decided Peter's attack was a fake. Now you've decided Will Starbuck was a mistake, too, and that for some reason Peter was supposed to find the wire."

"That seems fairly clear."

"Why?"

Merry hesitated.

"The false attack on Peter should have been enough to confuse the police, in the killer's mind," he said. "Why try another one? You've already worked out that whoever shot Peter didn't really intend to kill him—and I agree with you. So why try to kill him a day or so later?"

"Because maybe I'm all wrong," she said, in a very small voice.

"Trust your intelligence, Meredith," Ralph chided. "Peter wasn't even on-island when Will was hit, and anybody who wanted him should know that."

"You think Will was meant to hit the wire?"

"You shouldn't rule it out. What might Will know?"

"I haven't the faintest. And it's impossible to ask him. But what you say makes sense, Ralph. The guy chose a day Peter was out of town."

"Who knew he was gone?" Ralph asked.

She sat down and bit into her toast. "Same set of suspects, basically. Peter Mason has a small group of friends, but it's a tight network."

"Find out what Will might know. And find that man the Jacoby woman is afraid of."

Merry dropped her toast, startled as always by Ralph Waldo's uncanny ability to read her mind. Her grandfather picked up the piece of bread and set it on her plate.

"It's just an idea. She says she ran into her ex-husband's thug on the ferry Sunday night. But he hasn't shown up at her door. Maybe he tried to get at Lucy Jacoby through Peter Mason. What could hurt her more than hurting the man she loves?"

Merry sat very still, her mind working.

"There's a pattern of sorts," Ralph continued. "Peter runs with the Jacoby woman every Monday, Wednesday and Friday. And lo and behold, this week there's blood shed on Monday, Wednesday, and Friday."

"If you believe Rusty died in the early hours of Monday

morning," Merry said. She set down her napkin and willed herself to think. Was Ralph onto something?

"You're going round and round with the folks you know," Ralph said. "Try the ones you don't."

THE HELICOPTER WITH Will's gurney, Tess beside him, lifted from the helipad at six o'clock that morning. Peter and Rafe stood with the wind from the blades whipping their hair about their heads until the glass bubble beat its way into the air and out to sea. Neither of them said anything for several long moments. Then they turned and walked to the Rover.

"I'll drop you at the farm before I fly over to Boston," Rafe said. "You get some sleep, okay?"

Peter shook his head. "I've got a date with the detective. Bacon and eggs at my place, seven sharp."

HE HAD SEVERAL voicemail messages on his cell. He listened to them as he moved around the kitchen, throwing open the refrigerator door and rummaging through Rebecca's carefully organized stores. Sunday was her Quaker day of rest, and he was on his own for Merry Folger's breakfast.

George's voice, tentative and filled with affection, asking after his safe arrival. Walt Sargent, at the Ocean Spray depot, confirming receipt of the flatbed filled with cranberries from Tuesday's harvest. Peter pulled out half a loaf of Rebecca's oatmeal bread and set it on the counter, found some of her raspberry jam, and then went for the eggs. Someone had ended a call without a word. He'd do a Southwestern omelet with some of the salsa and cheese, throw a couple of sausages on the fire, add some of the last of the green peppers from the garden. He listened to hesitant breathing and more dead air. He stood up, suddenly alert to the silence on his phone. Lucy Jacoby shot into his brain, a sudden reminder of her fear. Then he heard the voice.

"And now what do I say?"

He froze.

"It's so odd to hear you, Peter, even on voicemail, after all this time."

She was amused, distant, like a fund-raiser for the Boston Symphony. He closed his eyes and turned toward the counter, gripping the edge painfully.

"You sound so much like yourself. Never mind. I suppose I should say hello. It's Alison. Sky Tate-Jackson, whom it seems you now *pay* to be your friend—or is it your lawyer?—tracked me down here in San Francisco." A short laugh. "Couldn't you have called the Alumni Office if you needed to reach me? At any rate, he told me about—your brother." A pause, as she cast about for something appropriate to say in sympathy, and abandoned the attempt. "*Your lawyer* asked me to come back East to discuss the whole thing. I'm not sure why that can't be done over the phone, but he's good at arguing otherwise." Peter imagined her fighting to keep down her irritation. "I arrive tomorrow night at seven thirty-five. Cape Air." There was an instant of uncomfortable silence, then: "Oh, Peter, I'm sorry for sounding so—It's just been—rather difficult. Until tomorrow—"

Automatically, he hit the "save" button on his phone and replayed that voice—her voice, like the current of a cool, dark river, a voice drowned in calm. He listened for the trace of New York that lingered metallically in her vowels, and found it. A shakiness in his gut that was part euphoria and part terror: He would talk to Alison again.

He listened a third time to the message and half willingly, uncertainly, copied down the time of her arrival. He glanced at his watch. Tomorrow meant today, and he had less than twelve hours to wait. She hadn't asked him to meet the plane; probably hadn't known whether he'd want to. For an agonized instant he wondered if she hoped he would skip it, then reminded himself she'd given him the information. And the choice. Very like Alison.

San Francisco. She'd gone almost as far away from him as she could go. He ran one fingertip over the trailing numbers and wrote *Alison* above them. Alison in San Francisco. The city—its moody weather and jagged seas, the plunges and peaks of its streets, the very shaking foundations—would suit her perfectly.

He looked up as the sound of tires on gravel filtered into the kitchen through the open back door. Merry Folger had arrived.

## Chapter 29

"IT'S A SHAME you don't write for television," Merry said. "Because this stuff about your family is great material."

She was staring out the kitchen window at the dog Ney, who sat under a young maple tree in the yard. He snapped periodically at the green horseflies that came in off the marshland and targeted his thin, short-haired skin. Presently Peter would whistle him inside for the remainder of a steak bone coated in sausage grease; for now, he seemed content to sit in a last pool of summertime warmth. Merry had never owned a dog. She yearned, suddenly, for something warm and contented to hold in her lap, something to put her arms around; or perhaps she yearned to be held herself. She winced, and shifted away from the window. She was too tired, and she needed all her intelligence right now. "So it was Hale who told Max what Rusty was doing."

"Yes."

"But he has no idea who gave Rusty the details of Max's merger plans."

"No."

"You trust this guy? You really think he's got nothing to do with Rusty's murder?"

"By the way he acted, I'd say Rusty's blackmail threats had less impact on him than they did on Sky. His career is only so important to him. And besides, I have George's word he was with her in Greenwich the night Rusty died."

"A wife's word isn't worth much," Merry said. "I knew I should have gone to Greenwich. I'd know better if I'd seen and talked to them myself."

"Can't be everywhere at once," Peter said. "You're just going to have to trust me."

"I wish that were easy." She closed her eyes and leaned her head against the cool panes of glass that separated her from Ney's summer idyll. "We found the car, Peter."

"What car?"

She saw that he was startled by her admission that she couldn't trust him. Trust was a tenet of Peter Mason's. He didn't seem to understand it had no place in a murder investigation.

"Rusty's Jeep," she said.

"Rusty had a Jeep?"

"He had a credit card. With a credit card, apparently, you can have anything."

"So it was rented."

"From Over Sand Vehicles. Under the name of Ribeiro, of course."

"Where'd you find it?"

"Wondered when you'd ask that. In Gibbs Pond."

There was a silence. "In Gibbs Pond?"

"Well, even a Jeep can't walk on water."

"What made you look there?"

"It seemed the closest place to deep-six something that weighs a ton. Particularly if you know the area well."

She turned to face him. The chumminess of the flight

over water and the Westchester drive seemed a distant memory.

"Let's talk about your family," she said. "The woman in the photograph. Why would she be with your dad?"

"A secretary, maybe."

"Uh-huh. Could be."

"Or a business associate."

"How about we try lunch date. Or steady date. Or call girl. Or mistress."

"That's enough." The words were sharp and bitten, like a lash across her cheek.

"Is it? You call me here to make a clean breast of the family history, but you're still trying to keep the dirty socks in the closet."

Involuntarily, his lips twitched at her mixed metaphors. "I didn't call you here. You came."

"You know what I mean. You're not helping. You're obstructing. Look at the facts. Look at the picture, for God's sake." She picked up her reading glasses, cast aside on the breakfast table, and settled them on her nose. "This is a very expensive broad we've got here. Leggy, too." She heard the tartness in her voice and despised herself for it, knowing he would hear feminine spite and dismiss what she was saying. "Your brother brought it for a reason. He was coming to see you. Put two and two together—he thought he had something to tell you about the woman in this picture."

"Perhaps. Or maybe he loved her, and kept the picture for old times' sake. How can I say?"

"He sure didn't carry this out of affection for your dad."

"Granted."

"Taken with everything you've told me about your

family, I'd say the odds are even she's the famous source you're looking for. She knew Max; Rusty apparently knew something about her. So I suggest we figure out who she is."

He considered this a moment, the brows furrowed over his gray eyes. "Malcolm didn't know her."

"So Malcolm said. I wonder." She paused, and looked at him speculatively. "Another thing. I'd like to find out what Lucy Jacoby's real name is, and why she wants you to believe she was married to an Italian count."

Peter, in the act of opening the back door for Ney, stopped in his tracks. "Her real name?"

"Well, it's not the one she's using, that's for sure."

"You can't be serious."

"Unless she's managed to get to Italy and back without showing a passport."

"How do you know?"

"Called the Department of State a couple of days ago. Asked if they'd ever issued a passport in that name. They said no."

"Maybe it was under her maiden name."

"So Jacoby's the last name of the Italian count?"

Peter paused, and then smiled, grudgingly.

"Not bloody likely, as they say," Merry said with satisfaction. "There's a driver's license under Lucy Jacoby in the Massachusetts system, issued five years ago."

"The year she came around the Point."

"Could be perfectly normal, as you say, because she moved here then; or it could mean she changed her name. For a lot of reasons."

"Like?"

"Say Jacoby is her name: maybe there never was an

Italian count. She never went to Italy, and so she never needed a passport. Or say Jacoby's a name she just adopted: maybe her husband—if she has one—is such a creep she's trying to keep him off everybody's screen by making up exotic stories and alternate personalities," Merry said.

"None of that has anything to do with Rusty," Peter countered. "Don't you think you're losing your focus? Whatever the nature of her marriage, if Lucy changed her address, why wouldn't she change her name? It's probably a grandmother's, or a middle name."

"I'd be obliged, all the same, if you'd ask. She'll tell you if she'll tell anybody."

"I'll find out what I can."

"Good. Look, I've got to get some sleep. Thanks for breakfast." She pulled off her glasses, picked up her decrepit bag, cast one last look out of the window at Ney under his tree, and turned to go.

Peter was studying the photograph of his father. "You're right, you know," he said. "Rusty brought this for a reason."

"Once or twice a week, I'm right about something," Merry said, "but lately I've been hoping I'm wrong. Like today."

"What do you mean?"

"The idea that you know something about that woman has been driving me crazy. I keep thinking maybe Rusty actually got to the farm, and showed you the picture, and it made you mad enough to kill him. You worry about the car being traced, so you dump it in the pond, throw his stuff in the sea, and hightail it back to bed."

There, she'd come out with it. She waited for him to react.

For a moment, Peter seemed stunned. Then the warmth faded from his face and his expression grew remote. "And what about this?" he said, tapping his left shoulder.

"Maybe you got somebody to do it for you," Merry said carefully. "To confuse me. I have to think of every possibility, Peter. You understand."

"No," he said, "I don't. I thought we were working together."

She picked up the photograph. "Tell me the truth. Is this a picture of Alison?"

He threw back his head and laughed at that. "No," he said. "Alison was a pretty woman, no doubt about it, but she's never looked like this in her life. This takes a lot of money, Merry, and that's something she never had. You can see her yourself—she arrives on a plane tonight."

"Sky's work?"

He nodded. "He hopes Alison can identify the source. You can show her the picture when you meet her tomorrow."

WHEN MERRY HAD left, Peter dragged himself upstairs and settled himself carefully on his bed, favoring his left arm. He was exhausted, but the detective's words were reeling in his head. He picked up Rusty's photograph and studied the image of his father. He recognized the expression on Max's face; he had been happy, and amused. But whether he knew the woman well or had met her for the first time, Peter couldn't say.

He studied the leggy broad, as Merry had dubbed her, and, not for the first time, wondered what it was that he found familiar. Her form in the breathlessly tailored dress? The sleek helmet of chin-length hair? Perhaps she tugged at his memory simply because he thought that she ought to. But when he tried to define the indefinable, it shifted away from him like a half-remembered name. He thrust the picture aside and closed his eyes. He needed sleep almost as much as Merry. He had Alison to face, tonight.

He had reached the semi-drowsing state where thoughts enter the mind and depart ungrasped when suddenly he shot upright in bed. *Mayling Stern*. Merry had found a Jeep in the pond, but she hadn't said whether the bumper was damaged. What had Mayling's Mercedes hit—and where?

THE WIND OFF the Atlantic blew Mayling's glossy black hair against the grain, a faint but inexorable tug that annoyed her. She was stretched out on a wrought-iron chaise this Sunday morning, reading the *Times*, and her garden was filled with the white noise of surf, punctuated by occasional birdsong and the muffled roar of private jets departing every three seconds for the mainland. They made her think of Sky, and she looked up at the arch of blue above her head whenever they passed.

She had spent a good part of the past hour studying a fall fashion supplement that had arrived that morning with photo spreads of her latest collection. Towering, wraith-like girls strode across desolate landscapes with identical expressions of solitude on their faces. There was even a picture of Mayling, aloof and unsmiling, amidst a covey of models; her eyes were opaque, unfocused, but only she would see that. And Sky.

Sky saw everything.

The unoiled gate in the white picket fence swung open, breaking her peace, and she looked over her shoulder, her heart racing uncontrollably. She composed her face, waiting for Sky to turn the corner of the house and break upon her. But it wasn't him.

"Detective Folger!" She rose from her chaise. "I thought you were Sky, surprising me."

"He's still in New York?"

"Yes. I'm going back myself in another few days."

Merry's lithe frame crossed the lawn. As she held out her hand, Mayling half-consciously compared the detective to the women stalking through her clothes in the *Times* supplement. The effect of sunlight on Merry's blonde hair was almost blinding; against her dark skin and brows, it gave the effect of a photographic negative. *She should wear sage-colored linen*, Mayling thought, *but she never does*. Then she came out of her dream and remembered why the woman was in her yard.

"More trouble," she said.

"May I sit down?"

"Of course."

Merry settled on the chaise opposite Mayling's and glanced at the *Times* spread. She knit her brows. "None of those clothes looks real, except yours."

"I wish the people who count thought so. The reviews were faint in their praise."

"Then ignore them. What women buy is more important than what critics say."

"Money always counts, unfortunately. But you didn't come here to talk about the rag trade."

"I don't know enough to sound intelligent, anyway." Merry met her eyes. "On the subject of your life here on Nantucket, however, I can hold up my end."

"You saw Sky Friday."

"Mr. Tate-Jackson is concerned about the mangled front end of your car."

"Your evidence people have already dealt with that. They showed me a warrant yesterday."

"He's also worried about the button you lost from your sweater. The hours you can't remember, the night Rusty died. And the letter you were reading when Peter walked into your studio the next day. Did you know Rusty was blackmailing Sky before his body was found?"

"No!" Mayling said. "You're all wrong! I had no reason to kill Rusty, even if everything else you know is true."

"The button, the bumper, the letter—all of it?"

"I didn't read the letter from Rusty until Labor Day. He was already dead."

"Peter caught you reading something, and said you looked like you'd seen a ghost. Did you mistake him, at first glance, for his brother? Insufficiently dead and back for revenge?"

"I wasn't reading the blackmail note when Peter arrived," Mayling said. "Sky didn't show it to me until that night. When he knew it didn't matter anymore."

"Because Rusty was dead."

"That's when I began to be afraid, Detective."

"That Sky had killed him?" Merry asked.

"Yes. He was late getting here, you see, the night before."

Merry frowned involuntarily. "The airline attendant remembers him arriving at eight. And Sky says you failed to pick him up. He had to take a taxi home."

"He may have," Mayling said. "I don't remember. He told you about my health issues?"

"The blackouts."

She nodded. "I showed up here around eleven-thirty, and Sky helped me to bed. He gave me a sleeping pill and said he was going out for a walk on the beach. I woke up around eight-thirty the next morning and realized he'd never come to bed at all."

"Did you ask him about it?"

"He told me he'd slept on the couch. And that I'd crashed my car the night before. I don't remember doing it, Detective. I've been wondering, for days, if Sky did it himself—when he ran over Rusty. While I slept, drugged, at his hand."

"Would Sky shift the blame for murder like that?"

"I don't know," Mayling said. "That's the most horrible thing of all. I can't bear to be with him, because of not knowing. And I'm too terrified to ask."

"Mayling," Merry said, "what were you reading when Peter found you that morning?"

She hesitated, blushed, and then looked away. "Sky's letters," she said. "He gets them, from his mother, every week. He never opens them. But I do."

She focused on the sea, letting the glare off the waves flood her sight. "I fill a kettle with water and wait for it to steam. Then I lift the envelope flap carefully with a nail file, read the letter, and put it back in the drawer where he keeps all of them, unopened. I keep hoping she'll change her mind. But we'll never know, will we, if he doesn't read them?"

"Change her mind about what?"

She smiled bitterly. "Me. The mongrel whore from the garment district who's not fit to marry her son. She's never accepted our relationship. She never will."

Merry sat up. "After all these years of living together?"

"You'd have to know Gwendolyn Tate-Jackson. A direct descendant of the New York Junker class, the Knickerbocker Club, the Four Hundred. I met her once," Mayling said, "so I know what she is capable of."

"Racism."

Mayling laughed abruptly. "Sky brought me home to her Park Avenue apartment to announce our engagement. She made me wait in the kitchen with the housekeeper while she told Sky what she thought. Horrible, vituperative things. Sky never went back."

*But he never married you, either,* Merry thought.

"I won't force myself into a family that doesn't want me," Mayling said. "I've told Sky I'll never marry him while his mother hates me so much. It would have a terrible impact on our kids."

Merry looked at the clothing designer a moment in silence. "Then she's won, hasn't she?" she said.

## Chapter 30

THE SMALL PROP plane out of Boston was the kind that didn't have a stewardess or in-flight catering; and at takeoff, the right engine tugged so wildly in a different direction from the left that the pilot aborted the attempt, taxied off the runway, and pulled down a technical manual from the shelf above his head.

Alison could see all of this because there was no curtain—much less a door—between the cockpit and the seven passengers, who'd been distributed in their seats according to weight. Panic surged from her feet to the roots of her hair as, his consultation finished, the pilot brought the plane back around to face the runway.

*I'm going to die*, she thought. *He looked at the owner's manual, for God's sake. Why did I ever, ever, come back?*

In the course of her constant travel she experienced all the stages of behavior common to terminally ill patients: Denial (*I'm not really here, I'm really in my own bed*); Anger (*I'm too intelligent to be this afraid*); Bargaining (*If you just let me live this time, God, I'll never get on a plane again*); Depression (*I've spent my whole life in pursuit of success, and my last meal will be airplane food*); and finally, Acceptance (*I've placed my life in the hands of a stranger, and that's okay, really, that's fine*).

The plane bumped and surged down the runway, both engines working in concert this time, and tentatively, diffidently, lifted into the air. Allison's panic increased. She gripped the bottom of her seat and wished desperately for in-flight catering. She hated flying without a drink.

PETER WAS LEANING against a pillar, losing a battle with his calm, when she appeared at the gate, and for several seconds, he looked past her. He was searching for a college kid with long, unstyled hair and a graceful dancer's frame, wearing jeans or a loose sundress with a cardigan sweater. He was looking for the past, and the present arrived.

"Peter!"

The voice riveted him, as it always had. He cast about wildly.

"Here!"

She stood barely ten yards from him, a wide grin on her face, any strangeness banished by the sudden joy of seeing him.

The years had dealt indifferently with Alison, writing lines across her forehead, sharpening the jut of her cheekbones, shafting her dark hair with premature strands of gray. The dancer's body looked now like an athlete's—less graceful than it was strong. She was dressed in black linen capris and a leather jacket; her flats were discreetly Italian and very chic. She had become the sort of woman he would admire from a distance and find disturbingly self-sufficient. He walked toward her and didn't know what to say when he arrived.

He settled for the safest gesture of his genteel childhood—the airy brushing of cheek against cheek, as though he were an art dealer and she a very special client. "You look wonderful."

She saw the arm in the sling then. "Take a fall from a horse?"

"Something like that. I'll tell you about it later. How was the flight?"

"Godawful. They always are. I'm never so thankful, or breathless, as when I emerge alive from a plane. I didn't actually expect you to meet me, Peter, but it's good to see you. I remember this airport isn't that far from town. I hope I'm not inconveniencing you with the drive . . ." She was speaking rapidly, trying to fill silence, a cover for her nervousness, he knew.

"Not at all," he said. "I'm parked right out front. Is this your only bag?"

"I've learned to travel light," she said.

What he heard was, *I'm not staying long.*

SHE DIDN'T SPEAK much in the Rover, just let the setting sun strike her cheek in lengthening red rays. The soft island wind flooded the open window with the scent of the sea and the faintest whiff of pine and heather off the moors. Peter, still steering and shifting with one hand, gave her a few bad moments; but the Old South Road was straight and empty enough for erratic driving, and she relaxed. It had been so long since she had smelled these smells and felt this tranquility emanating from the very shingles of the houses. Unbeknownst to herself, she sighed deeply, and Peter gave her a look from the corner of his eye.

"You must be worn out. It's a long trip from California."

"Made worse by fear of flying," she said. "I'm completely

drained when I get off a plane. I can barely walk. But this place makes up for everything. It's so restful, Peter. I know I'll sleep well tonight."

"Where are you staying?" he said.

"I hadn't thought about a hotel, to tell you the truth— I got Sky's call and caught a plane in a matter of hours." Too late, she heard how her words must sound to him—as though she were fishing for lodging. She bit her lip and looked at him quickly. He was gathering himself to open his home to her, and she could see the effort it cost him.

"You're welcome to stay—"

"How about if we try that historic brick place in town?" she broke in hurriedly.

He was silent an instant, regrouping. "The Jared Coffin House."

"That's it."

Constraint fell between them. He downshifted at the rotary and struggled with the wheel.

"What happened to your shoulder?"

"Somebody took a shot at me," he said casually. His gray eyes flicked over to hers, then moved back to the road. "What took you to California?"

*End of conversation about the killer*, Alison thought, and drew in a sharp breath. "I'd run out of alternatives. I'd tried everywhere else. And I managed to get a job, one reason I stayed."

"Doing what?"

"News reporting. For the second-largest newspaper in the state." She laughed. "Trust me to choose a dying profession. Print journalism has the half-life of a dead fish, particularly in California, where anything that happened yesterday qualifies as history. I don't know,

Peter—sometimes I think about going back to school, getting a law degree, maybe—and then I wonder whether I'm too old."

"Never ask that question, Alison. Assume you can do anything, and you will."

She studied his set face an instant, wondering what nerve she'd touched, then stared out at Orange Street. "Peter, this town has grown so much," she exclaimed.

"Nantucket has become the Hamptons," he said wryly. "You left at the right time."

"I'll always miss this island," she said impulsively. "I'll carry it with me forever."

Her words wrung Peter's heart.

"The things we've loved deeply never leave us, Alison," he said. "That's their special curse."

This time, she didn't dare look at him.


A WEEK AFTER Labor Day, and a Sunday evening at that, Alison had the pick of the rooms at the Jared Coffin House. Peter left her there with her luggage; she was still on California time and thought it too early to eat. For his part, he was flushed with weariness, the only word he could put to the sense of loss he'd felt during the ride into town. Alison was a stranger, complete in her own life, and the woman he'd loved was just a memory.

He threw the car into gear with his good arm and maneuvered his way up Centre Street, searching for a spot to turn around. Then he idled an instant in the road, and came to a decision. He would visit the house.

Mid-September twilight was coming down over the streets of town, and with it, a briskness to the air. Yellow light spilled out of a few windows, and straggling

tourists—a father with a child trudging at his heels, a
mother following along behind—ducked down the cob-
blestones in search of home. The season had come to its
natural end. Houses owned by off-islanders, like children
left too late on an empty playground, showed lost and
darkened faces to the street. He urged the Rover farther
and farther into the dusk, until the sidewalks dropped
away and the terrain began to climb. He was on the Cliff
Road.

The Mason house stood—as it had for a century and
a half—on high ground overlooking Nantucket Sound.
Lonely women had paced its hallways and hung by its
windows, waiting and craning to see the first small flare
of a sail on the horizon. Whale oil had paid for its wood
and bricks, shipped over the seas to the island; and whale
oil had filled it with treasure, a monument to the power
of Nantucket's captains and the Mason name. Now his
father's estate kept the empty house habitable; only the
Whitney children ran through its rooms, and then only
for a few weeks each summer. His mother had not come
to the island since her husband's death.

He turned off the ignition and sat a moment in the
stillness of the gravel drive, the hedges and the height
of the roof walk dreaming in the darkness. The sun had
gone down completely now, and he moved like a memory
himself, through the opening in the hedge and down the
walk of crushed quahog shells. The hydrangeas—dark
mounds of secret coolness—were pocketed with last
blooms. He heard the surf, far below off Jetties Beach,
and the tearing cries of gulls diving toward evening.

At the doorway he stopped, and craned his neck back
to stare up at the windows: the last light was glimmering

off the old panes. The keys to the house were in the Rover's glove compartment, but he had no desire to walk through the empty rooms. Instead, he turned and made his way around to the back terrace, and the lawns that stretched to the fence at the cliff's edge. Beyond it, Nantucket Sound swept to the horizon, alive and wavering under a rising moon.

He stopped at the edge of the flagstones and pulled up a wrought-iron chair. A flaking of rust came away in his palm. Uncaring, he turned the chair toward the sea. He was alone in the midst of the world and the night, and he was at peace.

Here on this lawn he had beaten George at croquet, with the set she'd been given for her eighth birthday, rocketing her bright orange ball from the terrace to the fence until she howled with disappointment. He had trained his first dog—a chocolate Labrador named Mud Pie—to dig up his mother's roses. In the shadow of the hedge his father had taught him how to swing a golf club; he had chipped a ball through the kitchen window. He had set off firecrackers near the hurricane cellar and thrown water balloons at Rusty's head from the safety of the roof walk. Now George's children rediscovered the rituals of generations of Masons, unaware that the endless days of their summer months were already passing into memory. He envied and pitied them at once.

He stood up and walked slowly down the lawn toward the sea. This was where the tent had stood, and the dance floor with the carefully draped tables; here the guests flown in from New York and the jazz orchestra. He ignored their ghosts and moved beyond, to the circle of moonlight falling on the grass just past the tent's farthest stake. Long after the fireworks had ended and the guests had gone home—when the others had fallen into bed and a dreamless sleep—he had danced with Alison in the moonlight, a slow, endless waltz that had ended in their lovemaking. The earth had been damp with the falling dew and tangy with salt spray; her skin had still held the heat of her sunburn. The surf had broken in tumult against the pilings of Jetties Beach, and he had desired nothing so much in his life as her skin under his hands.

The first two years after it all ended, when he was living in this house alone, he had returned to this spot as a tongue seeks a damaged tooth, probing the pain. He had never failed to find it. He shivered now in the darkness and turned back to the house. The emptiness of the place was too vivid. His father was gone, Rusty was dead, and his mother estranged; Alison had moved beyond him. It was time for Mason Farms, and sleep.

Halfway to the terrace he stopped, alert to a change in the listening stillness of the empty house: he was no longer alone. The throbbing in his left shoulder mounted to a crescendo of warning. Someone was sitting in the wrought-iron chair he had left on the terrace.

"Hello, Peter," Alison said, her voice low and filled with calm, like darkness made human. "So you came back, too."

## Chapter 31

MERRY'S EXPLORER CAME to a rolling stop next to the weathered obelisk standing in the center of upper Main Street. She jumped out, her arms filled with late dahlias culled from Ralph Waldo's flower beds. Six o'clock on a Monday morning, a bright September day by the look of things, and ten hours of solid sleep had cleared her head. She glanced back down Main to the business district, searching for too-observant eyes; but there was little traffic abroad as yet. The town was gripped in the early stillness she loved. Quickly, she hiked her right leg over the wrought-iron chain that set the war memorial off from the cobblestoned street and laid the dahlias at its base in a plastic vase of water. Twelve years ago on this day, Billy had pushed Rafe away from an IED in Fallujah. Her father wouldn't come here, she knew; Billy's name wasn't even on the memorial, at the police chief's request. John Folger had hated the Iraq war. The death of his son was an unforgivable waste, not something to venerate.

Merry had mixed feelings about the war memorial. Billy was buried in Arlington National Cemetery. This was the only place on Nantucket she could place late flowers tended by the grandfather Billy had loved. She reached out a hand to touch the rough stone briefly, her throat constricting, and then she turned to go.

She had been awakened from her nap the previous evening by a call from Rafe, holding vigil with Tess at Mass General. His time for conversation was short. He needed clothes for Tess—of course, she had flown out on Will's helicopter with nothing—and a shirt or two of his own. He'd tried to reach Peter, but the guy must have taken the phone off the hook—nobody at the farm was answering. Would she stop by the Greengage and pick up some things? And then drive out to the farm, maybe, for his? Whenever she could manage it. He'd pick 'em up from the Cape Air kiosk at Logan that evening. Or maybe, if Peter planned to come over to the hospital, he could bring the clothes with him . . .

There was no change in Will.

So here she was, groping for Tess's spare key in the hiding place behind a shingle, letting herself into the kitchen of the deserted Greengage. It looked far different today than it had the previous week, when Merry had met Tess over her melon salsa and muffin tins; the stove was cold and the room unlit. Tess had been called out to Cottage Hospital Friday night in the midst of her dishes; Sammy and Regina had cleaned up after her. The large pots were upended, like discarded party hats, to drain on the counters. After the brightness of the fall day, the half-light of the kitchen dampened Merry's spirits.

A light tapping on the panes of the back door made her jump, and she turned around quickly. A boy's face was framed in the glass. At the sight of her it took on an expression of caution and reserve she recognized. He'd have seen the Explorer outside, with its Nantucket police shield.

"Hi," she said as she hauled open the door. "What can I do for you?"

"Is Will home, ma'am?"

"Nope." She smiled at him, hoping he'd relax. "Who are you?"

"I—I go to school with him. Will he be back soon, d'ya know? It's kind of important."

His voice broke embarrassingly on the last word. A *boy on the verge of being something else*, she thought, *and pretty bad at it.* Broad shoulders that were no match for his skinny waist and legs. She studied his face, not knowing this one, but conscious she had seen him before. Then it dawned on her.

"You're the football player," she said.

He flushed. "Yeah."

Merry stuck out her hand. "I'm Detective Folger."

"Sandy Stewart," he said. "Is Will's mom around?"

"Come in, Sandy, and have a seat." She opened the door and stood to one side. "Will had an accident Friday night and had to go to the hospital."

"He did?" Sandy's eyes widened, and to her surprise, he looked over his shoulder. "I wondered why he missed the game Saturday. You sure it was an accident?"

Merry's eyes narrowed.

"Why do you ask?"

"Is he gonna be all right?"

"He's got a fractured skull, and he's in a coma. They flew him to Boston for tests. I don't know much more than that." She took a gamble and leaned confidentially toward Sandy. "Somebody staked a wire across the path Will uses through the moors. You know anything about that?"

Fear filled his eyes.

"Will's had a rough time getting back into school since his dad's death last year, hasn't he?" Merry persisted. "If this accident was a trick, Sandy—played by the football team, maybe?—a lot of people are going to be asking questions. Particularly if Will doesn't make it. You can tell your buddies I said that."

Sandy tried to speak, but no sound came. Instead, he lunged for the door.

"You're wrong, you know," he shot over his shoulder. "Totally wrong." Then he was gone, pedaling furiously toward school on his bike.

"IT'S LIKE NOTHING I've ever seen." Alison was staring out over the bog's tangle of maroon vines and scarlet fruit that ran from her feet to the line of marshland in the southwest that marked the verge of Gibbs Pond.

"I know." Peter was quiet for an instant, caught short by his love for this bit of land and his way of life. "You'll have to stop by tomorrow, when I'll be wet-harvesting again, and see what the red tide really looks like. In spring, when the vines are in flower, it's spectacular in a different way."

"What color are they?"

"Pinkish-white. They look like long-necked birds—hence the name, or one theory of the name, at least. 'Crane-berries' became 'cranberries' over time."

"It's a haven, isn't it, Peter?"

"The bog?"

"The house, this land, the unobstructed view, even the distance from town. You must feel utterly alone on earth, and master of it."

"I do," he said. It was like Alison to see the freedom in his solitude. He was thankful for that.

He had risen early to tend to the sheep, feeling Rafe's absence keenly. By midmorning he had been at the Jared Coffin House, hoping Alison had conquered jet lag and the weariness that must have come on the heels of their nocturnal walk through the back streets of Nantucket town. He had found the woman he knew again, some-where in the darkness—not the object of his passion, but the best friend he had missed inexpressibly through the years. No one had known him as well as she, before or since; and in his heart of hearts, he thought no one ever would again.

He had told her about Rusty's death—and his illness, the bitterness that had filled his blackmail letters; his banishment and loss. She remained silent through most of it, her head down as they passed the unlit and shut-tered houses.

"He was warped," she said finally. "I thought I could take it—the coldness, the way he enjoyed humiliating me—because I thought he needed me. Why else would he have done what he did to you? Why else would I—" She looked up at him then, her face composed. "Rusty needed no one."

"That's all past, Alison," he had said, very quietly, and they had walked on.

He shook himself out of reverie and turned to look at her now, all her ghosts banished, her face alive in morn-ing sun. It was incomprehensible that she had never been here with him before, and unthinkable that she should ever leave. As she would, all too soon.

"Let's eat," he said.

He handed her the photograph from Rusty's water-logged gym bag when she had finished her tuna fish sandwich. They were sitting on the wooden deck at the back of the saltbox, and Alison had discarded her sandals. Ney lay blissfully under her chair while she traced slow circles in his fur with the tip of her big toe. Whenever she stopped, Ney raised his head in outrage, cocking one ear in her direction, and then sank down with a clink of his tags as her foot resumed its perambulations across his stomach. The dog had accepted her immediately.

Her brow furrowed as she studied the photograph of Max Mason and the unknown woman. Then she went still. Schuyler Tate-Jackson was right. Alison knew who the woman was.

"I only met her once," she said. "When she walked up to our table in a restaurant downtown—and threw what your mother would term *a scene*."

Peter's lips twitched.

"I assumed she was one of Rusty's discarded women. We had an annoying tendency to run into them in the most unlikely—and likely—places. But I was wrong. She wasn't his girlfriend at all. She was your father's."

Peter reached for the photograph. He had half expected this; Meredith Folger had made it plain. His eyes slid over the woman leaning into the car. She couldn't have been much older than Georgiana at the time. He glanced up and found Alison watching him, her eyes holding something like pity.

"Rusty was afraid of her. I think she was threatening to confront your mother."

"Why would that bother Rusty?"

"I don't know," Alison said. "I never saw her again. I wasn't supposed to know about her existence. Rusty figured the less he told me, the better."

"But you're sure he was frightened," Peter said.

"Oh, yeah," she said. "He wouldn't take her calls, he wouldn't speak of her; and he never told me why."

"When was this?"

"Right before I left him."

"You left him?"

"You didn't know?"

Peter shook his head.

"Right after Thanksgiving. I heard he went to Brazil a couple of weeks later. We never spoke again. Not that I was easy to find—I was running from my own demons."

Something in his face must have challenged her to name them.

"Guilt," she said. "Shame. Loss. The knowledge that I had been a fool, and nothing could fix it."

He looked down at Ney, feeling no sense of victory. When he met her eyes she was fine again.

"This woman," he said. "Did you know her name?"

"It wasn't a real one," Alison said. "A nickname, I suppose. Now, what was it? Something odd, something made up, like Bambi. Or Sunny. Or—no, was it—"

"Sundance," Peter said.

WHEN THE PHONE rang he was expecting Rafe and news of Will. But it was Lucy Jacoby on the line.

"I kicked myself for staying away when your brother died. I won't make the same mistake twice. How is Will?"

"You heard," Peter said. "I should have called you."

"Of course you should have. But you've probably been

trying to find whoever did it, and personally, I think that's more worthwhile." She hesitated for a moment. "There were some pretty gory stories running around school today. I heard he was in Cottage Hospital, but I figured you'd know the truth. How bad is it, Peter?"

"He's not coming out of the coma," Peter said gently, "and they've flown him to Boston. I'm planning to head over there myself today."

"Poor kid. Peter—it wasn't—he didn't try to kill himself, did he?"

"Good God, no. Where did you get that idea?"

"I'm so glad," Lucy said. "Listen, I have something for Will. A book of short stories. They say people in comas can hear what you say to them. Tess could read to Will. It might help bring him back."

"That's good of you, Lucy. Drop the book by after school and I'll take it over tonight. In a few days, if we're lucky, he may be able to read it himself."

MERRY FOLGER HAD her feet up on her desk and her chair at a dangerous angle, rocking on two legs. Clarence Strangerfield's forensic report was spread before her, and it told her things that, unfortunately, she had already guessed. The footprints taken from Peter Mason's driveway matched in size, although not in shoe style, the prints left two nights later under the tree near his house, where someone had waited for him to walk the dog to the barn. Any closer identification—without a pair of suspect shoes—was impossible. She reflected on the sloppiness of this particular murderer, and wondered what it meant. Were the prints someone else's, left by the killer to frame an innocent person? Or did they betray a serendipitous quality, opportunities seized, without time to cover one's tracks, as it were?

And then there were the fingerprints.

"Yo, Merry!"

She looked up. Matt Bailey stood at her cubical. "There's a kid outside wants to see you."

Her chair came down with a clunk. "Threats, unfortunately, work better than promises," she sighed, and walked out to the station entrance. Beyond the double doors, squinting in the sun, Sandy Stewart was straddling his bike. She walked over to him.

"I think I know why they hurt Will," he said, without preamble. His face was stony and his voice flat, signs he was here because he had no choice. He reached around for his school backpack and swung it off his shoulder. "They made a mistake," he said, pulling out *Thirteen Reasons Why*. "It should have been me."

*Chapter 32*

PETER HAD LEFT three messages for Rafe over the course of the morning, and none had been returned. He told himself that meant nothing—Will might be just the same, and Rafe and Tess taking some much-needed rest. Or Will could be in the midst of the tests the Cottage Hospital had flown him to Boston to receive. He pushed aside the thought that Rafe was riveted to the boy's bedside, unaware of Peter's calls, because Will was fighting for his life.

So he leaped for the phone when it rang again, and again he was disappointed.

"Peter!"

"Buck," he said, his voice flagging.

"Well, am I ever the consolation prize today," Buck Maplethorne said, nettled. "You'd think I was trying to sell snowplows in June, with all the response I've been getting."

"No harm meant, Buckie, I'm just waiting on someone else's call, that's all."

"Well, I won't keep you. Just called to say your rented beater's come in, so you're all set for harvesting tomorrow, and you can come by the nursery anytime to pick it up."

"Thanks," Peter said.

He left Alison on the deck with a book and Ney settled at her feet, took the battered Ford that served Mason
Farms as an all-purpose hauler, and drove off without a
thought.

MONDAYS IN MID-SEPTEMBER were quiet at
Maplethorne's, with the summer folks gone and the
island hunkering down for wet weather. Peter found Buck
unloading ficus trees bound for his greenhouse.

"Here already? Hey, I've got a great snowplow I can
sell you. Cheap." He grinned, his broad face betraying
none of the financial worries that had beset his life since
starting the business. Peter was one of his best customers.
He placed orders in winter, when the off-islander petunia
market was long gone.

Buck led him to where the yellow metal beater sat
under a tree, awkward and purposeless on dry land. "It's a
beaut. And you're only paying the five days. Have it back
to me by five on Friday and we're set."

"Could you help me get it into the truck? I can't lift it
alone with this arm."

"Hey, you're not lifting it at all. Daniel!" he yelled,
cupping his mouth with one hand in the direction of the
greenhouse. Buck's seventeen-year-old son came at a trot.
"Let's get this beater into Mr. Mason's truck."

Daniel nodded abruptly in Peter's direction and bent
to his task, with utter disregard for his back or the proper
mechanics of lifting. The yellow metal frame rose triumphantly into the air and settled onto the floor of the old
Ford. Buck winked at Peter. "Wouldn't want you to have
to get it off the truck when you get home, either. You wait

for one of your crew, you hear me? Say, how are you driving that thing with one hand?"

"Recklessly," Peter said. "Thanks a lot, Buck. I'll see you Friday."

"Wait a sec," Buck Maplethorne said as Peter climbed carefully into the cab. "I'll be forgetting my name next. I found that rose you wanted."

"You did?"

"Yep. At least, I found out what it's called. Getting the rose'll be a bit trickier."

"Can't we order it?"

"If it were a commercially grown hybrid, sure. But it's not."

Buck was intent upon enjoying his tale. Peter turned off the ignition and opened the truck door. "Go ahead, Buckie."

"Well, first I looked online in commercial catalogues, but it didn't match any of the pictures. The rose you gave me looks like it's got some Hybrid Perpetual in it, and that scent—there's Musk rose in that flower's genes. So then I hunted around the heirloom rosarians' stock, but the color's too modern for an old rose. Finally I took a photograph and sent it to the American Rose Society."

"Something that would never occur to me."

"They got back to me this morning. It's a cross of the hybrid tea Tropicana and the hybrid musk Cornelia."

"A remarkable piece of detective work. What's its name, by the way?"

"Sundance," Buck said. "But the kick'll be to find it. The horticulturalist who hybridized it has never put the rose on the market. We'll have to contact her directly. There's probably only a few of these bushes in existence."

"You know who cultivated it?" Peter thought he could name the woman himself.

"Lady by the name of Betty Scott," Buck replied. "Lives in Westchester County somewhere."

"I know," Peter said. "I'm sorry, Buck, but I've got to get back to the farm."

He was gone before the nurseryman could answer.

MERRY PULLED UP to the saltbox on the moor and scanned the blank windows. Rafe was right. Peter wasn't at the house—probably somewhere in town with Alison Miller. She stifled a vague sense of unease and told herself that there was nothing unusual in Peter's sightseeing with a friend. But the short hair on the back of her neck was tingling uncontrollably.

She had come for Rafe's clothes and should have headed straight for the barn. She was bound for Lucy Jacoby's house as soon as she got the clothes to the airport. But she followed the tingling on her neck and walked around the back of the house, searching for some sign of life, something she couldn't identify.

Ney pulled himself to his feet, stretching luxuriously in greeting as she mounted the three steps to the deck. She saw the emptied iced tea glasses and the deserted chairs ranged around a mortally dangerous photograph. They had been here not long before, and they had left in a hurry. With a sense of foreboding, she opened the cover of a book of short stories dropped carelessly on the table near the snapshot of Max Mason and the woman he had loved. She saw the name on the flyleaf and began to swear.

She ran back to the Explorer, heart pounding, and threw it into gear.

*Lucy Jacoby.*

Who had inadvertently left a blackmail letter addressed to Sundance in the copy of *Thirteen Reasons Why* that she'd given to Will.

Who had knocked Will off his bike that same evening, desperate to search his backpack while he lay concussed on the moor nearby.

Lucy, who had probably spent a weekend of suspense and remorse, wondering where the book had gone.

Lucy, whose fingerprints on a bottle of wine matched the prints left on a wooden button from a sweater she claimed to have given away.

Lucy, dressed to the nines, leaning against Maxwell Mason's car in a photograph taken ten years ago.

Lucy, who had stopped by Peter's house, and found Alison Miller—the one person who could positively identify her as Sundance, link her to Rusty, and define her motive for murder.

Merry roared from the moors into Milestone Road, and turned toward Tom Nevers Head.

## Chapter 33

Up in the cool dimness of her loft bedroom, Lucy had Rafe's nine-millimeter Browning—the one she had taken from the barn the night she shot Peter Mason— trained on Alison, whose hands and feet were bound. Forty minutes had passed since they had unexpectedly met on Peter's deck.

Lucy looked very different from the girl in the bruised photograph of Max Mason's limousine that lay on the table between them—she had changed her hair and everything about her style—but just glimpsing the picture made her blood run cold.

She had recognized Alison immediately.

Alison had not recognized her.

The two women drank iced tea and chatted about books, Will Starbuck, and the island. Then Lucy suggested they take a drive through the moors. Peter had abandoned them both. There was a pumpkin farm out toward Tom Nevers. Had Alison seen Tom Nevers?

Alison couldn't remember.

Lucy left the book she'd brought for Will on the table with the empty iced tea glasses, so that Peter would know everything was fine. He might think she'd driven

Alison back to town or even to the airport. With luck, he wouldn't look for the woman for hours.

It was only later, in Lucy's car, that Alison realized who she was.

"I'M NOT GOING to hurt you," Lucy said now, laying the gun down on her bookcase. "It's just that I need some time. So I can get off the island before anybody knows." She turned to her closet and pulled a suitcase down from the top shelf.

Alison shifted slightly to ease the strain in her shoulders. Her wrists were painfully snug in the small of her back. "But I know, Lucy," she said quietly. "And I doubt you'll ignore that."

Lucy's hands stilled for an instant, and she looked at her with wounded and naked eyes. "I know you think I'm dangerous because of Rusty. But it was just a moment that happened." Her voice faltered and broke. "You don't have to be afraid of me."

"That kid in your class wasn't afraid of you," Alison said, "and he's in a coma."

Lucy flinched and dropped the pair of jeans she had been distractedly folding. "That was a mistake."

"Are you saying you didn't mean to stretch a wire across his path? Or that you meant for Peter to hit it?"

"I mean that he wasn't supposed to be hurt. Nothing's gone right since Rusty came back. Since the night I got his letter."

"Rusty blackmailed you."

"Yes." Lucy glanced from the skylight to the window. Fearful of discovery, she had drawn the shades. "Or at least, he tried."

"Tell me what happened," Alison suggested.

"I recognized him on the Fast Ferry. I don't think he recognized me. I hid in the women's room, and when the boat docked, I thought I'd lost him. But he came right here after he picked up that rental car—he had my address."

"How did he find you?"

"Sky Tate-Jackson, maybe. He used to email Rusty. Probably kept him updated on Peter, and Peter's friends. Rusty would recognize the name Lucy Jacoby. My full name is Lucy Jacoby Scott. It wouldn't have taken him long to hunt me down."

"Why did you come to Nantucket in the first place, Lucy?"

"Max loved this island," she said. "And I thought I could hide on the edges of things. Invent a new life. My father had left me some money—even Grandpa couldn't take that away—and I could live well here. With my books, my garden, and my classroom. Five years—I had almost begun to heal."

"And then Rusty came back."

"Did you mean to kill him?" Alison asked.

Lucy stared at her an instant, as if seeing again Rusty's silhouette in the fog. "When he showed up here, I offered to drive him to Peter's for the night. I couldn't stand to have him in my home. My car was in the shop—I'd ridden my bike to and from the ferry. But Rusty had rented the Jeep." Her voice quavered momentarily, then recovered. "I drove, since the fog was bad and he didn't know where Mason Farms was. He laughed at me all the way over to Peter's, saying he had half a mind to tell him who I was that very night—that I'd been in love with Max, and now I was in love with Peter."

As if remembering time was short, she scooped a heap of T-shirts and shorts into her arms. She threw the clothes, willy-nilly, into the suitcase. "He called me Max's mistress. It wasn't like that—some crass exchange of sex for money. But Rusty could make anything dirty, even memories."

"I know."

"When we got to the farm, I made him open the gate. I looked at him in the headlights, and thought of all I'd lost—Max, my old life with my grandparents, and now the new life I'd been building. My quiet friendship with Peter. I'd never wanted anything more than that. I was *Lucy* to him, not Sundance, not someone who'd caused his family pain. I couldn't let Rusty tell him anything about me.

"He was standing in front of the car, in the headlights, unlatching the gate. And I . . ." Her voice trailed away, then became stronger with memory. "I hit the gas. As hard as I could, as if that would end it faster. He flew into the air and landed on the hood of the car. The impact cracked the windshield."

"Is that what knocked him out?"

"Probably. I screamed—there was his body sprawled in front of the windshield—and threw the car into reverse. Rusty slid off the Jeep and didn't move, like he was dead. I got out and checked him—and then I realized. He was only unconscious—but when he came to . . . he'd have one more reason to blackmail me forever."

"So you killed him," Alison said.

"I helped him die. I dragged him by his ankles up the driveway and put him facedown in the ditch. I made sure the water came up over his hair. And then I got out of there as fast as I could."

There was a silence.

"I understand how you must have hated him," Alison said.

At that moment, they both heard the quiet scrape of metal on metal. Someone was working at the back door's lock.

Lucy whimpered once. Then she pulled a cotton running sock and a scarf out of her drawer, and gagged Alison.

MERRY HAD HER service revolver cocked as she inched her way through Lucy's back door. She threw a glance around the kitchen alcove, felt rather than saw the stillness of the empty main room, and flattened herself against the wall of the loft stairs. She began to creep toward the lowest step, holding her breath.

"I'm armed," a quavering voice called out.

Merry halted, her black brows crinkling.

"I have a hostage. I'll shoot her if you come any closer."

"Don't make this worse than it is, Lucy," Merry said.

Overhead, a bedspring creaked. Merry listened for the direction of the footsteps, one set pulling, the other dragging, and knew they were nearing the edge of the loft.

At that moment, the front doorbell rang.

All three of them froze.

Merry recovered first and swung around to the foot of the steps, her gun trained on Lucy Jacoby's head.

"Lucy! Are you there?"

Peter Mason's voice on the doorstep.

"She's armed and dangerous," Merry called. "We have a hostage situation."

She kept her eyes on Lucy and the woman who must be Alison. Lucy had locked Alison's neck in the crook of her left elbow. Alison's face was grotesquely distorted by a gag, and her eyes were wide with fear.

"Let her go, Lucy," Merry said. "This won't get you anywhere."

The front door was dead-bolted. She could hear Peter running to the rear of the house, where she'd forced the kitchen lock. "Stay out, Peter. I've got back-up on the way."

But he had already slid into the kitchen and was walking up quietly behind her.

"Why don't you let her go, Lucy," he suggested, "and we'll sit down and talk about all of this."

"Oh, Peter!" Lucy's voice rose hysterically. "Why weren't you there when I needed you?"

"Get out before you fuck this up," Merry muttered.

"I know her better than you do." Peter came calmly to Merry's side and stared up at the two women. "What do you want us to do, Lucy?"

"I need safe passage to the airport and a plane out of here."

"Let Alison go first," Merry said encouragingly, "and we'll talk about it."

Lucy shook her head and released the revolver's safety catch with an audible click. She placed the muzzle against Alison's skull.

"You're better than this." Peter moved slowly toward the stairs. "You can't change the past, but you can stop being Rusty's tool. He screwed up your life once. Don't let him do it again, Lucy. Say no. Say *enough*."

"I want a plane out, Peter."

Merry watched Lucy's gun begin to shake. She felt sweat break out on her own chest, aware of how volatile the Browning could be. If Lucy's finger moved the trigger—

"You could stop running." Peter mounted the first step. "You could be rid of fear. You haven't felt that kind of peace since the day he first blackmailed you, years ago, or the night you killed him."

"Stop right there!" she cried. "Don't come any closer."

"Let Alison go, Lucy." Peter took another step. "Nobody's going to hurt you anymore."

Without warning, Lucy shoved Alison to the edge of the staircase. Feet and hands still bound, Alison fell at her feet.

*A perfect shield*, Merry thought.

She grabbed Peter by his wounded arm and forced him behind her.

She was halfway up the stairs when Lucy fired.

## Chapter 34

LATER, WHEN THE English teacher's body had been taken away and Alison had been driven to the station to deliver her statement, Merry found Peter in the yard behind the house. He was standing near Lucy Jacoby's roses, and she didn't like the look on his face.

"Hey, Peter," she said.

He glanced around. "Hey. Thanks for being here when it mattered."

Polite, even when he thought she'd driven Lucy to her death. Merry considered the woman lying inert in the body bag. She wished she'd been able to talk Lucy down. But for what? Life in prison?

"When did you realize she'd killed Rusty?" he asked, breaking into her thoughts.

"A couple of things came together. I located a Lucy Jacoby by searching computer records under partial names. That told me her last name was Scott, and her original license was from New York. I remembered how Malcolm Scott looked when we showed him that photograph last week."

Peter nodded. "Rusty must have taken the picture the summer Lucy was involved with Max. He probably told her he'd show it to my mother. She was pretty young—really loved my dad—and didn't want to lose him. So to keep Rusty quiet, she gave him what he wanted—Max's takeover plans."

"Until your brother-in-law, Hale, told your father what Rusty was doing to him," Merry mused. "That must have been a lousy day for Lucy."

"Max would have figured it out: If Rusty could blackmail Hale, he could blackmail anybody. Max probably confronted Lucy and she probably broke down. Told him about the pictures, the threats, how Rusty had used her. That would only have made my father even more insanely angry at my brother." Peter's expression was harsh. "And then there's Malcolm Scott. Obviously Max told him what had happened—both about the affair and the blackmail. And when my father dropped dead a few weeks later . . ."

"Scott blamed Lucy. For thirty-five years, Max Mason trusted Malcolm Scott, and it turns out Scott's granddaughter was the one who nearly destroyed the company. I guess that's why he cut her off. A mixture of pride and shame. But her grandmother . . ."

"—Must have quietly stayed in touch. Hence these roses." Peter paused. "There's no doubt, I suppose? Lucy really did kill Rusty?"

"Her fingerprints matched the ones on the button we found near his body."

"Ah."

"That alone wouldn't be enough," Merry said, "We knew she'd owned the sweater, and she could have lost the button at your bog any time. But then there was Sandy Stewart."

"Who?"

"Friend of Will's. Lucy gave Will a book on Friday, but she'd left something in it by mistake—Rusty's blackmail letter, addressed to Sundance."

"So it was Lucy who hurt Will?"

"She wanted to get the book back, Peter." Merry stepped closer to him, disturbed by the remoteness of his expression. "That's why she knocked him off the bike. Only she got it wrong—Will had loaned the book to Sandy without even reading it, poor kid. And Sandy found the letter. He came to the police station this afternoon."

Something in Peter's face stirred. "Is there any news about Will?"

"Rafe called. In all this mess, I completely forgot to tell you. Will has come around. But there's one thing." She hesitated. "He'll need some rehab. Motor skills, stuff like that. The kind of thing you'd be great at helping him with, once he gets back from Mass Gen."

She was pleased to see some life stir in Peter's eyes.

"Look," she attempted, "I'm sorry it worked out this way."

"I am too," he said. "Lucy deserved to be left alone."

His voice cracked. Merry reached tentatively for his sleeve.

"She's at peace, Peter," she said. "It's you who has to find some."

He laid his palm fiercely on hers, holding it fast to his sleeve. She felt a thrill course through her body and fought the impulse to jerk her hand away.

"I thought, for one instant, that she had shot Alison. Then I thought she had shot you. And I was as destroyed by one possibility as the other."

She stepped back in confusion.

"Congrats on getting through your first homicide case, Detective."

"I'd be happy never to have another one," Merry said. "It tears me apart."

"That's why you're good at it." Peter looked at her intently. "You allow yourself to feel. Nobody ever said it'd be easy. But the hard things in life are the only ones worth doing."

He broke off a rose and handed it to Merry. "Lucy believed these were good luck."

The image of the English teacher's shattered skull and sightless eyes swam in Merry's mind.

"Her grandmother created that flower, and named it Sundance."

"The woman painting in the garden," she remembered. "Are you going to break the news to the Scotts?"

"I owe Lucy that," he replied. "I want to tell Betty how much she loved her roses. I don't suppose you'd come with me?"

"To Chappaqua?" Merry said, startled.

"It's a quick trip if you fly Cape Air straight into Westchester County. And you interviewed Malcolm about this case. It might help him to hear the end from you."

Peter was watching her carefully. Merry understood suddenly that he was asking for her support. Not Alison—not Rafe da Silva—not his sister, George. He wanted her.

She lifted the rose to her face and breathed deep of its scent.

*The hard things in life are the only ones worth doing.*

"Of course I'll come with you," she said.

Continue reading for a sneak preview from the
next Merry Folger mystery

# DEATH IN ROUGH WATER

*Prologue*

THE NIGHT WIND was blowing unusually cold for late
May, and the stars were blotted out by a bank of cloud.
Captain Joe Duarte took the measure of the waters, felt
the plunge of his deck, and knew he should head for port.
The mounting weather made black sea and sky one, a
pitching cocoon through which his trawler labored and
rolled. The *Lisboa Girl* had just crossed over what Duarte
knew as the Leg—part of the intricate underwater landscape of the Georges Bank he'd been fishing since the age
of fifteen. He had turned sixty-eight three months past,
and though much had changed in the fifty-three years
he'd been on the water, he still called the Bank's bottoms,
its gullies and peaks, by the old names made familiar from
decades of studying charts in storm and sun: Cultivator
Shoals, Billy Doyle's Hole, Little Georges, Outer Hole.

The younger men, using location indicators fed down
from the stars, thought in signals instead of words. They
moved over the crags of the seabed as a blind man feels
Braille, sensing the humps and dips that clutched at their
nets. Had they been told to head to the Leg instead of
following a GPS, they'd have been lost.

The captain knew the Georges Bank like the profile
of a beloved woman, something no locator on a screen

could ever replace. It was an ancient shelf of the North American continent, inundated by glacial ice melt twelve thousand years before. The Georges Bank sat more than sixty nautical miles off the present coastline and was larger than the entire state of Massachusetts. To Joe Duarte, it was home. The charted names of the bottoms remained with him like the Portuguese words of his childhood, artifacts of a vanished age. Like his boat. And himself, for that matter. He was among the last of Nantucket's commercial fishermen, and the last of the Duartes to go down to the sea, something they had been doing in Portugal and the New World for over five hundred years.

The *Lisboa Girl*, three decades old and Joe's second trawler, was one of only two remaining draggers to call Nantucket home. She was an Eastern-rigged wooden vessel, meaning that her pilothouse was aft and she launched her nets over the side rather than to the stern. A more dangerous and old-fashioned boat to fish from than the steel-hulled Western-riggers—in heavy seas like this, she'd have to come to a stop and turn broadside to the wind to prevent the net from drifting under the hull and fouling the propeller.

The captain pulled open the pilothouse porthole and stuck his head into the rising wind. It was time to quit fishing and head for port. His rheumatic bones ached, and his eyelids stung with weariness. Maybe it was time to quit for good, like all the rest.

Nobody his age worked a trawler anymore. The younger men skippered boats that cost hundreds of thousands of dollars and carried insurance that drained them of thousands more. Fishing from an island port like Nantucket tacked a surcharge on everything they needed to survive. They weren't fools. They had left long ago for the mainland ports of Hyannis and Provincetown, Gloucester and New Bedford, and the Nantucket fleet slowly died.

Joe Duarte had watched the others go with a grim pride. His boat was paid off. He'd inherited his house on Milk Street. He could afford to stay in the town where he was born—where, at fifteen, he learned his trade from his father and grandfather, and had the youth whipped out of him by the bitter cold of winter fishing. He found the mainland ports too crowded and the towns too suburban. Returning to the harbor of a January night, past Great Point Light arcing its reassurance into the early dusk, he saw the glow from hundreds of Nantucket windows rising out of the midwinter Atlantic with a surging of the heart and a gladness born of deep love. He knew the value of what he had earned with his blood and his years.

*Only I've no one to give it to,* he thought. *So much for pride. All it buys is loneliness. I've got to call Del. Blood is blood, after all.*

"Holy Christ, would you look at that!"

Jackie Alcantrara, his first mate, was bent over the gray face of the fish-finder, studying the shifting shapes of the schools twenty-five fathoms below. The image rippled like a field of summer wheat. "It's cod, Joe. A friggin' fish convention. Let's go." He moved to the door of the pilothouse impatiently, shouting orders to the two crewmen on the night watch.

Joe Duarte squinted in the glare of the working lights. It was impossible to see much of the Atlantic beyond, but he could feel the pitch of the waves, grown sharper in the last few minutes, and the wind that was tugging at his sparse white hair. They were heading into fifteen-foot seas, over sharp peaks on the sandy bottom, and the net would be torn to shreds. There were no other boats in sight. They were one hundred and fifty miles from land.

*Loneliness is a kind of death. I gotta call Del.*

"Jackie!" he yelled over the din of the gantry winch, which was paying out the net and the pair of half-ton steel doors that dragged it to the bottom. "Jackie!"

The mate turned to him impatiently, bullet head thrust forward in resentment. He had been a captain himself until last year, and taking orders from Joe was something he fought every day.

"Get the net outta the water, *now*!"

"What the hell are you talking about, old man?"

"I won't have a couple thousand dollars' worth of new net torn apart in a gale, you understand? Get it up!"

Jackie stood stock-still, his jaw working fiercely, his overdeveloped upper body emphasizing all that was squat and Cro-Magnon about him; then he turned and drove a hand flat against the pilothouse wall with a shuddering violence.

"Christ *Almighty*," he said. "When are you gonna go home and die, old man? Tell me that! There's ten tons of cod down there, more than we've seen in months, more than anybody's seen at one time in more trips out than we can count. We're making money here, and you talk about a net!"

*The bastard. I'd never have spoken to my captain like that. No respect, these days. No gratitude. I'd better call Felix Harper, too.*

On the one hand, everything Jackie said was true. For years, cod on the bank had steadily dwindled. During the day, they hung around in the mid-depths where only the huge factory ships could reach them; but at night, they dropped back to the bottom, and the *Lisboa Girl* dropped her nets after them through all the hours of darkness. Joe was turning his back on money. But he could sense the weather's gathering menace, and no amount of fish was worth the safety of his boat and men. Jackie was young. He would learn from the weather, from the ones who didn't come home, from the sudden silences on the radio frequencies in the midst of an unexpected gale.

"First Mate Alcantrara," the captain shouted into the wind, "for the last time, *bring in the net,* or I will do it for you." He ducked back into the pilothouse and counted to five. Then he looked through the porthole for Jackie. The mate had gone over to the crewmen and was shouting and gesturing; but still the net was being paid out. *Bullheaded young cuss.* A huge wave broke over the bow as the *Lisboa Girl* dove into a trough, spraying the men standing midships by the gantry.

Joe abandoned the pilothouse and reeled his way across the heaving deck, his hair instantly wet from the blown seas, his face turning red with suppressed rage.

"Tell me what I have to do to get an order obeyed here," he said to Jackie. The mate shrugged and looked away, muttering into the storm. Joe turned to a younger man working the winch. "Get that net back on deck, Lars, double-time, you understand?"

"Sure, Cap'n, if you say so." The blond crewman glanced at the first mate. "But there's an awful lot of fish down there."

"There's a lot of bones, too," Joe said through his teeth, "and not all of them ancient. Bring it up."

Lars, a Norwegian incorrectly known around Nantucket as the Swede, turned back to the controls and eased the lever through neutral into reverse. The winch gave a groan audible even over the force of the wind, and the net started to wind wetly out of the water.

"That's it," Jackie burst out beside him. "I'm through. There's nothing worse than a man who's too afraid to make money. Why don't you stay home and leave the cod to people who know what they're doing?"

Joe Duarte's rage hiccupped inside of him as he shot a look at Jackie's ugly face, but it was quickly replaced by a terrible weariness. He *was* old, too old to be walking a sea-slick deck in the pitching dead of night, too old to slam an obnoxious twenty-eight-year-old on the jaw, too old to weigh whether the catch or his life was more important.

"You think you know what you're doing, huh?" he said. "You think you know how to run a boat?"

"Damn sight better'n you do, old man," Jackie retorted.

"At least I've got a boat to skipper," Joe said, with satisfaction, "instead of a wreck at the bottom of Cape Cod Bay. You didn't learn from that bit of trouble, did you, Jackie boy? You never learn anything. Your skull's too hard and your brain's too small. You can get off my boat, and good riddance."

He had expected the first mate's scowl of rage and the words bubbling at his lips, had expected him to take a swing at him, even, sealing the fate of their sundering after a year of strained partnership. But he hadn't expected the look of horror that washed over the man as he stared at something behind Joe himself, over his head, or the cry of warning that was torn from him too late.

*Oh no. God, no. Del.*

The full force of the net's steel otter door, rising much too fast from the roiling sea, caught the captain in the back of the skull. It was a massive blow that knocked sense from him with the swiftness of a snuffed candle. He crumpled at his crewmen's feet, at the base of the gantry, the otter door swinging wildly overhead as the Swede struggled to secure it. Jackie reached for Joe Duarte just as the boat heeled over, wallowing in a trough and pitched sideways by the weight of the swinging door. But the stunned man slid out of the mate's reach, into the water, his white head another bit of froth on the surging waves.

"Joe!" Jackie cried, the howling of the wind drowning his voice. "Joe!"

But the old man was gone.

*Chapter 1*

"IT COMES AS no surprise to any of us, dear friends,"
Father Acevedo was saying, "that Joe Duarte stayed in
the water rather than attend his own funeral. He used
to say that if the Lord wanted him at Mass instead of on
the Georges Bank on Sunday, He'd have sent the fish to
church." He paused for the anticipated laughter. "I think
we know where the fish are today, dear friends, and we
know that Joe Duarte is right where he'd want to be."

The sentiment, however apt, failed to strike a note of
cheer in the crowd. It *missed*, somehow, like the funeral
conducted without a body, like the blowing gusts of fren-
zied rain that hammered the first summer flowers into
their muddy beds. Father Acevedo meant well. He was
Portuguese himself, born and raised on the Cape, and
his father had fished with the Provincetown fleet. He'd
known Joe Duarte for six years. But when a man was lost
at sea, fear cut deep in the hearts of his confederates, a
fear hard to laugh off. No one who fished for a living
wanted to die for it.

Detective Meredith Folger scanned the faces lining
the pews and aisles of St. Mary's. A few shocked smiles
met the priest's sally, but most of the mourners simply
looked uncomfortable. She caught the eye of Jackie

Alcantrara—Joe Duarte's first mate, the one who'd jumped into the Atlantic after him and come back empty-handed. He'd taken a knock on the head, and the hospital had shaved his skull; the man looked more like a bull than ever, she thought. His heavy-featured face had gone white under his tanned skin, and he wasn't laughing. Merry dropped her eyes to her lap and wished the funeral Mass were done.

Joe's relatives had come from all over Massachusetts—the Ed Duartes from Gloucester, the Luis Duartes from Mattapoisett, and up front, behind the first pew, the Manny Duartes out of New Bedford, the ones his daughter, Del, had been living with. They were all fishermen. A good number of townsfolk had also braved the rain to say goodbye to Cap'n Joe, though few among them still made their living from the sea. There were Portuguese names all over the island, but they tended to be printed on the sides of pickup trucks rather than boats. Not a family among them failed to fish every summer, however—for pleasure or sport, or the occasional killing in the Japanese tuna auctions.

Father Acevedo beamed all around and raised his hands, signaling the end of his homily, and the congregation rose for the Prayer of the Faithful. Merry craned for a look at Adelia Duarte as she stood in the first pew, her two-year-old, Sara, singing a quiet nonsense song to her doll, and marveled again at her calm dignity. She had been absent from the island almost three years, since the pregnancy that had alienated her father. To return under circumstances like these must be an unbearable strain. Yet she showed no signs of the gnawing guilt and regret that her neighbors probably hoped to see—none of the remorse of the prodigal daughter, eyes downcast and shoulders trembling, all hope of reconciliation lost. She had yet to endure the post-funeral reception, when the wives of her father's friends would invade the house with their casseroles and sympathy, sincere or false, a suffocating flock of femininity blessed with men safe and alive.

Merry smiled, and just as swiftly smoothed her features back into anonymous solemnity. Everyone in the church was trying not to stare at Adelia and her baby, and failing miserably. She was too much her father's child to care what Nantucketers said or thought about her life; she was probably looking forward to the struggle.

She had, after all, chosen to wear red today.

"A PRETTY ENOUGH little thing," Jenny Baldwin was saying, her eye on Sara Duarte, who was wandering wide-eyed through the forest of adult legs filling Joe Duarte's living room, "though rather small. But then she *is* illegitimate, and I always find that babies born out of wedlock are *not* robust, don't you? And where did she get that red hair?" she continued, not waiting for Merry's response. "Not from the Duartes, certainly."

"Agnes's hair was auburn," Merry said, recalling Adelia's mother.

"Was it?" Jenny said vaguely. "She died before my time, I'm afraid. Too bad. If she'd lived, perhaps Adelia wouldn't have been quite so—unrestrained. But a girl raised as she was . . ." She clicked her tongue in mock sympathy and raised one eyebrow in the general direction of the red dress. She was the sort of woman who'd learned to click her tongue before she'd learned to form sentences. "Of course, Tom and I were always ready to do anything we could for her—"

"If you'll excuse me, Mrs. Baldwin," Merry said, her own black brows lowering, "I'd like to talk to Del, and I haven't much time before I'm due back at the station. You understand."

"You were great friends once, weren't you?" Jenny Baldwin said, her bleached blue eyes awash with interest.

*She's wondering if I know who the baby's father is*, Merry thought with distaste. "Yes," she said, "but we've grown far closer since she left the island. Absence has a way of revealing your true friends."

She set down her club soda and crossed the room in search of the red dress, which seemed to have vanished into the kitchen. She had been less than frank with Jenny Baldwin, but anger brought out her contrary streak. Del Duarte was a childhood friend. They had grown apart during the past decade, some of which Merry had spent at Cape Cod Community College, the Massachusetts Police Academy, and her first tour in New Bedford. By the time she'd come back to Nantucket six years ago, Del had her own life. Her pregnancy took her off-island three years later. Merry had no idea who'd fathered baby Sara.

A wall of bodies obscured her view. She eased her shoulder past stocky, weathered Tom Baldwin, Jenny's husband, raising her hand to the small of his back and hoping he'd ignore her. Instead, he turned his head and smiled.

"Merry!" he said. "Good to see you."

"And you, Tom. Where've you been hiding?"

"Oh, inside a foundation or two," he said, his tanned skin crinkling at the corners of his eyes. He'd made more money than most during the recent development boom, and from the look of the signs around town announcing his current projects, he'd plowed the profits back into his business. Merry doubted he'd been inside a concrete cellar for years.

"I hope no one commits a crime today," he said, glancing over at her father, the police chief, who stood surrounded by a knot of Joe Duarte's older friends. From the way he held his hands in the air, spaced about eighteen inches apart, Merry knew John Folger was regaling them with the tale of his latest near-conquest of an elusive bluefish. "With Nantucket's finest trapped in this room, they'd get clean away with it."

"We left Ralph Waldo by the phone."

"How's your granddad doing?"

"Very well, thanks. He never seems to get any older." At eighty-two, Ralph Waldo Folger was competent and eager enough to resume his duties as police chief—relinquished to his son some twenty years before—so that Merry and John could attend Joe Duarte's funeral. She knew he'd be safely tucked up in his favorite armchair, one eye on the storm and one ear on the police radio.

"Sad about Joe," Tom said, twirling the ice cubes in his drink, "but at least he lived a long life."

"Right," Merry said shortly. Tom Baldwin would consider sixty-eight young once he reached it.

"I don't suppose Adelia will be staying on the island long," he continued. "The house should sell quickly, this time of year—"

"—and on this block of Milk Street," Merry finished. "I know. Everyone says the same thing. *Perfect* summer cottage for a young investment banker from New York.

But I haven't had a chance to talk to her long enough to find out whether she's planning to sell or not." She caught sight of Del through the space left by a turning head, and with a smile for Tom Baldwin, wove her way toward the kitchen.

It was like Joe Duarte's daughter to be calmly scrambling an egg in the middle of chaos. She stood by the stove, her long dark hair a shining band against the brightness of her dress, the only cheerful thing in an otherwise drab bachelor kitchen. It was a galley space, narrow and dark, with an ell for a small Formica-and-steel table with three outmoded chairs. The stubby refrigerator was rounded and domed in the mode of the 1940s, the counters were badly fauxed marble, and the linoleum on the floor was bleached of its original color—yellow, probably. A frieze of brown age spots overlaid the wallpaper like the back of an octogenarian's hand; Joe had apparently intended to strip it from the walls, since one section was torn off and hung to the floor with the pathetic droop of a three-day-old lily. The young investment banker from New York would have to sink some money into the place. Merry touched Del lightly on the shoulder, and Del turned to her with an expression partly of relief and partly of weariness.

"*Eh, filha,*" she said, "Good of you to come. It's been too long."

*Hey, girl.* The affectionate Portuguese phrase stripped away the years as suddenly as a breath of wind. Merry reached out to hug Adelia. "You look great," she said. "I can't tell you how sorry I am about Joe."

Del looked beyond her to the crowded living room. "Can you believe this circus?"

"It's like a bad joke—'How many people can you fit into a Nantucket cottage?'"

"Depends how many have eaten today, right?" Del said, laughing. "Joe'd have thrown them all out an hour ago."

"Or left them the house and camped on the boat."

"But that's what it means to be dead," she said, glancing up at the ceiling. "He's a captive audience somewhere, for the first time in sixty-eight years." Her eyes shifted quickly to the egg drying in the pan. "Whoops. She likes them soft, salmonella or no. Sara!"

She reached for a plate and scraped the egg onto it. Tom Baldwin shouldered his broad chest through the kitchen door, Sara Duarte giggling on one arm. "Here she is!" he said, swooping her into a chair fitted haphazardly with a booster-seat cushion. He turned to Adelia, one hand reaching for the plate. The Baldwins had no children, Merry remembered, but it must not be from choice, Tom clearly enjoyed them. He smoothed Sara's deep red curls, the color of mahogany, and settled himself into a chair, fork at the ready. Merry leaned against the wall and smiled at Del. She didn't smile back.

"I'll feed her, if you don't mind, Tom." Adelia took the fork out of his hand and stood over his chair, her lips compressed.

"Sure," he said, rising quickly. "Just thought you could use a hand."

"I'm never too busy to feed Sara," she said, and sat down. Tom looked at Merry, shrugged, and backed out of the kitchen.

"Feeling a little tense?" Merry said, drawing up the remaining chair as Adelia lifted a forkful of egg toward Sara's obliging mouth. "Or did Tom hit a nerve?"

"Tom's just being Tom," she said wearily. "Hale and hearty and bending over backward to show everybody that Sara would love to have a daddy. That poor Del has her hands too full, trying to raise her kid alone. Why didn't she put her up for adoption, like everyone told her to? So couples like the Baldwins, poor guys, could have a baby of their own? But no. Adelia was always so stubborn, so bullheaded. Never knew what was good for her, and never would listen when people tried to tell her. *Que pena.*"

"You don't really believe they think that, Del," Merry said.

"Oh, I *know* they do." Adelia put down the fork in frustration. "And I've got a headache that will not quit."

Sara kicked her feet against the tabletop, wanting another forkful of egg, then gave up and reached for it with her fingers.

"Okay, so maybe I'm a little raw," Del said, sitting back in the chair. "But you don't know, Mer, how hard it is to come back. To look like I don't give a damn. I can't even cry for Pop in peace. I can't lose it in public. Everybody'd nod and say I feel as guilty as sin. So I try to be a rock instead. You know, half these people are here out of nosiness. They want to see how I handle Sara. And how bad I feel."

"So how *do* you feel?"

"Pretty lousy," she said, laughing shortly. "You know me. I always felt guilt over things I only *thought* of doing, never mind things I've actually done. I can't get it out of my head that I didn't call him on his birthday. I *should* have called him, Merry. It was three months ago. I thought about it that day, *and I decided not to.* Can you believe that? As if he'd be around next year to call instead. I'm such a fucking idiot."

"Del—you can't think like that."

"Then I guess I can't think at all."

Merry was silent for a moment. She'd known Del for twenty-odd years. Despite the distance that had grown between them, she was probably Del's closest friend on Nantucket. And she knew that if their roles were reversed, she'd have felt the same way. Never mind that Joe Duarte hadn't called his daughter in years; he'd had the last laugh. He'd *died*, the ultimate upping of the ante in a war of silence.

"It'll be over soon," she said, reaching for Del's hand. "You'll be home in New Bed before you know it."

Del squeezed her fingers in response, released them, and drew a deep breath. "Well, yeah, that's what I'd like to talk to you about," she said. "I'm thinking of staying."

"Here?" It was the last thing she'd expected. "So you're not selling the house. From the way the real estate talk is going, you've got at least ten buyers in the living room alone. Do you want your old job back?"

"With Tom?" Del shook her head. Three years ago, she had been Tom Baldwin's personal assistant, and was, by all accounts, invaluable. She was smart, efficient, and organized—the last something Tom had struggled and failed to be.

Del reached for a napkin to wipe Sara's face. It was smeared with egg, like the sunrise smile of a clown. Sara pursed her lips and leaned away, her hands balled into fists.

"He hired a sub for me when I left, and he's not gonna fire her just because I'm back in town."

"Even if you could stand it," Merry said.

Del grinned. "Yeah, there's that," she said. "I'd probably go nuts. Too much a part of the past, you know?" She looked at Merry, weighing her words. "I've got a better idea. I'm going to take Pop's boat out and fish."

"You? *Fish?*"

"Swordfish, actually. You know what they're getting for harpooned ones? It's like a yuppie craze. Somebody figured out that a harpooned fish dies quicker and tastes better than one caught by the long-liners' nets. Whole Foods pays through the nose for it, all over the country. So do restaurants."

"And God knows we have enough of those." Nantucket's restaurants were expensive, trendy, and geared to a moneyed crowd. "But Del—a harpoon?"

"I've thrown one before," she said, smiling. "You know how Pop was. He wanted a son and he got me. So he tried his best to turn me into a boy. I've been throwing a harpoon with him on the weekends since I was ten. He'd leave the *Lisboa Girl* at dock and take out the *Praia*—his thirty-footer—with me in the bow to spot. We caught a bunch over the years. You learn the knack. And you never forget the thrill."

"Aren't swordfish pretty scarce?"

"Used to be," Adelia said, "but lately the stocks have been recovering. Some of us think that's due to the shift from longline to harpoon fishing—swords aren't being overfished as badly as they used to be. My cousins in New Bed harpoon on the side. I went out with them a couple of times to get my arm back in shape, and it reminded me how much I missed being on the water. Pop used to say the harpooner's arm was passed down through the blood, you know, ever since the whaling days. Knowing the sea and loving it is something Duartes are born with."

She paused and looked at Merry soberly. "Pop's dead. I can't bring him back. But now he's gone, I miss a lot of things I thought I'd forgotten. Like hard work and cold spray and the fight to the death. I want Sara to grow up a Duarte."

"You think you can make a living?"

"I hope."

"If the swords play out, you can always switch to tuna." The Japanese paid exorbitant prices—up to twenty thousand dollars a fish—for prime bluefin tuna at auction.

Del shook her head. "They're even scarcer than swords."

Merry ran her fingers through her blonde hair—still damp from the rain and the persistent humidity that came with it—and decided to concentrate on essentials. "Who's going to crew for you?"

"I haven't figured that out," her friend admitted. "I'll think about crew tomorrow. There has to be some guy on the island who's strong enough to work for a woman."

"I'm not so sure," Merry said carefully. "Precious few are willing to take orders from one."

"Nothing's changed down at the station, eh, *filha?*"

Merry was one of the few women on the Nantucket police force.

Adelia's sudden smile was like a snapshot of childhood. "Come fish," she said. "We could be the only girl crew on Nantucket. Think about it. We'd be a tourist attraction."

"We Folgers like to say that police work is handed down through the blood. Something we're born with."

"I was afraid of that. Got any ideas about crew?"

"I might. Give me a few hours." She paused, and eyed the baby. "You'll need child care."

"I know." Adelia lifted Sara out of her chair and straightened the hem of her dress.

"She's beautiful, Del," Merry said, squatting down to Sara's eye level. She had the meltingly soft skin and the faint flush of rose in her cheeks that come with the two-year-old's territory. Her eyes were Merry's exact shade of green. She smiled slowly at Merry and reached a hand out to squeeze her nose.

"Yeah. She's a sweetheart. Gives nobody trouble," Adelia said soberly. "Hard to believe she comes from me."

Merry rose and brushed off her skirt. "What are you doing tonight? After this crowd clears out, I mean."

"Having dinner at your house, if I'm lucky."

"Good. I know just the person to take care of Sara." She gave her friend a swift kiss, touched a hand to the child's head, and was gone.

# TRAVEL THE WORLD FOR $9.99

PASSPORT $9.99 TO CRIME

**PARIS**

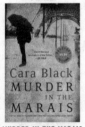

**MURDER IN THE MARAIS**
Cara Black
ISBN: 978-1-56947-999-5

**ITALY**

**DEATH OF AN ENGLISHMAN**
Magdalen Nabb
ISBN: 978-1-61695-299-0

**AMSTERDAM**

**OUTSIDER IN AMSTERDAM**
Janwillem van de Wetering
ISBN 978-1-61695-300-3

**CHINATOWN, NYC**

**CHINATOWN BEAT**
Henry Chang
ISBN: 978-1-61695-717-9

**SLOVAKIA**

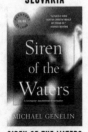

**SIREN OF THE WATERS**
Michael Genelin
ISBN 978-1-56947-585-0

**SOUTH KOREA**

**JADE LADY BURNING**
Martin Limón
ISBN: 978-1-61695-090-3

**GUADELOUPE**

**ANOTHER SUN**
Timothy Williams
ISBN 978-1-61695-363-8

**ALASKA**

**WHITE SKY, BLACK ICE**
Stan Jones
ISBN: 978-1-56947-333-7

# The first books in our most popular series in a new low price paperback edition

### DENMARK

**THE BOY IN THE SUITCASE**
Lene Kaaberbol & Agnete Friis
ISBN: 978-1-61695-491-8

### HOLLYWOOD

**CRASHED**
Timothy Hallinan
ISBN: 978-1-61695-276-1

### LONDON

**SLOW HORSES**
Mick Herron
ISBN: 978-1-61695-416-1

### WWII BERLIN

**ZOO STATION**
David Downing
ISBN: 978-1-61695-348-5

### ENGLAND

**THE LAST DETECTIVE**
Peter Lovesey
ISBN: 978-1-61695-530-4

### WWII EUROPE

**BILLY BOYLE**
James R. Benn
ISBN: 978-1-61695-355-3

### SWEDEN

**DETECTIVE INSPECTOR HUSS**
Helene Tursten
ISBN: 978-1-61695-111-5

### AUSTRALIA

**THE DRAGON MAN**
Garry Disher
ISBN: 978-1-61695-448-2

### LAOS

**THE CORONER'S LUNCH**
Colin Cotterill
ISBN: 978-1-61695-649-3

### CHINA

**ROCK PAPER TIGER**
Lisa Brackmann
ISBN: 978-1-61695-258-7

### ENGLAND

**WOBBLE TO DEATH**
Peter Lovesey
ISBN: 978-1-61695-659-2

### ITALY

**CONVERGING PARALLELS**
Timothy Williams
ISBN: 978-1-61695-460-4